Mrs. Trollope

The Young Heiress

A Novel

Mrs. Trollope

The Young Heiress
A Novel

ISBN/EAN: 9783337047375

Printed in Europe, USA, Canada, Australia, Japan

Cover: Foto ©Andreas Hilbeck / pixelio.de

More available books at **www.hansebooks.com**

THE YOUNG HEIRESS.

A NOVEL.

BY

MRS. TROLLOPE,

AUTHOR OF

"WIDOW BARNABY," "ADVENTURES OF A CLEVER WOMAN,"
"MRS. MATHEWS," ETC., ETC.

LONDON:
CHAPMAN AND HALL, 193, PICCADILLY.
1864.

THE YOUNG HEIRESS.

CHAPTER I.

IT is not very often in our money-loving and industrious country that we see a house, which has the appearance of being absolutely abandoned by its owner, and apparently permitted to fall into decay as rapidly as its nature shall permit, without any interference from the hand of man either to hasten or delay it. But such was a few years ago the case with a large, dull, heavy-looking mansion in the county of Cornwall.

Yet although there might have been many, who would probably have been well pleased to occupy so roomy a dwelling at the low rent for which it might probably have been obtained, nobody came forward to bargain for it; the reason for which perhaps might have been found more in the imaginations of those who turned away from it, than in any prudent consideration for their own interest; for the house really was a good and convenient house, and the garden attached to it, though curiously matted over by a vigorous growth of weeds, was spacious enough to have been both pleasant and convenient.

But the house had an ill name, and nobody, as it seemed, had mental courage enough to set about giving it a better.

The circumstances which led to this evil reputation are well known to me; and as they have appeared to me to possess some interest, I have been tempted to record them in the following narrative.

The name of the family who were the last inhabitants of this

2

house was Rixley. At the time my narrative must begin, it consisted of only four individuals; namely, a father, with one son, one daughter, and one female servant to wait upon them. Mr. Rixley, the father, was at this time about fifty years of age; his son was fifteen; his daughter, twelve; and the servant who attended them, about forty. Mr. Rixley was one of those people whom some persons declare to be very handsome, while others aver that they are greatly the reverse. It was, however, a matter of fact, which admitted of no dispute, that he was a tall, well-grown, well-proportioned man with regular, and decidedly handsome, features. The difference of opinion concerning his looks could only arise among those, who suffer their imaginations to be the fool of their other faculties, or else worth all the rest. In short, among those people who were in the habit of seeing more than was absolutely in sight, Mr. Rixley did not appear well-looking, because the various expressions of his countenance—and they were very various—seemed to indicate passions and feelings that were sometimes doubtful, often bad, but never good.

His son inherited his form and his features, though by no means the expression of his countenance; but his daughter resembled him not at all. She was small for her age, and very delicately and symmetrically formed ; and her features and complexion were likewise of a delicacy and refinement which, in comparing her to her father, could only suggest the idea of contrast, instead of resemblance.

As to the fourth personage who composed this small but very various household, by name Sarah Lambert, she, too, had been, as well as her master, very strikingly handsome; but ill health, or ill temper, or both together, had worn her almost to the thinness of a skeleton ; and the magnificent black eyes, which had probably, in the days of her beauty, been the most aidful feature in producing it, had now an almost frightful effect as they glared from her thin and sallow visage.

Helen Rixley was (as I have said) about twelve years old at the time my narrative begins, and her half brother three years older. The mother of the boy had been the mistress of his very dissolute father, and had died when her child was about two years old. Within a month after her death, Mr. Rixley left his home at the Warren House, as it was called, and which was not then quite so desolate as it became afterwards ; and, after the absence of a month or two, announced by a letter to his housekeeper that he was married, and that his house and garden were to be set in order, as he should return to it with his bride in the course of a week or two.

The house and garden were, accordingly, put into very nice order; and in the course of a week or two, the master of it arrived with his bride, and a very young and a very lovely bride she proved to be.

Who, or what she was, he never announced to anybody; and yet he had no reason to be ashamed of her, for she really was as innocent as she was young, and as good as she was beautiful.

The shame of the marriage—if shame there was—did not rest with her, poor girl, but with the hard unfeeling female relative who urged her into it.

She had been left an orphan by the early death of both father and mother, who had made a miserably imprudent marriage; the father being a young fortuneless officer on the eve of being sent to the West Indies, and the mother, the equally fortuneless daughter of a clergyman, who had performed the duties of a curate in a village near the young man's last English quarters.

A few years' service abroad sufficed to terminate all the mortal cares of the young father, and the young mother returned with a baby to England, with no provision but a tiny pension, and no relative to assist her, save a maiden aunt, who proclaimed, and considered, herself as the most noble minded of women for giving her shelter.

The young widow, however, did not trouble her long, and moreover contrived, during the few years she lived, to pay a very sufficient remuneration for the maintenance of herself and her child, by means of selling her very clever water-colour drawings to a Bond-street furnisher of costly albums.

The maiden aunt showed no very affectionate kindness, perhaps, in placing the little orphan girl in a sort of apprenticeship to a good school in the neighbourhood of London; but, as a measure of prudence, she could have done nothing better, and moreover, by a happy chance, the desolate child did not encounter any of the cruelties and hardships which are often said to attend such a position. The object of so placing her was the hope that it might enable her to get her bread as a teacher in the school, or as governess in some private family; and being exceedingly well taught, and, moreover, exceedingly apt to learn, it is probable that this result might have been easily obtained, had not another mode of maintaining her been offered, and eagerly accepted by the maiden aunt.

2—2

It chanced that in one of the short and far-between visits of Helen Herbert to the country-town residence of this old lady, she was seen, and very passionately admired, by Mr. Rixley, who was then still a young and decidedly a very handsome man. Nevertheless, the young Helen did not admire him by many degrees so much as he admired her, and would very greatly have preferred returning to her promised post of teacher at the school to the becoming Mrs. Rixley.

Had she been a few years older she might have made more resolute and more successful efforts to decide this question for herself; but she was only seventeen, and the habit of obedience was still so inveterate in her that she yielded with but little resistance, and arrived in due time at the Warren House in the character of its mistress.

Perhaps in these its best days the said Warren House had nothing very beautiful or exhilarating in its aspect; but whatever was the cause, it is certain that the young and lovely Mrs. Rixley was not in any way enchanted or exhilarated by finding herself there.

In fact, the only thing that appeared greatly to interest her in her new home was the beautiful little boy whom she found trotting about there with just about the same degree of licence and of favour as we usually see accorded to a domestic pet. Nothing, in fact, could more accurately describe his condition than the words of the old song—

> "Now fondled, now chid,
> Permitted, forbid,
> It was leading the life of a dog."

But even this degree of favour was accorded more by the servants of the house than its master; for though the bright-looking little seraph was suffered to come and to go, when the parlour door happened to be open, without absolutely being kicked out of the way, it was but rarely that his hard natured father deigned to look at him, and never from the hour of his birth, which had cost his unfortunate mother the loss of family and friends, had he ever been seen to bestow a caress upon him.

This wretched mother had lived in the most perfect seclusion of the Warren House; but during the two years which preceded her death, she had learnt to welcome the departure and mourn the return of her seducer, on whose affections, although she continued to be called by his name, and to appear to be mistress of his house, she had evidently ceased to have any hold within a very few months of her residence with him.

As long as she lived, poor young creature, her beautiful child had been her idol, though she could scarcely feel him to be a consolation; but it seemed to be the pretty boy's fate to make the mournful seclusion of the Warren House endurable to its female inhabitants; for when a real Mrs. Rixley took possesion of it, his pretty ways occasioned her the only pleasure and amusement she seemed capable of feeling.

Nor did her fondness for him cease, when she had a child of her own to share it. The birth of her little girl was, nevertheless, an event of immense importance to her. Had she ever loved her husband, the evident loss of his affection, of which she was made fully aware within a very few months after their marriage, would doubtless have, in a great degree, poisoned the happiness which the birth of her little daughter occasioned; but, as it was, she too, like her still more unfortunate predecessor, learnt to welcome his departure from home with as keen a feeling of joy as happier wives welcome a husband's return.

As to the cause of his long and frequent absences she knew nothing. He used his house much as a traveller might use a well-known inn, coming and going without ceremony, and without thinking it necessary to give notice either of the one or the other.

The Warren House was a very isolated mansion, being at nearly a mile's distance from the parish church, and rather more from the little village to which it belonged; and the detached mansions of the few gentlemen's families resident in the neighbourhood were at a somewhat greater distance still. The reason of this sort of isolation was obvious, arising from the immediate vicinity of a wide-spreading rabbit warren, which had given its name to the house occupied by Mr. Rixley, and its dreary aspect to the land immediately surrounding it.

The remoteness of its situation must always have rendered it a lonely and unsocial sort of dwelling; and its present owner's manner of life had, of course, rendered it still more so.

The doubts which were speedily circulated respecting the first Mrs. Rixley's right to the name not only kept these few and distant neighbours from coming near her, but seemed left as a legacy to the second Mrs. Rixley also; and the village doctor was for a long time the only one of their neighbours who ventured to bring his wife to call upon her.

But the sort of suspicion which at first appeared to attach to her wore away by degrees: her little girl was taken to church to be christened, and was duly entered in the register as Helen, the daughter of George Rixley and of Helen, his wife; whereas, in the case of little William, the ceremony of christening in the parish church was omitted altogether; and this difference was considered to be a very satisfactory proof that the second Mrs. Rixley had better claims to the civility of the neighbourhood than the first.

But as this satisfactory event did not take place till nearly a twelvemonth after the real Mrs. Rixley was installed in her mansion, the visits of her neighbours were neither made, nor received, perhaps, very cordially; and, excepting in the case of Mr. Foster, the apothecary, and his family, these visits never led to any great intimacy. The habits and manners of Mr. Rixley himself were not, indeed, such as to lead to intimacy; for although he occasionally returned the hospitalities he accepted by giving, about twice a year, a very ostentatious dinner to those whose dinners he had eaten, the repulsive stiffness of his manner was never relaxed towards any one.

He was no sportsman, and, therefore, never met his neighbours in the field; he never mounted a horse, and, therefore, never made a morning visit; and, moreover, he was so often absent for weeks and even months together, that, excepting at these formal dinner parties, he was very rarely seen by his neighbours at all.

There was but one amusement or occupation to which he was known to be attached, and to this one he certainly was attached even passionately, and this was BOATING.

The Warren House at Crumpton was situated in the midst of a mile or two of tolerably level, but very lofty and bleak table-land, which reached to the edge of one of the boldest cliffs on the coast of Cornwall; and it was on the turbulent element over which that bleak cliff hung that the master of the Warren House found the only recreation which its neighbourhood seemed capable of affording him.

A frightfully steep flight of rude steps, rarely trod by any feet but his own, and those of the out-of-door servant, who *sometimes* cleaned the shoes of the family, but *always* took care of the fine boat belonging to its master, led from a dip in this cliff to the rocky beach below, where, in a curiously tranquil little creek, was erected a large and very costly boat-house, so well placed and so firmly constructed as pretty safely to defy the storms of that stormy coast.

And in this boat-house dwelt the thing that was very

decidedly dearer to Mr. Rixley than either wife, mistress, child, or any other thing whatever.

But his pleasure in it was savagely solitary; for though the boatman who always accompanied him, and another sailor who often did so when the battling breeze was too strong for one alone to combat—though both these men were highly paid and highly valued servants—the idea of their sharing his pleasure no more entered his head than the idea that the sails, the rudder, or the oars enjoyed it.

That Mr. Rixley loved the sea at all times and in all variations of weather was clearly proved by the many hours he passed upon it in heat and cold, in storm and calm, in sunshine and in torrents of rain. A violent thunder-storm, indeed, was his especial delight; and the only state of atmosphere which ever kept him for a whole day on shore when at Crumpton was that of dense and hopeless fog, or perfect calm. But it was evident that this dislike of a fog arose in no degree from any consciousness or fear of danger; for never was his eagerness to embark so great, and so evidently uncontrollable, as when imminent risk of life was not only threatened, but positively present with him.

Upon these occasions it was his invariable habit to bestow a very liberal largesse on the boatmen on leaving the little vessel, and another on the following morning, if, on re-visiting the boat-house, he found his darling craft well secured, and in all respects well cared for.

But he was most sternly arbitrary in exacting their obedience on occasions when the state of the elements was such as would have made it only commonly prudent, had they refused to risk their lives in compliance with his commands; and he had very correctly calculated the price at which they would consent to run the risk he proposed to them. That price he paid without a moment's hesitation; and had these nautical slaves of the purse more fully comprehended the desperate wilfulness of the man they had to deal with, they might easily and habitually have extorted a much heavier tax than he had ever paid.

Once, and fortunately only once, the life of the assistant boatman was sacrificed to the sort of brutal intrepidity with which Mr. Rixley defied all the dangers of a tremendous storm, for the sake of enjoying the godlike sport (as he called it *to himself*, for he never expressed that, or any other of his strange peculiarities, to mortal man) of rising out of the depths of a sea chasm, in order to ride aloft on the foamy crest of a sea wave.

Once, while enjoying this pastime, he saw the man, who was engaged on some manœuvre at the head of the boat, fairly knocked over by a wave, and then washed into the sea by the same wave on its return. All the efforts made by Mr. Rixley and the other man to save him were vain; and the poor fellow sank before their eyes to rise no more.

This event, of course, made a good deal of noise in the neighbourhood; and the rashness of Mr. Rixley was also, of course, much blamed; but when a donation of two hundred pounds to the poor man's widow was paid into the hands of the village lawyer, with instructions to settle one hundred and fifty of it upon his little orphan girl, and to place the remaining fifty in the savings' bank in the name of the widow, as a fund to supply her immediate wants, there was not a voice to be heard discussing the tragical event that was not loud in praise of the brave gentleman's noble generosity; and the accident by no means tended to make the fishermen, or their sons either, less willing to accompany the Warren House squire whenever he asked for their services. He had shrewdly guessed that so it would be, and was by no means inclined to quarrel with the adventure.

But, notwithstanding the lavish liberality with which Mr. Rixley repaid all services rendered to him in pursuit of this darling amusement, he was neither greatly loved nor respected by a single individual among those he employed. Even his fearlessness, which in most cases is a very highly-esteemed quality by all whose lives are passed in the presence of danger, had in no degree endeared him to them. Had any among them been nice in expressing distinctions, he would have been oftener called rash than brave by them; and very justly, for the mental condition which deserves the name of courage was as unknown to him as the sensations of a fainting fit; and if he laughed aloud while his attendants turned pale with fear, it was only because his inordinate enjoyment of vehement sensations made the fitful blustering of the roaring wind, and the mad dancing of the foaming waves, more agreeable to him than the loveliest stillness which heaven ever permitted to rest upon the bosom of a summer sea.

It will easily be believed that in this his favourite—or rather his only—pastime, his wife and children had no share. In fact, they had very little more of his society when he was dwelling at the Warren House, than when he was absent from it; and, fortunately for her happiness, his wife was by no means disposed to mourn over this neglect as one of the evils of her destiny; but, on the contrary, to consider it as a most important alleviation of her unhappy position; and such it certainly was.

Neither was she, for the most part, in any way annoyed by the interference of her husband in the arrangement of her domestic concerns. She hired servants and dismissed them, according to her own judgment, will, and pleasure, he having told her in a very peremptory manner, upon the first occasion of the kind that offered, that she must never again trouble him by any reference on such a subject.

Once, indeed, it happened, a year or two after their marriage, that the servant who attended on the children was dismissed by him, in consequence of her having, as he said, answered him impertinently; but this interference was by no means exercised rudely, as far as concerned his wife, whatever it might have been to the servant he dismissed; for with much more civility and observance than he was in the habit of showing her, he apologised for having put her to inconvenience by this sudden dismissal, adding that he had made the best atonement he could for it by making inquiries in every direction for a well-recommended nursemaid to take her place, and that he had succeeded in hearing of a young woman who had already filled a similar situation, and of whom he had received so high a character as to make him expect that she would be a perfect treasnre to her and to the children.

The time of most ladies might have hung heavily upon their hands in the situation in which Mrs. Rixley was placed; but it was not so with her. The education she had received became a great blessing to her. She had inherited her mother's talent and taste for drawing; and the teaching she had received in the art had been excellent, and excellently well put to profit: she was as good a linguist as any young girl could be who had never left her native land, and who had never had time or opportunity before her marriage to read anything beyond her class-books. She had an excellent ear, and had been justly considered as the best pianoforte-player at the school; and she could have sung too, and very sweetly, had any one ever wished to hear her.

But not even all this most fortunate treasure of resource would have sufficed to occupy her time so completely as it was occupied, had she not speedily taken a mother's interest in the beautiful, but utterly neglected child, whom she found running about her husband's house as the acknowledged son of its master, but receiving no more notice from him than if he had been a foundling left at his door.

There were many vices deeply rooted, and deeply hidden too, in the heart of Mr. Rixley; but their concealment was for the sake of convenience, and did not in any case proceed from hypocrisy, for no man could well be more indifferent to the opinion of his fellow creatures. Mr. Rixley was a rich man, and rich men may easily gratify their whims, and their passions too, without exposing themselves to any penalty enforced by the laws. Had he been a poor man the case would have been widely different. But although he could do, and did do, pretty nearly all the evil which it suited his inclination to achieve without making himself amenable to the laws, he was aware that if all his transactions were known, it would in all probability be productive of inconvenience to him; and he, therefore, did a great many things that nobody knew anything about but himself.

Farther than this, however, his hypocrisy did not go. He did not think it necessary to affect a virtue when he had it not, for he would not have given up a sail in his boat, or any other gratification to which he was attached, for the sake of being considered as the most virtuous man in existence by every human being of his acquaintance. And therefore it was that his wife discovered, before she had been twenty-four hours in his house, that he had a heart as hard as a stone, and not a thousandth part so much amiable feeling as the cat who lay on the hearth-rug and caressed its kitten as it ran over her.

On the whole, perhaps, it was well for her that this discovery was made so speedily, and so decisively. Had she loved the man to whom she had been given as a wife, the case would here again have been very different; but as it was, it was far better for her to understand him thoroughly, and understand her own position also at once.

In achieving this she made no blunder whatever.

He remained with her for about a fortnight after their return home as the most impassioned of lovers, and as she thought, poor young thing, as the most disagreeable of men; and then he left her; why, or whither he went she knew not at all, and certainly cared not much. Her childhood though not unprofitably spent, had never been childishly gay, and had never been youthfully happy, and now the quiet stillness of her almost solitary home was infinitely less shocking to her than it would have been to most girls of the same age.

In the course of this honey fortnight he had besought her to

tell him if there was anything she wished for, which his house
did not contain, and which the neighbouring little town could
not supply, adding that he was writing to a friend in London,
who would execute any commission she would give with all
possible attention to her wishes.

In reply to this obliging offer she had answered very readily
that she should be greatly obliged to him if he would subscribe
to a library for her, and make arrangements for a regular
transmission of a book-box for her, about once a month.

The request was complied with, amidst abounding caresses,
and the standing order given in consequence of it having never
been rescinded, she had continued in the enjoyment of this very
consolatory indulgence to the day of her death.

And it was well she had it, for she wanted that, and every
other consolation within her reach, to enable her to endure the
many painful features of her strange destiny. She was indeed
very speedily released from the oppressive fondness of her ill-
matched mate, and not unfrequently from his presence also for
many weeks together, and for this she was very truly thankful.
But nevertheless her life was a painfully strange one for so very
young a woman. Her good and steady friend, Mrs. Foster, the
worthy wife of the village doctor, often told her that she might
easily put herself upon a more intimate and pleasant footing
with the ladies of the neighbourhood, if she would show them
any indication that she wished it, for they were all disposed to
like, and think well of her. But poor Mrs. Rixley had no
courage to try the experiment. It is true that her husband
never enquired what she did during his absence, but she felt
very reasonably certain, that if anything like intimacy were
established between her and her neighbours, his cold and
repulsive manners to them would be a ceaseless source of
embarrassment, and annoyance.

And so she lived on in her studious solitude, her dearly
loved step-child, and her own darling little girl being her pastime as long as their babyhood lasted, and her well-instructed
pupils afterwards.

That she should dearly love her own, and only child, and be
dearly loved by her in return, was certainly not very extraordinary, nor in any way out of the common course of things;
but there was something more than common in the attachment
which existed between her and the little William. Pity for
his neglected condition had first opened her young and truly
feminine heart to the motherless and neglected boy, and his

bright beauty, and bright intelligence had rapidly increased this pitying tenderness, till her love for him very nearly, if not quite, equalled the love she felt for her own child; while, on his part, his devoted affection for her seemed to call forth, and keep in full action all the energy of his excitable and ardent spirit.

CHAPTER II.

My retrospect ought to have been condensed into the reasonable bounds of one chapter; I have, however, exceeded this, and must give another to it—but my narrative is still retrospective.

A manner of life so unvarying as that of Mrs. Rixley cannot be exposed to any change, however apparently trifling, without such a degree of attention being excited by it, as to make it appear of some importance. And so it happened with the recluse of the Warren House when her nursery maid was dismissed by her husband, and a stranger introduced in her stead.

Had Mrs. Rixley's life and occupations been less isolated, and less abundant in opportunities for solitary and fanciful lucubrations, she would probably have been satisfied by perceiving that this new attendant upon the children appeared to understand her business extremely well, and was regular and attentive in the performance of it; but though these valuable qualities were by no means overlooked, or undervalued by her meditative young mistress, this did not suffice to prevent her fancying that the young woman had something strangely capricious in her disposition, although this supposed caprice never interfered with the performance of the duties assigned to her.

For a long time, however, the idea that this Sarah Lambert was subject to occasional fits of ill-temper greatly lessened the confidence which her general good conduct was calculated to inspire; for poor solitary Mrs. Rixley was grievously tormented with the idea that if the deep gloom, which sometimes appeared so legibly stamped on the handsome and expressive features of this important functionary, were to seize on her while walking with the children on the "beetling cliff," she might be strangely tempted to save them and herself also from all future human ills, by tossing them over the rock, and flinging herself after them.

But by degrees these vague imaginings in a great degree wore themselves out, and well they might, for the woman's devotion to the children was unbounded, and if any danger could be rationally feared from her attendance on them, it must have been found in the risk they both ran of being, in nursery phrase, spoiled; for it was very evident that if left wholly to herself she would have indulged them much beyond the limits of discretion.

But Mrs. Rixley was not wholly wrong in thinking, and in feeling, that there was often something singularly puzzling in the aspect and manner of this young woman. Most people would have allowed her to be extremely handsome, though there were many, of whom her mistress was one, who thought that the expression of her magnificent eyes was more startling, than agreeable.

These marvellous eyes were large, long, dark, and lustrous, and there were moments, for instance when they were fixed with almost passionate tenderness on the little William, when neither her mistress, nor any one else could deny that they were the most beautiful eyes they ever beheld.

But Mr. Foster, who was a "travelled man," having been a navy surgeon in his youth, explained the mystery of this unwonted brilliancy, and vehemence of expression, by pronouncing very confidently that the eyes were Greek eyes, and that, though it was possible one of her parents might have been English, it was quite certain in his judgment that the other must have had a different origin. Whether he were right or wrong in this conjecture was never likely to be known, for no one ever heard the tall, dark-eyed, grave-looking Sarah Lambert talk of herself, or any one belonging to her.

To her mistress she was respectfully obedient, and rigidly observant of her wishes, as respected the arrangements of the nursery; but there was a coldness in her manner which not all the familiarity arising from lengthened service, or sympathy of feeling concerning the children, could remove. Whether this manner arose from dislike, or from respect, it would have been difficult to say, but whatever its cause it was not agreeable, and the less so from the striking contrast which it formed to her manner with the children, which was always fondly caressing, and sometimes almost impassioned in its tenderness.

Mrs. Rixley's studious habits—for the solitary life she led had converted more than one of her pursuits into studies—often prevented her from leaving the house in the morning, even in the most tempting season of the year; for as the children advanced in age, her occupation as sole instructor to them both constantly employed four or five hours of the early part of the day, and when they were dismissed to their sports in the garden, she was wont to sit down either to read, or to draw, and would often remain thus engaged till the daylight failed her.

Upon one occasion when this had happened three or four days successively, without her having taken any exercise at all, she began to feel that she wanted the fresh air, and that she had sat still too long.

The day had been warm, and the children having been indulged with a long evening ramble had gone both of them early to bed, so it was alone, and not with the sturdy little William trotting as usual by her side, that she set forth to take a moonlight walk upon the cliff.

The breeze from the sea was deliciously cool, without bringing any chilling quality with it; and she strolled on, and on, till she had far exceeded the usual limits of her evening walk.

At length she reached the point where the steps, leading to the beach and the boat-house, were situated, and for a moment she felt a strong inclination to descend them; for although her strangely-tempered husband had never once invited her either to accompany him in his boat, or even to walk with him to the beach, which formed the most attractive feature of their residence, she had found out, and enjoyed its beauty in that happier portion of her existence, during which his absence from home left her free from any risk of meeting him, either on the cliff, or under it.

When she took the children with her to the beach, she availed herself of an approach somewhat more circuitous, but much less dangerous; but when alone she had so often taken this shorter way, that she no longer felt any fear in treading it.

But now, though the moon shone brightly, she hesitated when she reached the point where the opening in the cliff, looking more like a dark chasm, than a stair, yawned at her feet, and after the doubt of a moment she discreetly turned away, determined for this time to be contented with looking on the moon-lit sea from the heights, without attempting to approach it more nearly.

This resolution was the more easily taken, because there was a little hollow sheltered nook, at no great distance from the place whence the steps descended, which was well known to her as offering the most commodious seat imaginable from whence to look out upon the ocean, and the bold sweep of towering rocks by which it was bordered. To this nook she now turned her steps, and having seated herself in the turfy hollow, she rejoiced in the prudence which had brought her to a spot so every way enjoyable, instead of seeking the doubtful pleasure of a scramble down the cliff.

She had not, however, enjoyed this snug position long, before she became aware that the almost certain solitude which had often rendered it so agreeable as a resting-place, was not quite so certain by night, as by day, for ere she had been seated many minutes, she distinctly heard voices discoursing aloud at no great distance from her. She speedily became aware, however, that the speakers were approaching the summit of the cliff by the steps from which she had just before turned away, and she rejoiced anew at the discretion which had prevented her meeting them, and this not only because she wished not at such an hour to meet any one, but because the doing so, even by broad daylight, would have led to the awkward necessity of the ascending party going down, or the descending party going up, for to pass each other would have been pretty nearly impossible.

Her satisfaction, moreover, was the more complete, because there was now no sort of necessity that she should be seen by the approaching strangers at all; for nothing could be more easy than for her so to place herself within a few feet of the place where she was sitting, as to be quite beyond the reach of any passing eyes.

The change of position necessary to ensure this did not occupy a moment, but the manœuvre had not been long accomplished, when a voice vibrated upon her ear, which she instantly knew to be that of her husband.

He had been absent from the Warren House nearly a month, but as he had condescended to tell her when he left it that it was his purpose to be absent for two, she was as much surprised as chagrined at his unexpected return. Had she not believed his continued absence certain, she would have been far more likely to betake herself to the safe solitude of her bed-room than to have wandered within reach of his so well-known haunt, as the steps leading to his boat-house.

She rejoiced, however, most sincerely, that the timid fit had seized her, which had prevented her meeting him, face to face, where it would have been next to impossible for him not to offer her the assistance of his arm; and it was now so long since anything so nearly approaching conjugal kindness had passed between them, that the necessity for it would probably have been equally disagreeable to both parties.

The rocky crag which so effectually prevented Mrs. Rixley from being seen from the path above the hollow nook in which she had placed herself, in no way impeded her being able to see the persons who traversed it, and she soon perceived that the companion of her husband was a woman.

Unfortunately for the reputation of the gentleman, the frequency of this sort of companionship with persons of the very lowest class was too notorious for his wife to be ignorant of it, and the pain arising from seeing him thus approaching to within a few feet of her, with his arm thrown round his companion, arose chiefly from the disagreeable consciousness that accident had now made her a spy upon his actions, while fully aware that the peaceful tenor of her existence was the result of her careful avoidance of everything approaching to interference with his mode of passing his time, either at home or abroad.

So genuine was her wish to preserve herself in this state of ignorance, that as the pair approached her place of conceal-ment, she actually closed her eyes that she might not by possibility recognise the woman who was his companion.

"Almeria! you are an idiot!" were the first words which she distinctly heard, as the pair approached her. They were uttered in the deep voice of her husband, and though they indicated reproach, there was something in the accent with which they were uttered, which showed plainly that whether idiot, or not, "Almeria" was not an object of indifference.

"You know," he said, "that let who will come into the house, you are the only one, either in it, or out of it, for whom I really feel attachment. Then why cannot this content you? You cannot have forgotten that I told you, from the very first, that desperately as I was in love with you, I never would sub-mit to be tormented by a woman's jealousy. Have you forgotten this?"

If his companion replied to this question, it was either by a sign, or a whisper, for no sound was heard by Mrs. Rixley, who would gladly, poor lady, have submitted to the fatigue of walking a dozen miles before she slept, could she equally well have escaped hearing what was to follow. But so it was not to be.

"Now just tell me, Almeria, will you," resumed Mr. Rixley, in a tone that might have been heard distinctly, even had he been less near to his concealed wife, for the pair had now reached a point of the path that was almost exactly above the unfortunate lady's head, "just tell me how you think it happens that the doll of a woman I have got at home is suffered by me to go on there, year after year, as the mistress of my house?"

"The question is easily answered," replied his companion. "She remains there because you cannot help it. She remains there because she is your wife!"

These words caused the concealed Mrs. Rixley to start so vehemently, that had she been less completely out of sight of those who were passing along the path above, the movement must have betrayed her. It was not, however, the purport of what was said which caused this emotion, but the sound of the voice which spoke it—a voice so perfectly familiar and well-known, that she felt it impossible she could be mistaken as to the person to whom it belonged, and yet a second thought told her that mistaken she must be, for how was it possible for her to believe that this "Almeria," so earnestly assured that she was the only one for whom her husband felt any real attachment, was Sarah Lambert, her nursemaid?

It was not very wonderful, perhaps, that her curiosity to ascertain the real truth upon this point was too pungent to permit her submitting to the cautious restraint which she had hitherto imposed upon herself, and she was in the very act of stepping forward from beneath the overhanging bushes which concealed her, when the loud voice of her husband, immediately above the spot where she stood, showed her that instead of walking forward as she supposed they had done, they were standing still within about four feet of the top of her head. She made this discovery however in time to arrest the imprudent movement she was going to make, and it was probably fortunate that she did so, for the tone of her husband's voice as he replied to the fair "Almeria" by no means indicated any very gentle mood.

"Again, I tell you, that you are an idiot!" he exclaimed. "Yet it is I who am an idiot," he added, "for believing that you mean what you say. You know better, Almeria! you know as well as I do that if she were ten times my wife, I would manage to get quit of her if she troubled me. But she does not trouble me. On the contrary, her remaining to all intents and purposes my very contented and obedient wife, and your very unobservant and contented mistress, makes her invaluable to us both! Moreover she teaches the children well, and it costs me nothing. Moreover she keeps the house well, which is very convenient. Moreover every girl in the parish might appear a beauty in my eyes without her ever finding it out, or caring a rush about it if she did, and that too is very convenient. And very convenient would it be for all of us, if you had common sense enough to follow her example in this particular."

"It shall be my study to do so," replied the deep-toned and impressive-voice of Almeria, alias Sarah. "I ought to be able to do it," she added, "for I know two receipts for it. The one is that I should cease to love you. The other, that I should leave your house, and hide myself where you should never see me more."

"And if you ever attempt to achieve either the one or the other," replied Mr. Rixley, "I swear by all that is sacred, that I will murder you first, and myself afterwards! Beware of me, Almeria! I am not one who can be safely trifled with! You pride yourself upon your strength of mind, and firmness of character. And I have listened to your boastings till I believed you to be all that you seemed to believe yourself, and have almost worshipped you accordingly. And have you not ruled me, and led me, as if I had been your slave, instead of your master? Do you not know for, and by whose pleasure it is that these two children, for whom I do not care a rush, are kept here in high style and state, instead of being sent off to some cheap school, where I should never hear their voices again? Have I not told you a thousand times over, that I hate children? And have I not given up my own will in this, in order to gratify yours? Why do you seem to shudder thus as you hang upon me, Almeria? Perhaps you think me a monster because I love them not? Ungrateful woman! If I love them not, it is because they are not yours! It is hateful to me to remember that the puling girl of my puling wife must inherit all I possess, except forsooth what I may be pleased to leave by will to your hopeful darling the boy, who is the very image of his vulgar mother, and to my fancy, the most disagreeable brat I ever encountered in my life!"

"Take your arm from my waist, George Rixley! I will sit

here no longer! The night wind from the ocean chills my limbs . . . . and your words chill my soul! Let me go, I say. I will sit here no longer."

These words, uttered in the clear voice of her stately nurse, gave the first intimation to her greatly embarrassed mistress, that the pair from whom it was so important that she should remain concealed, were not, as she had imagined, pausing in their walk, but actually seated, almost close to her.

She positively feared to breathe, lest her hiding-place should be discovered thereby, and so great was her terror of the consequences which might follow such a discovery, that had not her husband obeyed the mandate of his mistress, and moved on, it is highly probable that his unfortunate wife might have betrayed herself by falling insensible upon the spot where she stood, and thereby calling their attention to her.

But she immediately heard him reply, in accents of tenderness such as she remembered to have heard in years long past, "Chilled, dearest! come then! and come quickly! Why have you let me detain you so long!"

And then she heard no more, save their retreating footsteps towards the Warren House.

The effect of this most unexpected discovery upon Mrs. Rixley was as painful—fully as painful—as if she had loved her husband, though the pain was of a very different kind. She found herself in the position which is, perhaps, of all others, the most painful to a conscientious mind, that is to say, she knew not what she *ought* to do, for she knew not, among many conflicting feelings, which were the most purely dictated by her duty, and an uncompromising sense of what was right.

There was something terribly repugnant to her delicacy in continuing to associate with the woman who called herself Sarah Lambert, on the same terms of well-satisfied and approving esteem as formerly. This course would not only be repugnant to her conscience, but would, moreover, require a degree of constant self-command, and even of hypocrisy, which she did not believe she had the power of practising. Yet, on the other hand, how could she venture to risk her own safety, and, what was far dearer still, the safety of the children, by proclaiming her knowledge of the infamous position which their nurse held in the house? It had been made clearly evident to her, by the direct avowal of her husband, that these unfortunate children owed the asylum granted them in the house of their father to the influence of this woman, and if she permitted her own feelings to rob them of it, what had she to give them in its stead?

Through the long hours of the dreadful night which followed this discovery, the unhappy Mrs. Rixley never closed her eyes in sleep, nor even for a moment ceased to meditate with the most intense anxiety on the miserable position in which she found herself involved. The consequence of this feverish watchfulness, and the miserable uncertainty of purpose which ceased not to torment her during every hour it lasted, proved too much for her strength both of body and mind, and when Sarah Lambert as usual entered her room with the little Helen on the following morning, she found her in a raging fever, and perfectly delirious.

The violence, and the suddenness of this seizure, puzzled the worthy Mr. Foster greatly. But it was in vain that he questioned Sarah as to the manner in which she had spent the preceding day. Sarah knew nothing of her having taken a late evening walk; and when cautiously questioned by Mr. Foster as to the possibility of her having been startled, or in any way agitated by the unexpected return of Mr. Rixley, she gave a very satisfactory reply in the negative, assuring the apothecary that to her certain knowledge, her mistress had gone to bed, not only without having seen her master, but also without having been made aware of his return, as she herself, as well as all the other servants, very distinctly declared that they had neither seen, nor spoken to her after the return of Mr. Rixley, stating, moreover, that to the best of their knowledge and belief, she had retired to rest before his return, which was not till a late hour in the evening.

This illness, though it was both violent, and lingering, did not prove fatal; but the unfortunate Mrs. Rixley never fully recovered her health, or spirits. To decide upon a difficult, and very doubtful question without any counsellor to assist the judgment, must ever be a painful and arduous task, and sad indeed were the long and dreary hours devoted by the suffering invalid to the question of whether it were best, and wisest, to run all hazards, and insist upon the dismissal of her husband's mistress from the office of constant attendant upon herself and the children, or to suffer things to continue as they were, and endeavour to forget all she had seen and heard.

That she at length decided upon this latter course might perhaps have been partly owing to the conduct of Sarah Lambert during her long illness. Had she been her sister, instead of her rival, she could not have shown more devoted attention, or more unwearied care; and when, upon at length leaving her room, and resuming by degrees the task of instructing the children, she discovered that the strangely mysterious "Almeria" had, notwithstanding all her attendance upon herself, contrived to supply her place with them, she felt no doubt, that she "might have better spared a better" person.

The result, therefore, of all poor Mrs. Rixley's deep meditations was, that everything, excepting the state of her own health and spirits, remained in the same state as before her illness; but she never completely recovered from the effects of the shock she had received, and within two years after her eventful moonlight ramble she died, leaving her only child and its almost equally dear little brother, with no human being to love and cherish them, save the guilty woman whose disgraceful connection with their father rendered her pretty nearly the last person in the world, to whose care they ought to have been confided.

CHAPTER III.

"Dear, dear Sarah! Pray do not tell me that I must not go in the boat with papa!" cried the eager William, who, notwithstanding his fifteen years, and his almost manly stature, was still wonderfully obedient to command, at least when the command was spoken by the omnipotent Sarah Lambert, omnipotent alike from her absolute and uncontrolled power in his father's house, and from his own grateful and devoted affection to her. Nor was this devoted affection more than she deserved, both from him and his sister also, for everything like pleasure or even comfort, which they either of them enjoyed, was owing to her influence, to her exertions, to her stedfast purpose, and to her stedfast will.

The reader must content himself with being told that several years have worn themselves away between the conclusion of the last chapter, and the beginning of the present one, and great and important changes had taken place in the apparent situation of Mr. Rixley during this interval.

For the first year or two after the death of his wife, his establishment at the Warren House underwent but little change. His intercourse with his neighbours, indeed, which had never been very frequent, had now nearly ceased altogether, although he was much less absent from the neighbourhood, than he had been during the lifetime of his wife.

But this falling off of neighbourly intercourse was not very extraordinary, for his young daughter had still too much the appearance of a mere child to be visited, except by friends as intimate and as warmly interested for her as the young Fosters, and he was himself much too unpopular to be sought, and much too unsociable to seek anything approaching to friendly intercourse with anybody.

But during this first year or two his two children had enjoyed the advantage of receiving lessons from the curate of Crumpton, who, by the recommendation of Mr. Foster, and the influence of "Almeria," was permitted to attend them for three or four hours every morning.

No person could be more capable of advancing the education of these sadly-placed children than was this good Mr. Bolton. He was an excellent scholar, according to the English acceptation of the phrase, and, moreover, as it happened, he was an excellent French scholar too.

He was still almost a young man, though the father of a large family; and though his object in accepting the moderate stipend offered for the hours he thus devoted to the Warren House was to obtain a greatly-needed increase to his small income, he soon found himself so much interested both for the boy and girl, that his friendship became as valuable as his instruction.

When Sarah Lambert first learnt that the curate of Crumpton was anxious to find pupils, she made one of those resolute attacks upon her "*master*," which seldom altogether failed of success, in order that William might have the benefit of instruction thus fortunately within his reach; for his father had long ago declared that *nothing* should induce him to place the boy at school; the final answer which he had given to her remonstrances on this subject being, that he had rather be hung, drawn, and quartered, than submit to having his affairs, and his conduct, examined into and judgment passed upon him, by masters and ushers, mistresses and maids, through all the successive schools and academies, which her silly fondness for him might lead her to recommend.

"There is at least one holy axiom, Almeria," said he, "that I have never lost sight of through life,—'*let not thy left hand know what thy right hand doeth*,' and you, of all the world, should be the last to quarrel with my respect for it, for it has saved you from much that you would not very patiently have endured!"

He spoke truly—and she knew it. He spoke resolutely too; and when she was aware that he did so, the contest ended, for Almeria loved not to speak idle words. And thus it was that his son William had completed his fifteenth year, and his daughter Helen her twelfth, without receiving any more finished education than it had been in the power of his wife and the curate to give them.

But as both the children were quick, intelligent, and docile, they were considerably better informed on many subjects, and in all respects greatly more intelligent, than those who had apparently enjoyed much greater intellectual advantages. But a very sudden alteration now took place in Mr. Rixley's manner of living: and though he gave no reason for it, not even to Sarah Lambert, it could scarcely be doubted that pecuniary misfortune must be the cause of it. But upon no occasion had he ever adhered so scrupulously to his system of secrecy as he did now. He gave Mrs. Lambert, as he now always called her, at least when there was any one present to hear him, very sudden, but very explicit, orders to dismiss every servant in the house, only permitting a woman in the village, who had formerly lived with him as cook, to do the work of the house as a day-servant; adding, however, as he gave this permission, that it was highly probable that when Helen was a year or two older she would have to fill this place herself.

"But this," he added, "will depend upon circumstances. It is possible that I may never be obliged to place her in the situation that Rebecca Watkins holds now; but it is not only possible, but very probable, that I may, and if the necessity, or what I shall choose to consider as the necessity, comes, be very sure, Mrs. Lambert, that I shall not shrink from it."

He said this sternly, and resolutely; and Sarah Lambert felt at that moment (and it was the first time that she had ever felt it distinctly) that her influence with him was no longer so omnipotent as it had been.

If before this conviction reached her heart, a choice had been offered her between feeling it, or losing the power of feeling anything, by yielding herself instantly to sudden death, she would have chosen the latter. But no such choice was offered; and the pang that shot through her heart and brain at that moment might have won pity from any being of a nature less flinty than that of the man who inflicted it.

At the time this narrative actually begins, however, this *necessity* had evidently not arrived; for though everything approaching to the appearance of a gentleman's establishment had been broken up, the footman, cook, housemaid, and regular gardener dismissed, and the reverend tutor paid off, with a formal written notification that his attendance upon the young people would be no longer required, yet still the daily attendance of the "maid of all work" was permitted; and no tasks were as yet assigned to the delicate Helen but such as were apportioned by Sarah Lambert, and these, most assuredly, were no heavier than might h..ve been enjoined to an accomplished young princess of the blood royal, whose education was not yet completed.

Although nothing in the least degree approaching parental love was now, or indeed ever had been, demonstrated by Mr. Rixley towards either of his children, his conduct towards them was by no means equal. To the boy he was always either brutally severe, or else so negligent as to make it almost doubtful whether he had not forgotten his existence altogether.

To the girl also, he was frequently very sullenly cross, but neither absolutely brutal, nor forgetful; for it . frequently happened that after one of his long absences from the Warren House, which since the dismissal of his servants had again become both long and frequent, he would desire that she might be brought to him: and when she came, he looked at her much as he might have done at a horse that he was about either to buy or to sell. Upon these occasions Sarah Lambert never failed to bring forward the young William also, secretly flattering herself that his handsome person, bright intelligence, and frank, joyous manner must, in time, win the heart even of his unnatural father.

And even after she had given up this hope, she still persevered in her system of making William accompany her to the parlour when commanded to bring Helen. For some time the only notice, which this sort of enforced entry produced, was a surly frown, and to this the light-hearted lad was so accustomed that he did not greatly heed it; but it sank deep into the heart of Sarah Lambert—so deep, that the passionate love she had once felt for Rixley was so rapidly growing into hatred, that nothing prevented her leaving him but the idea that his children would suffer more than he would by her loss.

Of this quiet, but most complete change in her feelings towards him, Mr. Rixley was completely unconscious. He had known, only too well, how successful his influence over her had been in overcoming and stifling all her early principles, and all her purest feelings: and he triumphed in the consciousness of having perverted and subdued a mind so powerful, and a heart so warm.

But, although he knew much, he did not know all the peculiarities of her character, nor was he aware how far the same resolute firmness of temper which had led her to conquer every obstacle, and crush every virtuous feeling, in order to give herself to him, might lead her in some new direction, upon her discovering that she was no longer of the same importance to him as formerly.

He did, however, perceive that she was very obstinately resolute in her determination of bringing the son of the pretended Mrs. Rixley as often into his imperial presence, as the daughter of the real one: and this provoked him greatly; for he not only had given to this, his sole legitimate child, the privilege of being christened and registered at the parish church, but he had actually made his will, and left her everything he possessed.

This last act, indeed, was not performed without the pleasant consciousness that it would be annulled if he should chance to marry a second time, and become the father of a legitimate son.

In truth his only reason for making this will at all, was because he was very particularly anxious to guard against the possibility of his brother's inheriting, as heir-at-law, whatever property he possessed.

Mr. Rixley was a great hater; he certainly might have very fairly been said to hate many persons with an intensity that might have secured to him the admiration of the great moralist himself; but all his other hatreds were but minor passions in comparison of that which he cherished against his brother; the original cause of this master passion may be explained hereafter, but it had nothing to do with the events which I have at present to relate.

The having made this will, however, whatever the motive of his doing it, had given his daughter considerable importance in his eyes, and it was this feeling which caused him to summon her to his presence in the manner above mentioned.

As to the poor boy, he had been from the hour of his birth so little cared for, or indeed thought of, by his father, that nothing but Sarah Lambert's ill-judged pertinacity would have been likely to have made him of sufficient importance to be the object of positive dislike. Having been repeatedly told by those who had given the boy all the instruction he had received that he was more than commonly rapid in learning all that they attempted to teach him, Mr. Rixley conceived the bright idea of procuring for him the place of usher at the grammar-school of a neighbouring town, and it was with this view that he still continued to allow the visits of Mr. Bolton, the curate, in the capacity of a tutor.

But he became so irritated by the observation of the once omnipotent Almeria, upon his want of affection for the boy, in thus condemning him to a sedentary occupation in a close school-room, which his active temperament would, she said, so assuredly make peculiarly painful to him, that he suddenly changed his purpose, and protested with an oath—both oath and protestation being addressed to the pale and gloomy-looking Almeria—that the boy should cost him no more for lessons, but should learn to be a sailor.

"Perhaps," he added, with a sneer, "that trade may suit his *temperament* better: and, at any rate, I can teach it myself, which will suit my present system of economy greatly better than paying Mr. Bolton."

That Mr. Rixley was in earnest in saying this, was in some degree proved, by three days passing away without their seeing the good curate; but during that interval no further mention had been made of the new project of education.

On the fourth, however, upon Sarah's taking the two children into the parlour, the salutation of their father was not, as usual, addressed to Helen, but to the boy.

"William!" he said, "what would you say if instead of having Parson Bolton to make you study Latin and Greek, I were to take you in hand, and make a sailor of you?"

"I should say, papa, that I liked it very much indeed! And I would not let Helen get before me in Latin, either, for I would sit up at night to write my exercises," was the boy's reply.

"Come along then!" returned his father, with a greater approach to good humour in his voice than poor William had ever heard from him before.

"Won't it be nice for me, Sarah?" said the boy, turning to

the constant friend who he felt sure would rejoice with his rejoicing.

But in this he was disappointed, for Sarah Lambert knit her dark brows, and said, "No, William! I do not choose that you should go on the sea in such weather as this. It is blowing fearfully! It will be a storm. I will not let you go, William."

And then it was that the boy said, "Dear, dear Sarah! Pray do not tell me that I must not go in the boat with papa!"

CHAPTER IV.

Mr. Rixley had been so long accustomed to submit himself in many things to the influence of Sarah Lambert, at least while under the immediate influence of her commanding, or her beseeching eyes, that he heard this appeal, and saw the arbitrary shake of the head which rejected it, without testifying either surprise or anger. Nevertheless, after the interval of a moment, he turned suddenly towards her, and fixed not exactly an angry, but very decidedly an inquisitive glance upon her countenance.

Her pale cheek was for a moment crimsoned, and, contrary to the usual result of an enquiring look from the man who fancied himself her master, she did not return his glance, but fixed her eyes upon a flower that she held in her hand.

At that moment they mutually misunderstood each other most completely. Mr. Rixley fancied that she feared having offended him by the blunt wilfulness with which she had opposed his proposal to the boy, and *she* thought that he had detected the dark feeling of suspicion with which she had heard him propose to take his young son with him upon the sea in weather which none but a practical sailor could have encountered without certain suffering, and probable danger.

They were both mistaken, however; for Sarah Lambert neither feared, nor heeded, the possibility of his being offended by her refusal, nor did *he* guess how dark was the suspicion which had flashed upon her mind upon hearing his proposal to the boy.

He looked at her frowningly, nevertheless; but not as he

would have looked had he suspected the truth; and said rudely
enough, "How can you be such an idiot, Sarah Lambert?
Because it pleases you to stand there looking at a rose, or a lily,
or whatever it is you are holding there so daintily, you want to
make this great huge giant of a boy do the same. I suppose
you are giving him lessons in needlework? How does he get
on with his stitching, Mrs. Lambert?"

"No, papa! no! Sarah does not want to make a coward of
me! Don't be angry with her because she loves me! Only
tell her that there is no danger, and then she will like my going
almost as much as I shall like it myself."

"Very well, sir, I will obey you," replied his father. And
then turning towards her with what he intended for a smile,
but which she read aright as a sneer, he added, " I beg to assure
you, Mrs. Lambert, that there is no chance whatever of your
young darling's being exposed to any danger, and I therefore
flatter myself that you will be so obliging as to let him go."

"Then let us all go!" said Sarah Lambert, with an air of
great animation, "I am no great coward myself, and as to the
gentle-looking Miss Helen, I can assure you, sir, that she is
likely to turn out a perfect heroine. There is no such feeling as
fear in her nature! You will like to go in the boat, my dear,
will you not?"

"I should like to go anywhere with you, Sarah," replied
Helen, creeping lovingly to her side, and passing her arm under
that of her faithful attendant and dearly beloved friend.

"Intriguing sorceress!" muttered Mr. Rixley between his
teeth, but in a tone so low that the children heard it not, though
Sarah Lambert did, for he took care to be close to her ear as he
uttered the words.

She started, but immediately recovering her self-possession,
she said, addressing them both, but without paying the least
attention to their father, who nevertheless stood by in silence,
as if expecting her final commands, "No! we will neither of
us go. This weather is not fit for an excursion on the water.
Hush! Do you not hear the raging wind. It is not right
for us to leave the house in such weather, and therefore we will
not do it."

Both the boy and girl did as she bade them do. They did
listen to the wind, and became so seasonably aware of its violence, that they signified their conviction, like reasonable beings
as they were, that "they thought it would perhaps be better to
stay at home."

"Curse her!" muttered Mr. Rixley in a deep whisper.

"What great events from trivial causes spring!"

Unimportant as this scene appears in the repetition, it was productive of very important results to the parties engaged in it.

The rage of Mr. Rixley appeared for a moment to be perfectly uncontrolable. He stamped with his feet, he clenched his fists till his nails lacerated the palms of his hands, and again he uttered curses both deep and loud against HER, for so only was the object of his wrath designated. "Leave the room," he said, distinctly addressing the two children, "I wish to speak to Mrs. Lambert on business."

Sarah Lambert, on hearing these words, released the hand of Helen, which was fast locked in hers, bent down and kissed her forehead, and said, in a very gentle and composed voice, "Go, my dear;—go, both of you into the school-room. I will come to you almost directly."

Helen immediately prepared to obey her by walking towards the door, but having reached it paused for a moment to wait for her brother. But the obedience of the boy was less prompt; he remained stationary, and as it were rooted to the spot where for the first time he heard the sound of his father's harsh voice raised to unmitigated violence, and uttering curses against HER whom he loved himself with all the gratitude and all the fondness of his warm enthusiastic nature.

His father turned towards him with an uplifted arm. "Go, William!" said Sarah Lambert, very quietly, but fixing her eyes upon him with a look that had more of entreaty than command in it; and he obeyed her instantly.

To the school-room they both went, William's arm round the waist of his sister, and her head resting against his shoulder as they walked.

On entering the room he placed her in the cushioned chair which had been her mother's constant seat, and having closed the door placed himself before her, and remained for a moment silently looking in her pale face.

"Helen!" he said at length, "I do not wish to have any secrets from you, and I do not choose that you should think me any better than I am. You are my sister, you know, because the same man is your father and my father, and as we have neither of us any other brothers or sisters, we ought not to live like strangers together, the one not knowing what is passing in the heart of the other. And you don't know yet, Helen, what is the greatest and strongest feeling in my heart."

"Yes, I do, William!" replied the little girl, affectionately, "your love for me, and for Sarah Lambert is the greatest and strongest feeling."

"No, Helen, it is not," he replied, gloomily and sternly. "You are mistaken, you are deceived in me, and that is exactly the reason why I am now determined to open my heart to you. I will not let you love me upon the strength of a mistake and a blunder, and from believing what is no better than a lie. I certainly do love you, and Sarah, both, dearly, dearly! But you have got a very mistaken idea of me, Helen, if you think *that* sweet gentle feeling is the strongest feeling of my heart. Hear the truth at once, and then all the love you may be able to feel for me afterwards I shall cherish and delight in, because it will be fairly my own, without cheating; but first listen to me and believe what I say—the greatest and strongest feeling of my heart is *hatred of my father!* Yes, Helen, hatred of your father, and my father."

"That sounds very shocking, William!" replied the poor girl, looking frightened, but at the same moment stretching out her arms to embrace him.

"Then you think you can love me still?" said he, kneeling down before her, and fondly returning the kiss she impressed upon his forehead. "How very glad I am that I have told you the truth, Helen! I don't feel now as if I were so very wicked, and the reason for that is, that I am no longer conscious of deceiving you, and of appearing better than I really am."

Having said this he sprang upon his feet, and strode with a hurried step up and down the room.

"What do you think he is saying to her all this time, Helen?" he exclaimed, after continuing his walk in silence for a minute or two. "I suppose you know who he meant by HER? When he uttered in that horrid voice the words 'curse her,' you understand that he meant to curse Sarah Lambert?"

Helen did not speak, but she bent her head in reply in a way which made her brother fully understand that she agreed with him in his interpretation.

"HER, Helen!" he repeated—"HER! Sarah Lambert! The being who has watched over his dying wife, and the motherless children she left, more like an angel than a woman! It was three years ago and more that your dear mother died, Helen, and you were a very little girl; too little perhaps to remember much about it now; but I remember it all! I remember how day after day, and night after night, she would sit watching by your dear pale mother's bed, and only steal away from time to time just to see that you and I wanted for nothing. Ay, and she was very kind to him too, ungrateful tyrant as he is. I have seen her gentle ways with him a thousand times, when he has been as sullen as a bear to her in return! Yet now he curses her!—Helen, I hate him."

"Do not say so any more, William—not even to yourself," replied the little girl, looking pale with terror, " I am sure it must be very wicked to say so, or I should not feel so frightened at hearing it. Promise me that you will not say it again," she added, coaxingly, and repeating her caress.

"There is no occasion that I should say it again," he replied, springing upon his feet, while the heavy gloom which had seemed to settle on his young brow vanished completely. I have spoken the truth, and you are no more likely to forget it than I am. I wanted you to know the truth, Helen, and you do know it, and yet you love me still. I feel now as if I did not much care for anything—nor will I care for anything, as long as he does not drive Sarah away from us. But she shan't stay to be ill-used. He had better not use her ill, Helen! He had better not! I do assure you it would be very dangerous, for I hate him already quite enough : and if he makes me hate him more by ill-treating her, I think I should kill him—I do, indeed! But don't look so frightened, child. Good gracious, how pale you are! How can you be such a fool, Helen? Do you think I am going really to kill him this very minute?"

"I wish you would not talk in such a very dreadful way, William! " said the poor girl, actually trembling from head to foot. "If you really love me, you never will talk to me in such a very shocking way again. What do you think Sarah would say, if she could hear you?"

"Why, I think it is very likely, my dear, that she would say just as you do, that it was very wrong to talk about such shocking things as killing. But I can tell you, Helen, what she would *not* do. She would not turn as white as a sheet, lips and all, as you have done.—There is no silly girl-like weakness in Sarah Lambert! If she told the real truth like me, she would be sure to say, that if a wicked man was shot, it would be no more than he deserved. But I think it is very likely she would not say it, though she might think it, for fear, you know, that it might set me upon shooting him,"

This was said with the gay boy's usual lightness of manner; but poor little Helen was in no humour to laugh at it. Her father's violent language had frightened her, and her brother's wild talk frightened her again; but this was not all, for she was frightened also, because she thought that Sarah stayed a great deal too long in the parlour, considering what a very bad humour her father was in: and, perhaps, she was right.

CHAPTER V.

Mr. Rixley remained silent for a minute or two after his children had left the room, as if listening to the sound of their retreating footsteps; and then he said in a voice so low as to be almost a whisper, "Sit down, Mrs. Lambert."

Had he cursed her again, and in the same fierce tone of angry violence as before, it would not, perhaps, have affected her so painfully as these civil words thus civilly spoken. It was the first time he had ever addressed her as "Mrs. Lambert," when they were quite alone, and it was also the first time that she had ever felt convinced in her inmost heart that he had ceased to love her. Perhaps he was not altogether unmindful of the effect likely to be produced upon her by this change, and it might be that he felt more disposed to produce such an effect than to avoid it.

Be this as it may, he was instantly obeyed, which, heretofore, had not always been the case when he had addressed a command to her. It is probable that the young William was right, when he said that Sarah Lambert would not turn pale upon hearing him talk of shooting and killing, yet her always pale cheek had become much paler now; but there was, moreover, a strong expression of resolute endurance in her eye, which, from its sternness, might have frightened the bold boy himself, had he seen it.

"It is high time that we should understand one another, Almeria;" said Mr. Rixley, as soon as they were both seated, "and depend upon it," he added, "that it will be as much for your advantage, as for mine, that we should do so."

These words, slowly and deliberately spoken, together with

the act of seating themselves, which they did in two chairs exactly opposite to each other, afforded the strongly-moved, but strongly-minded Sarah Lambert, quite time enough to decide upon the line of conduct she should adopt in the new position which she plainly saw opening before her.

Notwithstanding the many excellent and noble qualities with which Nature had endowed this unfortunate woman, the vehemence of her feelings, whether excited by what was evil, or by what was good, had hitherto for ever overpowered the dictates of her judgment, but it was so no longer with her. She was at that moment quite as certain as if the words had been already spoken, that it was the purpose of her master to dismiss her, of her lover to declare that she had outlived his liking, and of the man, for whose sake she had sacrificed all that made life precious, to inform her that for the future their paths must be as widely apart as possible.

All this she felt, and knew, as if by inspiration; but by the time her now haughty-looking master had placed himself in his chair, she was perfectly prepared for it all.

"We are neither of us fools, Mrs. Lambert," said Mr. Rixley, cutting his nails, as he spoke, with a penknife which he had in his hand, "we are neither of us fools, and therefore whatever business we may have to settle is not likely to detain us long. Though you do not choose to let your nurseling, Master William, hazard his precious safety by taking a sail with me, I happen to think the day exactly fitted for it, and I shall be off directly; so you must excuse the want of ceremony, if I settle the business I have to do rather abruptly. How long is it, Mrs. Lambert, since you and I began making love?"

Many great and important acts have been performed that demanded less strength of mind for their achievement than was required to enable "*Mrs. Lambert*" to reply to this question in the manner she did.

"A very long time, Mr. Rixley! There is no denying that," she said, in an accent which betrayed no more emotion than if she had been discussing the length of time it had cost her to hem his last dozen of pocket-handkerchiefs; "and I own to you," she added, "that I am well pleased at your giving me an opportunity of speaking to you on the subject of my situation in your family. I know I am useful in the house, and I know I am useful to the children; and I think it would be a great folly in you to send me away, merely because my love-making days are over. You do me no more than justice in saying I am not a fool; but a fool I must be, if I felt it necessary to give up my situation as your servant, because we have both of us grown tired of love-making."

"I am sure I don't want to send you away, Mrs. Lambert, if you can really be contented to stay as a servant, and nothing else; but nothing else you ever can be again, I promise you. The folly has lasted too long already, and the consequence is, that you decidedly give yourself very unwarrantable airs with me. What the devil was it to you, Mrs. Sarah Lambert, whether that long-legged scamp of a boy that you have been dandling for the last dozen years got a ducking or not? Much it would have hurt him! I tell you fairly I don't like such a dictatorial style from you any longer. It is high time it should be left off."

"Dear me, Sir!" replied the once splendid and omnipotent Almeria, in an accent, and with an attitude in perfect accordance with her situation as a long-trusted and faithful attendant upon the children, "I should have thought that you had seen enough of women, and children, to know that a nursling is dearer to the nurse than anything else in the whole world, that is to say, of course, after her love-making days are over. But if you will let me stay on, Sir, as nursery governess and housekeeper, I will do my duty by the children, and never trouble you by reminding you of the days that are past and gone. And I am sure, Sir, if you take another to manage your housekeeping, you won't find it answer."

Mr. Rixley looked at her with a suspicious glance for a moment, as if he did not quite know whether she was in earnest; but there was a quiet business-like composure in her manner which reassured him; and, moreover, he had recourse to a little rapid mental logic, which speedily convinced him that there was nothing at all extraordinary in her being willing to continue to remain in the house upon the terms she herself proposed.

"Why should I suspect her of being more pigeon-like, and constant, than I am myself?" thought he. "She is much too clever a creature, and that I ought to know by this time, to want to go on for everlasting, as if there was no such thing as growing old. And it is hard to say what I could do without her, either as to the housekeeping, or the children. I had better take her at her word, and try her, at any rate. It will be easy enough to get rid of her afterwards, if I find she plagues me."

These wise thoughts passed rapidly through his brain, and were acted upon immediately.

"There is a great deal of truth in what you say, Mrs. Lambert," he replied, after the meditative silence of a minute or two: "I certainly do think that it would be very great folly for me to send off such a useful person as you are, for no worse fault than making a fuss about the great boy that you nursed; so you have my free leave to stay, provided you never get bothering me by going back to old times, or any nonsense of that sort—you understand?"

"Yes, Sir, I understand perfectly," was her reply.

"Very well then. Let us say no more about it. The boy may go on with his Greek and Latin if you will, and be an usher if you can find anybody to take him. I shall not trouble him, or any of you, much, for my affairs require my being a good deal in London just now."

"Very well, Sir," replied Sarah, very meekly. "I will endeavour to keep everything in good order during your absence."

"Do so, old lady! and if you never plague me with any old nonsense about yourself, nor any new nonsense about the boy, you may live, and die too, in the old Warren House, without my doing anything to prevent it."

As he said these words he clasped and pocketed his pen-knife, raised his tall person from the chair in which he had been reclining, and walked out of the room; but he left the door open behind him, and therefore if he had turned his head round he might have seen her; for which reason she remained for a minute or two perfectly motionless in the chair in which he had left her.

But he passed on, turned the corner from the passage into the hall, and was immediately out of sight. And then she moved her limbs, and drew a long breath.

The moment after, she heard him open the house door, and slam it after him; and then she drew another long breath, and rose from the chair; but she held fast by the back of it, as if fearing that her strength might not be sufficient to enable her to stand without it. But this faint feeling did not last long, and the moment it was passed she moved off with a hurried step towards her own room, her only fear being that she might meet some human eye before she reached it. She had the good luck to escape this, for William and Helen were obediently waiting for her in the school-room, and, having reached the shelter she sought, she noiselessly closed the door and locked it.

and then threw herself upon the bed, and for a few moments
she so far gave way to her weakness, both of mind and body, as
to burst into a convulsive fit of weeping. The tears she shed
were scalding hard-wrung tears, but they were beneficial to her.
Had she not wept, she might have become delirious.

CHAPTER VI.

Why, or wherefore, it might be difficult to tell, but it is
certainly a fact that the propensity to different passions differs
as much in different human beings as their form and features.
A keen-eyed, and nice-fingered phrenologist might point out
with great accuracy the effects of this variety of temperament
as manifested by the form of the head within which the agents
of these various passions are at work; but this only shows the
effect of their greater or less activity, and not the cause of it.
Why it was that the woman, who is best known to the reader
as Sarah Lambert, though frequently under the influence of very
powerful passion, was in no degree subject to *jealousy*, I cannot
tell; such, however, was the fact.

Mr. Foster, the apothecary of Crumpton, was perfectly
correct in his judgment, when he stated it as his belief that
Sarah Lambert was of Greek origin. Her mother was a Greek,
and had come to this country as the wife of a certain Thomas
Lambert, the comely captain of a merchantman, who had fallen
in love with her at Corfu, and married her there, greatly to the
scandal and displeasure of her family, who considered their
handsome but portionless daughter as having greatly degraded
herself by the connection.

The comely captain, however, did not very long survive his
nuptials, but lived long enough to bring his handsome wife to
his native town, which was Falmouth, where he established her
in a very comfortable, well-furnished little mansion; but the
worthy man died when his daughter Almeria was only five
years old, leaving her and her mother with little or nothing to
maintain them, save the rent of their pretty house, which was
let as furnished lodgings, the widow and her child contenting
themselves with the little back parlour, and the kitchen below
it.

Their means of living, however, were occasionally increased by the handsome Widow Lambert's condescending to cook for, and wait upon such single gentlemen as came to lodge with her, and could afford to pay her for doing so.

But, notwithstanding this condescension on her part, she did not neglect her little girl, and gave her quite as much, or rather more education, than was necessary for her station.

This unfortunate girl was very handsome, and her mother was very proud of her beauty, and long persuaded herself that it was absolutely impossible that so beautiful a girl, who could play music, and speak French, could fail of getting a husband rich enough to keep her like a lady; and to take them both back to their own bright mother country with wealth and grandeur enough to make all their kindred there both proud and happy to receive them.

And if admiring lovers had been all that was necessary to realise this dream, poor Mrs. Lambert would only have awakened from it to welcome the reality. Neither were there wanting several eligible proposals of marriage to the beautiful Almeria; but her obstinate refusal to accept any of them, though long tolerated by her admiring mother as a prudent expectation of something better still, at length became a source of perpetual struggle between the mother and daughter. The tempers of both were violent, and as year after year passed on, the continued strife between them became so ceaseless and habitual, that the lives of both were embittered by it.

Yet still the beauty of Almeria continued as striking as ever, and again and again her hand was sought for in marriage by men whom her mother approved, but to none of whom she could be persuaded to listen. It was in vain that Mrs. Lambert—whose temper was become as gloomy as it was violent—it was in vain that she explained the deficiency of their little income to supply their daily wants, and the daily dress of her admired daughter, for the only answer she could obtain was the sturdy repetition of the often pleaded defence, "Mother, I do not love him!"

"Nor will you ever love any man! It is not in your nature to love," was the answer she had more than once received from her angry parent. But Almeria herself was of a different opinion, and rather felt conscious that it was because she could love, and love passionately, that she shrunk with such deep abhorrence from the idea of giving herself to one whom she loved not.

It is scarcely possible to imagine a more dangerous process for such a character as hers, than that to which she was thus perpetually exposed. She felt in her very heart of hearts that she was right, and not wrong — virtuous, and not vicious — in refusing to become the wife of any man she could not love; yet, notwithstanding the truth and purity of this theory, it was, by the unfortunate concurrence of the circumstances around her, likely to lead her to the reverse of all that was virtuous in principle, and right in practice.

Matters were in their very worst state between herself and her mother; money was scarce, and debts abundant: and, moreover, a wealthy merchant, who offered to provide for her mother, as well as to make a handsome settlement on herself, was earnestly beseeching her to marry him, when a yachting excursion, in which he was engaged, brought Mr. Rixley to Falmouth.

The purpose of the party, with whom he was engaged, was to make a long rambling cruise, but the wind fell to a dead calm when they were off Falmouth, and they came on shore to escape the bore of close quarters, and useless sea-room.

The rest is soon told, and the less it is dwelt upon the better. Mr. Rixley appeared to Almeria the *beau idéal* of all she had been looking for in a lover; and, to say the truth, her home had become so miserable, that even had she admired him less, he might have succeeded in winning her heart. But, as it was, all the indifference of her past life seemed like a well-preserved magazine of gas, that blazed into a brightness proportioned to its former darkness the moment that the flame had reached it.

Mr. Rixley, with all his ardour, and all his impassioned vehemence, was not a man capable of returning, or of comprehending such a love as that which Almeria Lambert bore him. But he certainly thought her by far the handsomest woman he had ever seen, nor was he at all insensible of the pleasure of being passionately beloved for himself, and himself alone. He knew perfectly well that his wife neither did, nor ever had loved him, nor had he ever had much faith in the disinterested attachment of poor William's mother, though in point of genuine attachment she might perhaps have held the middle place between the passionate love of Almeria, and the something more than mere unimpassioned indifference which was felt for him by his wife.

Certain it is, however, that coarse and unrefined as had ever been every attachment he had hitherto felt, and totally incapable

as he was of comprehending the powerful character of the unfortunate Almeria, or of appreciating the strength of her mind,
or even her devoted attachment to himself, he was nevertheless
fully aware that he was loved now, as he had never been loved
before; and being conscious, moreover, that he was no longer
in the flower of his youth, his vanity was as much touched as
his affection, and he was desperately determined not to lose the
gratification of so splendid a conquest.

The manner in which he brought her into the house has been
already stated, as well as the position she held there. Although
he was infinitely more capable of awakening all that was evil
in the unfortunate woman's character, than of appreciating
what was good, he was far from being insensible to the
gratification of being her idol as well as her master; and
though his dissolute manner of life led him during the years
which followed into many passing intrigues, it could scarcely
be said that she ever had a rival. Had she been as prone to
jealousy however, as she decidedly was the reverse, it is possible
that the case might have been different; as it was, she felt
herself as undoubtedly certain of his continued love for her, as
of her own unvarying love for him.

It is certain, indeed, that not all this undoubting confidence
in his attachment either did, or could prevent her being a very
miserable woman. She had no natural propensity to hypocrisy
in her, yet her whole life was a cheat, and the consciousness of
this galled her pride even more than it awakened her remorse.
The certainty, however, that the man she adored, rather than
loved, was an object not only of indifference, but dislike to his
wife, was an endless and ceaseless source of consolation to her,
and without it, as she often told herself, she would rather have
died than lived.

Another source of consolation arose from a cause of precisely
an opposite character, namely the strong sympathy which
existed between her unfortunate mistress and herself in their
feelings towards the children. She knew that here at least she
was a blessing and a comfort to her, and the knowing this was
a more constant support to her under the many miseries of her
degraded position (although she guessed it not) than all her infatuated confidence in the attachment of her master.

It is a commonly received belief that love is blind, but there
could not easily be found a stronger illustration of the truth
of this, than the manner in which Almeria Lambert so long
witnessed the hard indifference of Mr. Rixley towards his

children, without feeling her attachment to him lessened by it.
He had told her that if the children had been hers, he should
have loved them; and she so implicitly believed the assertion
that she only pitied, where she ought to have hated him.

As to her own attachment to them, which partook of the
same characteristic devotedness and warmth of heart which so
long sustained her love for their father, she accounted for it to
herself, by remembering that the children were his.

In short from the hour in which she had first seen him, to
that in which he had just left her in the manner I have
described, she had been living as completely in a state of
delusion respecting his character, his qualities, and his feelings,
as if she had been held under the spell of an enchanter's wand.

Now, for the first time, she saw him such as he really was,
and the doing so very nearly destroyed her.

The firmness of her own attachment had communicated a
like firmness to her faith in him.   She had never for a moment
felt the sensation of jealousy, for this is a passion that for the
most part owes its birth to suspicion, and suspicion was foreign
to her nature: nor was it jealousy that tortured her now.   Had
she believed him to be still the same glorious being which her
ignorance and her imagination combined had led her to paint
him, and if so believing she had learnt that he no longer loved
her, but loved another, the conviction, if it had really reached,
might have really killed her . . . . but it would not have cured
her of her love.   But now the frightful truth flashed upon her
with the clearness, and almost with the rapidity of lightning,
that she had been living under a delusion from the hour she
had seen him first, till within a few short moments of the
instant when she had seen him last.

The revulsion occasioned throughout her whole being by this
discovery was fearfully violent, and its effects were fearfully
lasting.   To follow the course of all the terrible thoughts
which chased each other through her throbbing brain, as the
conviction of the delusion under which she had lived, settled
itself as it were upon her very heart and soul, would be a futile
attempt; and the sequel of my story will do more towards
making this vehement process understood, than the most
laboured description of it.   Yet even while crushed to the
earth by the blow which had fallen upon her, the dauntless
spirit of the unfortunate woman seemed to rise within her in
defiance of the cold-blooded contempt with which she had been
treated.

But for a considerable time she felt as if her intellect was confused, and that although she had much to do, and that very strong measures were to be taken, she would have been about equally at a loss to say what her object was, or what the means by which she proposed to obtain it. By degrees, however, she became more collected, and more calm; one proof of which was, that she resolutely determined to avoid taking any sudden resolution as to her future conduct.

"Could I," thought she, "during the course of the coming night sleep but for one short hour, the puzzling confusion of thought which now besets me, would cease, and I should not decide one moment to do that which I should decide against doing the next."

She rose from her bed, and for a few minutes indulged herself by standing bare-headed at her window, and receiving the fresh strong gale from the sea upon her forehead. And then she soliloquised again.

"I will first make a difficult, but not very important resolution," thought she; "if I have sufficient self-command to keep that, I may look forward with something like confidence in my own strength for the future."

And after a few minutes of consideration this first resolution took for its object the occupying the remainder of the passing day exactly as she would have done, had the most important catastrophe of her life not fallen upon her.

To achieve this, the first thing she had to do was to seek the children, and to speak to them as if she were still the same tranquil-minded and contented being they had ever known her. This might be somewhat difficult, for instead of tranquil-minded, her head was throbbing as if a set of fulling hammers were at work within it. Yet what was this, when compared to the task which was to follow after? For had she not to see, and hear, and speak to, the man who for a dozen years had perseveringly deluded her into the belief that he had loved her, even as she had loved him? And as she remembered this, the thought of instant self-destruction flashed across her mind as an alternative offering most tempting relief.

It was surely more a Greek than an English feeling which followed, and which at once and for ever chased every idea of self-destruction from her mind.

"Destroy myself?" she muttered bitterly, "and so save the villain from all further pains and penalties from his infernal acts? No! By the God that made me, I swear that I will cherish my own life with all the tender caution of a coward keeping guard over his own safety, and all the wakeful watchfulness of a mother protecting a precious child. Yes, Rixley! I will live till I have taught thee to know that a wronged woman's hate may be more difficult to conquer than her love.

From this moment Mrs. Lambert found no farther difficulty in sustaining the part she had assigned herself. In all respects, save one, she was guided, as she had ever been, by the kindly feelings of a very affectionate heart. She could not feign to love William, and his sister Helen more dearly than she really did love them, therefore with them she had no change to make; and as to the being before whom she was never again to appear, save as the thing she was not, how could the playing such a part be anything but joy and gladness to her? Should she not deceive him? Would not her every look and word be false? And should she not taste all the sweetness of vengeance as she fooled him? And might she not worm herself into the hidden mystery of his changed heart? And might she not torture him then?

The smile was a very fearful one that sat upon her still handsome features, as she thus prepared herself for the task that lay before her; it was not a false smile, however, but a very true one, inasmuch as it spoke a feeling of deep contentment from contemplating the work that lay before her, and with it a consciousness of the unshrinking strength which she felt within her, wherewith to accomplish it.

CHAPTER VII.

She found William and Helen very quietly seated in the school-room, the turbulent feelings of the boy soothed into forgetfulness of everything painful by the clever device of Helen, who after suffering his first vehement burst of anger against his father's offensive words to the beloved Sarah to exhaust itself, had restored him easily to his usual happy state of mind by making him read the "Lay of the Last Minstrel" to her as she sat at work.

Mrs. Lambert praised them both for being so well employed,

and with such perfect composure of look and manner, as almost made them forget that anything had occurred to vex her.

I have now related all that I know respecting the unfortunate Almeria Lambert up to the moment at which the feeling, which, when she was innocent, had proved strong enough to overthrow all that she knew was right, had been converted, after many years of guilt, into another feeling quite strong enough to stifle that to which it owed its birth; but which, nevertheless, was not of the quality likely to lead either to fitting repentance or fitting atonement.

Yet still the character of the woman remained a mixed character; it was by no means wholly bad, for there was no selfishness in it: and there was still an immensity of that deep devotion to those whom she could still love, which redeems human nature from much that is contemptibly little, though it cannot save it from much that may be fearfully bad.

The day passed on, to all appearance much as former days had done; William prepared his exercises for the clergyman's evening visit. Helen had been ready for it before the scene in the parlour took place; and she now settled herself very steadily at the pianoforte, in order to achieve a final and decisive victory over a difficult lesson.

The habit of Mr. Rixley was to dine alone when his mornings, or rather his whole days, were passed on the sea, and he did so now; his son and daughter, however, were ordered to come in with the dessert; and as no order of his was ever disobeyed, they appeared before him, although both of them would infinitely have preferred remaining to perform the very hardest tasks that the school-room could offer than partake with him the finest fruit that was ever spread before a mortal.

Upon this occasion, however, he treated them both with rather more than ordinary civility; nay, he even condescended to speak to the boy as if he were a reasonable creature capable in some degree of understanding him.

"There! that will do in the way of crunching, and peeling, and munching. Let alone the walnuts, William, and listen to me. I wish to speak to you about your future prospects, if you are not too great a fool to understand me."

The boy coloured, pushed the offending plate from him, and fixed his fine intelligent eyes upon the face of his handsome, but stern-looking father; but he said nothing.

"That means that you will listen I suppose; but it would be more civil if you said so," said Mr. Rixley.

"I will listen," said the boy.

"Thank you, young Sir! you are excessively polite and obliging, not to say condescending and amiable. However, it may be as well to mention to you that if you do not listen now, you will never have an opportunity of doing so at all, for most certainly I shall not take the trouble of speaking twice to you upon a subject which I consider as being much more interesting to you than to me."

The boy looked steadily at him, but did not speak.

"You heard me this morning offer you the choice of becoming a sailor, or remaining a book-grub and becoming an usher. You heard me offer you the choice, I suppose?"

"I heard you say something about it, Sir," replied William, quietly.

"It was very obliging of you to listen so attentively," returned his father; "and I presume you also heard your stupid old nurse object to it, even though I proposed to teach you the trade myself?"

The face of William became as red as scarlet on hearing this disrespectful allusion to one whom he loved at once as a mother and a friend; but he replied firmly, "If Mrs. Lambert objects to it, Sir, I should object to it too. I hope I shall never do anything that Mrs. Lambert objects to."

"Very well, my independent young Sir; then an usher you shall be to the end of your days; and I hope you will have themes to correct, and boys to flog, to your heart's content."

William had been looking steadily in the face of his father from the time that this conversation began; but on hearing these last words, the expression of his features suddenly changed, and a smile, that might have been construed into a look of rather saucy defiance, succeeded to the subdued and quiet air with which he had hitherto listened.

But the change in the boy's face was neither more sudden nor more striking than that which was perceptible in the father's. A sort of dry and hard indifference had seemed to be settling itself on the features of Mr. Rixley, but this was now changed to a look of brutal rage. His face was flushed, his brow contracted, his full under-lip was compressed for a moment by his large white teeth, and the glance which shot from his eyes had something vastly more like hatred than paternal love in it.

"You sneer at me, do you, Master William Lack-name? Pray do you know who you are? Perhaps your dearly-beloved

Mrs. Lambert may have mentioned the fact to you; but if she has not, I will. I plainly perceive that it is high time you should know who and what you are. Did Mrs. Lambert ever disclose this interesting secret to you?"

"I don't know what you mean, Sir," replied William. "I don't think that Mrs. Lambert ever told me any secret."

"Very discreet. Very right. Very proper on the part of Mrs. Lambert. But the reasons which kept her silent do not affect me; therefore, Master William, I desire you to understand now, and to remember for ever, that, according to law, you are no son of mine; and, therefore, whatever I do for you is a matter of grace and favour, and not to be sneered at. Do you understand me, Sir? I never was married to your mother. She was my mistress, Sir, and not my wife. Do you comprehend what I am saying to you?"

The effect of this announcement upon the poor boy was terrible! The cruel words seemed to have turned him to stone. He uttered not a syllable; but, having looked steadily in the face of his savage father for a moment, as if to read there some trace of jesting falsehood, he crossed his arms upon the table before him, and hiding his face upon them, uttered one sharp cry of such deep anguish, that the frightened Helen rushed from the room, and, flying to Sarah Lambert, exclaimed, "Oh! come to poor William this very moment, dear Sarah! I believe papa has said something that will kill him! Something about his mother .... Come with me, Sarah! Oh, if you had heard him groan as I did, you would not like to keep away from him!"

Sarah Lambert divined the truth in an instant.

"He has told him, has he?" she said; and then added, in a muttered murmur to herself, but too indistinctly for Helen to understand her words, "It follows quick. This is part and parcel of what has gone before. There is something brewing— something in the wind." And as she spoke she seized Helen by the hand, and hastened with her into the parlour.

"Oh! you are come to see the *dénouement*, Mrs. Lambert, are you?" said Mr. Rixley, as they entered. "Did Helen tell you that I have announced to this young hero the blot in his escutcheon? I rather wonder, by the way, that he has never found it out before, for I really believe that pretty nearly everybody in the parish knows it. But people sometimes are vastly discreet, when there is no earthly reason for their being so, and vastly the reverse when there is. Not that I mean to blame you about it, Mrs. Lambert. It was quite right and proper that you should say nothing on the subject without my orders."

All this was said *sotto voce* to the greatly excited, but very quiet-looking Mrs. Lambert, as she stood looking at the sobbing boy from a distance, while his sister hung fondly over him, whispering in his ear, "For my sake, dear, darling William! look up again! Never mind what he says. Remember how we have seen him use Sarah! Surely we ought not to mind anything he says to us, after that."

Her words were not heard in vain. William not only looked up, but rose from his chair; and, taking the hand of his sister, which she had laid upon his arm, pressed it to his lips.

"Come into the garden with me, Helen!" he said, without appearing conscious that there was any one else in the room. "A walk under the lime-trees will do me good."

She, too, at that moment, seemed neither to see or remember any one but her brother, and hand in hand they walked out of the room together.

"Certainly that boy is the most audacious cub that ever was hatched," said Mr. Rixley, following them with his eyes; "and it would serve him perfectly right if I bound him apprentice to a tinker. My fool of a wife was the first who turned his head by her ridiculous petting; and there is no denying that you have had some share in it too, my sage old lady."

"I am sure if I have, Mr. Rixley, it has been done from mere idle thoughtlessness, and not because I fancied that a boy in his situation ought to be too much humoured and indulged; quite the contrary: for I know, of course, that he must make his own way in the world, and that he ought to be made to under-stand it."

This was said so precisely in the tone in which a cold-hearted and cautious confidential servant would have been likely to answer under the circumstances, that Mr. Rixley felt instantly relieved from all fear of opposition in his projects from the interference of the over-fond nurse.

"Quite true, Al——. You are perfectly correct in your notions on the subject," said he, looking at her with very grave approbation; "and if you are to go on living here, as my house-keeper, I shall consider it as a great advantage that you should no longer behave to him as if he were my son and heir. There has been a great deal too much of it already. But things, as you must plainly perceive, I think, must all be put upon a new footing now. I am going to be married, Mrs. Lambert."

People who have taken the trouble of studying perhaps the most powerful, though not the most obvious, peculiarity in the female character, cannot but have perceived that a very strong and resolute power of self-control is at their command, when circumstances call upon them to exert it. It is needless to enter into the philosophy of the subject; but it might be easily shown that this sort of passive power often very effectually supplies their want of strength, both moral and physical, in other respects.

There were at that moment two very opposite feelings at work within the heart of Mrs. Lambert, which between them made her think it was still worth while to live, in spite of all the misery that weighed upon her.

The first—decidedly the first—of these, was the hope of obtaining revenge, in some shape or other, upon the man who had so basely treated her; the second was the hope that she might still be able, in some degree, to guard the children she loved from the sorrow and the suffering which their unprincipled father was likely to bring upon them.

She knew that they had hitherto profited greatly by her influence; but that influence, as she was now informed upon the best authority, she possessed no longer; and most women, upon becoming aware of this fact, might have been tempted to withdraw themselves from a scene where they could no longer hope to be useful, and where they were very sure of being wretched.

But Mrs. Lambert had a proud, and stiff, and sturdy spirit within her, which would have made the destroying herself by a bold leap from the cliff into the sea a much easier and a greatly less painful task than the seeking relief by quietly withdrawing herself from the man who had destroyed her.

But it required no long meditation to make her feel that if she still hoped to play an important part in the drama of Mr. Rixley's future life, it must be done under the shelter of a mask as deceptive as that which he had worn when persuading her that, with all his faults, he was a noble-minded being, who deserved her love.

And such a mask she felt that she had the skill to fabricate, and the courage to wear.

Nor was she mistaken in thus estimating her own powers. She knew, for she had already, poor soul, been often obliged to practise it, that she was capable of that sort of patient persevering self-control which could enable her to "look like the innocent flower, but be the serpent under it."

And as a proof of this she now heard the man, whom but
yesterday she had believed to be devotedly attached to her,
proclaim his intention of being married to another, without
manifesting, by any outward or visible sign whatever, that she
was either surprised or pained by the intelligence!

He was himself, however, probably a little surprised, though
certainly exceedingly well-pleased, by the quiet and perfectly
contented, if not exactly delighted tone, in which she replied,
"I cannot say that I am at all astonished at hearing it, Mr.
Rixley. It is no more than I expected; and, of course, it is no
more than is right and proper. Had it happened a few years
ago, I dare say I should have thought differently about it; but
women outgrow the follies and fancies of their youth much
sooner than men do, unless they happen to be very great fools
indeed; and, as far as I am concerned, I must say that if the
lady is a real lady, and has got a good fortune, my opinion is
that it is the very best thing you can do, both for yourself and
Miss Helen."

"I am very glad to hear you say so, Mrs. Lambert," replied
Mr. Rixley, very cordially, "and it just confirms me in the
opinion I have always had of you. Some women, and a good
many of them, if the truth must be spoken, are good for nothing
on earth after their youth and beauty are over; but that's not
the case with you by any means."

"I am sure it is very kind of you to say so, Mr. Rixley," she
replied, without moving a muscle; "and it is easy to reconcile
oneself to grey hairs, when one hears an old friend speak as
you do now. I think, Mr. Rixley, that the good opinion and
friendship of such a man as you are, are better worth having
than the young love of all the men in the world. Women, you
know, grow old a great many years before men do; and I am
quite convinced that all the women who have common sense
enough to remember *that*, spare themselves a monstrous deal of
vexation!"

"I tell you what, Almeria—I beg your pardon; I ought to
call you Mrs. Lambert, and so I will henceforward, for you
deserve to be treated with respect, and you shall have it from
me, at any rate. But this is what I was going to say, Mrs.
Lambert. I did not intend, when I came down here this time,
to say anything more to you in the way of confidential talk,
than merely that I was going to be married; and, to say the
truth, I was more than half afraid that you would fly off in a
passion, as so many women do when they hear that an old

friend is beginning to think of the main chance a little, instead
of going on love-making to the end of his days. But you, my
dear good soul, are such a capital first-rate creature, that I feel
inclined to tell you a great deal more about myself than I ever
did before; and I have no doubt you may be very useful to me
in many ways. Do you think you shall have patience to hear a
long story?"

"Oh, dear! yes, Sir. I am quite sure I shall find it very
interesting, if it is about yourself; for I do assure you that you
are quite as interesting to me now as you were when we
were both younger, though, of course, in a different way," she
replied.

"Very well! that is just as it ought to be. But I won't
begin now. I will wait till those tiresome children are gone to
bed, and then I will tell you a great many things, Mrs. Lambert,
of which you have no notion as yet, I promise you. And there
is a good chance that you may be useful to me, with your
clever head, for there are one or two points upon which I
have not quite made up my mind, and I shall like to have your
opinion."

<hr>

CHAPTER VIII.

"Now, then, old acquaintance!" began Mr. Rixley, as soon as
he found himself *tête-à-tête* with Mrs Lambert. "I presume
there is no danger of our being interrupted? Rebecca Watkins
is gone, I suppose?"

"Yes, Sir. I locked and bolted the door after her a quarter
of an hour ago," was the satisfactory reply.

"Now, then, sit down, Mrs. Lambert, and you shall hear a
great deal more about me than I ever told you before. I think
you will be rather surprised to find that you don't even know
my real name."

"Is not your name George Rixley, Sir?" said his companion,
fixing her large eyes upon him with a look in which there
seemed to lurk a suspicion that he was jesting.

"You don't believe me?" he said, laughing. "But I am
telling you nothing but the truth, Mrs. Lambert. My name is
George, certainly, and once upon a time my name was Rixley,

too; but it is so no longer.   My father's name was Rixley; but my mother was a Beauchamp, and her only brother, who died a bachelor, left me his estate on condition that I took his name: so I am now George Rixley Beauchamp, instead of George Rixley.   This name and fortune, however, did not come to me till I was thirty years old; and my father, being both devilish strict and devilish poor, I had led but a hard sort of life till old Beauchamp died; for, as he never would tell anybody what he intended to do with his property, I could not borrow a shilling upon my chance of the estate.   And what made my condition worse was, that I have a detestable younger brother, who was bred a parson, and who was a prig and a hypocrite from the hour he was born.   If ever any man had a good right to hate another, I had a good right to hate him; and hate him I did, and hate him I do, and hate him I shall, as long as I have life enough left in me to love or to hate anything."

This profession of fraternal hatred was uttered with a degree of fervour, which left no doubt of its sincerity.

The blood of his greatly excited auditor seemed to curdle in her veins.

"The man is giving the last touches to the portrait of himself which he has drawn this day!" thought she, with a sort of mental shudder, which did not, however, in the very least degree affect her outward demeanour.   She looked at him, indeed, with a stedfast composure of features, which gave to her pale face the aspect of a bust of marble, as motionless and still as if actually made of stone, yet having, like the portrait busts of Hiram Power, such an expression of living intellect, that "one might almost say the *marble* thought."

But Mr. Rixley, as he called himself, was in no condition to speculate upon what was passing in the mind of his auditor. He was thinking, feeling, living, wholly in himself, and for himself; and all that he was conscious of in the condition of his companion was that she was a creature devoted to, and wholly dependent upon him, who might be useful, but who was infinitely too helpless and forlorn to do him any possible harm.

There was, therefore, no drawback to the pleasure with which he recounted a history of which he was himself the hero, and in the detailing which he might safely indulge himself by expressing his most hidden and most detestable feelings, without a shadow of fear that this egotistical outpouring could do him any injury.

"There is no need," he resumed, "that I should waste time in telling you all his diabolical ways of making me appear like a demon, and himself like an angel; it is enough that I should tell you that he did so, year after year, till everybody belonging to me, excepting my old uncle, who, luckily for me, had a natural antipathy to parsons, I do verily believe, thought I was too bad to live, and most likely prayed for my death."

"They must have been very wicked, then!" said Mrs. Lambert, who, as he stopped and looked at her, as if to ascertain the effect he was producing, felt herself obliged to say something.

"Wicked?" he repeated, with an oath. "Yes, Goody Lambert, I think you are tolerably right there. I don't think there was one of the set that did not deserve to be burnt alive. I think it may be taken as a proof of my having a very good temper, for in the midst of all this lecturing and torment I actually found time to fall in love. I did, upon my soul! deeply, madly in love! And now I will make you understand why, and how, it came to pass that I hated, do hate, and ever shall hate, my odious and every-way detestable brother. This girl, this lovely girl, for she was lovely, Mrs. Lambert, lovelier ten thousand times over than ever you were, though she had not your great bright Greek eyes—this girl refused me, and married my brother!—she did, upon my soul!"

And having reached this climax, Mr. Rixley Beauchamp paused in his narrative apparently to take breath, for he was very highly excited, and actually appeared gasping from vehement passion.

Mrs. Lambert was greatly more self-possessed and composed. His fierce eyes were fixed upon her, however, and it was evident that he expected her to say something in reply. It is probable that she might have preferred remaining silent, but she was not in the mood, notwithstanding the tranquillity of her aspect, to yield to any such self-indulgent suggestion, and she said in a voice which, considering the circumstances, was marvellously steady and passionless. "And no great wonder that you hate him, Sir! He seems altogether to have done quite enough, I think, to justify your hatred."

"Enough! yes, enough! and to spare, my good woman, for he seemed to live only for the purpose of making himself appear an angel, as I told you before, and me a demon! But now I must get on with what I want to tell you, for this part of my story makes me still feel as if I should go mad, when I think of it. The next thing that happened was, of course, that he had a son and heir born to him, and I had the gratification of hearing it pretty plainly hinted that our rich uncle Beauchamp was very likely to settle his estate upon this very particularly beautiful boy! But now, Almeria, the scene suddenly changed, for our half-witted, old mummy of an uncle died at last, making me his sole heir! For a few years I was happy enough, as you will easily imagine, for my blessed brother was as poor as a rat, being disappointed in his hopes of getting a living, having a new baby born to him every year, and my father's affairs getting into worse condition every day he lived. But this state of felicity did not last long for me; my father died, and my mother's settlement, though not a large one, was quite sufficient to make her feel rich, when my father and his extravagant ways were removed; and then she went to live with her darling youngest son, and they all seemed to be living in Paradise together, and I will leave you to guess how much I enjoyed seeing it. I really believe I should have gone mad, if I had not just at that time taken a violent passion for boating. I was invited to join a cruising excursion on board Sir Solomon Jones' yacht, and we were caught in a gale that very nearly swamped us. Every one of the company, except myself, were not only as sick as cats, but they all, more or less, showed the white feather, and the sailors on board did me the honour of declaring that I was the only man amongst them. It was this, I believe, that first put the fancy into my head . . . . and then you know, as long as I remained in London or at Beauchamp Park either, I was sure to see and hear something of the man I hated, for as long as my mother lived, they continued to reside in London, where the hypocrite parson had at last got appointed to a chapel. So, upon reading in the newspaper a description of this place, I came down to look at it, and bought it immediately. The scheme answered perfectly; for by means of calling myself Rixley, and leaving out the Beauchamp, I altogether escaped the bore of being known in the county as Beauchamp, of Beauchamp Park. I brought down a devilish pretty girl, and called her Mrs. Rixley. She was the mother, you know, of your precious nursling, Master William. But I took this idiot mother to sea with me one stormy day, merely because she was the greatest coward I ever knew in my life, and I thought it would be good fun to hear her squall, and see her drenched in the spray, but I had no notion of its killing her, which it certainly did, as I dare say you have heard."

"I am no great gossip, Mr. Rixley," replied his deeply disgusted auditor, who felt, as she listened to him, a fresh pang of self-reproach for having been beguiled into loving the vile being to whose autobiography she was so demurely listening. "I am no great gossip, as you well know, and all I remember to have heard on the subject was that the first Mrs. Rixley died in consequence of a cold which she caught in boating."

"And I suppose my baby fool of a wife heard the same story," rejoined Mr. Rixley, "for though I often tried to coax her to go out with me, I never could persuade her to put her foot in the boat; and I must say, Mrs. Lambert, that you were fairly worth ten thousand of either of them, for though the only way I could ever give you a sail was the making you get up in the middle of the night when the moon shone, we have had many a spanking voyage together: and nothing was ever so cleverly managed as the nursery night-work! My idiot of a wife, fancying that nobody but herself could take sufficient care of her precious daughter either by night or by day, soon rendered our having separate rooms a matter of necessity; and then, as you may remember, Mrs. Lambert, I positively forbade that the boy should be made such a milksop of, as to sleep in the room with a nurse, and this left us pretty tolerably at liberty, you know— and, upon my soul, you showed yourself a heroine upon more occasions than one. I never saw any woman in a boat behave like you! It is a devilish pity you should ever grow old, for I don't expect that my young lady wife that is to be, will ever handle a rope as I have seen you do."

"If I had been a LADY, Mr. Rixley," replied his companion in a tone of the most philosophical indifference, "the chances are that I should never have handled a rope either. My father had been a hard-working, and very brave sailor in his youth, and it was very natural that I should take after him."

"It may be very natural, Mrs. Lambert," he replied, "but it does not always happen, for all that. I am sure my pretty doll of a daughter is not at all like me, and that is one reason, I suppose, why I care so little about her. And now that just brings me round to the point I wanted to come to. The fact is, Mrs. Lambert, that I shall not be contented unless I have a son. That hateful brother of mine has one, and, moreover, he is one of the finest-looking young fellows that you ever saw in your life—just such a grown fellow as William is. But as to

Helen, she is like nothing on earth but her mother, and she, as
you know, was never well, and died at last quite young. Now,
if Helen dies young, whom must Beauchamp Park and my ten
thousand a-year go to? After all I have told you, Lambert,
you cannot feel much at a loss to guess why it is that I am
anxious to have a legitimate son."

"Oh dear, no! Mr. Rixley," she promptly replied, "I
comprehend your motives perfectly!—And you have fixed upon
the lady, have you?"

"Yes, to be sure I have," he returned, laughing, "I should
have thought that you knew me better than to fancy that I
should have talked about it, before it was all settled. And a
devilish lovely young creature I have chosen, I promise you—
so young, indeed, that I don't at all relish the thoughts of
presenting Miss Helen to her. She must dislike the idea
of being called *mamma* by a girl very nearly as tall as
herself."

"But how will you be able to manage, Sir, so as to prevent
it?" said Mrs. Lambert, in a tone of friendly anxiety.

"Why, it does not seem very easy just at first thinking of it;
but a clever head like mine, especially if assisted by another
clever head like yours," he replied, "may be able to find both
the will and the way. I don't think there is any great need of
my dwelling upon the fact, that I would rather sell every acre
of my uncle's property, and throw the money into the ocean,
than let my detested brother, or either of his children, have it"

"Why, certainly, Sir, after what you have told me, I can't
think it very likely you should wish for that: neither is there
any danger that it should be so, while you have children of
your own," replied Mrs. Lambert.

"Children! *A child*, I suppose you mean? You don't
imagine, you half-caste Greek Jack Tar, do you, that I intend
to bequeath my grandfather's long-descended Beauchamp acres
to a bastard? Upon my soul, if I thought you had really any
such notion in your head, I would turn you out of the house
this instant, and never let you enter my presence again!"

"And very proper it would be that you should do so,"
returned the resolute woman, with the most stoical apathy, "I
was only thinking of Miss Helen, Sir."

"Very well, then. It is all very natural that you should
think of Miss Helen, and if I were to die to-morrow, the whole
of my Grandfather Beauchamp's fine property would go to her.
But this does not satisfy me, Lambert. Just think, what would

happen, if you please, in case that girl should die! She is as like her mother as one egg is like another, and I think it very likely—very likely indeed—that she may die early. Look at her little delicate hands and feet, Lambert, and then look at mine, and you will see at once that she does not take after me, in any way, but after her mother, who, though she lived the most healthy life possible, always in the country, you know, and never keeping late hours, or anything of the kind, died before she was thirty, or near it. The girl will do the same, and then the son of that d—d ungrateful woman who scorned my love, and of the detested brother who supplanted me, will become my heir! You may have some notion how detestable this idea is to my soul, by the fact that I already, though in pretty stout health, and not yet fifty years old, have made my will. I have, upon my soul, Lambert, I have made my will, and left everything I have in the world to Helen, which I did on account of my not being over sure that I might not, some coal-black night or other, get washed overboard among the rocks; and then, you know, they might have made out, perhaps, that the girl was just as illegitimate as the boy, and as they would all, of course, be leagued together against her, you may guess what sort of a chance she would have had against them all. But for all that, Mrs. Lambert, I have no more intention of leaving the Beauchamp property to that wry-faced girl, than I have of leaving it to you. My intention is to marry, and a devilish fine young creature I have fixed upon, as I have told you."

"And upon my word, Sir, it appears to me that you could not possibly do anything better," replied the attentive listener, without changing either in look or manner the perfect composure of her demeanour. "And how soon will the marriage take place?"

"Why that is just what I can't exactly tell you; and it is upon that very point I shall want your advice and assistance," he replied. "I have made my offer, and have been very graciously accepted; but I would much rather settle everything about Helen, and where she is to live, and who is to take care of her, and all that sort of plaguing business, before I actually settle the day. And now what I want to ask of you is, whether you would yourself be ready and willing to take charge of her?"

The resolute composure of the unhappy woman had lasted her to this point so well, that her voice had never for a moment faltered, nor had her complexion changed; but now she suddenly became as red as scarlet, and her eyes, which had been steadily fixed on the face of her master, now sought the ground, as if she had no longer sufficient courage to look at him; and as to her voice, she trusted it not, but remained perfectly silent.

"Why, what the deuce is the matter with you, woman?" he exclaimed. "By Jove, one might think I had asked you to murder, instead of take care of her! What makes you colour up in that ridiculous way? And why do you sit there as if you were struck dumb? Why can't you answer a civil question civilly, and without keeping one an hour waiting for it?"

But Almeria Lambert was not a woman to be terrified, or overpowered, by rough language; on the contrary, this rudeness from her master at once restored the courage, which had almost failed her upon being made to remember that the protection thus asked towards the being she most fondly loved could not be given by her, without degrading the object of this fond affection.

It was a dreadful thought, and as true as it was terrible; but she had been already called upon to stifle and conceal the strongest feelings of her soul, and had obeyed the call with a degree of courage which made her, as she felt, the master of the heartless wretch who tortured her. This thought at once restored her self-possession, though this last pang was sharper perhaps than all which had preceded it. "You must excuse me, Sir, if for a moment I felt half frightened at the idea of your trusting the care of your heiress to me. It would bring such a deal of responsibility with it!"

"Don't be a fool, Lambert, and make mountains of molehills!" he replied. "In the first place I am not dead yet, if you please to observe, and in the next, you may as well remember that I intend to have a male heir before I die, so that your chance of having so important a personage as my heiress upon your hands, is but small."

"True, Sir! that is very true indeed! I forgot *that*," she replied with energy, "and it makes a great difference as to my saying yes, or no, to your proposal. Then if I say yes, Sir, I may take it for sure and certain I suppose, that as soon as ever you have got a son born, you will destroy the will you have made, making Miss Helen your heir?"

"Yes, to be sure you may. But what a queer woman you are," was the reply. "I should have thought, considering what a great affection you have ever professed for her, that you would have rather seen her a great lady, and an heiress, than not."

"And so I should still, Sir," she replied with great readiness, "if it were not so plain to see that you would rather leave your estates to a son than to a daughter. And, besides, Mr. Rixley, I feel quite sure that you will never leave either of the dear children in poverty. If I did not think *that*, I could not of course find it in my heart to wish for you to have a son."

"Well, Goody Lambert, I would rather hear you talk in that way, because it is no more than natural, and though I won't bind myself by promising anything fixed and certain just at this moment, you may set your heart at ease about my not leaving you all three to starve. A pretty riot you would be kicking up, if I did, wouldn't you, old lady?"

"Why, of course, Sir," she replied, now perfectly restored to composure, and to the part she intended to perform, "I should not rest very quietly in a starving condition, with a darling boy starving on one side, and a darling girl on the other, knowing, too, that their father possessed many thousands a year. But it would be nothing better than affectation, if I pretended to say that I have any such fears, for I have not. I dare say you will behave very handsomely. Only, Sir, there is one thing that puzzles me."

"Well! speak out; what is it?" demanded her master.

"You must promise not to be angry, Mr. Rixley," she replied, "for without that I had rather keep silence."

"Don't be a fool, Mrs. Lambert. I don't believe a word about your being afraid, so out with it. What is it that has puzzled you?" said he.

"Why, it is this, Sir," she replied, with a sort of respectful curiosity in admirable keeping with the part she was performing, "I cannot guess why it was that you dismissed your servants, and gave over living like a gentleman, just about the very time you made the will you tell me of, making Miss Helen a great heiress. I can't understand why you should have told me just then for the first time that it was very likely Miss Helen would, one day or other, have to take the place of Rebecca Watkins in the house."

"You shall not puzzle your old brains long about that, Mrs. Lambert," he replied, "for I will explain it at once. My purpose then, was exactly the same as my purpose now. When I gave you this notice, I had made up my mind to do exactly what I am about to do now, that is to say I had made up my mind to marry; and I had also made up my mind that in case I should have a son, I would make a will by which, as in duty bound, I should leave the whole of the Beauchamp property to my son, making, however, such a provision for the girl as her penniless mother's daughter might have a right to expect; and that shall be enough for her to live upon, with you for a companion, Mrs. Lambert. And if she does not like that, she may make herself a teacher in a school, as her mother was before her. Why do you look at me so sharply, with your great eyes? Are you going to grumble at what I have said?"

"Pray, Mr. Rixley, do not say I look sharply at you," returned Mrs. Lambert, with exceeding meekness. "If you were to say that I looked as if I were listening with great attention, you would show that you understood me better. I have done my duty to your children since I was hired to attend upon them, and I sincerely wish to do so still; and it must be plain to you, that in order to do this, it will be necessary for me to understand what your intentions are about them."

"Yes. That is true enough, certainly," he replied. "But you need not talk about *them*, Mrs. Lambert. Let things turn out as they will after my marriage, you will have little or nothing more to do about HIM. I have completely made up my mind that he shall be an usher in some country school or other. Everything that Parson Bolton has told me about him proves that it is exactly what he is fit for, so you need not give yourself any farther trouble on that subject. For the present, however, everything may go on exactly as it does now, only you won't have many more visits from me, I suppose, before the marriage takes place; not that I mean to give up my dear boat, not a bit of it, I promise you! When I am once safely married I shall make no scruple of coming down to the Warren House for the sake of a sail, though I shall not think it necessary to bring my beautiful wife with me. She never saw such a rough-looking barn of a place as this since she was born, and the party she would find here would startle her a little too, I suspect. Don't you think so, Mrs. Lambert?"

This question was asked with a gay laugh; and, therefore, Mrs. Lambert laughed too. But she was probably conscious that her muscles were more likely to rebel in making this attempt, than in performing anything else she could require of them; she therefore very discreetly pulled forth her pocket-handkerchief and applied it to her nose.

The device answered even beyond her hope, for Mr. Rixley Beauchamp laughed aloud as he looked at her, and exclaimed, " What a discreet personage you are becoming, Mrs. Lambert! You do not choose that even I should see how greatly you feel amused at the idea of the future Mrs. Beauchamp's coming to pay a visit at the Warren House, and finding *you* here ?"

" Well, Sir! And if such a thought did come into my head," she replied, " I am sure it was very natural."

" To be sure it was, old friend! And don't fancy I am going to be angry with you for that. Not a bit! I won't say that I should exactly like to make the experiment, for the style and station of the future Mrs. Beauchamp is considerably more in accordance with the style of Beauchamp Park, than of Crumpton Warren House, and the place itself, as well as the live stock she would find here, might produce rather a disagreeable effect on her nerves."

The conversation then turned on the minor details of household economy; all of which he seemed to have studied and arranged on a very modest style of expenditure; but this was not a point that, as far as she herself was concerned, was at all likely to excite the most excitable feelings of her vehement character. It would not, indeed, have been easy for Mr. Rixley to have touched on any subject whereon she could have listened to him with so much genuine indifference. In fact she herself possessed, although he did not know it, quite as large an income as she required to maintain her. Her mother's death had put her in possession of about sixty pounds a year, which sum was transmitted to her by half-yearly payments, through the agency of a Falmouth banker. This money had hitherto been spent by her in a manner to make the pretty strict economy of Mr. Rixley as little injurious to the comfort of his children as might be. Among all the lamentable faults of this unfortunate woman's character, there was no mixture of sordid selfishness : and the reason she had never mentioned this little independence to her master was solely that she might be able to employ it for the use or gratification of the children, without being told, as she frequently was on all occasions of expenditure, that he did not wish his children to be over-indulged.

Perhaps it was fortunate that this branch of his discourse was so little interesting to her: for its discussion produced a look of such genuine weariness on the features of the miserable Almeria, that the self-occupied brute felt very comfortably persuaded the communication of his intended marriage, which he had somewhat dreaded to make, had not affected her very strongly : for that it was evident she was made more tired than angry, by his long statements respecting his future intentions concerning his children, and their future manner of life under her superintendence.

Nothing could be more accordant to her wishes than that he should so think; and when he taxed her with being so tired of his long story as to be very nearly asleep, she confessed that he was quite right, and that anything he might wish to say further in the way of directing what was to be done about keeping up the garden, and the boat-house, when he was away, would be much more accurately remembered by her if he would be so good as to let her hear it the next day, when she would not feel so sleepy.

He immediately agreed to this, telling her that she might take herself off as soon as she pleased; but adding, with a significant nod, accompanied by an equally significant laugh— "Your falling to sleep when I am talking to you of all my own affairs, is a pretty plain proof, my ci-devant beauty, that it is high time I should take me a wife. I suspect it is a sign that we are neither of us quite so young as we have been."

"Perhaps it is, Sir," replied Mrs. Lambert, very quietly ; " I wish you good night, Sir; and I shall be ready to hear all you may be pleased to have to say to-morrow."

CHAPTER IX.

"THANK heaven!   That is over, and never, never, never, can it come again ; " soliloquised the unhappy woman, as soon as she had shut herself up within the shelter of her own room. "And this is the man to whom I have sacrificed my youth, my innocence, my happiness!   But my misery, my frightful, frightful misery, is not all his fault!   Let me be just, even in this hour of bitter agony!   It is not his fault, but mine, if I have debased myself to the lowest pitch of degradation and infamy, in order to indulge a tender passion for such an animal as that! Had another painted him to me, as he has now painted himself, would I not have expended my last breath in denouncing that other to the world as a liar and a slanderer? But what is there that human malice, or human invention could have attributed to him, that could have exceeded in vileness what he has recorded of himself? What has become of all the rainbow-colouring with which his accursed falsehoods beguiled my judgment, and made me fancy that all the shame and sin that surrounded me was in truth intellectual superiority, and devoted affection? Oh fool! fool! fool! And it is for this man, for this cold, hard, selfish villain, that I have sacrificed myself, soul and body! In this life, and in the next! For ever, and for ever, and for ever!"

It would be in vain to attempt to follow the wretched woman through all the fearful meditations of that dreadful night. It is probable that even her reason was in some degree shaken by the vehemence and the vainness of her self-reproaches, and by the intensity of the indignation, and the hatred which seemed to overflow and submerge her very heart and soul as she dwelt upon the systematic villany by which she had been deluded, and destroyed.

To say that her once passionate love for her master was turned into as passionate hate, would be but a weak description of the feeling to which she now appeared to yield, and devote herself, and which seemed to resemble in its deep intensity the fanatic vehemence of a half-crazed religious enthusiast, about to atone for all past sins by a phrenetic devotion of himself to present suffering.

The light of the early morning sent its cold pale beams into her chamber before she had for a moment closed her eyes in sleep. She started almost in terror as she perceived this: for her aching head had been working at intervals throughout the night upon what she might best do for the interest of the children, and had pretty well decided that her best course would be openly to advocate their cause, and to shame the unprincipled father into securing to each of them such a provision as might secure them from the misery of absolute poverty.

But she knew that this could only be hoped for as the result of her resuming such a degree of influence over his mind as might induce him to listen to her on this important theme with fear, if not with affection. But this again could only be hoped for by her being still able to subdue her own feelings with the same success which had hitherto attended her efforts to do so; and this she felt could not be done if she met him with her head aching, and her pulses throbbing, as they did at present.

She rose from her bed, and, looking at her face in the glass,
positively started, at perceiving the havoc which one night of
vehement suffering had produced on her appearance. It is
no fable which states that the colour of the hair will change in
a single night. The hair of the unfortunate Almeria Lambert
was peculiarly rich and abundant, and had been very nearly
black; but now one side of her head was almost as white as
silver.

Vanity had nothing to do with the emotion which this discovery occasioned: her first, in truth her only thought upon the
subject came in the shape of alarm lest HE should discover it,
and suspect in consequence the sincerity of that indifference, the
assumption of which was the only possible means by which she
could gratify the burning longing for revenge which had become
the strongest feeling of her nature; for all her other feelings,
even those which her repentant heart now told her were the
best and purest she had ever felt—namely, her love for the
children she had nursed and cherished, as if they had been her
own—even her love for them called upon her to take vengeance
against their unnatural father. It has been said, truly enough,
that we are all disposed to

> "Atone for sins we are inclined to.
> By damning those we have no mind to;"

and it was probably for this reason that the enormous proportion
of selfishness which the present plans of Mr. Rixley Beauchamp
displayed, caused them to raise so fierce a feeling of anger, and of
hatred in the heart of Mrs. Lambert, for she had no selfishness
in her. If, by sacrificing everything she had in the world, she
could benefit those she loved, or in any way increase their happiness, the doing so would have given her more keen gratification,
and more really heart-felt joy, than any other thing that could
have befallen her.

To her own personal gratification and convenience, she was
very nearly insensible, and still more nearly indifferent; but to
minister to the pleasure, the happiness, the gratification in any
way of those she loved, seemed to make earth a heaven to her.

By the slight sketch which has been already given of her
early history, it may be easily perceived that the broad boundary
line between right and wrong had never been very clearly
pointed out to her: and the miserable result of this has been
sufficiently shown. But even this deficiency, lamentable as it
was, would not have brought her so low as she had fallen, had

it not been that her imagination was as super-abundantly active,
as the moral sense was torpid.

The sort of mystery in which the goings and comings of Mr.
Rixley were involved, the remarkable incongruities in his mode
of living, the lavish expenditure which attended all the arrangements in which his nautical amusements were concerned, and
the close economy which he exhibited on almost every other
occasion, would all have suggested to most people, as they
certainly did to his very miserable wife, that his resources were
precarious and uncertain, if not absolutely disreputable; nay,
even this last idea often, and very painfully, suggested itself to
her, in consequence of the very evident repugnance which he
displayed on every occasion, where there seemed a probability
of meeting strangers, to accept any of the rare invitations
addressed to him.

But no such reasonable thoughts ever suggested themselves
to the unfortunate Almeria, though she too had her meditations on the subject. She had fabricated a romantic theory of
her own, by which she contrived to convert all the selfish
caprices of her master into so many proofs of his noble nature,
and his arduous struggles to maintain his family, without
sharing the anxieties of his (probably) very uncertain position,
either with his wife, or with herself.

She had, in fact, persuaded herself, purely by the workings of
her own imagination, that Mr. Rixley was a merchant, and not
always a very prosperous one, and that when he left them, it
was solely to attend to his mercantile concerns; and that when
he lavishly spent money upon his boat, and its costly accom-
paniments, it was both because some lucky speculation had
answered, and also because the moonlight hours which he spent
in that dear boat with her, were the happiest of his existence!

It is not very difficult to imagine, therefore, what her feelings
must have been, on learning that the man who had perpetually
reproached his gentle, meek-spirited wife, because her very
humble housekeeping was not humble enough, had been for
years living in the uncontrolled enjoyment of an income of
many thousands a year; that the only reason for his having
married at all, was for the sake of gratifying his fiend-like
hatred of his brother, and that *now* the dearest hope of his life
was that by the birth of another child he might be able, at his
own death, to leave his beautiful, innocent, motherless daughter
in a position too obscure for her ever to profit, in any way, by
the wealth and station he himself enjoyed!

As to her own share in the terrible exposition of this long-drawn tale of treachery, hatred, perfidy and hypocrisy, she saw —she understood—she felt—it all; but, nevertheless, when contemplating the whole series of his life's dark history, she was hardly conscious that she was thinking of herself, and yet her share of it was not the least tragical part of the drama.

It was thus that the long-deluded woman passed the hours which immediately followed the discovery of her having bound herself, body and soul, to a much viler being than any she had ever conceived it possible could exist, and that too by the sacrifice on her own part of everything that might have left her the comfort of self-respect to console her in her misery.

That she was in no degree blind to the sin and degradation to which she had submitted herself by yielding to her unbridled passion for the man she now so deeply detested, was proved by the melancholy depth of her conviction, that, with all her tender pity and devoted love for the poor friendless Helen, she could only bring her to shame and woe, by cherishing, and watching over her! The more she meditated on this terrible idea, the more its questionable truth became evident, till every other sorrow and regret seemed swallowed up in the feeling, nearly approaching to despair, which it brought with it.

Yet still she felt that the destiny of this dear child was not decided, and could not be decided for many months, or it might be for years to come. It might be that she would inherit the whole of her father's noble property, and if she did, her less fortunate brother would most assuredly be also well provided for by her. And for a few moments while these pleasant thoughts held possession of her mind, her spirits were soothed, her throbbing pulses became hushed, and she fell into a deep sleep which endured for an hour or two, and which probably saved her from absolute madness.

Her waking from this sleep was certainly terrible; but, nevertheless, the good effect of it was not lost; for though profoundly wretched, she was in perfect possession of her reason, one proof of which was that the most fixed and stedfast object of her thoughts, from the moment that she roused herself to a perfect consciousness of her situation, was the finding some protection for Helen, less injurious than her own.

Mr. Rixley Beauchamp meanwhile enjoyed a night of undisturbed repose. It was some time indeed since he had felt so completely at ease in his mind, and so every way comfortable as he did on retiring to rest that night. Not that he had ever been tormented by any scruples, or by any doubts as to what he should do, in order so to arrange his affairs as to leave him at perfect liberty to follow his own wishes, and his own will, in every respect. But he was not altogether without a feeling of uneasiness as to the manner in which "old Lambert" might receive the news of his intended marriage. This uneasiness, however, was now passed, and over. The woman had behaved, as he was quite ready to allow, admirably well, and he was a lucky fellow for having secured the services of such a steady sensible person to take charge of his plagues of children.

It was with this comfortable thought that he turned himself snugly round upon his pillow, and went to sleep.

It was not the custom of Mr. Rixley Beauchamp to breakfast with his children. Strong coffee, and new-laid eggs, could in no way be considered as fit provender for them, and notwithstanding the revolting fact that William was very nearly as tall as his father, it was considered by that father as much more seemly that he should continue the wholesome habit of eating a bowl of bread and milk with his sister in the school-room, than that he should be deluded into fancying himself a gentleman, and a fitting companion for himself.

So the master of the house, as usual, took his coffee and eggs in solitary state, a part of that state consisting in his being waited upon during the meal by Mrs. Lambert.

His first glance at her countenance on that morning, though it had no mixture of fear in its expression, had something of curiosity in it. He did not feel quite sure as to the temper in which he should find her: for the temper of Mrs. Lambert had never been an *even* temper, her secret thoughts having sometimes led her to be very sad, while her secret feelings, while believing herself the only loved one of the man she loved, had oftener led her to be joyfully serene, if not exactly joyously gay.

But Mr. Rixley Beauchamp, though he certainly did not meditate upon the subject very deeply, was nevertheless quite aware that the news he had communicated to her on the preceding evening must necessarily have made her perceive that her position was greatly changed, and he did not feel quite certain that she would behave as well to-day as she had done yesterday.

He had, however, the very great satisfaction of perceiving that her countenance expressed nothing in the least degree

6

approaching to ill-humour; and so well pleased was he by the discovery, that he told her to sit down by him and let him explain to her exactly what he intended to do about Helen. •

"As to the boy," he added, "we need not waste our time in talking about him. His fate is settled and sealed. He shall be an usher in some country grammar-school. Bolton says that he is the best scholar he ever had, and that's a proof, you know, that he is fit for the business. Moreover, my dear Lambert, to tell you the truth, I don't think he is fit for anything else. He is a milk-sop, Lambert. If he had been a fine spirited fellow, such as I was at his age, I should very likely have got fond of him. But I never came down here in my life, that I did not find him either coaxing and kissing my idiot of a wife, or else looking at Helen as if he were quite ready to hold her doll for her, if she was tired of holding it herself. In short, I hate the boy, that's the truth; and that's one reason why I rather enjoy the idea of his being an usher, for I'd much rather sweep the streets myself."

Had Mrs. Lambert permitted her master at that moment to have seen the expression of her countenance, it is possible that he might have come to a different conclusion respecting her state of mind. But she was far too much self-possessed to hazard any such experiment as looking at him, being, on the contrary, very particularly engaged at the moment in rincing his coffee cup preparatory to its being replenished.

"As to the girl," he continued, "I don't say that I have any dislike to her, for I really have not. She is certainly very pretty, and that, you know, is the best thing that a woman can be; and if I have no son, she will be my heiress, and in that case, of course, I shall bring her forward, and see that her education is properly finished. But meantime, Lambert, I intend that she shall remain here with you. For the next year or two, this will be quite as well for her as the finest school I could put her to; and if I am so fortunate as to have a son, I will leave a couple of thousand pounds in your hands, which will be quite enough for your adopted daughter, *Helen Rixley*. For, mind you, Goody Lambert, she is never to hear the name of Beauchamp unless I should fail to have a son. Do you understand me?"

"Yes, Sir, perfectly," replied Mrs. Lambert, in a tone, and with a manner that expressed the most dutiful attention to his words.

"I shall not sell this place at present," he resumed, "and I shall let you remain here as long as I keep it, and what may happen afterwards, will depend very much upon your conduct, and that of the girl."

"And I hope, Sir, that you will find no cause to be displeased with either," was her respectful reply.

"And I hope so too. But I shall not stand upon much ceremony with either, if I see, or hear of anything that I disapprove," said he, rising, and taking up his hat, which lay in a chair near him. "I am now going to my boat to enjoy my last free sail for a long time, perhaps, for immediately after my marriage I shall probably only stay here for a few hours, if I come at all, for it will only be to settle with the Falmonth banker about the payment of the sum I shall allow to you and Miss Helen, for your housekeeping, and it may be that I shall even manage that by writing. However, in case I should be drowned to-day, Goody, remember there lies my will in that old desk yonder. I have taken good care that neither my dearly beloved brother, nor any of the cursed imps belonging to him, shall profit in case of my sudden death, either by sea or land. When I am married, and have a lawful son born, alive and thriving, it will be a different affair; but till that happens, I will keep guard over it as carefully as if it secured the property to myself, instead of to pretty Miss Helen. And now good morning to you, Mrs. Housekeeper. I suppose you have not forgotten the orders I gave you at dinner yesterday about letting me have a good boat luncheon packed for me this morning?"

"Oh, no, Sir! It is quite ready, and I suppose old John may follow you down with it?" said Mrs. Lambert, looking at him with an expression of such placid obedience that he rewarded her with a very cordial and merry slap upon the shoulder, exclaiming at the same time, "That's right, old woman! You are a trump now, as you always have been. It used, you know, to be the queen of hearts, but now, by Jove, I think you are the ace of clubs, for you are as powerful in your place as Hercules himself could be! But don't forget, if you please, that another proof of your power must be displayed by getting ready a first-rate supper for me when I come back to-night; for I mean to see the moon rise, I promise you, and I shall be as hungry as a wolf."

CHAPTER X.

To most women it would have been a relief to find herself alone after such a scene as the above, but it was not so to Almeria Lambert. She had been exerting every faculty to enable her to act a part—a most difficult part; and she had been perfectly conscious the whole time that she had acted it well, wonderfully, admirably, astonishingly well. This conscious success had sustained her strength, and made her feel for the time that hers was the predominant spirit, and that the tyrant villain she so deeply hated was still her slave.

But no sooner was the unhappy wretch alone, than all the deep and desperate misery of her condition rushed back upon her heart, and completely overwhelmed her. It must have been a hard-hearted being who could have looked at her then, without compassion. All the illusions of her life had vanished as suddenly as if charmed away by the wand of an enchanter. She saw, with terrible clearness, *what* she herself had been, and *what* the being for whom she had made herself the wretch she was! The idea of looking at the pure and innocent girl who had been consigned to her unholy guardianship was dreadful to her, and she rose from the chair into which she had fallen when her master left her, and with a rapid movement closed the door, and locked it.

And then she re-seated herself; and then with a sort of hard composure which had greatly less of sober reason, than of desperate resolution in it, she set herself to think upon the future. That the fearful passion of revenge was busy at her heart, cannot be doubted; and yet it came in such a questionable shape that she knew it not, for it seemed to herself that her only wish—her only thought—was how she could make *atonement* for the grievous sins she had herself committed.

But whatever of good, or whatever of evil, might have been at work within her during the next dreadful hour or two, no fair judgment could have been passed upon her either for the one, or for the other; for assuredly she was not in the full possession of her reason.

Meanwhile the unfortunate children of a most guilty father sought what naturally seemed the best and only solace within their reach, namely the comfort of an unrestrained discussion in the school-room between themselves, respecting the cruel scene of the previous day.

Their childish breakfast had been placed before them by their umwhile nurse, with an intimation that if they wanted anything more, they were to apply to Rebecca Watkins for it, for that she should herself be too much engaged to attend to them.

And having said this, she left them to their melancholy talk, and she sighed as she remembered how melancholy it must be. "And yet," thought she, as she silently turned away, "how blessed is their condition, when compared to mine!"

"I don't think we shall trouble Rebecca Watkins to give us any more breakfast," said Helen, with a melancholy smile, "I don't feel as if I should ever be hungry again."

"And it is I, my poor Helen, who am the cause of all you suffer!" cried William, striking his forehead with his clenched fist. "I!—I who would gladly give half the years of my life if I could be an honour and credit to you during the other half! But instead of that, my very existence is a disgrace to you! How much better would it have been for you, Helen, if I had never seen the light of day!"

"How can you talk such cruel and hard-hearted nonsense, William!" exclaimed the poor girl, bursting into tears. "You must know so very well, William, that you are the person I love best in the world! You must, and you do know it, and yet you have the heart to wish that you had never been born! Isn't this being cruel?"

"No, no, no!" replied the unhappy lad, his pale lips trembling with emotion. "It is because I love you, as well as you love me, that I wish I had never been born; and I believe that both you and I too ought to wish that I was dead, for then at least I could not be a disgrace to you!"

"Why," said she, "do you say such dreadful words to me, William? Why should you be a disgrace to me? All the shocking things papa said last night, cannot make any real difference in you. If it is all true, it is no fault of yours. And perhaps it is not true, perhaps he said it only because he was in a passion. You know when papa is in a passion, he always does say shocking things. But considering how old and tall you are, William, you ought to know better than to mind it so very much."

"It is only because you are not so old, my poor Helen, that

you do not mind it more. Not only am I between three and four long years older than you are, my poor child, but for hours and hours, Helen, when you have been a-bed and asleep, I have been reading, reading, reading all sorts of books! You know what a quantity of books poor mamma used to read, and I too read them all, and a great many more besides that I have got from Mr. Bolton's library, and I know a great deal better than you do, Helen, what my situation really is. I wonder if your dear mother knew the truth? If she did, she must indeed have been an angel to behave so like a real mother to me!"

And here the unhappy boy once again buried his face in his hands, and sobbed like a girl.

It was in vain that Helen threw her arms around his neck, and endeavoured to comfort him by her endearing caresses; for so strongly had the painful idea taken possession of him that the close affinity between them was, and must ever be a disgrace and injury to her, that the caressing repetition of the name of brother, by which again and again she fondly addressed him, seemed instead of a comfort, to be a torture to him; and when at last he raised his head and looked at her, she was positively frightened at the altered expression of his features, and the look of gloomy misery which she read in his eyes.

"Helen!" said he, with great solemnity. "You must never call me by that name again! It is a disgrace to you, and can only be a pain to me. Could any act of mine do you any sort of service, Helen, I think that I would gladly give my life to achieve it. But as it is between us now, sweet love, my best advice is that you should never call yourself my sister. The fact is—and you should thank God for it, Helen—the fact is that we cannot feel alike towards the man that we both call father. I am far—oh! very far—from wishing that there should be any sympathy between us on this subject!"

And here he paused, and for a moment or two remained profoundly silent, but then added in an accent which made her tremble,—"HELEN! I HATE HIM!"

*　　*　　*　　*　　*　　*

Helen was by no means a weak-minded young girl. She was, on the contrary, a very intelligent, and a very reflective person for her age; and minds so constituted are not apt to experience the painful sensation of terror, lightly. But it was terror that she felt at that moment, for the whole aspect of her brother seemed changed, and one of the noblest and most intellectual countenances that ever was looked upon seemed

suddenly to be metamorphosed before her eyes, and to become
the type at once of the most vehement rage, and the most
bitter suffering.

Nor were the delicate features of Helen deficient of expression
in their turn, and her look of mingled fear and woe seemed to
recal her brother to a better or a calmer state of mind, for he
took her hand gently and kindly in his, and said, "Do not let
me frighten you with my violence, Helen! And whatever may
happen to me, dearest, remember always that if I had loved
you less, I should have borne the degradation which has fallen
upon me better. I did so dearly cherish the thought of being
your friend, and your protector through life, that the suddenly
being informed that I am in a condition too degraded to permit
of my being so, has overpowered me. But love me still,
Helen! Though I may be forced to leave you, and though
our destinies, if I continue to live, must, perforce, be sure to
throw us very widely asunder, let me, to my very last hour,
believe, that notwithstanding the stigma that is upon me, you
will still remember me with affection."

Helen's reply to this may be easily imagined. She threw
her arms around his neck, and told him, while a shower of
tender tears poured down her cheeks, that no sister ever loved
a brother more fondly than she loved him, and that she did not
believe that any girl living could have a brother, who so well
deserved her love.

"Bless you, my Helen!" he replied, while his manhood,
stout as it was, could not prevent his eyes, too, from shedding
some drops which showed that there was still left some of that
tender softness of nature, which in the midst of all his lightness
of heart had so effectually endeared him to the small circle
within which he had lived, save with the one exception of his
unnatural father.

Had his situation and prospects been less miserable, he might
indeed have been considered as an individual peculiarly favoured
by nature, for he certainly possessed in no common degree the
qualities and the faculties which are most calculated to insure
happiness. With a form and features of very uncommon
comeliness, he had a constitution, both of mind and body,
indicative of a degree of firmness and vigour, that seemed to
promise success in whatever he undertook; and the enthusiastic
affection, with which his very heart and soul repaid kindness,
rendered him a being that it seemed impossible *not* to love.

But the hard chance, which made him find in his own father

a being from whom his heart shrank with abhorrence, seemed to have changed his nature, and what under other circumstances would have constituted the noblest feature of his character, now appeared forcing him to desperation and to sin.

Hatred was now almost as busy at his heart, as love; and he was so conscious of this, that he shrunk from the look of earnest and affectionate enquiry which his sister fixed on his strangely-altered features.

"Let me leave you now, Helen!" he said; "I am no fit companion for you, in any way. I cannot go to Mr. Bolton to-day. Let me be quite alone! I will walk. Perhaps the dreadful thoughts which seem to have taken possession of me may leave me, in the stillness of a solitary walk. I shall not come home to dinner, Helen, so do not wait for me. Tell poor dear Sarah Lambert that I love her dearly, and the more dearly, Helen, because I know she will always love you. God bless you both!"

And with these words he turned away and left her.

Poor child! She little guessed at that moment how fearfully important she would learn to consider every word he then said to her! And yet her heart sank within her as she lost sight of him, and she wept long and bitterly; for the solitude in which he left her was, for several hours, perfectly uninterrupted.

<hr>

CHAPTER XI.

Mrs. Lambert meanwhile sat herself down in the parlour as soon as her master had left it, and remained there perfectly alone for nearly an hour. She could not, however, have been said to be perfectly idle, for if her limbs were at rest, her brain was at work, and on themes, too, of such deep importance, that instead of remaining thus silent, and thus still, for one hour, she would willingly have continued thus deeply meditating on the future for many. But this could not be. She had much to do, and a will still stronger than her wish for meditation, to make her do it.

For a moment she paused before the door of the school-room, and she longed to open it; but she did not yield to the temptation, for she neither wished to waste her time nor to agitate her spirits; and she passed on to the kitchen, where all necessary preparations were made for the substantial supper which her master had ordered to be ready against his return.

She, moreover, gave such instructions to Rebecca Watkins as she thought sufficient to supply the wants of the less important portion of the family for the day, and all this being accomplished in a very steady and business-like manner, Mrs. Lambert put on her bonnet and shawl, and set off upon a walk to the parsonage.

She was no stranger there, for both the young people, without having any such intention, and in fact without being conscious of what they were about, had impressed the Bolton family with a very decided feeling of respect for Mrs. Lambert.

Innocent as angels of the nature of her real position in their father's house, they had ever spoken of her to their kind friends the Boltons with the truest respect and affection, and though the good clergyman and his wife did not see her often, for Mrs. Bolton was as devoted a mother as Mrs. Lambert was a housekeeper, all the intercourse which had ever been between them was of the most friendly kind.

When, therefore, she now knocked humbly at the parlour door, she was greeted with a friendly smile both by the good clergyman and his wife, when she opened it in compliance with the hospitable command " Come in! "

After the first words of salutation had been exchanged, Mr. Bolton, fixing his friendly eyes on the face of the visitor, exclaimed, " You are not well, Mrs. Lambert! and you are not only looking unusually pale, but you look harassed and unhappy. I trust that nothing is the matter with either of my dear pupils? "

If it had happened that her master had made the same discovery while she had waited upon him during the morning meal, it might have annoyed her greatly; but now the observation was a relief to her, for it at once offered an opening for the communication she wished to make, and for the dismal tale she had to tell.

" My looks, then, are a faithful index of my mind," she replied, "I am, indeed, harassed and unhappy, and to a gentleman like you, Sir, and to your good lady too, your knowing this will be more likely than anything to make you listen to me."

" Sit down, Mrs. Lambert," was the kind reply, "and if we can either of us be of any use to you, be very sure that we

shall not shrink from any trouble it may bring with it. There
is nothing the matter with the young people, is there?"

"They are both well in health, Sir," she replied, "and yet it
is on their account that I am so miserable. As to myself," she
added, withdrawing her eyes from Mr. Bolton's face, and fixing
them on the ground, "I neither want nor wish for aid from any
one. I have forfeited all right to the friendship of the good,
and my pecuniary situation is such as to render their pecuniary
assistance unnecessary."

Mr. Bolton changed colour, and most involuntarily started as
she said this. The unfortunate Mrs. Lambert both saw and
understood this perfectly. Had the unhappy woman not been
the mistress of her every way vicious and unprincipled master,
she might have been cited from one end of the country to the
other as the most perfect pattern of an excellent servant that
could be found in it. She herself knew this as well as Mr.
Bolton did, and it was this consciousness of her own merit
which enabled her at once to perceive that the nature of her
self-accusation was already understood.

The silence of a moment followed, and then Mr. Bolton
raised his eyes and said, as he directed them towards his wife,
"If you wish to consult me as a clergyman, Mrs. Lambert, and
as the minister of your parish, it would be better perhaps that
I should see you alone."

"You will cease to think so, Sir, when you shall have heard
what I am going to say," she replied. "If it were of myself,
and my own affairs, that I was about to speak, I should receive
your rebuke with equal deference and obedience; but in that
case, Mr. Bolton, it would not have been necessary, for I should
never have presumed to speak to you on the subject at all. But
it is concerning your pupils, Sir, and of their very terrible position, that I wish your advice, and perhaps your assistance, and
that of your lady also. Fear not that I should make any
further reference to myself. You have understood the words I
have already spoken as I intended you should understand them;
and this, as far as I am concerned is all that is necessary."

The wretched woman felt that the worst part of the task she
had set herself in seeking this interview was now over, and she
at once felt restored to all the cool, deliberate, and resolute
self-possession which made so remarkable a feature in her
character.

"Go on," said Mr. Bolton, after the pause of a moment.

"My master is not, as I believe, in any respect the sort of

person that he is considered to be in this very neighbourhood,"
she resumed. "In the first place, he is not known here by his
real name; in the second, instead of being in the necessitous
circumstances which he has affected, as an excuse for his parsi-
monious manner of living, he is a man of distinguished family,
and the possessor of a large and long descended property ; and,
in the third, the fine noble-hearted boy who has had, amidst all
his misfortunes, the great good luck of having been your pupil,
Sir, has, in fact, no right to any name at all, his unfortunate
mother not having been the wife of his father."

"Your statement respecting Mr. Rixley's real name and circumstances is quite unexpected, certainly; and I believe the
whole neighbourhood to be as much in the dark on the subject
as myself," replied Mr. Bolton. "But it is otherwise respecting
what you tell concerning his son, for most persons, I believe, are
aware that he was never married to the poor boy's mother. I
love the lad most sincerely ; and most truly rejoiced should I
be, were it ever to be in my power, to assist him in any way ;
but I will frankly confess to you, Mrs. Lambert, that having for
so many years avoided any personal familiarity with Mr. Rixley,
and remained so perfectly in ignorance of all the mysteries
which seem to be attached to him, I have no wish whatever to
become more acquainted with him now than I have hitherto
been; and I shall be obliged to you if you will excuse my not
listening to any further details about him."

Mrs. Lambert remained silent for a moment : and, notwithstanding all her self-possession, she felt utterly at a loss how to
proceed ; but, fortunately for her, and for the helpless being
whose cause she meant to plead, her pale and sunken features
assumed an expression of such deep and true despair, that the
kindly heart of Mrs. Bolton was too profoundly touched to
resist it.

"Perhaps, Stephen," said she, addressing her husband, almost
in a whisper, "perhaps you might do good by listening to what
she has to say."

The intellect of Mr. Bolton was an intellect very greatly
superior to that of his wife, but it would have been difficult to
have found anywhere a heart of finer quality than hers. One
of the good gifts belonging to that heart was its true allegiance
in all ways to her husband, and it was rarely indeed that she
uttered any word which might be construed into the expression of
an opinion different from what had been previously given by
him. But when this rare occurrence did take place, it invari-

ably produced, as all rare occurrences do, a considerable effect, and the words which I have given were no sooner spoken than the countenance of the clergyman underwent a marked change; its cold, and almost stern expression relaxed, and he said, "My good wife is right, Mrs. Lambert. Go on, and tell me everything you wish to say. My reason for stopping you arose from my dislike to hearing anything like secret communications respecting the affairs of my neighbours, in which I can do no good. But if you think I can be useful to the children or to yourself, I am quite ready to listen to you."

"I beg you to believe, Sir, that I know what is due to you, and to your lady, better than to ask assistance from either of you for such a person as myself. Neither do I require assistance from any one. But concerning these unfortunate young people I have the double reason arising from their great need of help, and the consciousness of my own unfitness to render it. May I not add that the great kindness which they have hitherto received, both from yourself and your lady, has seemed to justify my asking the help which they so greatly need from you?"

"Yes, Mrs. Lambert, you are right, quite right. Let us hear in what way you think we can be useful to them."

This permission, to speak freely, seemed for a moment only to impede her power of speaking at all, for on receiving it she raised her hands to her eyes, and remained, as it seemed, lost in thought. But then she began by stating to them, with scrupulous exactness, precisely the narrative which she had received from her master on the preceding day, apologising for the strength of the language she used when describing his hatred towards his brother by saying that as she earnestly desired to make them comprehend his real feeling and his real motives, she preferred repeating the precise words in which he had expressed them, however painful it might be either to speak, or hear them.

Having rapidly, but very accurately repeated all he had told her of his early life, she alluded to the commencement of her own fatal acquaintance with him as slightly as was consistent with her purpose of making them acquainted with the facts, and the only portion of the narrative that she dwelt upon in which she was herself concerned, was that which first followed her domestication in his family; but she only did so sufficiently to make her auditors comprehend that, during this time he had succeeded in persuading her that notwithstanding his frequent absences from the Warren House, he was still devotedly attached to her.

"I mention this," she continued, "in order to enable you in some slight degree to understand the effect which his recent disclosures have produced. It was only yesterday, Mr. Bolton, that he communicated to his unfortunate son the wholly unsuspected fact of his illegitimacy. The effect of this disclosure upon the young man was terrible—very, very terrible! I have always been aware that he was a highly sensitive, and very noble-spirited boy, but I certainly should never have anticipated that he would have felt such agony at being made acquainted with this stain upon his birth. That the blow fell the more heavily from the savagely unfeeling way in which it was given, cannot be doubted; and the fearful and desperate glance of hatred which it produced—it was but one glance! for the boy never raised his eyes to his unfeeling father again—will never pass from my memory! But Mr. Rixley only sneered at him."

And here for a moment the miserable woman covered her face with her hands, and remained silent; when she removed them she was perhaps paler than ever, but there was an air of stedfast and immovable composure in her features which seemed to indicate that the most terrible part of her narrative was over, and that whatever remained for her to tell would be spoken with more calmness. "It was yesterday also," she continued, "that he for the first time informed me of its being his purpose to marry immediately, adding that he had selected a bride, beautiful, high-born, and wealthy. He added also that he was greatly enamoured of her, but that he had reasons, stronger still, for deciding upon again enduring the matrimonial yoke. 'I marry,' said he, 'wholly and solely in the hope of having a son, for I will not leave it within the reach of possibility that my hateful brother should inherit my estate.'"

And then in a perfectly clear and steady voice, Mrs. Lambert went on recapitulating all that the reader already knows respecting his having guarded against the danger of his brother's succeeding as heir-at-law, in the case of his sudden death, by having made a will bequeathing the whole property to his daughter.

Having reached this point of her narrative, Mrs. Lambert paused, and remained silent for a minute or two, with her hand pressed upon her forehead, as if her memory had lost the thread connecting what she had said with what she was about to say.

"But I see not how I can be of any use in these affairs," said Mr. Bolton, more from a wish to assist her in recovering her memory than from any desire to check her narrative.

"Pardon me, Sir, for being so prolix," she replied quickly, and with every appearance of being in very perfect possession of all her faculties. "The nature of the assistance which I hope to find from the benevolent kindness of yourself and your lady will be sufficiently evident. Having informed me, as I have stated, of his having taken this precautionary measure, which he seemed to laugh at, however, as he mentioned it, he went on to inform me that it was still his intention to keep his present, and his future family, in ignorance of the obscure marriage which he had formerly contracted, and which death had fortunately dissolved, and to be equally reserved on the subject of his having two children inhabiting a remote house, which they, none of them, knew he possessed. 'As to the boy,' he added, 'I shall immediately make an usher of him'—and then, at the same time, I think it was, he told me that I was to continue at the Warren House to take care of his daughter, adding that he should provide for the maintenance of us both. And it is concerning this last announcement, Sir, that I want your advice and assistance. Had I been . . . other than what I am . . ." said the unhappy woman, bursting in tears, "I would have accepted the precious charge with joy and gladness, and while waiting upon her with all the duty of a servant, I should have loved her with all the tenderness of a mother; but as it is! . . ." And here she stopped, and the first tears she had shed during the interview escaped from her eyes, and rolled down her pallid cheeks.

For a moment her auditors both remained silent, but even so they both managed to reply to the appeal made to them in a way that very clearly showed that they felt the force of it. Both Mr. Bolton and his wife fixed their eyes upon the carpet and gently shook their heads. But this mute avowal that they both agreed with her in opinion as to the impossibility of her being permitted to take charge of their dearly beloved Helen, was not all the answer she received. In a voice of deep sympathy, and of very earnest kindness also, Mr. Bolton hastened to reply, "Mrs. Lambert, I am quite sure that I speak the sentiments of my wife, as well as my own, when I tell you that your conduct upon this occasion is exactly everything that it ought to be. We know wonderfully little of Mr. Rixley personally, considering how many years we

have been neighbours, and how long I have been employed
to assist in the education of his children; but all we do know of
him must naturally lead us to wish that we may know nothing
more, and most especially that we may not be led by any
circumstances into the necessity of holding personal intercourse
with him. You will easily understand this, Mrs. Lambert, and
I feel confident that you will carefully avoid the either doing or
saying anything that might lead to this. But on the other
hand I do not scruple to tell you that we all love these most
unfortunate young people too sincerely to shrink from doing
everything that may be in our power to help them. Tell us
candidly, and without any scruple or hesitation, what it is you
would yourself wish that we should do for them."

This challenge, far from appearing to embarrass the hitherto
almost trembling visitor, seemed to inspire her instantly with
courage and confidence.

"I will tell you, Sir," she replied. "I have already told you
all I know concerning them, and I will now tell you what it is
I dare to hope from your kindness to beings so utterly helpless,
and so miserably unprotected as they are about to be. Let me
begin, however, by speaking of myself, as the doing so will
tend to remove embarrassment in many ways. I received upon
the death of my mother a sum of money which enabled me
to purchase an annuity of sixty pounds for my natural life.
This income is fully adequate to the supply of all my wants,
and I possess, moreover, a small house in Falmouth, a couple of
rooms in which will suffice for my own accommodation, and the
rent of the remainder will assist my income. I have said thus
much to prevent the pitying kindness of your hearts from being
wasted upon any thought of me. In reply to your frank
question, Sir, as to what I would wish you to do for the unfortunate young people for whom you have already done so
much, I frankly answer that I wish—nay that I dare venture
to hope—that you will extend to them all the personal protection which circumstances may enable you to bestow. Mr. Rixley
set off this morning upon a water excursion, leaving orders
that supper should be prepared for him against his return this
evening. It will be my office, as usual, to wait upon him at
table, and I expect that he will take that opportunity of
explaining to me what it is his precise purpose to do respecting
the children. He has already informed me that he intends to
leave the Warren House to-morrow morning, and that it is his
purpose to leave me sufficient credit at the Falmouth bank to

enable me to keep house, and provide for them as I have already done since the death of their mother. Some distinct and specific instructions on the subject of his unfortunate son I also expect to receive from him, and my earnest prayer to you, Sir, is that whatever funds are left at my disposal you will take the management of them, and do the best you can for the interest and protection of both these most innocent and unfortunate creatures."

Mr. Bolton remained silent for a minute or two after she had ceased speaking, and then said, "Your request, Mrs. Lambert, has so much that is vague, and yet so much that is important in it, that my reply must . . . ." and here the good man again paused, as if doubtful of what he ought to say; but presently added, "of necessity be vague also. I can make no promise more specific than that I will do all that may be in my power to serve them.

"But surely," he continued, "in the case of his son he will make his intentions known by a personal communication with himself? William must be, if I mistake not, nearly seventeen years of age. He looks even more, but I well remember that he has always been remarkably tall, and in every way advanced beyond his years. But even at seventeen he surely ought not to be treated as a mere child, and left in the care of his nurse. It is evident, Mrs. Lambert, from the position in which Mr. Rixley proposes to leave you here, that you are still likely to have considerable influence over him, and I trust you will exert it for the purpose of preventing this cruel injustice. William Rixley has great abilities. Not only has he learnt everything that it was in my power to teach with more brilliant rapidity than I have ever before witnessed, but he has on many occasions shown unmistakable symptoms of a noble spirit, and a highly susceptible sense of honour. I earnestly advise you not to let his father depart leaving orders that this boy should be placed as usher in a country school. It is utterly impossible to conceive any situation less suited to his temperament. I think it would kill him, Mrs. Lambert! For Heaven's sake do not let this unnatural father set off upon this project of marriage till he has conversed with his son upon the nature of his future career!"

Mrs. Lambert listened to all this with the most respectful attention, but her complexion changed from pale to red before she answered it.

At length she said, "I beseech you, Sir, not to judge of my

wish and will to obey you strictly upon every point concerning which your kindness and compassion will lead you to bestow your invaluable advice, by what I am going to say in answer to your present proposal. But in order that you should understand me, it is necessary that you should be told that, till yesterday, this unfortunate boy has been left in total ignorance of the miserable circumstances of his birth. Till yesterday he believed his mother to have been his father's lawful wife. I was present when his unfeeling father told him in the most abrupt and brutal manner the disgraceful truth, and never can I forget the terrible effect which this truth produced on the unhappy boy. Rage and—can we wonder at it—hatred also flashed from that bright and youthful eye. Do not, I conjure you, Mr. Bolton! Do not insist upon my again bringing this father and son together face to face! Most solemnly do I assure you that knowing the father's reckless brutality as I now know it, and having witnessed the vehement emotion of the son as I saw it then, I dare not risk making myself the agent for procuring such a meeting. Wait, Sir! wait till the first dreadful shock is over, and then, if circumstances should seem to render it desirable that they should meet at all, the danger of their doing so may be less."

Mr. Bolton listened to her gently, and with great attention, but when she had finished he shook his head in a way that very plainly showed he did not agree with her.

"Mrs. Lambert," he said, "I must frankly tell you that I think you wrong. You are evidently terrified at the idea of their meeting, from fearing that some personal violence might arise between them, from one side or the other. But trust me there is a good deal of feminine weakness in this fear. Nay! do not look ashamed of it! Your spirits must have been dreadfully shaken during your late interviews with this hateful man, and we can scarcely wonder that very wild fears for the future may mix with more substantial ones. But I really believe that if you will consider the subject dispassionately you will agree with me in thinking that this young man ought to see and converse with his father before this projected marriage takes place. It may be too late afterwards."

"That is true, Sir, very true!" replied the pale and almost ghastly-looking woman, in an accent of deep respect; for the sudden flush which the idea of a meeting between a father and son had sent to her face very speedily passed away, and left her as pale as ever.

7

"I have not seen poor William since I carried in breakfast to himself and his sister in the school-room this morning, but I will now return to the house, and, if he is not gone out upon one of his rambles, I will tell him exactly what you say. I am sure there is no person whose opinion he will be so likely to listen to as yourself."

"The sooner you seek for him with this object the better," rejoined the worthy clergyman; "and therefore I will now wish you good morning; but not without assuring you that I justly appreciate the motives which have induced you to pay us this visit."

"I will go, sir: I will go immediately," she replied. "Let me only add one word for the poor friendless girl who is to be consigned to my protection, but whom I love too sincerely to hazard her happiness, and her respectability, by taking charge of. Her fate, by her father's statement, is still very uncertain. Should he have no male heir it is his purpose—and if I understood him rightly he made his will with this object—for this friendless girl to inherit his large property. Such being his intention, it is impossible to doubt that it must be his intention, also, immediately to make such a provision for her as may enable any person who takes charge of her to provide suitably for her home and her education. I have already explained with sufficient clearness why I cannot be that person. But you, Sir! .... You and your excellent lady!...... I dare not dictate to you, but should you, when I have withdrawn myself to the obscurity which my degraded condition demands, should you then find this dear child wholly unfriended, yet rich enough to insure those who befriended her from loss, may I not hope that wholly friendless she will not be permitted to remain?"

"Be very sure, Mrs. Lambert, that both my wife and myself appreciate your motives in this application to us. In my soul I believe that they do you honour; but you must not insist upon an immediate answer from either of us. Give us time to talk the matter over together, and I think it very likely that your view of the case may be adopted by us. But at present I will pledge myself to nothing, Mrs. Lambert. You will doubtless have a final conversation with your master before he leaves the Warren House, and the result of this may enable us to decide upon the degree of assistance which we may have it in our power to offer you."

This was too reasonable to be controverted, and the unhappy

woman took her leave with assurances of the deepest gratitude for the unmerited kindness with which her terrible narrative had been received.

〜〜〜〜〜〜〜〜〜

CHAPTER XII.

IT is needless to follow the wretched Mrs. Lambert through all the hours of that dreadful day. There were moments during the course of it in which she could remember nothing but the sort of phosphoric brightness which still rested on her recollections of her first years of union with the man who now so recklessly threw her from him as an idle toy, no longer possessing the power of amusing him. But if there were moments given to the memory of the delusions which formerly surrounded her, there were long hours bestowed upon the recollection of the scenes of yesterday, and the preponderance of the latter, over the former, was in accurate, and very natural proportion to the recent freshness of the one, and the blighted and blasted memory of the other.

But it is indeed needless to follow all this, and scenes less visionary have now to be related, which must necessarily throw into the shade all the useless regrets of the sinning, but more sinned against, Almeria Lambert.

*　　*　　*　　*　　*　　*

Poor Helen had passed very nearly the entire day alone.

William had left her for the solitary walk which he had predicted would be so useful to him ; and Mrs. Lambert had, in many ways, too much to do to permit her giving more than a few moments at a time to Helen ; so that long before her father had re-entered the Warren House after his lengthened excursion along the coast, she had quietly crept to her little distant bedroom, said her prayers, gone to bed, and fallen asleep.

. William returned an hour or too before his father, and, though looking pale and miserable, he accepted the supper Mrs. Lambert had prepared for him, but not till she had assured him that his father was not in the house; for the poor boy seemed to dread the sight of him.

"I would rather go supperless to bed, Sarah Lambert, than

run the risk of meeting him!" said he, with something very like the shudder of abhorrence passing over him.

"There is no danger of that, my dear boy," she replied, in the tone of iron composure with which she habitually concealed every emotion too strong to be safely made manifest. "Your father intends leaving home to-morrow; at least an hour before your usual time of rising. He is going to be married, you know! He is going to visit the lady he is in love with! I have told you that, already, William, and you may be therefore very sure that he will not delay setting off upon so agreeable a commission at all longer than he can help. So you have only to keep in your room, my dear boy, till about six o'clock in the morning, and then you may come down stairs without any fear whatever of meeting him."

"Till six o'clock in the morning?" replied William. "Very well! And now then, good night, dear old friend! Nobody in the whole world, I believe, ever loved me excepting that angel woman who taught me to call her mother, my pretty Helen, who ought to have been my sister, but who shall never have the shame of calling me brother, and yourself, dear Sarah! Good night!"

And having said these words with very evident emotion, he pressed a silent kiss upon the forehead of his nurse, and left her.

He had evidently been much more strongly affected by all that had happened during the last twenty-four hours than his sister had been, and it is, therefore, by no means extraordinary if he did not sleep quite so soundly.

Mr. Rixley returned to the Warren House very punctually at the hour when he was expected, and it was soon evident that he came fully prepared to do honour to the supper he had bespoken. He both ate and drank heartily, and when he had finished his meal, but not till then, he invited Mrs. Lambert to sit down with him, saying, "It will be better, Goody, to say all that there is left for me to say to you to-night; for there is nothing bores me so much as having anything to do in the business line, when I have got to set off full speed in the morning. However, I believe I have already told you nearly all that is necessary for you to know. I have left an order at the Falmouth Bank, which will enable you to receive fifty pounds quarterly, for the maintenance of yourself and Helen. You seem to wince, my beautiful Almeria? But this is quite enough I promise you, and most decidedly I shall allow no more. You must remember, if you please, that the chances are at least a thousand to one against Miss Helen's inheriting the Beauchamp property, and you may depend upon it she will hear of me, should I be sufficiently unlucky to want her as an heir; and, in the meantime, I strongly advise you, for her sake, never to breathe a word to her, or to anybody, respecting this very improbable contingency. As to that detestable giant of a boy," he continued, "I have already told him, and you too, what I intend him for. Take care, Mother Lambert, that with as little delay as possible you make an usher of him. There are lots of schools—free schools, and tight schools—in Devonshire and Cornwall, both, where a single word from his dear friend Parson Bolton would get him admitted immediately; and that the said Parson Bolton may not have the disgrace of standing godfather to a *sans culotte*, this order upon Kingwood's Bank will not only pay your first quarter, but serve to fit you all out in the independent line. And now, good night, old lady! This may probably be the last time that you and I shall be *tête-à-tête* together, and my farewell advice to you is not to trouble yourself, or indulge yourself in any romantic love fit for that gawky boy, for take my word for it you will only be disappointed."

The master paused, but the servant uttered no syllable in reply; she only raised her eyes, and looked at him.

He returned the look, and laughed.

"Yes, yes! Mrs. Lambert," he resumed, "I understand your great Greek eyes perfectly. You think I am jealous of the hobbydehoy, but you were never more mistaken in your life. As far as my peace of mind is concerned, I give you my word of honour you might bestow your mature affections upon every boy in the parish, if you liked it, without causing me any Othello-like sensations whatever. I speak wholly and solely for your own use and benefit, because I happen to know that ladies who are no longer in their *première jeunesse* are rather apt to fall in love with gentlemen who are. You understand French, you know, so I need not explain myself farther."

A little interval—a very little interval—elapsed before Mrs. Lambert spoke, and then she only said, very quietly, "Thank you, Sir. I am quite sure that you intend that what you say shall be useful to me, and I think it is very likely in one way or another, that it may be so. But you forget, Sir, how late it is, and I have not finished my packing yet, for I did not know how much linen you would choose to take with you?"

"*All!* you foolish woman! ALL! What should I leave

linen here for? For tinder? Or do you think it might be convenient to help out Master William's equipment before he takes possession of his ushership, and so save you a little stitching, Mrs. Sarah? and make him look, perhaps, a little more like a gentleman than he ever did yet, eh?"

"No, Sir, not that," she replied, "only I don't know what to do about making room for it. If you take all your things, Sir, I must look about for a larger box."

"Very well! look away, then," he replied, "I dare say you will find lots in the store-room. I have got to pack my writing-desk before I go to bed, so bring me my glass of white wine negus, and then be off."

Having said this, he lighted a cigar, which he smoked while she cleared the table, and obeyed his command that she should place his desk, which was deposited on a distant table, upon the one before him. When she had done this, he nodded his head and mumbled "Good night!" without, however, removing his cigar; but before she had closed the door of the room after her, he remembered his negus, and called out, "I say, Lambert! don't forget my negus." In answer to which she replied, "No, Sir," but without re-entering the room.

On reaching the kitchen she found the faithful factotum Rebecca Watkins still there, though it was considerably later than her usual time of leaving the house. "How comes it that you are here still, Rebecca?" said she. "I thought you were going when I took in my master's supper."

"And so I was going," she replied, "but just as I was passing the bottom of the stairs to go out, who should I see coming down but Master William, looking so unaccountable pale, that I believe I started outright at the sight of him, and that made him smile, poor young gentleman, but looking for all the world like a ghost all the time. And then I asked him if I could do anything for him, or get anything for him to take, seeing that he looked so poorly, and his answer was that he would not trouble me, but that he really was going into the cellar to draw a tumbler of beer, for that he was so remarkable thirsty after his walk, that he did not think he could get to sleep without it. And thereupon I offered to draw it for him, but this he would not hear of, upon no account. I tried to take the tumbler he had brought down stairs with him out of his hand, but he would not let me have it, and seeing he was so determined, I gave it up, but I was determined, on my side, that I would not go home till I had told you how ill I thought he was looking, that in case you heard him moving in the night you might go to him. But I knew it would vex him, like, if he thought I was watching him, and I, therefore, crept back into the kitchen and shut the door, so that he could not see me, and then I do believe that I fell asleep in the chair I sat down upon, for I never heard him go up again."

"I think he was only tired, Rebecca," replied Mrs. Lambert, "and there is no great wonder in that, for I know he has been taking a very long walk to-day. However, I shall be sure to remember what you have told me, and take care to look after him if he should be unwell."

"Now, then, I shall go away easy," replied Rebecca, "but, upon my word, I tell you no more than the truth when I say he looked ill, for I don't know that I ever see'd a young lad look so deadly pale in my life."

"I hope you will find him looking better when you come to-morrow, Rebecca, but you will do no good by staying any longer now, for I would not have him disturbed on any account. Nothing that anybody could do for him would do him as much good as a sound night's rest."

"Good nights," were then again exchanged between them, and they parted, Rebecca Watkins going to her home, and Mrs. Lambert to the school-room, where she sat down to meditate deliberately, as she told herself, during a few uninterrupted moments, on all that had happened to her during the last eight and forty hours.

If the steadiness of her deliberation might have been judged of by the steadiness of her demeanour during the next quarter of an hour, it was steady enough, for not only was she as pale as marble but as motionless too. Apparently, however, she gave way to no vehement emotion; she 'shed no tear, she breathed no sigh,' but at the end of that quiet, or, at any rate, motionless interval, she suddenly roused herself, as if then recollecting for the first time since she had left her master's presence, that he had commanded her to do many things which were still undone; she got up from the chair on which she had placed herself, and having for a moment closely pressed her aching forehead with her hand, she seemed suddenly to shake off the sort of dreamy stupefaction which had been creeping upon her, and employed herself in making the negus which had been ordered; having done which she carried it to the parlour and placed it on the table at which her master was still sitting, arranging sundry papers in his writing-desk.

He took no notice whatever of her entrance, but when she was in the act of leaving the room, he said, "What have you been so devilish long about? Are my things packed, Lambert? I am going to bed this moment."

"Everything shall be ready," she replied, and closed the door behind her. But everything was not quite ready yet, for she had to go into his bed-room before he entered it. Many of the things which he had ordered to be packed were still there, and it was with a hurried step that she now mounted the stairs to his apartment. She succeeded, however, in accomplishing all she had to do there before he entered the room, but met him on the stairs as she descended with her apron full of various articles which she was about to put in his travelling trunks.

"You have not finished yet?" he exclaimed impatiently. "Upon my soul, Lambert, it is quite time that I should give you up, for you are grown into a cursedly tedious old drone."

"I shall have plenty of time, Sir," she replied, as she passed him.

And so she had, and she faithfully kept her promise of having everything he had ordered neatly packed; and then she too went to bed.

CHAPTER XIII.

At her usual early hour on the following morning the faithful Rebecca arrived at the Warren House, and let herself into the back kitchen by means of the key which had for years been confided to her in order to enable her to make her frequent exits and entrances without troubling the scanty household.

As usual, too, she performed her morning duty of making the fire and putting on the kettle, and then repaired to the parlour in which the master of the house had supped on the preceding evening, and began to put it in order for his breakfast.

But before she could make the room look tidy she had rather more to do than usual, for the carpet was covered on both sides of the chair in which he had sat with fragments of various written papers, of which it seemed that he had disembarrassed his writing-desk which he had left standing on the table exactly opposite his chair.

Having carefully removed all these minute fragments, and thereby restored the room to its ordinarily neat aspect, she prepared to lay the cloth for breakfast, for she knew that "the master" was to set off early on his journey to London.

But she felt almost afraid to move the writing-desk lest it might have been expressly left there by its choleric owner in order to be ready for his further use in the morning; and having stood meditating on this doubtful point for a moment, she laid the still-folded cloth on the table determined to consult the housekeeper before she ventured to remove the very handsome and important looking desk.

She did however all she could in the way of preparation that did not interfere with this prudent resolution; she took away an empty tumbler which stood upon the table, removed every particle of dust with her checked apron, and then placed the tea-tray with pretty nearly all that was needful for breakfast beside the table-cloth, in order to be perfectly ready to obey the orders of Mrs. Lambert as soon as she should receive them.

Nor did she wait long for the appearance of this important functionary, for she entered the room almost at the moment that she had completed these preliminary operations.

"Oh, goodness! I am so glad you are come down, Mrs. Lambert!" exclaimed Rebecca, pointing to the table, "for I was come to a stand-still, because I did not know whether I ought to move that grand-looking box, or not. You know that it always stands yonder upon that table from the time master comes into the house, till he goes out of it again, and I am sure I don't know if he would choose that anybody should put hands upon it besides himself."

"You go on laying the breakfast, and never mind about the box," replied Mrs. Lambert, seating herself in a chair near the door. "Only take everything else off the table," she added.

"And so I have, Mrs. Lambert. I have taken away a dirty tumbler, and the plate that it stood upon, tea-spoon and all, and I have swept away lots of bits of paper both from the table, and the carpet round about, but I would not do any more till I had got your orders."

"Well, Rebecca, then I think you had better leave the desk where it is and lay the cloth at the other end of the table," was the reply.

Rebecca immediately set to work to obey her, and while she

was thus employed, Mrs. Lambert said, "Have you seen Master William, Rebecca? He is always stirring before this time, but I have neither seen nor heard him."

"Nor I either, Mrs. Lambert," replied Rebecca. "But I am not a bit surprised at it," she continued, "for I am positive sure that the poor young gentleman was not well when I saw him just before he went to bed last night. You know I told you so, Mrs. Lambert, didn't I?"

"Yes you did, Rebecca, but I can't say that I minded you much, for I knew that he had been taking one of his over-long walks, and that was quite enough to make him look tired. However, I'll go and see if anything is the matter with him."

"And that is just what I think you ought to do," was the rejoinder, "for I won't believe that he is right well till I see him again, and he tells me so."

"Finish what you are about, then," said Mrs. Lambert, leaving the room as she spoke, "and I will come back again with news of William, directly."

She kept her word, for she did come directly, and in as short a time as it was well possible for her to have mounted the stairs, and come down again. "Ill!" she exclaimed, as she re-entered the parlour, "It does not seem very likely that he should be ill. But he is neither in his bed nor in his room, Rebecca, and the strangest thing of all is that his window, which opens upon the top of the porch is thrown up, and that he is gone that way is clear, for one of his sheets is made fast to one of the posts of his little bed, which he has drawn close to the window, and it is plain that he has let himself down by the help of it."

"But what in the wide world could have made him do such a trick?" replied Rebecca. "What should he have run away for in that fashion, Mrs. Lambert?"

"Because his father had used him brutally!" replied Mrs. Lambert, covering her face with her hands.

"Poor boy! Poor boy!" responded Rebecca. "To think that such a fine, handsome, kind-spoken young gentleman should hazard his dear precious young life for that!"

"Gracious God, no!" replied the other, vehemently. "I don't believe any such thing. There is nothing in the whole world so unlikely! But we are two fools for being frightened about him, Rebecca Watkins. I'll bet you what you please, that he is only gone upon another of his long walks. He has always been as mad about walking as his father about sailing.

. . . . And here comes the chaise for my master! Don't say anything to anybody, Rebecca, about William's getting out of the window. It will only give people a notion that he is a wild sort of boy, and that he is not. Mind what I tell you! He is the very best and gentlest human being that ever God made. He might do many wild madcap things in sport, but that is the very worst of him."

At this moment, the old servant, who was gardener, shoe-black, and head boatman of the establishment, presented himself at the door. "Is master ready?" said he.

"He has not had his breakfast yet, at any rate," replied Rebecca, "so the chaise must wait his pleasure, as, of course, it ought. But if he is late it is not our fault, for we have got everything ready for him."

"Do go up to his door, John, will you?" said Mrs. Lambert. "Go to his door, and tell him that the chaise is come."

The man hastened to obey her, and mounted the stairs, not exactly with a light step, but certainly not with a slow one, the two women remaining below, too much occupied, as it seemed, with the strange escapade of William to enable them to think much of anything else.

But their talk on this subject was very speedily interrupted by the return of John, who rushed down the stairs with a step as rapid as that with which he would have descended from the top-mast to announce the sight of land after a calm, though nothing could be less alike than the countenance with which he would have announced that joyous fact, and that with which he now addressed the two women who were awaiting his return.

"He is dead!" he exclaimed, in an accent which would have carried terror to the stoutest heart. "He is dead, and as cold as a stone!"

Rebecca Watkins uttered a loud scream, while Mrs. Lambert sunk into a chair in perfect silence, but looking herself as pale as the corpse her fellow-servant described.

"But, maybe, he is not outright dead, Mrs. Lambert?" said Rebecca. "Maybe he is only swooned away like, out of an accident? Didn't we ought to send right away for the doctor, Mrs. Lambert?"

"To be sure we ought!' responded both the other servants; 'and that without losing another moment!" added Mrs. Lambert.

"Mr. Foster will be here in the twinkling of an eye, I'll

answer for him," exclaimed John, seizing upon his hat, and darting out of the house without waiting for further orders.

"But mercy on me!" exclaimed Rebecca, trembling in every limb, "it is not right for us to stay down here, doing nothing, is it, Mrs. Lambert? Didn't we ought to go up stairs together, both of us, to see if there is any good to be done? How can we be sure that John mightn't have blundered? Didn't we ought to go up, Mrs. Lambert?"

"Most certainly we ought, Rebecca," replied the other, with greatly more composure; though she, too, still looked very pale: "the only objection to our going together," she added, "is our having to leave the house-door open. It won't do, you know, to keep the doctor waiting when he comes."

"Well, then, what can we do?" said Rebecca, "I wouldn't go up first by my own self for all the whole world, and I don't suppose you would either? What a pity it is that Master William should be out of the way just at this moment!"

"It is, indeed!" replied Mrs. Lambert, with a sigh, "I would give a great deal to have him by me at this moment. Not that I mind about going up, Rebecca. I will go up directly, if you will promise to bring up the doctor the very minute he comes. You must not keep him here talking, remember, because if any good can be done, of course it must be done directly. If he really is dead it must have been in a fit, and the only chance will be to bleed him immediately."

"Yes, sure," replied the still shaking Rebecca, "that is what will be done, I'll engage for it; and don't you be feared that I shou'd keep back the doctor from doing it."

Having received this reiterated promise, Mrs. Lambert left the kitchen, and repaired with a slow, but perfectly steady step to contemplate the dead body of the man whom she had once, and that at no very distant date, loved with a devotedness of affection, but very rarely met with in any class.

But even then she lost not that wonderful power of self-command, which had enabled her for so many years to retain an aspect of perfect tranquillity in a situation, which, to most women, would have rendered the attempt to do so absolutely impossible. She now entered her master's bedroom with her usual steady step, and, having reached the bed, stood gazing on the lifeless form, which lay stretched upon it, with a degree of solemnity which precluded the possibility of accusing her of anything like indifference, or lightness of feeling, but which spoke at the same time the most perfect self-possession and calmness.

The man who had so lately been the personification of everything that was vehement and wilful, now lay stretched before her in a way that proclaims the idle nothingness of all human passion more impressively, and more convincingly, than all the sage, and all the priest have taught.

The deep philosophy of the lesson was not lost on the half-educated woman. She could not tremble, and totter, and faint, as the majority of women of her own rank might have done; but she felt that she stood face to face with the greatest mystery which has hitherto been revealed to us throughout all the startling wonders of creation!

Where was that spirit now, which had possessed the skill of seeming to be one thing, while it was another? Was it gone where it would be for ever stripped of that power? And would it henceforward inhabit regions more fitted to its real nature than to its assumed one? Or was there in sin a quality, analogous to weight in matter, which took it and its belongings, *of necessity*, and by a primal law of nature, down deeper, and deeper still, to a lower stage, a lower department of Nature's workshop?

Almeria Lambert had certainly been taught, after a fashion, to speak French, and to play on the pianoforte; but, nevertheless, she was a very ignorant woman; and when her fancy once set sail, she had neither rudder nor compass to help her, and during her fits of speculation, would often have been at a loss to have told either which way she was going, or by what means she hoped to obtain the goal she had in view.

But on the present occasion, at least, the vagueness of these imaginings was certainly beneficial to her, for however wild the whirlwind of thought which seemed to drive her on, it had decidedly the beneficial effect of taking her from the ghastly scene before her, or, at any rate, of enabling her to contemplate it with infinitely less of mere feminine weakness than Rebecca Watkins could have done.

Mrs. Lambert, however, was not long left to her solitary meditations beside the body of her late master; for John had been a fleet messenger, and Mr. Foster obeyed the startling summons with all the promptness which such a summons is sure to produce in a neighbourhood too scantily populated for exciting incidents of any kind to abound.

Moreover, the really kind-hearted village doctor no sooner

heard old John's panting announcement that "Squire Rixley had died of a fit during the night," than his thoughts flew to the children, both of whom he had ushered into the world, and both of whom seemed to him, as well as to all others, to have so wonderfully little claim upon the kindness of any one in it.

When, therefore, the grey-headed messenger added to his intelligence, "the housekeeper's best respects, and hopes that his honour would be pleased to come over to see if anything could be done in case the poor gentleman should not be dead outright," Mr. Foster seized his hat and strode off to the Warren House without a moment's delay, but with a much stronger feeling of interest for the children than for Mr. Rixley himself, whether he were dead or alive.

As to this latter question, the first glance of the experienced doctor's eye settled it, as far as he was concerned; and the first words he spoke as completely removed all doubt from those around.

"There would be no use in attempting to bleed him! His blood will never flow again," said Mr. Foster, gently laying his hand on the shoulder of Mrs. Lambert, who was still standing beside the corpse, with a countenance that had more the expression of deep reverie and meditation than of vehement emotion.

"You had better come down stairs, Mrs. Lambert," said he. "I am sure the poor children must want you to be with them at such a moment, and you can do no good here! But where *is* William? Does he know that his father is dead?"

"We can't find Master William, Sir," said Rebecca Watkins, who, together with old John, had followed the doctor up stairs.

"Master William, Sir, must have set off upon his usual morning walk long before old John went up to call my master," said Mrs. Lambert, "and, therefore, of course, he can know nothing about it."

"Yes, indeed, poor young gentleman," added Rebecca, "it is likely enough that by this time he may be miles off; bird shooting, maybe, as he often is by times in the morning. And it was plain that he was more than usual early to day, 'cause we know that he got out of the window of his room to prevent disturbing anybody."

Mrs. Lambert knit her brows, and said hastily, "Nonsense! That is no proof that he was out earlier than usual, for it is what he has been in the habit of doing for years."

"No, sure," said John, with a look of astonishment. "Well,

now! to think of my never finding that out, and I coming so constant almost before daybreak!"

"Well, well, his being absent now is of no great consequence; for he could do no good to anybody here," returned Mr. Foster. "Let us think of poor Miss Helen. I suppose she is asleep still, Mrs. Lambert? But I should like to see her, if you please, as soon as she gets up. I think the best thing will be for her to come to our house directly; it will be less dismal for her, poor child, than staying here; and I suppose we shall soon learn what is to become of her afterwards. But I don't believe that there is anybody in the whole county that knows anything about Mr. Rixley's family. It is just possible that his bankers at Falmouth may, but that we shall easily find out; and if he has ever made a will, I think it is more likely to be with them than with anybody else. But I suppose, upon this point, you know nothing, Mrs. Lambert?"

"I certainly cannot say that I *know* anything about his will, Sir, except that I have heard him say that he had made one," replied Mrs. Lambert.

"I am glad to hear it," returned Mr. Foster. "If we find a will, it will, doubtless, make everything easy."

This conversation did not take place, however, as the parties stood round the dead man's bed; but Mr. Foster, having seen that Rebecca Watkins and old John had reverently covered the body, drawn the curtains, opened the window, and closed the door, had led the way down stairs, and seated himself in the dining-parlour.

"Let me see poor Helen before I go," said he, as soon as he had received this agreeable information respecting the will; "and as soon as I have spoken to her I will myself ride over to Falmouth, and inquire at the bankers, whether they are in possession of any document that may be of importance to these poor friendless orphans. But I should like to see poor Helen first."

"I will go to her immediately, Sir," replied Mrs. Lambert, turning to leave the room as she spoke; but ere she had reached the door, the unconscious Helen appeared at it.

"Is papa gone, Sarah Lambert?" she said, meeting her nurse in the doorway, and before she had become aware that Mr. Foster was in the room.

But before Mrs. Lambert could answer, the friendly doctor had hastened forward, and, taking her hand, led her to a chair, and placed her in it,

Helen looked surprised, but, nevertheless, greeted him with her usual friendly cordiality. "I am always glad to see you, Mr. Foster," she said, with a smile, "provided you do not come because somebody is sick, and I don't believe that anybody is sick now. Where is William, Sarah Lambert?"

"Do not be alarmed because you do not see him, my dear Helen," said Mr. Foster, "for I dare say he is perfectly well, though he does not happen to be here. But I am very sorry he is not here, too, for I have sad news to tell you, my dear, and I know it would be a comfort to you to have your brother with you, and I shall be very glad when he comes home. But I cannot wait for that before I tell you what has happened, for it is quite proper you should hear of it immediately."

These words, vague as they were, prepared her, as the friendly speaker intended they should, for something both sad and sudden; and this was all by which he thought it necessary to preface the words, "Your father, my dear young lady, is dead! He has, apparently, died suddenly during the night; probably from apoplexy."

"My father dead?" she exclaimed, suddenly changing colour; "and where is William? Sarah Lambert! tell me where William is gone? Pray let me see him directly."

"You shall see him, my dear child, as soon as ever he returns to the house," replied Mrs. Lambert; "but I do not think that will be for some hours yet, for I fancy he has set off quite early upon one of his long walks."

This answer seemed to satisfy Helen, or, at least, to silence her; but it appeared to surprise Mr. Foster, for he said, "How very strange it was, that he should have set off without seeing his father, almost at the very moment that the chaise which is now at the door must have been expected to take him from home. He had not quarrelled with his father, had he? If he had, poor lad, he will be dreadfully sorry when he comes home, and finds what has happened."

"Quarrelled!" said Mrs. Lambert, indignantly, "Oh, dear no, Sir! nothing could be further from his thoughts than that, poor dear boy. But my master never chose that anybody should take leave of him when he went away, or make any fuss of any kind when he came back; and, therefore, there was nothing at all extraordinary in William's setting off to take a walk this fine morning."

"No, indeed," returned Mr. Foster; "in that case, he can neither blame himself nor be blamed by anybody. I was going, my dear Miss Helen," continued the kind-hearted apothecary, "to do my very best to persuade you to go home with me to my house; but now I will say nothing about it, as I can perfectly well understand that you wou'd not like to be out of the way when your brother returned. I must go now, for there is more than one sick person in the parish expecting me; but I shall call again before I go to Falmouth, and then I hope he will be returned, and that he will join with me in endearouring to persuade you that it will be much better for you, just at present, to come down and stay a little while with Mrs. Foster and the girls, than to remain here."

The only thing which poor Helen clearly understood at that moment was, that Mr. Foster meant to be kind to her; and it was probably more the grateful feeling which this idea produced than anything approaching grief for the death of her father, which drew forth the tears which now filled her eyes.

"You are very kind!" she said, with rather an hysterical sob.

"Take care of her, Mrs. Lambert," said the apothecary, kindly; "but that I am very sure you will do, without my telling you; and I say, Mrs. Lambert," he continued, in a whisper, "don't let there be any nonsense about her going to look at her father. She is quite hysterical enough already, without that."

Mrs. Lambert respectfully promised to obey his instructions, and the friendly apothecary took his leave.

CHAPTER XIV.

The sudden death of the master of a house, and the father of a family, can never occur without plunging all the survivors connected with him into a state of great agitation and excitement. Whether his loss be lamented with affection, or deplored only as the breaking up of domestic ties, it must necessarily be the prelude to many painful scenes.

It may be fairly hoped that few men die leaving so little trace of affectionate regret behind them as Mr. Rixley of the

Warren House; but on the other hand it may be fairly hoped, likewise, that few men die leaving those to whom they had given existence, and who depended on them for the support of it, so completely at a loss to guess what was to become of them.

In the present case, however, it was only on poor Helen that this desolate feeling fell with all its weight. Had she ever loved her father, had she ever been permitted to love him from the hour of her birth to that of his death, this dismal feeling of desolation could not have fallen so heavily on her; for then her thoughts would have had more than one direction in which to turn themselves, and their heavy gloom would have been softened into tenderness, and relieved by tears.

But nothing in the slightest degree resembling tears now came to the relief of Helen, as she thought of her father. She remained in the chair in which Mr. Foster had placed her perfectly motionless.

Rebecca stood looking at her with a pitying eye, her arms a-kimbo, and dolorously shaking her head; old John had followed the doctor with the civil intention of opening the house-door for him; but before the house-door was reached, Mrs. Lambert called him back.

"I want you immediately, John," said she, earnestly, "I want you to go, without a moment's delay, to Mr. Bolton; tell him what has happened, and beg him to have the great kindness to come here directly."

The old man moved off with a step rapid enough to prove that he, too, thought this was the most proper measure that could be taken; and when he was gone Mrs. Lambert went to Helen, and drawing a chair close to her, sat down, and passing one hand round her waist, parted the hair upon her drooping forehead, and said, "Look up, my darling child! You must recover yourself, Helen! You must not let this terrible event overpower you so completely! I hope and trust that your good friend, Mr. Bolton, will be here directly. The seeing him will, of course, be a great comfort to you, but I should not like for him to see you so perfectly miserable as you look now, for it would be enough to make him despair of being useful to you."

"Where is William, Sarah Lambert? Where is my dear, dear brother? I should not look miserable if he were here. It is William I am thinking about and nothing else," replied Helen, in vehement agitation.

"Depend upon it, my dear child, William will be here again in a few hours, so do not make yourself miserable about that."

"Do you really think so, my dear, darling Sarah Lambert?" returned Helen, suddenly throwing her arms round the neck of her nurse, and eagerly kissing her. "If your words do but come true, Mrs. Lambert, you shall find that whatever happens to us I shall try to behave as I ought to do. If William and I are not parted, I am sure I can bear anything. And you, too, Sarah Lambert! I must not be parted from you, my dear, dear nurse. And if we three are together, we will never mind about wanting money, or anything of that sort, for I am quite able to work, and so is William, and so are you. It is quite impossible that anything very terrible can come to us if we are all left together."

"Your good and wise friend Mr. Bolton will tell us all that we ought to do," replied Mrs. Lambert, "and you, and William too, will, I am quite sure, be always ready and willing to do whatever he says ought to be done. I am sure we can neither of us doubt his kindness to William, for he really seems to think him the very best, as well as the very cleverest boy he ever knew in the whole course of his life. I have heard him say so over and over again, Helen."

"And so have I, Sarah Lambert," replied Helen, with energy; "and it was true, too, and I don't believe he ever will see any one equal to him if he lives a hundred years. But where is he, Mrs. Lambert? Where is he? Oh! his absence at this moment is dreadful!"

"It is certainly very unfortunate, my dear child," replied Mrs. Lambert, whose perfect calmness of manner formed a strong contrast to the vehement emotion manifested by Helen; "very unfortunate!" she repeated, "and yet, after all, my dear, it is of no great consequence, you are certain of seeing him in an hour or two."

"Oh! if you could but convince me of that!" returned Helen, clasping her hands, "if you could but convince me of that, you would no longer have any reason to complain of my not behaving well!"

"Well then, my darling child!" returned Mrs. Lambert, fondly kissing her, "you will be everything I wish you to be before the evening. But you must begin to show your intention of behaving well to-night, by eating some breakfast this morning. I should not like for Mr. Bolton to come and find you as pale and as shaking as you are now."

Poor Helen answered nothing, but, dearly as she loved her nurse, she felt greatly relieved by her leaving her quietly alone while she employed herself in preparing the table for breakfast, for then she could indulge herself by placing the back of the chair upon which Mrs. Lambert had been sitting exactly before her, and having crossed her arms upon the top of it, she leant her aching forehead upon them, and, suffering her abundant curls to fall forward, enjoyed for a few moments the comfort of knowing that the tears might flow without being seen by anybody.

The preparations for breakfast meanwhile, went on, and in the course of them, Rebecca Watkins asked the housekeeper if she should now remove the writing-desk, and cover the table, as usual, with the table-cloth.

"No, Rebecca! no!" answered Mrs. Lambert, with some quickness. "Let it remain exactly as it is. The table is large enough. The last thing he ever did was using that desk, and there let it be left till Mr. Bolton comes."

The few minutes which had elapsed since Helen was left to herself, appeared to have been beneficial to her, for when Mrs. Lambert took her by the hand, and led her to the table, she had not only ceased to weep, but she held up her innocent young face to her kind and watchful Sarah Lambert for a kiss, and it was bestowed with a degree of fondness that could scarcely have been greater if it had been given by a mother to her child.

"And you do really think that William will return before the day is over?" said Helen, preparing to eat her breakfast, and at the same time nestling close to the chair in which Mrs. Lambert had placed herself beside her.

"Don't be angry with me, Sarah Lambert," she added, "for plaguing you with the same question so over and over again; but nothing does me so much good as hearing you say that you feel *sure* he will be back to-night."

"Well, then, dearest," replied her indulgent comforter, "I will keep on saying the same words again, and again, and again, till you have got him back again."

Helen turned her beautiful eyes upon her with a look that seemed to speak more gratitude than the promise deserved, but it was not so, if its value was to be estimated by its effect; for when Mrs. Lambert presently repeated with a smile, "He will be back again before night, Helen," the gentle girl really looked as if she only wanted that assurance in order to console her under every possible misfortune—past, present, or future.

Helen and her loving nurse were not left long, however, to either give or receive consolation solely from each other, for considerably before Mrs. Lambert had hoped to see him, Mr. Bolton entered the parlour.

They both rose up to receive him; he looked, good man, not only hurried, but agitated, and, having noticed poor Helen with gentle and paternal kindness, he turned to her nurse and said, " Let me speak to you alone Mrs. Lambert for a few minutes."

She curtsied her acquiescence, and saying to Helen, " Wait for us here, my dear child, till we come back again," she preceded the clergyman into the school-room.

" This occurrence is frightfully sudden! awfully sudden! Mrs. Lambert! Have you had any reason during the time you have known him, for supposing that Mr. Rixley had any propensity to apoplexy ? "

" Unless occasional violence of temper might be so considered, Sir, I should certainly say *not*," replied Mrs. Lambert.

" Did any scene of unusual vehemence occur between you after you left us yesterday ? " said Mr. Bolton.

" Unusual ? " repeated Mrs. Lambert, thoughtfully. " No, Sir; I should certainly say not. He remained in his boat for many hours ; but I have no reason for thinking that he injured himself in any way by this. On the contrary, he eat a more than usually hearty supper; but he sat up very quietly for more than an hour afterwards, arranging the papers at that writing-desk. When he went to bed he left it on the table, exactly where you will find it when you re-enter the room, Sir, for I have not let anybody touch it since. He told me himself some days ago that his will was in that desk; and it is there, Sir, that I hope you will find it."

" It is not I who must look for it, Mrs. Lambert," replied the clergyman. " We must immediately put seals upon all his personal effects; and then take measures, without loss of time, to inform his nearest of kin of his death, and of the state in which all his property here is left."

" Yes, Sir," she replied; " that is what I thought must be done; and I trust, for Miss Helen's sake, that it will be you, Sir, who will have the kindness to write to his family."

" It may, perhaps, be best that I should do so," he replied. " Meantime, Mrs. Lambert, I would wish that if the late Mr. Rixley was in the habit of employing any attorney in this neighbourhood, that person should be sent to immediately, in order to witness the putting seals upon all receptacles containing papers, money, or plate."

"This shall be done directly, Sir," she replied. "Old John will easily find a messenger to ride over to Falmouth to Mr. Lucas. But who is it that must send for him? Would it be asking too much, Sir, if I begged of you to take the trouble of writing a line to Mr. Lucas in your own name, desiring him to come to the Warren House?"

It would be no great trouble, Mrs. Lambert," he replied. "But where is William? I think it would be better that he should write this note."

"Unfortunately, Sir, William is not at home," replied Mrs. Lambert.

"Not at home! Where is he, then?" inquired Mr. Bolton.

"I don't know, Sir," she replied. "He was gone before I was up this morning, and I suppose he has set off to take one of his long early walks."

"I am sorry for it," returned Mr. Bolton. "I should have wished to speak to him immediately. But it cannot be helped, and we must not waste time by waiting for him. Give me pen and ink and paper, Mrs. Lambert, and I will write at once, not only to Mr. Lucas, but to Mr. Rixley's family also. I think you told me that he had a brother. Can you give me his address?"

"No, Sir, that I certainly cannot," she replied; "and I do not believe that I have ever heard him name it. But I think that if you were to direct your letter to the Rev. Mr. Rixley, Beauchamp Park, *to be forwarded*, I think it could hardly fail to reach his brother."

"But did you not tell me that the family name was Beauchamp?" demanded Mr. Bolton.

"No, Sir," she replied; "Rixley is the family name of my late master. He himself took the name of Beauchamp, when he succeeded to the Beauchamp property on the death of his maternal uncle. His brother, therefore, I presume, must still be called Rixley."

"True, true. I will then direct my letter to the Rev. Mr. Rixley," returned Mr. Bolton, preparing to use the writing implements which she had brought him.

"But his daughter and heiress," rejoined Mrs. Lambert, almost in a whisper, as if afraid of interrupting him—"his daughter and heiress will, of course, take the name of Beauchamp. She will be Miss Beauchamp, of Beauchamp Park."

"Upon my word, Mrs. Lambert," said Mr. Bolton, holding his pen suspended while he spoke to her, "I think you draw your conclusions respecting Helen's heiress-ship from very uncertain authority. I sincerely hope that you have never given her reason to suppose that you have any such idea in your head."

"Never! Mr. Bolton, never!" she replied, with great earnestness. "I should be quite as averse to having any such notion suggested to her as you could be yourself, Sir, or, perhaps, more so, for I know better than any other person can do how little dependence can be placed on any statement made by her father. If my master really did make a will, I think it will be found in his writing-desk. But I certainly feel that it is very possible he never made any will at all. Gracious heaven!" she exclaimed, after the silence of a minute or two, "it is *very* possible!" and as she said this she clasped her hands together across her forehead, with a much greater appearance of agitation than she had yet shown. "And if it be so, if it *should* prove so, Mr. Bolton," she added, "what is to become of Miss Helen? She will be worse off, oh! greatly worse off, than she has ever been! Who is there to feed her? Who is there to take care of her? Is she to be indebted for her daily bread to such a one as I am?"

And then, for the first time since old John had announced the death of her late master, the wretched woman shed tears; nay, despite all the self-command on which she so justly prided herself, she wept bitterly; and there was an expression of such deep despair on her pale harassed features, that the kind pastor's heart ached for her. He seemed to forget, for the moment, her own statement of the guilty life which she had for so many years been leading, and to remember nothing but her faithful attachment to the orphan child she had nursed.

"Do not torment yourself, Mrs. Lambert, by fancying a misfortune which certainly, from what you told me yesterday, does not seem probable," said he. "Did you not say that your master had positively stated to you the fact of his having made his will, and also that he had left his property to his daughter?"

"Most assuredly he did!" she eagerly replied; while her own statement, thus simply repeated to her by Mr. Bolton, seemed to reach her with all the force of incontrovertible authority. "He not only said it," she continued, earnestly, "but I believe in my heart that then, at least, he spoke the truth. But there is something so very dreadful, Sir, in the bare possibility of its proving otherwise, that I felt as if I had not strength to bear it! But I not only remember his words, I remember also the dreadful feeling with which they were uttered; and, therefore, it is that I do believe they were said in earnest! If he has made his will—and, thank God! I do believe he *has* made it—it was no love for his sweet innocent child that made him do it. It was only hatred to his brother!"

"This may be so," said the clergyman; "but it will be better for us not to remember it, Mrs. Lambert. You reprobate his hatred for his brother; and yet you seem to be giving way to a similar evil feeling towards himself. I will not deny," he continued, seeing her dark eye flash with indignation—"I will not deny that he has given you great and terrible cause to dislike him, and to shudder at his name; but it is our duty as Christians, Mrs. Lambert, to conquer all such feelings, and to forget them."

"Forget them!" she replied, again pressing her clasped hands across her forehead. "Forget them! God forbid!"

"Fie, fie!" said Mr. Bolton, shaking his head. "You know not what you say!"

And feeling that this was no moment for reasoning with her, he resumed his pen, and wrote the following letter to "The Rev. Mr. Rixley:"—

CHAPTER XV.

"7th September, 18—.

" Sir,

"It has become my painful duty to announce to you the sudden death, in my parish, of a gentleman, who I am told is your brother. This gentleman, whom for many years I have known as Mr. George Rixley, has been residing, at intervals, during that time, at an old mansion that he has purchased here, known by the name of the "Warren House," he has made himself very little acquainted with the neighbourhood, but I learn from a servant who has lived with him many years, and

who seems to know more about him than any one else, that
though the name by which he has been known here was that of
his father, it is not the name which now, of right belongs to
him, he having for some years assumed that of Beauchamp, in
consequence of inheriting the property of a maternal uncle. I
mention these circumstances that there may be no doubt left
upon your mind respecting his identity. All other particulars
respecting him, and the children he has left, will be more easily
explained to you, Reverend Sir, if you answer this letter, as I
presume you will do, in person.

"Mrs. Lambert, the housekeeper, to whom I have before
alluded, tells me that she has no doubt that her late master left
a will, as he has himself, more than once, stated this fact to her.
She has even pointed out to me the piece of furniture in which
she believes this document is placed. It is a moderate-sized
writing-desk, and I shall forthwith have it conveyed to the
parsonage house for greater security, where I hope it will be
opened by your own hand. It will be desirable, of course, that
this should be done as speedily as possible, in case the will, said
to be deposited in it, should contain any instructions respecting
his funeral. Should I not be fortunate enough either to see or
hear from you before the thirteenth of the current month, the
remains of your brother will be interred in Crumpton Churchyard
on that day.

"I remain, Reverend Sir,
"Your obedient Servant,
"STEPHEN BOLTON,
"*Officiating Minister of Crumpton.*

"Please to address to me,
"Crumpton, Cornwall."

Having written this letter, Mr. Bolton read it aloud to Mrs.
Lambert, and then sealed and dispatched it by a trustworthy
messenger to the post-office at Falmouth, together with a note
to Mr. Lucas, the attorney, requesting to see him immediately.

Having performed this necessary business, Mr. Bolton proposed returning to Helen, and the housekeeper accompanied him
accordingly into the parlour. They found her sitting exactly
where they had left her, and on seeing Mr. Bolton re-enter the
room, she again rose up, but made no step in advance to meet
him, and in fact looked so miserably ill as to suggest the idea
that she was too weak to make the exertion.

"My poor dear Helen!" said the clergyman, taking her hand
and replacing her in her chair, "the shock you have received

has been too sudden, and too violent for your strength; but you must rouse yourself, my dear child, and not sit thus gloomily meditating upon what has happened. I think, Mrs. Lambert," he continued, "that the best thing I can do will be to take her to the parsonage. You will have a good deal to do here to get everything in good order preparatory to the arrival of Mr. Rixley, who will be here in a day or two, I have no doubt, and it will be better for Helen to remain quietly with us till he comes. You will send down whatever you think she may want, and may feel quite easy about her, for you know she will be well taken care of."

"Thank you, Sir, a thousand times for your thoughtful kindness! It will indeed be a great comfort to see her removed from this dismal house," replied Mrs. Lambert, every feature in her speaking face bearing testimony to her sincerity.

"Helen, dearest!" she continued, taking the hand of the pale girl between both of hers—"Helen! Do you hear the great kindness of Mr. Bolton?"

"Indeed I do hear it," replied Helen, while tears of gratitude started to her eyes, "and I am most grateful for his goodness to me. . . . But, William, Mrs. Lambert? You cannot think I would go away without seeing William, do you?"

"Your coming to us need not prevent your seeing him, Helen," said Mr. Bolton. "I believe the dear boy knows that there is no place where he would be more welcome than at our house—for we all love him. But even if he had any doubt upon the subject, which is not very likely, Mrs. Lambert, you know, can easily make him understand that we are all expecting him, yourself included, Helen. Will not this suffice to make your mind easy on that point?"

Poor Helen looked greatly at a loss how to answer. She certainly did not wish to appear either ungrateful or unreasonable, and yet it was very evident that the arrangement did not quite please her. For a moment she was silent, and then she said, "If I do not thank you as I ought to do, dear, dear Mr. Bolton! it is not because I do not feel your kindness. But there is something so strangely dreadful in all that has happened since William took leave of me last night, that I don't think anything would do me so much good as the seeing him again the very first moment that he comes home. After I have seen him for one single moment, Mr. Bolton, and that he has kissed me once more, and wished me good night, as he used to do, I would rather go to your house ten thousand times over than stay here, but I *must* just stay to see him first, if you please!"

"No, Helen! No! I must have my way in this," replied Mr. Bolton. "It is not right, my dear child, at least in my opinion it is not right, that you should remain here."

"Now Helen, I am quite sure that you will resist no longer," said Mrs. Lambert.

She spoke this earnestly, and most assuredly with perfect sincerity; but it was easy, for Mr. Bolton at least, to see that it was not without a bitter pang that the unhappy woman felt the stern necessity of parting with the innocent young creature whom she had so carefully cherished, and so fondly loved. But she remembered that it was she herself who had first pointed out this necessity, and a moment's thought had sufficed to make her deeply thankful that she had pleaded against herself so successfully.

Helen listened respectfully, as she always did, to every suggestion of Mr. Bolton, and after the silence of a moment, she said, "If you think it is better for me, Sir, I am ready to go. But somebody will come and tell me when William comes home?"

Mr. Bolton undertook to promise that this should be done, and then her bonnet and shawl being given to her by Mrs. Lambert, the kind clergyman passed her arm under his own, and led her from the Warren House, little thinking that she should never re-enter it again!

    *   *   *   *   *   *

Nothing could be more truly amiable than the manner in which the orphan girl was received by Mrs. Bolton; and had it not been for the eager wish which still seemed to pursue her for the return of her brother, her young nerves would soon have recovered their tone; but as hour after hour of that long day wore away without bringing him, or any tidings of him, not all the kindness with which she was surrounded could avail to tranquillize her.

At a few minutes before eleven o'clock at night Mrs. Lambert came to the parsonage, but it was only to beg that the family would not sit up any longer, as she now considered it as quite impossible that William should return that night.

It was painful to witness the agitation with which Helen listened to this announcement, and the more so, because those who felt this friendly pain had not a word to say in the way of hope or consolation to her.

This most ill-timed, and unfortunate absence was indeed so perfectly unaccountable in every way, that neither of those kind friends who stood around the sobbing girl could suggest any probable reason for it. Not only had William never before absented himself at night, but never upon any occasion had he suffered his passion for solitary rambling to beguile him to any spot sufficiently distant to prevent his returning to the house before the usual hour of closing it for the night.

Mrs. Lambert remembered all this, and remembering also the strange manner in which he had left it that morning, or rather during the preceding night, she could not help sharing in some degree the fear which had evidently taken possession of Helen, namely that he had fled from the hateful tyranny of his father without any intention of returning.

Nevertheless a moment's reflection sufficed to persuade her that in the present state of affairs there would be no great difficulty in getting him to return; she knew how devotedly he was attached to his sister, and felt not the slightest doubt that he would hasten back to her as soon as the news of his father's death should reach him ; and the suddenness of this event was so sure to make it talked of far and near, that she felt no doubt that the report of it would very speedily overtake him.

Notwithstanding the long and confidential conversation which had taken place on the preceding day between herself and Mr. and Mrs. Bolton, Mrs. Lambert felt that she could not with propriety speak as openly to Helen in their presence respecting the motive of William's departure, and the certainty of his return, now that the cause of his aversion to his home was removed, as she could do if they were *tête-à-tête;* she therefore said, respectfully turning to the clergyman and his wife, " If you will kindly permit me to attend Miss Helen to the room in which she is to sleep, I think I could persuade her to undress and go to bed quietly, and to-morrow she will, I trust, be more composed, and more reasonable."

This suggestion was immediately acted upon; the gentle Mrs. Bolton led the way to her neat guest-chamber, placed a light upon the table, gave a silent kiss to the sobbing Helen, and retired, leaving the pale but perfectly composed Mrs Lambert, and the orphan girl she so fondly loved, alone together.

No sooner was the door closed upon them than Helen rushed into the arms of her nurse, and wept upon her bosom as she had often done when terrified by the harshness of her father in days of yore; and, as in days of yore, her sorrow was soothed, and her caresses returned with the tenderness of a mother. The healing effect of this unrestrained indulgence of feeling immediately produced the benefit anticipated. Helen, though still looking very miserable, became composed and reasonable, and instead of turning with all the bitterness of despair from the friendly and consoling words that were addressed to her, she now became as eager to listen as Mrs. Lambert was to speak of her absent brother.

"Now you are my own dear reasonable Helen again!" said the loving nurse, placing the orphan girl beside her, and looking fondly in the lovely young face so confidingly turned towards her. "Now you will listen to reason, my darling child, and not to the inventions of your own frightened fancy."

"I will listen to you, my dear, dear Sarah Lambert!" replied Helen, fondly kissing her. "You never, as long as I can remember anything, have said to me any word that was not as kind as it was true, and as true as it was kind, and you never will, of that I am very sure! But it is strange his going away so, just at this terrible time, isn't it, Sarah Lambert? Do you think that anything passed between them—any violent quarrel I mean—after I was gone to bed? At what time did papa come home?"

"Very late, my dear child," replied Mrs. Lambert, "and I am quite sure there was no quarrel, for I must have heard it if there had been; and I give you my honour that I heard nothing of the kind. Indeed I believe that William must have been gone to bed before his father came home, but of this I cannot speak with certainty, because I was very busy."

"It is a great, great comfort to me to hear you say that, Sarah Lambert!" replied Helen, "for I was afraid—oh, dreadfully afraid—that they might have quarrelled, and that they might have fought!" and Helen trembled from head to foot as she uttered the words, and hid her face on Mrs. Lambert's bosom.

"Set your dear heart at rest for ever from all such thoughts, my child!" returned her nurse, very solemnly. "I am sorry that you should have conceived such, even for a moment. It was the will of God that your father should die, Helen, and therefore he is dead. The suddenness of this event must naturally make it a great surprise—a great shock—to you, but such cases are by no means very uncommon, and greatly less surprising, I think, than it would have been either to you or to me to see William fighting with him. I cannot imagine, my dear child, how so wild a thought could ever have entered your head."

"My dear, dear Sarah Lambert," replied Helen, almost cheerfully, "I feel and understand the truth of every word you say; but it is easy enough for me to explain to you how this wild and terrible thought came into my head. It came in two ways, Sarah Lambert. One way was from the horrible fierce and angry looks of . . . . of my poor father the last time I ever heard them speak together, and the other was from the look—the fearful look—of my dear tortured brother, after the frightful conversation in which his mother's shame and his own degradation were so cruelly announced to him. Oh, Sarah Lambert! can I ever forget the fearful change that came over my poor brother's face when he confessed, with such terrible bitterness, that he hated him who had brought this shame upon him, and then reproached him with it?"

"Yes, my precious child!" replied Mrs. Lambert, solemnly, "I trust that you will forget that, and all else that has tended to destroy the joyous happiness which ought ever to be the portion of childhood! Be ever pure and innocent of sin, my sweet Helen, and then the years that are to come will atone for all that was evil in those which are past; and that has been much, very much, my poor child."

"But for a great while, you know, I had my dear mamma with me, and always dear William, and always you! Ought I not to be thankful for all that, Sarah Lambert?" replied Helen, again laying her head lovingly on her nurse's shoulder. "And if my dear William comes back, and if you stay with me always, always, I don't think that I shall ever again complain of any-thing."

The unhappy woman, thus fondly "loved in vain," could not, with all the stern firmness of her character, prevent a tear from falling on the face of the loving, and fondly loved young creature from whom she was so firmly resolved to tear herself. But even at that bitter moment she remembered the will which her late master had taught her to expect would be found in his writing-desk, and instead of suffering more tears to fall, she cheerfully exclaimed, "My dear, dear Helen! Look up hopefully! We have all of us, in different ways, suffered a good deal of sorrow, I believe . . . . But I think the future will be better, Helen; and if it be so, if it indeed should be in any degree what I anticipate for you, I shall still be happy! Yes, Helen! happy, happy, happy!"

Helen very naturally thought that this burst of hopeful
gladness, so unlike the usual quiet sedateness of Sarah
Lambert's manner, arose from the vivid recollection of what
they had all suffered from the capricious violence of her father's
temper, now removed from them for ever; but having never
before heard her allude to her own share of suffering from this
cause, she felt that this dearly-beloved nurse had always had
more merit, as well as more suffering, than she had ever before
given her credit for.

Again she caressed her tenderly, and again she exclaimed,
that if William would but come back again, so that they might
all three live on quietly together at the Warren House, she
should be quite contented with her own share of happiness.

For one short moment—as the conscience-stricken woman
listened to this innocent burst of young affection, and read in
the sweet eyes that were fixed upon her, with all the eloquence
of sincerity, the confirmation of the feelings it expressed—for
one short moment, poor Sarah Lambert thought that the sins of
the wretched Almeria might be for ever buried and forgotten in
the grave of him who had caused them; but the vain illusion
lasted no longer, and, when it was past, she said, in a voice
which betrayed no weakness of any kind, but which was in
perfect accordance with the solemn wisdom of her words, "My
dearest Helen! neither of the three can reasonably expect, or
reasonably wish, that so it should be! You have several very
near relations, Helen, although you have been hitherto very
strangely kept in ignorance of their existence; and both the
law of nature and the law of the land point them out as the
persons to whose protection you must look for support, and
by whose authority you must be guided. And this will be
greatly more advantageous to you, Helen, than being left for
ever in the hands of your old nurse."

"Then their protection must be extended to that old nurse
also," returned Helen, while a bright flush dyed her cheeks, and
such a light flashed from her eyes as Sarah Lambert had never
seen emitted from them before.

"Concerning all that, my dear child," she replied, "we must
for a while longer remain in ignorance. The best good night I
can now give you, my dearest Helen, is the assurance that I feel
no doubt of your brother's return, as soon as he shall have heard
the news, which will be so quickly spread through the country
as to make it pretty nearly impossible that he should not hear
it soon. And now, then, sleep well, my darling child! Let

what will happen to either of us, I do not think that either will
ever quite forget the more than common love that there has
been between us." One more loving kiss was then exchanged,
and then they parted ;. the interview having produced effects as
opposite as it is well possible to imagine on the minds of each ;
for Mrs. Lambert left Helen with a feeling of deeper misery
than had ever, perhaps, rested on her mind before ; for never
before had she felt her to be so every-way deserving of her
devoted love ; while never had she felt such a profound conviction that the most imperative duty of her future life would be to
separate herself from her for ever! And on the other hand,
Helen laid her head upon her pillow, and dropt asleep, with the
delightful feeling that the old friend she so truly loved, loved
her most truly too, and that such being the case, there was little
or no danger that any new friends would have the power, or
will, to part them.

<hr>

CHAPTER XVI.

On awaking the next morning, the first thoughts of Helen
were painfully confused. It was a minute or two before she
clearly remembered where she was; and when, by degrees, all
the circumstances of her perfectly new position arranged themselves in her mind with all the grave reality of truth, she felt
as if she herself were as much changed, and as new as they
were. The influence of her father's stern temper, harsh
manners, and tyrannical will, had not only produced effects
uniformly painful upon very nearly every hour of her past
existence, but had apparently, in a great degree, changed her
very nature too. Not only had his fearfully unfeeling temper
made itself felt when living with his unhappy children, but the
crushing weight of his tyrannical caprices had been made to
bear upon them even in his absence; nor could all the influence
nor all the power of Mrs. Lambert neutralize the effect of it.

The very remarkable personal advantages of both the
children, as well as the terms of affectionate admiration in
which the Bolton and Foster families spoke of them in the
neighbourhood, was quite sufficient to have obtained for them

many valuable friends; and moreover, the manner in which they were left to grow up, under the care and companionship of servants, added a feeling of pity to the interest they were so well calculated to inspire. But all these friendly feelings were of no avail in benefiting the forlorn situation of the forsaken children at the Warren House; for never did its tyrant master leave it without reiterating his commands that no strangers, of any rank, were to be permitted to enter its doors, and that the children were on no account to be suffered to hold intercourse with any persons in the neighbourhood, save and except the clergyman and the apothecary.

All this had, of course, been submitted to without resistance, but not during the last year or two without a very painful consciousness of hardship and restraint. This consciousness had, on the part of Helen, been felt more on her brother's account than her own. There is a natural diffidence about young girls, who have had no companions of their own age, which renders it much easier for them to yield to such discipline than to attempt resistance to it; and it would have been almost as likely for Helen to have taken possession of her father's boat during his absence, as to have ventured to look in the face of any of the forbidden individuals who resided in the neighbourhood.

Poor William Rixley was exactly the sort of boy to attract attention, and to enjoy with keen delight the riding and the shooting which had repeatedly been offered to him by many whose kindly natures led them to witness, with real pain, the many privations to which "that magnificent-looking young fellow, William Rixley," was obliged to submit.

The only horses he ever rode were unbroken colts, lent to him by the neighbouring farmers, who declared that, somehow or other, the young chap could do more towards bringing them into order than they could; and one observing old man declared that the only likeness, as far as he could see, by which the young Rixley showed himself to be the son of the old one, was observable when the Warren House squire was enjoying a stiff gale at sea, and when his son was making a skittish young colt obey the rein, just as his father made the bounding boat obey the helm.

And the old man was right; for in this sort of enjoyment in danger lay the only point of intellectual resemblance between them. But the speculative eye of this old man was not the only one which watched the bold bearing of the beautiful, but

neglected boy, with interest; and very many were the friendly
hints which, directly and indirectly, he received, concerning the
readiness with which such, or such of his aristocratical neighbours would give him either hunting or shooting, by the loan of
a horse, or the *entrée* to a preserve. But all these friendly
hints, though they made his heart beat and his eye sparkle,
were one and all uniformly received with a sadly-whispered,
but most positive refusal.

It is very possible that the fear of his brutal father's anger
would not of itself have sufficed to ensure such constant
obedience; but it had been made plain to the capacities of both
William and his sister, that any transgression of the rules laid
down for the regulation of their melancholy existence would
infallibly be visited in such a way upon their much-loved
Sarah Lambert, as to cause her great annoyance: and this was
enough—always and for ever enough— to secure the obedience,
not only of the gentle Helen, but of the fearless William
likewise.

It was with wonderfully sudden strength and distinctness,
that all this rushed upon the mind of Helen, as she awoke the
next morning, and remembered that this terrible father *was
dead* and could torture them no more!

It is a lamentably false doctrine which teaches parents to
believe that their children ought to love them, and, in point of
fact, *must* love them, let them be treated as they may. Neither
children nor wives, however strong they may feel the tie to be,
which binds them to the tyrant parent, or the tyrant spouse,
are, in any degree, removed beyond the reach of ordinary
human feeling; and those do but delude themselves who
think it.

It was with nothing like a pang of sorrow that Helen
remembered she was fatherless; but neither was it with anything approaching the triumph of newly-liberated self-will. In
fact she thought only of William, and of Sarah Lambert; and
the only portion of these new-born thoughts which personally
concerned herself was that which led her to believe stedfastly
in her true and loving heart, that now that she need be afraid of
nobody she might do a thousand and a thousand things which
would be sure to please them both.

But that day, and the next, wore themselves away without
bringing any tidings of William; and poor Helen again began
to feel very miserable about him, notwithstanding all the arguments adduced by Mrs. Lambert, to prove that the cause of his

absenting himself being so well known to them, the certainty of that cause being removed ought to convince them that he would return as soon as the fact should reach him.

But the day following brought the Rev. Mr. Rixley to the parsonage, and the emotions produced by his arrival, and by the scenes which followed it, soon caused all lesser anxieties to be forgotten.

The Rev. Mr. Rixley was, in all respects, as totally unlike his deceased brother as it was well possible for one man to be unlike another. Yet he too had been, and indeed still was, extremely handsome; but in his case there was no combat between the fine regularity of his features and the expression of them.

No one could possibly deny that he was a very handsome man, and it was not likely that many could be found who could, with the envious perversity of his late brother, feel any doubt as to his being, as we may say of children, as good as he was handsome.

But, nevertheless, he looked as if his life had not been one of unbroken prosperity, for there was much more of anxious meditation than of triumphant success in the expression of his countenance.

But there certainly is a sort of freemasonry among good men as well as among bad ones, and the Rev. Mr. Rixley and the Rev. Mr. Bolton had not long sat face to face together before a sort of mutual feeling had been generated between them which led each to feel very sure that they should speedily both like and esteem the other.

Mr. Bolton evidently thought it proper to take it for granted that Mr. Rixley would be anxious to learn all the particulars which he could communicate respecting his late brother's very sudden death; and he expressed himself very much as if he had been making an apology, when stating how very little he knew personally either of his departed neighbour during his life, or of the manner of his death.

"It must, I am afraid, appear very strange and very un-neighbourly, Mr. Rixley," said he, "that a neighbour, of so many years' standing, and one too who, excepting the excellent lady, his late wife, was the only instructor of his children, should know so very little about your brother, as not to be able to tell you, with any degree of certainty, whether his health, previous to his late attack, was good or bad, but such is the case. Is it long since you last saw him, yourself, Mr. Rixley?"

"Yes, Sir," replied his new acquaintance, "it is many years since I last saw my brother, Mr. Beauchamp; but at that time he certainly had the appearance of being an extremely healthy man, and one whom I should have thought very unlikely to die from such an attack as this seems to have been. He went to bed, you say, apparently in perfect health. It must therefore have been some sort of fit which carried him off?"

"Yes, Mr. Rixley, I believe so. We have a very clever and experienced medical man among us who saw him after his death, and I understand that such was his opinion of the case."

The conversation then went on to the more interesting subject of the deceased gentleman's children, of whose very existence Mr. Rixley declared himself to have been ignorant till the receipt of Mr. Bolton's letter; but all discussion respecting them speedily and naturally ended by Mr. Rixley's saying, "My first business must be the examining the desk you have mentioned to me, in search of a will. If we find this, my path will of course be pointed out to me by its contents, and till I have made myself acquainted with this will, I think I would rather not see the little girl you have mentioned. The boy, I think you said, was not at home?"

"No, Mr. Rixley, he is not, and the circumstances attending his departure are very painful," replied Mr. Bolton. "Your estrangement from your brother will doubtless have made you less acutely sensitive respecting all particulars relating to him, than would have been the case had things been otherwise between you; but there was much in his manner of living which it is painful to remember, and to comment upon. This poor lad, who, if I mistake not, is about sixteen or seventeen years of age, is a natural son. But he is a boy that any father might be forgiven for being proud of. He has been my pupil for several years, and I have found in him not only very superior and rare ability, but a very noble, though certainly a somewhat fiery temper. He has never been an inmate with me, and, of the many hours we have spent together, the great majority have, of course, been devoted to study. Nevertheless, I think I know enough of him to say that he possesses many fine qualities, and a warm and generous heart. But, for all that, it is quite certain that he was anything rather than an object of affection to your brother; on the contrary, he was uniformly treated by him with very cruel neglect, and, on many occasions, with very cruel harshness also, and there is every reason to believe that he clandestinely left his father's house on the very night he died, in consequence of a most painful scene which had passed between them on the previous evening, the particulars of which have reached me; and they have left me fully persuaded that the poor youth quitted the house of his father with no intention of returning to it. Nor will you, Sir, greatly wonder at the vehemence of the poor boy's feeling when I tell you, that it was during this scene, and in the presence of his young, and greatly-loved legitimate sister, that the disclosure of his being a natural son was made to him, accompanied, as I am assured, by a degree of unfeeling indignity which amounted to insult. This scene took place in the evening; the unfortunate boy went to his bed-room shortly afterwards, and has never, I believe, been seen since by any of the family."

"Poor boy! he must have suffered greatly!" replied Mr. Rixley. "Such a disclosure, and so suddenly made, may well have produced such a result; and the poor fellow must be perfectly destitute, I presume."

"I presume so, too," replied Mr. Bolton, "save and except the conscious power of great ability which he must have carried with him. His father, it seems, had decided upon placing him as an usher in some country grammar-school. But with all his scholarship he was totally unfit for such a situation. And how he hoped to find the means of living, I know not. It is, however, almost impossible that the news of his father's sudden death should not reach him; and when it does, depend upon it he will immediately return to the Warren House."

"Yes, no doubt of it," replied Mr. Rixley, "and let us hope that the will you mention may make some provision for him. Of course I feel rather anxious to see this document. Shall we look for it, Mr. Bolton?"

"That is the desk, Sir, which is supposed to contain it," replied Mr. Bolton, pointing to an isolated box upon an isolated little table that stood before the book shelves on the opposite side of the room. "But I am every moment expecting a call from Mr. Lucas, the attorney, who has been occasionally employed by your late brother. I got him to put his seal on various depositories at the Warren House within a few hours after we discovered that its owner was dead, and yonder desk was among the number. I fully expected your arrival to-day, Mr. Rixley, and requested that he would call here, which he promised to do."

The conversation between the two clergymen then fell upon the peculiarly desolate condition of poor Helen; and Mr. Rixley asked some questions, though not with any appearance of very vivid interest, respecting the education she had received.

"As long as her admirable mother lived," replied Mr. Bolton, "I should really think she was as thoroughly well taught as it was possible for any young lady to be. But since that heaviest of all possible losses, her mother's death, fell upon her, she has had no instructor but myself."

"How old did you say she was?" demanded the uncle, but still speaking as if the question were asked only because it seemed necessary to say something about her.

"I do not exactly know," was Mr. Bolton's reply, "about thirteen, I think, or something more. She is a very lovely girl, and becoming more so every day, I think."

This sort of talk went on but a short time longer before it was interrupted by the arrival of the Falmouth attorney; and a very few minutes afterwards the important desk was brought forward, and the seal that had been placed upon it broken by the same legal hand which had affixed it.

<center>~~~~~~~~~~~~~~~~~~~~~~</center>

CHAPTER XVII.

WHEN the desk was opened every recess in it was found filled with papers, many of which the attorney's rapid and experienced eye discovered to be documents and memoranda of business-like importance; nor were they long in finding that most important one of which they were in search. This document was the work of a London lawyer, and not of Mr. Lucas; and the three gentlemen now bent upon its examination were all equally ignorant of its contents.

Mr. Lucas was desired to read it aloud, which he did, clearly and distinctly. It was not a long will, considering the great amount of property disposed of by it, the preamble occupying the largest portion. This preamble was evidently listened to with pain by both the clergymen, but probably not with much surprise by either. Mr. Bolton, indeed, almost felt that he had heard it before, so precisely was it in accordance with Mrs. Lambert's statement respecting the feelings and intentions of her late master.

It very explicitly stated that his only motive for making the will at all was as a measure of precaution, lest, by possibility, his brother, or any of his brother's children, might inherit his property in case he died intestate. The preamble then proceeded to state that this possibility might arise from the fact of his having a natural son, whose existence would, of course, be no impediment to the succession of his brother, or his brother's family to the Beauchamp estate; and that as his legitimate daughter was born under apparently similar circumstances, inasmuch as he had lived with the mothers of both in great retirement, and that both had been called by his name, he deemed it safest to bequeath his said property by will to his daughter Helen Rixley Beauchamp, commonly called Helen Rixley. .

Then followed in goodly legal style, and phrase, the important, "*give and bequeath*," followed by the enumeration of sundry estates familiarly known by the comprehensive phrase, "The Beauchamp property," all and every of which were bequeathed and settled upon his daughter Helen, and her heirs for ever.

The name of the testator and of three witnesses, with the seals of all duly appended then followed; having examined which, Mr. Lucas folded up the parchment, and for a moment held it in his hand, as if doubtful in whose custody he should place it; but this moment sufficed to decide him, and he presented it to Mr. Rixley, saying, "You, sir, as the natural guardian of the young lady, are the person in whose hands it would seem most proper to place this important document, till such time as the proper steps can be taken for proving it."

"If I can be of any use in proving the hand writing of my brother, I shall be ready to do it," said Mr. Rixley, composedly; "but I would rather not be troubled by having the custody of the will. Either Mr. Bolton or yourself, Sir, might, I think, with more propriety undertake the care of it."

"Mr. Lucas was the lawyer employed by your late brother while he was in this neighbourhood," said Mr. Bolton, "and I think the desk itself, and all that it contained, had better be consigned to his keeping for the present. He will, too, be certainly the most desirable person to be employed in transacting the necessary business at Doctors' Commons."

"If I am to take this desk and its contents into my charge," replied the attorney, "I must beg to have a catalogue of the said contents taken in your presence, gentlemen."

Little as Mr. Rixley appeared desirous of mixing himself in his late brother's concerns, he could not object to so reasonable a proposal, and the contents of the desk were accordingly examined, and catalogued. It contained a few letters and several bills, a few of these being apparently still due, but the rest having receipts appended to them in very proper business-like style. But, with the exception of the will, the only document of any real consequence which they found was a fully authenticated certificate of the marriage of the late William Rixley Beauchamp with the mother of the young heiress.

"This, too, is by no means an unimportant document," said the lawyer, putting it into the hands of Mr. Bolton.

"Certainly not," replied the curate of Crumpton, passing it to Mr. Rixley.

"There is nothing equivocal in this," rejoined the lawyer again, receiving it, and carefully replacing it in the desk. "This document, and the will together, places the young lady in perfectly smooth water." He then rose, locked the desk, and put the key in his pocket.

"I came here on horseback, Mr. Bolton," he said, "and I will, therefore leave this desk in your charge; but I will take an early opportunity of sending for it."

"I will not offer to spare you the trouble," replied Mr. Bolton, smiling, "for I would not wish to have any further responsibility thrown upon me respecting this important desk. I will, however, give it house-room till you send for it."

This promise seemed to satisfy the lawyer; and he took his leave as soon as he had received it.

The funeral was to take place on the following day; but notwithstanding the amiable physiognomy of Mr. Rixley, and the very decided opinion conceived by Mr. Bolton that he was an exceedingly amiable man, the interval which must of necessity elapse before they parted seemed longer than the curate of Crumpton knew how to employ.

The statement made by Mrs. Lambert respecting the estrangement between the two brothers had been very completely confirmed by the demeanour of Mr. Rixley, and, moreover, the fact that the so-recently-heard-of niece was endowed with the noble property which, but for her, must of necessity have belonged to himself and his children, caused Mr. Bolton to feel that the offering to present this obnoxious young intruder to her unknown uncle was but an unpromising device for enabling them to get through the remainder of the day in a manner as little painful to all parties as might be.

But a very few moments' reflection convinced the worthy

curate that, however little profitable, or however little pleasant it might be to bring these near, but unknown, relatives together, it was decidedly his duty to do it. All the circumstances of Helen's real position recurred to him. He remembered all the particulars related to him by Mrs. Lambert, as well as the personal confession which had been blended with the narrative; and he felt that, whatever might have been the conduct of his very worthless parishioner to his brother, it could not exonerate Helen's uncle from the obvious duty of protecting so near a relative, under circumstances which so clearly showed that such protection was very greatly required.

After the silence of a minute or two, passed in meditation as to the best manner of stating the case, Mr. Bolton said, "I feel considerable reluctance, Mr. Rixley, to the taking advantage of the accidental circumstances which have brought us together, in order to dictate, or seem to dictate, to you the line of conduct towards your young niece which I think you ought to pursue; and believe me, nothing but the persuasion that it is my duty, would induce me to do it."

"I am persuaded of it, Sir," replied Mr. Rixley, gently, but somewhat coldly. "Permit me, however, before you enter upon the subject," he continued, "to make you aware that the circumstances which led to the estrangement between my brother and myself, were of no common kind, nor are they such as I could easily explain in their full extent to anyone. I have, moreover, another observation to make, which is, that my brother's richly endowed heiress cannot by possibility require any sort of assistance which it is in my power to give. She will, of course, become a ward of Chancery, and proper persons will be appointed to take care of her. Were she poor, instead of rich, Mr. Bolton I might possibly feel, notwithstanding all that has passed, that it was my duty as far as my very limited means would permit, to assist her."

"Bear with me patiently, my dear Sir, even if I take the liberty of saying that I differ from you entirely. The very peculiar advantages which both nature and fortune have bestowed upon your niece, render her greatly more in need of your protection than she would be were she without them."

"I suspect there must have been some fallacy in the reasoning which leads to so startling a conclusion," replied Mr. Rixley, with a quiet smile. "I should think," he added, "that the same protection under which this young lady has been living since the death of her mother might easily be secured to her still. I know that her late father's residence here has been by no means constant, or even regular, in its periodical recurrence; for though I have not seen him, I have heard of him frequently."

This speech embarrassed the good curate exceedingly. He had no intention whatever of communicating the confession of the unhappy Mrs. Lambert to any one. He could not doubt that it had been made to him solely for the purpose of inducing him to find a more fitting protector for Helen than she herself could be; and could he have obtained this protection from her uncle without disclosing the principal reason which caused him to seek it, he would have been relieved from a very painful task. But he now saw, and felt, that this was impossible; and he, therefore, though not without great reluctance, distinctly stated to Mr. Rixley the reasons which made the removal of Helen from the neighbourhood an event so very greatly to be desired for her.

Mr. Rixley plainly showed, both by his heightened complexion and his kindling eye, that the depravity which could thus consign a daughter to the charge of a woman so circumstanced was felt by him as no light addition to all the foregone causes of indignation, which for years had been accumulating in his memory against his brother.

He positively shuddered as the clear statement of the facts developed to him all the hard corruption of heart which it was so well calculated to prove, and Mr. Bolton flattered himself that he had conquered.

Great, therefore, was his disappointment, when, withdrawing his hands, with which for a moment he had covered his face, Mr. Rixley said, "What you tell me, Sir, is very terrible, and I wish I could have died without hearing it! Unhappily I wanted no further proof of depravity in this man to justify the estrangement between us, which I have so vainly attempted to conquer, as far as my own feelings were concerned, for long, long years of life. It was his conduct to our angelic mother which first turned my heart against him; in comparison to which his conduct towards myself I can truly say as counted as nothing, although it has been marked with unceasing hostility on his part. And now, when I hoped that such painful—such guilty —feelings might be forgotten, and buried for ever, I have the misfortune of learning what is, perhaps, more atrocious than all which has gone before it! But I ought to beg your pardon for this weakness of lamentation and murmuring. It would have been fitter that I should have received this intelligence without making any commentary on it. But I am sorry to perceive that we draw a very different practical inference from it. It is evident that you think this crowning trait of infamy on the part of my brother ought to induce me to take his daughter to my heart and my hearth, and make her the companion of my own girl. Mr. Bolton, I cannot do this—it is repugnant to my feelings, and alarming to my conscience. How dare I bring an unhappy young creature, who has passed every hour of her life in such companionship, to be the daily and hourly associate of my innocent child? I dare not, I cannot do it!"

"If such be your view of the case, Sir," replied Mr. Bolton, gravely, "I will say no more. Heaven tempers the wind to the shorn lamb; and the pure and innocent creature who unfortunately inspires such feelings will not be the victim of them. I am as full of hope as you are of fear concerning her: and we will now let the subject drop. This is a heavy day for you, Mr. Rixley; nor is it without pain to me. But there are many hours of it to be got through yet; and I think it would do us both good if we could contrive to get a little air and sunshine without committing the obvious indecorum of being seen by the villagers. But I think if you would trust yourself to my guidance, I could take you down to the beach by a path that I have myself formed from the bottom of my garden, in which it is extremely unlikely that we should meet anyone."

"The doing so would be a great relief to me," replied the other, "for I confess to you that my head aches very severely." A statement to the truth of which the pallid countenance of the speaker gave ample testimony.

Mr. Bolton immediately rose, and prepared to lead the way; but Mr. Rixley retained his seat, and made a movement with his hand, which indicated that he had something more which he wished to say before they set out. Mr. Bolton obeyed it; and then, with a little hesitation and a little embarrassment, his companion said, "Do not, if you can help it, my dear Sir, consider me either capricious or inconsistent, if I tell you that *now* I should wish to see my niece. Till the question of her becoming one of my family had been fairly discussed and finally decided, I wished to avoid this; as, otherwise, my averseness to receiving her might have been attributed to personal prejudice against her. But there is now no danger that you should so mistake me, and therefore, by your good leave, I will see her."

Though, after what had passed, Mr. Bolton was inclined to

think this a very useless ceremony, and only calculated to produce pain to poor Helen, he, nevertheless, did not feel justified
in refusing to do what was asked of him; and being very sure
that he should find the unconscious heiress with his kind-hearted
wife, he went to the usual sitting-room of that truly-estimable
personage, and found Helen, as he expected, sitting close beside
her, and looking all the better for the consolatory talk to which
she had been listening.

During the short interval which had intervened between
leaving the uncle and finding the niece, Mr. Bolton had decided
that he would not as yet communicate to Helen the great change
which had taken place in her condition. He was well aware,
indeed, that no form of words which he could use in announcing
this, could possibly convey to the young girl the immensity of
the change which awaited her; but he wished her uncle to see
her unchanged in look and manner by any such startling announcement; and all he said was, "Come with me, my dear
Helen; your uncle wishes to see you."

"Have you heard anything about William, Sir?" was her
reply.

"Go, Helen! go, my dear," said Mrs. Bolton, gently, but in
a tone that had some authority in it. "I am very glad," she
added, "that he wishes to see you. He is the nearest relation
you have left, my dear child, and it is greatly to be desired that
he should take some interest in you."

"No! William is the nearest relation I have left, and no
uncle in the whole wide world can ever take so much care of me
as he would do, if he would but come home again!" exclaimed
Helen, somewhat vehemently.

"Come with me, my dear," said Mr. Bolton, extending his
hand towards her. "It is not behaving well to keep your uncle
waiting."

Helen's only reply to this was instantly rising from her chair,
and putting her hand in that of Mr. Bolton, which was extended
towards her; but not a word more was spoken between them
before the parlour door was opened, and Helen found herself
standing in the presence of her uncle.

CHAPTER XVIII.

The heart of the young girl beat painfully; but that of the relative before whom she was brought to present herself appeared, by his attitude and occupation, to be in a state of very perfect composure.

Mr. Rixley had taken up a book as soon as he had found himself alone; this might, in some degree, have been a matter of habit, but it was also a fair indication of the real state of his feelings towards the child he had sent for. His reason for sending for her was precisely what he had stated to Mr. Bolton. He felt no personal interest in her, and he would willingly have altogether forgotten her existence; a state of mind to which he flattered himself that his family, as well as himself, would very speedily attain: nor did he feel any misgivings as to the possibility that the approaching interview would make any alteration either in his wishes or intentions.

But in this he was mistaken.

Helen was very pale when she entered the room, and a feeling made up of one-third of youthful timidity, and two-thirds of averseness to the interview, caused her to show nothing of her magnificent eyes, save their long lashes; moreover, instead of approaching her uncle, she stopped short, and stood immovably still, within one step of the door.

It would be difficult to do justice to the feelings with which Mr. Rixley gazed at her.

In the first place, he had expected to see a little girl; but Helen, though little more than thirteen years old, was already as tall as the majority of women; and though very slight, there was an air of quiet, graceful firmness in her carriage, which, even more than her height, prevented her from having, in any degree, the appearance of a child. But this difference between what he saw, and what he expected to see, could only produce surprise; and it was a far different emotion that Mr. Rixley experienced. It was not like the effect of looking upon what was new to his eyes, but upon what was familiar. Most familiar, and most dear, did the features of Helen appear to her uncle; for they were the features of his mother. Most wonderfully striking, both in form and in expression, was the resemblance between his almost idolized mother and this lovely girl; and it was the more striking to him from the fact, that the late Mrs. Rixley had not only married at a very early age, but had retained her beauty in an extraordinary degree to the time of her death.

Such a resemblance to a mother, so freshly remembered, must have produced a strong effect on most men, especially when suddenly appearing before them for the first time; but in this case, it was no ordinary amount of feeling that was awakened. All the most interesting circumstances of Mr. Rixley's life had been influenced by, and mixed up with his mother. The untoward, and early-displayed temper of his brother, had of necessity led to such a difference in their mother's feelings towards them, as bound the younger to her with more than common love and devotion, while it produced feelings in the elder so nearly approaching hatred both to mother and brother, as to poison the peace of both.

The consciousness that this gentle mother, and ever-faithful friend, had often endured a sort of domestic martyrdom while watching over his interests, hda never left him, and her image lived as freshly in his memory as if he had lost her but yesterday. It was not very extraordinary, therefore, that this sudden, and most unexpected appearance should completely overpower him. For one moment he looked at her, as if actually gazing on a supernatural appearance, and there was a wildness in his eye that almost partook of terror. But in the next, he burst into tears, and, rushing towards her, caught her in his arms, and pressed her to his heart, as if he had found a long-lost daughter of his own. "Oh, my child! my child!" he exclaimed. "How came I to forget that, though you were *his* daughter, you were the grandchild of my angelic mother!— Helen! dearest, dearest Helen! You are her living image!— For God's sake do not hate me!—If you will let me, my sweet girl, I will be a father to you! My dear Anne will be a sister, and you will love your aunt, Helen, even if you cannot love me, for everybody loves her.—But I have frightened you, my dear one! Frightened you by my vehemence!—you will not, you cannot love me!"

"But I do love you. I love you already!" cried Helen, earnestly. "But you you must not weep because you have found me. I cannot bear to see your tears. And yet I love you the better for them. I see," she added, while her own tears flowed still faster than his, "I see that you loved your mother, just as I loved mine. For I can sit and cry by the hour together when I think of her! But indeed—and indeed—I ought not to cry now, for I feel that God has sent a great blessing to me, but though I do cry, I am very, very thankful!"

This most unexpected scene had passed before the eyes of Mr. and Mrs. Bolton with such astounding vehemence and rapidity, that for a moment they both looked bewildered; but nothing could be more genuine, nothing more cordial than the joyful congratulations which followed it.

Mr. Bolton, who but a few short minutes before had felt so heavy at heart from the failure of all his efforts to propitiate the good offices of the only person who could properly undertake the charge of the desolate young heiress, now looked and spoke as if every care he had in the world had been removed, and the two clergymen cordially shook hands together as if for the first time.

And truly it was for the first time that they had done so with any real and cordial sympathy of feeling; for on the only subject of personal interest that was in common between them, their opinions and their feelings had hitherto been greatly at variance. Mr. Bolton's earnest desire being that the personal charge of the orphan heiress should be undertaken by her uncle, while Mr. Rixley's earnest desire was that he might have nothing whatever to do with her.

Now, however, it speedily became evident that all their views, hopes, wishes, and intentions on this subject were in the most perfect accord, and the intercourse between them became cordial and unembarrassed accordingly. Nor was the gentle-hearted Mrs. Bolton in any degree less pleased than her husband by this additional gleam of sunshine which seemed to have fallen like a ray from heaven upon the head of the so lately desolate Helen, and no one that had looked upon the little party, that now sat so lovingly together, would have easily believed that the kindly feelings so legible in the eyes of all were not yet half an hour old.

It was strange that the sudden change of purpose which had been so seemingly resolute as that of Mr. Rixley's, should bring with it so much deep-felt delight; but never did a fine expressive countenance more unequivocally express happiness than his did as his eyes fondly rested upon his beautiful niece. "And your name is her name!" he exclaimed joyously. "How little did I anticipate the pleasure which this gives me!"

"Was your dear mother's name, Helen, then?" said his niece innocently. "And it was the name of my mother, too," she added.

"No, my child," replied her uncle, "her name was not Helen, but it was Beauchamp, and your name is Beauchamp."

"No, it isn't!" returned Helen, looking disappointed. "My name is Helen Rixley."

"She knows nothing about it as yet," said Mr. Bolton, replying to the inquiring glance of his new acquaintance. "There has been no time to tell her. When I carried your permission for her to come to you, I thought much more of that than of the . . . than of anything else, Mr. Rixley."

"I thank you. I believe everybody has behaved much better in this business than myself. I thank you much for letting me have the pleasure of announcing the real state of the case to Miss Beauchamp. For you are Miss Beauchamp, my sweet Helen, and you inherit the property, as well as the name of your grandmother's family."

"Do I?" said Helen, looking rather puzzled. "Why do not you inherit it, uncle? You are her son, and I am only her grand-daughter."

"You are a bad lawyer, Helen. As the child of my mother's *eldest* son, you inherit the property by your father's will."

"Oh! that is the law, is it?" she replied. "And I suppose the dear old Warren House is what you call the property, and if that is the case I hope you will sometimes come and live there with me,—and Mr. Bolton, and Mrs. Bolton, and all the dear children will very often come and see us. I know they will, because they are always so very, very kind. And when dear William comes back, he, and I, and dear good Sarah Lambert will all be as happy as the day is long!"

A shade seemed to pass over the countenance of Mr. Rixley at the mention of William, and a deeper shade still over that of Mr. Bolton at the name of Sarah Lambert; for they both felt that there were difficulties to be overcome before the young heiress could be established with all the decorum as well as with all the liberality and refinement which her position required.

A glance was exchanged between them, but for a moment they were both silent, and then Mr. Rixley said, "You may depend upon it, my dearest Helen, that all those who will have the management of your affairs before you become of age, will be anxious to do everything in their power to make you comfortable and happy. But you have a great deal more to learn about your own affairs before we shall be able to make you fully comprehend the great change which has taken place in your situation. For instance, my dear child, though it is quite true the Warren House has become your property, you will, I think, young as you are, agree with me in thinking that it will not be the most proper and suitable residence as your home, when I tell you that you are also become the posessor of a very noble mansion called Beauchamp Park, where your ancestors have lived for many, many generations, and where your grandmother, through whom you inherit the property, was born. This Warren House was bought by your father, comparatively speaking, a very few years ago."

"Well! I am sorry for that," replied Helen, with a gentle sigh, "because I don't think I shall ever like any other house so well—particularly the schoolroom, you know, Mr. Bolton, where we always were so very quite and comfortable, William, and I, and dear Sarah Lambert! However," she added, "I believe it would be very silly to care very much about a house. Of course we should grow to love any house, if we had the people we loved with us—and that I shall always have, shall I not, dear uncle?"

This was a very embarrassing question, and the more so because Mr. Rixley was a very sincere man, and would have found it difficult to say "Yes" when he meant "No." And he certainly was in no doubt as to the fact that it would not do for a young lady, aged thirteen and a half, the heiress of the Beauchamps of Beauchamp Park, with a clear revenue of ten thousand a year, to set up housekeeping with a runaway boy if she could find him, even though he was the natural son of her father, or with a nurse who had been that dissolute father's mistress.

All therefore that he could reply to this eager burst of affection was to tell her, kindly, but vaguely, that he thought she had a good chance, wherever she was, of being loved by the people around her, and therefore there was little doubt of her loving them in return.

But vague as this was, it was all he could venture to say, and Mr. Bolton spared him the embarrassment of discussing the arrangements for her future home at this early period of their acquaintance, by observing that it was time for them to set off upon their projected walk, if they meant to reach the picturesque spot he had mentioned; a suggestion to which Mr. Rixley readily agreed, and the two gentlemen set off together in a much better state of mind for tasting the beauties of nature than if they had done so before the introduction of Helen to her uncle. Nevertheless they had to converse on topics that were in no trifling degree painful to both. The idea that this dear and precious child should have been beguiled into loving her father's mistress with all the tender affection of a warm young heart, was very painful to Mr. Rixley, and he expressed his grief and indignation strongly.

"I can neither blame your feelings, my dear Sir, nor be surprised at the strength of them," said Mr. Bolton. "But let us be thankful," he added, " that you have been prevailed upon to see this dear child, and that her beautiful features have achieved the effect of recalling your honoured mother's image."

His companion was silent for a moment, but was evidently, and even strongly affected by these words; and then said, "Yes Mr. Bolton, I am thankful—very deeply thankful—and the more so when I remember how very near I was to passing by on the other side. Nothing will satisfy me now," he continued, "but removing her from the neighbourhood of this woman at once, and receiving her as a member of my own family."

"And that," returned the greatly comforted Mr. Bolton, earnestly, "that is precisely what I have ventured to wish, and to hope, from within about an hour after I made your acquaintance. And take my word for it, Mr. Rixley, the more you see and know of this poor child, the more you will rejoice at her having become known to you. Fortunately there can, I presume, be no difficulty in constituting you her personal as well as her natural guardian?"

"No, there will be no difficulty about that, I daresay," returned Mr. Rixley. "The funeral of her father is to take place to-morrow," he continued, "and on the following day I purpose setting off on my return to London, and will take her with me. Our home there is not a splendid one, for we are not rich people, Mr. Bolton, but I think we shall be able to make her comfortable, and she will have the advantage of being within reach of the best masters. Moreover, if you will venture to trust a father's report, you may have the satisfaction of believing that your young favourite will find a nice sort of sister in my daughter. But you must not take all this upon trust, my good friend, but must come up to see how we are going on, with your own eyes. We owe you much, Mr. Bolton, and I should be sorry to think that Helen should not still benefit by your friendship."

Their walk was both long and pleasant, for their conversation was in no danger of flagging for want of matter, and proved equally agreeable and satisfactory to both parties.

On their return to the parsonage, however, they found that poor Helen was again plunged in very bitter grief not only from the prolonged absence of her brother, but on account of the very unsatisfactory tidings which she had at length received from Mrs. Lambert.

Her nurse, who really seemed almost as anxious as herself, had promised, when she parted with her on the preceding evening, to get one of the many fishermen who lived in the village, to make inquiries in the town of Falmouth as to whether William had been seen there, for it had occurred to her as probable that if he had left his father's house with the hope of finding some employment which might maintain him out of it, Falmouth would be the place where he would in the first instance be likely to seek for it.

And this conjecture, as it seemed, had been perfectly justified by the result, for her envoy had returned with the intelligence, that the poor lad had been seen and recognized at Falmouth while in earnest conversation with a party of sailors at the port, during the afternoon of the day in which he had left the Warren House.

But her intelligence went no further, and could therefore scarcely be said to have afforded his anxious sister any consolation at all; for, as she truly said, he could not have remained many hours in Falmouth without hearing of the event which they expected would cause his immediate return upon his becoming acquainted with it, and his not returning proved only too plainly that he had not remained there long enough for the intelligence to have reached the town before he had quitted it, which reasoning, together with the profession of the persons with whom he had been seen conversing, went far towards proving that he had probably embarked and put to sea before the intelligence which it was hoped would cause his return could have reached him. Should this indeed be the case, how terribly distant, and how terribly vague, did her hope of seeing him again become!

This idea, which was much too well founded to be reasonably combated, affected her so deeply, that Mrs. Bolton thought it would be best for all parties that her uncle should not see her under the influence of a sorrow so vehement, and in which it was so perfectly impossible that he could sympathise; and therefore, at the earnest persuasion of her kind hostess, the weeping young heiress again laid her head upon her pillow, as little mindful of her newly acquired importance in the world, as if she had been three years old, instead of thirteen and a half.

CHAPTER XVIII.

On the morning of the funeral, Mrs. Bolton carefully guarded the door of Helen's room, in the hope that the poor girl might remain unconscious of what was going on till the ceremony was over, which, as it had been fixed for an early hour, she thought might be managed without any great difficulty. Not, indeed, that Mrs. Bolton so little understood either the feelings or the character of Helen as to suppose that she would either feel or affect any vehement grief on the occasion; but she knew that the poor girl had suffered, and was still suffering greatly from the absence of her brother, and even the scene of the preceding day with her newly-found uncle, though soothing and consolatory in no ordinary degree, had evidently caused her considerable agitation, and Mrs. Bolton was not at all mistaken in thinking that the more quiet she was kept during this last day at Crumpton, the more fit she would be for her journey to London on the morrow.

But fate did not second the kind intentions of the curate's wife, for within a few minutes after the arrival of the professional officials, with their hearse, and their mourners, at the Warren House, the quiet mansion of the village priest became the scene of a tumult which might have aroused a sounder sleeper than Helen.

She was awakened by the noise of many voices all speaking vehemently together, and started up in her bed to listen; for it instantly occurred to her that some news had arrived respecting her brother. She sprang instantly from her bed, dressed herself with the least possible delay, and, totally forgetting Mrs. Bolton's gentle injunction to remain quietly in her room till she came for her, rushed down the stairs, and on reaching the little hall at the bottom of them, found herself amidst a group of men, two or three of whom were sailors; and one of these was the favourite boatman of her deceased father.

Mr. Bolton and Mr. Rixley, who had been at breakfast in the parlour when the noise began, were now in the midst of them, and evidently endeavouring to comprehend what they were saying, which, from their all talking together, was no easy task.

"Is it about William? Does anybody know anything about William?" cried Helen, stopping short on the last stair but one, and thereby enabling herself, poor child, to be both seen and heard by those to whom she addressed herself.

The boisterous, and now brutal-looking fellow, called by his late patron, Commodore Jack, and known in the village as John Cummings, was the individual who undertook to answer her.

"Know anything about him?" he roared in reply, in the stupendous voice which he prided himself in making heard in the stiffest gale that could blow. "I know anything about him? I think we know enough! The infernal imp got up in the middle of the night, and murdered his father, and then jumped out of the window and started for Falmouth, where he got a berth on board some vessel that was short of hands, and he is now, doubtless, hugging himself for his exploit on the high seas. He thinks he has cheated the hangman, mayhap, but he will be caught, if there is justice either in heaven or earth, and I shall have the glory of seeing him hung before I die."

That these dreadful words were listened to with horror and dismay may easily be credited, but for a moment it was in awe-struck silence. And the next sound that was heard was that caused by the fall of Helen from the place where she stood, upon the stone floor of the hall.

There were by this time many persons assembled in this little hall, including the whole of the small household, with the exception of the nurse and her charges, with Mr. and Mrs. Bolton and their guest; but the majority of those who already filled the room, and many more who were endeavouring to force their way into it from without, consisted of the villagers, particularly that portion of them who gained their living as fishermen, and as sailors.

Several of this motley throng made a movement towards the prostrate and insensible Helen; but it was her uncle who first reached her, and raising her in his arms, carried her into the parlour.

Mrs. Bolton followed them, but the master of the house remained amidst his boisterous guests, who were greatly too much excited to listen to his gentle remonstrances and entreaties, that they would retire.

Finding that it was utterly impossible to get rid of them, he addressed himself to John Cummings, and in an accent of pastoral authority, desired to know for what reason he thus forced himself into his house, and on what ground he had dared to blast the character of an absent, but most estimable young man, by uttering the wild statement which had produced so alarming an effect on his young sister?

Notwithstanding the vehement excitement of the rude fellow he addressed, Mr. Bolton was too much respected in his parish for any inhabitant of it to answer him uncivilly, and even Commodore Jack took his hat off as he replied, "Please your reverence, I should not do what I am doing in regard to coming here, nor I should not say what I have said in regard to the wickedness that has been done, if I had not warrant for it. I trust your reverence will not be putting my late honoured master and patron under the ground this blessed day, before you have sent for the coroner and had the body properly examined; and saving your presence, Sir, it will be at your own peril if you do, for as sure as my name's John Cummings, we'll have him up again."

Mr. Bolton felt puzzled and looked distressed. "Will you tell me," said he, "on what ground it is that you have conceived this very strange and improbable idea? Mr. Foster, who is a very skilful practitioner, has seen the body, and if it had exhibited any appearance to justify the strange idea you have conceived, you may be very sure that he would have perceived it. Will you tell me, Cummings, what it was that first put this thought into your head!"

"Yes, your reverence, you have all the right to ask, and I hav'n't the leastest objection to answer. The reason why I think the sudden death of my late patron and master was nowise natural is this. The day before he died, or was put to death, he passed above ten hours in my company in his boat, and if I ever seed a man, gentle or simple, in the very topmost enjoyment of health and strength it was Squire Rixley that day."

"I have no doubt that your statement is perfectly true, John Cummings," replied Mr. Bolton, "but take my word for it, that no medical man would tell you that he was the less likely to die of apoplexy on that account. On the contrary, indeed, I think it very likely that many persons might think ten hours of

exercise, and perhaps of violent exertion, for the sea was rough,
and your master was famous you know, for never sparing himself—many people, I say, might think this very likely to be the
cause of the fit that carried him off."

"God bless your heart, Mr. Bolton! But you, Sir, d'ye see,
asking your pardon, are a parson, and sea-work that might
seem likely enough to a gentleman of your cloth to be darnation
difficult and dangerous, would come like child's play to such a
gentleman as Mr. Rixley. And then, Sir, by your leave,
in the next place, I can't find out that Mr. Foster, who
is no doubt of it, a first-rate gentleman in his way, I
can't find out that he ever did, as one may say, examine
the dead gentleman at all. He could not stay, as Rebecca
Watkins tells me, above a minute or two in the room, and that
minute or two most likely came very quick upon the death, and
everybody knows that it is not just at first like, that the
symptoms of poisoning shows themselves, and *that* I, for one,
know from more than hearsay, for I have seen with my own
eyes a dead man that was poisoned, both soon after the death,
and two days later, and the difference was no joke, I can tell
you."

"But why, if you have had this notion in your head, did you
not mention it earlier?" said Mr. Bolton. "Only as late as
yesterday morning Mr. Foster might, I know, have seen the
body without any inconvenience; but now the undertakers have
finished all their preparations, and such an examination could
not take place at present, without producing a very disagreeable effect. Mr. Rixley's own brother is here for the purpose
of attending the funeral, and such a circumstance could not
take place without shocking him greatly."

"I can't help that, Sir," said the resolute John Cummings,
" I hope I should be as loath as another to shock any gentleman's feelings, without due cause for it, and as to the charge of
delay on my part, Mr. Bolton, I think I can explain the reason
for my not having any suspicion at first, and then letting the
suspicion get hold of me afterwards. The reason was this,
Sir : We all of us, we Crumpton people I mean, know Rebecca
Watkins, who has been, off and on, a servant at the Warren
House for years and years, and a thorough good sort of body
she is, and one whose word I would take as surely as that of
anybody I know, for there is nothing like falsehood in her.
And she it was, please your reverence, who first put this question
into my head."

"What question?" said Mr. Bolton, rather impatiently. "You surely forget, John Cummings, that the funeral of your late master is very indecently stopped by the strange conduct you are pursuing."

"I forget nothing, your reverence," replied the man. "One thing that I can never forget is, that let him have been what he might to others, he was ever the sailor's friend. I forget nothing, your reverence; and if you had heard Rebecca Watkins say what I heard her say this morning, I greatly misdoubt if you would ever have forgotten it, either. We were all, that is a many of us, talking together upon this sudden and awful change from all the might of manhood, caring not a button for the stiffest breeze that could blow, and the horrid stillness of a corpse stretched helpless on the bed of death! 'Well now, to be sure,' said Rebecca Watkins, 'there must have been something queer going on among 'em all at the Warren House. There was the squire, the very day before the night of his death, going down to the beach, and into his dear boat, looking for all the world as if he intended to live for ever; and there was that dainty boy William, with his handsome face, and his eyes full of tears, making much of his sister, for all the world as if he expected that he never should see her again. Well then, what follows next? why who should I meet upon the cellar stairs, just as I was going to set off home for the night, but William? I axed him if I should draw some beer for him, for he looked as white as a sheet, and I truly thought that he had worn himself out with his walking, and hadn't strength enough to get down to the beer barrel and up again. But he only seemed to want to get rid of me, and said Thankey, thankey, Rebecca, it's your going home time. I wou'd rather draw the beer myself,' and then, your reverence, she went on to tell us that when she went back to her work in the morning, the first news she heard was, that Master William had let himself down from the window by the help of his sheets tied together, and was off, nobody knowed where. And then the next thing that come upon her was finding the master dead in his bed."

"Startling events both, no doubt of it, John Cummings. But I see not why you should fancy that there was any connection between them," replied Mr. Bolton.

"You have not quite heard all Rebecca's story yet," resumed the sailor, doggedly. "I don't rightly remember how the matter came out, whether the people about got to asking her questions, or whether it come out because her heart was too full to keep it in; but before she finished, she gave us plain enough to understand that there had been sharp and bitter words between the father and son. And now I have said my say about my poor master; he was the sailor's friend, but I won't answer for his never having done or said what he had better not. By Rebecca Watkins' account, who can hear through a key-hole, I suppose, as well as another, the squire was in a passion with the boy for some provoking trick or another, and then he twitted him with being base-born, which he didn't ought to have done, for certain, but the young chap, she says, was downright mad with rage, and she says, too, that if she don't greatly mistake, she heard him as good as threaten his life. Well, Sir, and what happens within a trifle more than twenty-four hours afterwards? Why, the father is found dead in his bed, and the son, after jumping out of the window, and scrambling his way by hook or by crook to Falmouth, is seen talking with sailors on the quay, and I'll bet fifty to one that he is sailing away by this time to the other side of the world, perhaps."

This long statement, which, though rapidly uttered, was pronounced with great distinctness, had been listened to with greedy ears, by the thick packed crowd who had forced their way into Mr. Bolton's hall, and a sort of groan was uttered at its conclusion which very plainly testified the deep interest which they all took in the narrative, as well as the general persuasion that what the speaker had uttered deserved the deepest attention.

Mr. Bolton was instantly aware of this fact; and thoroughly well knowing the self-willed temperament of the population, he felt that, however absurd he believed their suspicions to be, it would not do to attempt to extinguish them either by the voice of authority, or by the reasonings of common sense. After the pause of a moment he replied, " My good friends, I think you all know me too well to believe that I should be less anxious to discover the truth in this matter, than yourselves. I should not be doing my duty, however, if I concealed from you that I consider you to be utterly wrong and mistaken in your suspicions. I know William Rixley well, better, believe me, than it is possible you can do, and this knowlegde renders it, I may say, impossible for me to believe him guilty of the crime you all seem disposed to lay to his charge; for if this were not the case, I feel sure that you would indignantly reject such an imputation, thrown as it is upon an absent boy who has no power to defend himself."

"We don't want to be cruel or unjust towards man, woman, or child," cried a voice from the furthest corner of the hall, "but neither would it be right to pass over such strange things as we have heard without examining a little into them. I vote that we should none of us believe the young fellow to be guilty till such time as we have got proof against him."

"Agreed," cried John Cummings, in a voice that might have been heard from the mast head of a man-of-war. "Agreed! and the first thing to do by the way of getting at proof, is examining the body of the dead man. If he is found to have died by the visitation of God, why then, in God's name, let his body be laid peaceably in the earth, and let us pray, like good Christians, for the peace of his soul. But if, on proper examination, things should turn out contrary, and that poison should be found within him, why in that case we must have a proper coroner's inquest, and then after the jury shall have heard all the particulars, we shall get a proper verdict against the murderer, known or unknown."

"Ay, ay, no doubt of it," replied many voices in chorus.

"Then be it as you wish, my good friends," replied the clergyman. "I hope and believe," he continued, "that you will find yourselves altogether mistaken in your suspicious, but as this painful idea has evidently got possession of your minds, it is best that you should be satisfied on the subject, even at the cost of some inconvenience."

"And that is spoken like a reasonable gentleman," returned Cummings, "and it is what we expected, and looked for, from your reverence; and I thank you, Sir, in the name of the parish, and specially of all the sailors."

"But let me add one word to what I have already said," resumed Mr. Bolton, "It is proper that you should all of you know that the next of kin to the late Mr. Rixley is now in this house. This gentleman was his own brother, and of course nothing can be done in the business, either by you or by me, without consulting him upon it."

"I won't be baulked in the examination of the body for all the brothers on the face of the earth," said Cummings. "But we don't want to do nothing in the dark; contrary-wise altogether, so your reverence is welcome to tell just all that has passed here to all whom it may concern, and the whole world beside, so we will let you go, Sir, in peace and quiet, to make the communication in any way as you may think fit, and meanwhile we will, some of us, be off to look after the doctor, and then, if his judgment is, not clear against it, we must summon the coroner."

The invading party then elbowed and shouldered each other out of the house, and Mr. Bolton joined the anxious party in the parlour, conscious that he had nothing to tell them at all calculated to remove any of the painful feelings, from which he knew they must be suffering.

CHAPTER XIX.

THE spectacle that greeted Mr. Bolton on re-entering the parlour was by no means calculated to tranquillize the annoyance and alarm, which the scene in the hall had occasioned him.

The first object on which his eyes rested was the figure of Helen stretched upon the sofa, her lips and cheeks utterly colourless, and her eyes closed; her uncle was standing at her feet, gazing upon her death-like attitude and complexion, with a look of mingled love and alarm, that it was impossible to witness unmoved; while poor Mrs. Bolton, with all a woman's sympathy, and all a woman's terror, was unable to obtain even the aid of a glass of water for her, the only exit from the parlour being into the crowded hall, and opening the door which led to it, would have been like inviting further outrage and renewed suffering.

"Oh! thank God you are come, Stephen!" she exclaimed. "Are those dreadful people gone? What is it they want? What was it they said about William Rixley?"

"You shall know everything," he replied, "as rapidly as I can make myself understood. But tell me first, what we can do for that poor child. Is she still insensible? I could almost say that I hoped it."

And then, without waiting for an answer, he again left the room, speedily re-entering with water, and followed by a servant with a bottle of vinegar. The application either of one or both these remedies caused Helen to rouse herself, and open her eyes; but they seemed to close themselves again in spite of her efforts. The tears, however, which now began slowly to course each other down her cheeks, showed that she was no longer insensible.

"What is it all about, Stephen?" again exclaimed Mrs. Bolton, with very natural impatience. "Helen has been lying just as you see her, only more death-like still ever since her uncle brought her in; and he has been too much frightened about her to be able to explain anything to me. Why have all the fishermen rushed into our hall so rudely? And why does this poor child appear to be so dreadfully alarmed at seeing them?"

"She looks better now, Mr. Rixley," said the master of the house, addressing his guest, while at the same time he took the arm of his wife and passed it under his own. "I think we may safely leave her with Sally now, and I wish very much to speak to you."

The three then left the room together, and having entered the little library and closed the door, Mr. Bolton redeemed the promise he had given, by repeating, as succinctly as possible, everything that had passed in the hall.

Mrs. Bolton felt both shocked and terrified. She pressed her hand upon her forehead, but uttered not a word. Mr. Rixley, too, remained silent for a minute or two after the statement was made, and then said, "This is a very startling communication, Mr. Bolton; but I, as you must be aware, am quite unable to judge of the truth, or even of the probability, of it. Have the kindness to speak to me with entire frankness, my dear Sir, and tell me at once whether you think this horrible suspicion has any probability of truth in it."

"With the most perfect sincerity, Mr. Rixley, I answer you that I do not," replied Mr. Bolton. "I think William Rixley infinitely more likely to attempt his own life than that of his father, although that father so very little deserved the name. I have always known William to be warm-tempered and impetuous; but if he had attacked his cruel father at all, it would have been openly and in the face of day—not as a midnight assassin."

"I cannot help thinking," said Mr. Rixley, musingly, "that poor Helen is of a different opinion."

"Good Heaven, Sir!" cried Mr. Bolton, indignantly, "how is it possible you can have conceived such an idea? Let me implore you," he added, "to conceal it from her, for most truly do I believe that her love for this brother is such as to make such a suspicion a death-blow to her. She not only loves, but positively reverences him; and I have often heard her say that she thought William was born with a sort of impossibility of doing anything wrong. And upon my honour I have often, when I have heard her say this, been greatly inclined to agree with her. And so I am still, Mr. Rixley."

"Well, Sir," returned Mr. Rixley, quietly, "you and Helen must certainly be much better qualified to form an opinion of this unfortunate boy than I can be. In truth, I have never for a moment dreamed of forming any opinion of him at all. All I meant to say was, that there was a sort of agony expressed by the countenance of Helen the moment before she fainted, which I could understand perfectly if anything caused her to believe it possible that this much-loved brother was guilty of the crime laid to his charge; but which remains, in my opinion, perfectly unaccountable if she did not."

"I am sorry that you should have conceived such an idea," returned Mr. Bolton, "because I should greatly wish that you should do justice to the fine qualities of both these young people. However, it is infinitely more important that you should judge Helen rightly than her brother, for with him, poor fellow, it certainly cannot be expected that you should ever have much intercourse; and as to Helen, who will, I hope, my dear Sir, be constantly under your own eye, I can feel no serious misgivings as to your making any mistakes about her. Her nature is as clear and as pure as crystal; and you will find no difficulty, when you know her better, in understanding everything that is passing in her heart. But all such speculations are equally useless and ill-timed at this moment. I hope, Sir, that you agree with me in thinking that our best course must be to let these blundering sailors have their way about the examination?"

"Assuredly!" replied Mr. Rixley. "I much doubt, indeed, whether anything that we could either of us do or say would have influence enough to prevent it. But besides all other annoyances, my dear Mr. Bolton," added his new acquaintance, "you will have to endure me; for I cannot take this dear child away, nor should I, to say the truth, like to go myself, till this painful question has been set at rest."

His friendly host very earnestly and very sincerely assured him that the painful question, as he most justly called it, would be greatly more painful still, had he not the very important assistance and support of his presence. "But, to tell you the truth," continued Mr. Bolton, "I am very greatly inclined to make light of all the big words we have heard this morning.

Not that I at all doubt the sincerity of the zeal and affection expressed for your brother by that stalwart son of Neptune, whose exordium you listened to before you took charge of poor Helen. I am quite sure he was sincere, and himself believed every word he said. But I think you will find that he is mistaken, and that the result of the examination will be that the late Mr. Rixley Beauchamp died a natural death."

"I most earnestly wish it may prove so, for many reasons," replied Mr. Rixley; "but I do not agree with you in expecting it."

"May I ask you, my dear Sir," returned the curate of Crumpton, in an accent that betokened considerable surprise, "what reason you have for thinking so?"

"Indeed you may, and, indeed, too, I will answer with all sincerity," returned his companion, "though I am quite aware that I can give no very plausible reason for the faith that is in me. I think, however, that the primal cause for my adopting it, arose from the effect that man's statement had on poor Helen. My eye was upon her at the moment his words reached her ears; and I do not think I shall ever forget her look of agony."

"But do you not think that the mere fact of her hearing it stated that her father was murdered may account for her emotion?"

"No, Mr. Bolton, I do not," was the reply. "But add to it," he continued, "the still more dreadful fact that her brother was strongly suspected of being the assassin, and then all the misery expressed in that innocent and most lovely young face is perfectly natural, perfectly intelligible."

"I think the accusation alone is quite sufficient to account for the emotion you witnessed, without supposing that she believed it to be just," replied Mr. Bolton. "Don't you think so, my dear?" he added, turning to his wife.

Mr. Rixley watched her in silence for a minute or two, and then said, "Will you forgive me, my dear Mrs. Bolton, if I beg you to reply to your husband's question? Not that the opinion of either of us can be of the least real importance in the business, or signify to any of the individuals concerned in it. But you know dear Helen better than I do, and I should much like to hear your interpretation of the agonized emotion she betrayed. Women, you know, are often said to be the keenest observers."

"I certainly will not refuse to answer you, Mr. Rixley," she replied, "though I would rather not have had the question pressed upon me, for it is a very painful one. Had I, however, nothing but my own acuteness to enlighten me, I certainly should adopt my husband's opinion; but I am sorry to say that I have some reasons for thinking that you, my dear Sir, are very likely to be right in your interpretation of Helen's feelings. When Mr. Bolton first brought her home to me after her father's death, she was in a state of such vehement agitation that I really feared she was seized with fever, and was becoming delirious. But not for a moment did she say anything which could lead me to suppose that it was affliction for her father's death which caused this. The only name she uttered was that of her brother, and every hour of his lengthened absence seemed to bring her an additional load of misery. At length I almost scolded her for this violent grief about an absence, which was not likely to endure longer than many of his former rambles had done, and pointed this out to her, and then, after looking piteously in my face for a moment, she threw her arms round my neck, and with a fresh burst of tears sobbed out, 'Indeed, indeed if that was all I should not be so miserable. It is not so much his being away, though that is bad enough! But it is remembering all that happened before he went!' And then she endeavoured to describe to me the scene of which we had heard before from Mrs. Lambert, and in which the barbarous father of the unhappy boy insulted him in the presence of his sister by the most unfeeling statement that words could convey respecting his birth, and his abject condition. But as she went on with her description of the agony and despair into which this most unexpected discovery had plunged her brother, it was perfectly evident that what rested the most painfully on her mind was the boy's expressions of rage and hatred—for hatred was the word she used—for the treatment he had received. In short," continued Mrs. Bolton, shuddering as she spoke, "the impression she left upon my mind by her description of William's vehement resentment, joined to the agony I saw her suffer, as she dwelt upon the circumstance of his having absconded, do lead me very strongly to suspect that your interpretation of her conduct and feelings is less correct, my dear Stephen, than that of Mr. Rixley."

"I had forgotten that Helen had witnessed that terrible discovery scene," said Mr. Bolton with an altered countenance. "God grant that it may be found that there has been no poisoning in the case! Otherwise it is impossible to deny that the coincidence is most unfortunate! Poor Helen! No wonder, if she had this dreadful idea in her head, that his continued absence should be the cause of such severe suffering to her!"

Meanwhile the zeal of the parties, who had undertaken to summon first the doctor and then the coroner, did not relax. The first object was speedily accomplished. But the result of this was too important to be recorded at the end of a chapter.

CHAPTER XX.

PAINFUL as the whole of this strange and most startling investigation was to Mrs. Bolton, she never for a moment thought of herself, or regretted that hospitality to the unhappy orphan, which had so completely banished everything like tranquillity from their abode.

The state of poor Helen was indeed such as must have awakened pity in natures far less prone to it than was that of the kind and gentle Mrs. Bolton. But it would have been better for the suffering girl, perhaps, if in addition to gentle kindness, Mrs. Bolton had possessed more firmness of character.

The first symptom which Helen gave of having perfectly recovered from the faintness which had seized upon her, was throwing her arms round the neck of her good hostess, and fervently kissing her. The next was saying in a manner, so imperative, as almost to approach the tone of authority, " Mrs. Bolton, you must not try to prevent my knowing everything that is going on. Every word that John Cummings said in the hall, before I fell down the stairs, I *heard* and I *remember*, therefore, you see, it would be as vain as it would be unkind, if you were to attempt keeping me in ignorance. I will not be kept in ignorance, Mrs. Bolton. It would be quite in vain if you were to try to do it. I would find means to leave the house. I would indeed! Nothing shall prevent my hearing of everything that is done and everything that is discovered."

There was something so new and strange in the air of resolute firmness with which these words were spoken by Helen, that Mrs. Bolton's presence of mind was completely overpowered by it.

"You shall! You shall! Dear Helen," she replied. "Only you still look so very pale, that just for the present I am quite sure that you ought to think of nothing but keeping yoursel_ quiet."

It was a very scornful sort of smile that curled the lips of Helen as she replied, "It would be quite as easy to make me sit perfectly still with my hands before me, if my dress were in flames, telling me that the fire would burn still more fiercely if I moved. I will not deceive you, Mrs. Bolton, and don't you try to deceive me. It will not answer, for I *will* know every-thing!"

Poor Helen had very magnificent eyes, a fact of which Mrs. Bolton had never been so fully aware as at that moment, when they were turned upon her with a bright intensity of wilfulness that certainly would have suggested the idea of incipient fever to a more experienced person; but Mrs. Bolton's head was full of her own preconceived, and by no means erroneous opinion, that the imagination of the unhappy girl had already suggested to her all that was most terrible as the possible result of the inquiry which was at that moment going on at the Warren House; and, therefore, instead of dispatching a messenger who should bring the doctor with all possible haste to bleed her, she yielded to what was more like a command than a request, that a servant should be dispatched to the Warren House, and ordered to remain there till the result of the examination was made known, and that the moment he had learnt what it was, he should return and make it known to her.

For this result they had not long to wait. Nothing like pre-cipitation, nothing like rashness, nothing in the least degree resembling indifference, shortened the process; but the case was too clear to admit of hesitation in deciding that the late George Rixley Beauchamp had died from the effects of poison!

The still more important question, as to how the poison had been administered, was still unsolved, and on this point the eagerness of inquiry was, if possible, still more vehement than concerning the fact itself.

Mrs. Lambert had very earnestly besought permission to be present during the examination, and this was granted. It was not at that moment deemed necessary to have recourse to dis-section; for on examining the tumbler, which stood on a tabl' close beside his bed, it was found to contain quite enough of ' mixture with which it had been filled to show that poisc' been mixed with it, and no sooner was this fact distinc' by Mr. Foster, than every eye was turned towards Mrs. Lambert, and almost every voice addressed some question to her, all however having the same object, namely to inquire if she thought it possible that her unfortunate master had administered the fatal dose to himself, or, if not, whether her suspicion could rest on any individual as likely to have committed the crime.

She listened to them all, but seemed to wait till they were silent, in order to reply; and then she said, "I cannot wonder that you should all turn to me to explain this dreadful mystery, and if I cannot throw some light upon it, whom can we hope to find who can? I have not only lived in his family above a dozen years, but have always been treated, both by him and his children also, more like a friend than a servant. And yet," she continued, after the pause of a moment or two, during which she seemed meditating on the question that had been asked, "and yet I feel that I am quite as unable to answer you as the greatest stranger here. Some people have said that my master played high when he was in London, and that he sometimes lost large sums of money. Whether this were true or false, I have no means whatever of knowing. I know, indeed, that he sometimes came home from London in a good humour, and sometimes in a very bad one; but as to his being so unhappy as to want to kill himself, I cannot say that any such thought ever entered my head."

"And is there nobody, either young or old, Sarah Lambert, nobody in the whole world that you can think of, who was at all likely to do such a deed?" said John Cummings, looking at her sternly.

She only shook her head in reply, but in a way that evidently showed she thought the question a very idle one.

"There is no use, my good woman, in your looking so very disdainful about it," returned Cummings. "There will be other folks, besides you or I either, who will have to examine into this matter; and, may be, it may come into the heads of some of 'em, that the conduct of the dead gentleman's son may be worth inquiring into."

The face of Mrs. Lambert, as these words reached her ears, became for a moment as red as scarlet; her dark eyes seemed to emit an indignant flash, as she fixed them on the speaker; and there was both anger and scorn in the tone of her voice as she replied, "As to the other folks you talk of, I don't know who they may be; but this, I think, I can venture to say, John Cummings, that you won't find another—man, woman, or child

—sinful enough to utter such a thought as you have now spoken. But I am ashamed of myself for thinking it worth my while to answer you; for there is, I dare say, a great deal more folly than wickedness in your words, and I don't believe you would find another who would think it worth while to listen to such nonsense."

"For the matter of that, Mrs. Lambert," replied the man, with a sneer, "I don't fancy that we should be likely to find everybody exactly of your mind respecting that young gentleman. All the world may not think him such a beautiful fellow, and such a spotless angel, as you do. His poor father himself, for one, wasn't a bit blinded by his handsome looks; for I have heard him say, scores of times, that he wished he had never seen the light of day, for that there was no good in him."

"And because the father was an unnatural father, you take it for granted that the son must be an unnatural son, do you?" returned Mrs. Lambert, trembling with passion, and advancing her clenched fist towards him, as if it was her intention to knock him down.

"Come, come, Sarah Lambert," said another of the sailors, "don't you be after putting yourself in a passion. It's all very natural that you should take the part of the pretty boy you have nursed in any quarrel, or strife, that might chance to come between the father and son, but that is no reason why you should threaten to knock down John Cummings in that fashion."

"I ain't much afraid of Sarah Lambert's fist," said Commodore Jack, with a very disdainful smile, "and, to say the truth, I am not much afraid of her, and her anger, in any way; for I am quite sure that no proper inquiries will be stopped by it, and that is the business that we ought to be thinking of at this present minute. I certainly shan't take upon me to say that it was his young mis-begot son that murdered the squire; but for all that, it would be scarcely lawful, and by no means wise, for any of us to forget what we have all heard down the street yonder, concerning the desperate quarrel that there was between them. But for the matter of that, Sarah Lambert, you might all have quarrelled together for everlasting without any of us taking heed of the matter, if it had not been for the fact of his running away. What do you say to that, Mrs. Lambert?"

"I say," she replied, making a strong effort to recover her ordinary tranquil aspect, "I say that what you are pleased to call running away was no more than what he had done scores of times before. Nobody could ever accuse Master William of neglecting his school-work with Mr. Bolton, and he never would have got a long walk at all, poor boy, if he had not done it by what you are pleased to call running away. It was his common practice, Mr. John Cummings, to set off sometimes before it was light in the morning, that he might get a good walk before his eight o'clock breakfast."

"And was it his common practice to get out at the window, letting himself down by means of his sheets? Was that his common practice, Mrs. Lambert?"

Again the blood mounted to the temples of William's friendly advocate, and she was about to make some angry rejoinder, when she checked herself, and said in her usual quiet manner, "We are both of us very wrong, John Cummings, to dispute in this way over the body of our dead master. It will not be our task to say how, or by whose hands, this dreadful event has been brought about. If the doctor is of opinion that our master's death has been caused by poison, the solemn question as to the hand by which it was administered must be inquired into by those who are appointed by the law of the land for the purpose; and let us hope, for the sake of truth and justice, that those appointed to execute this task will be more cool-headed, and a little less in a passion, than either you or I. However, without any presumptuous wish to decide this question by my own judgment, I must just observe, that at any rate I have a better right to give an opinion about Master William than you can possibly have, for I doubt if you ever exchanged two words with him in the whole course of your life, whereas I have known every thought and feeling of his heart for longer than he can remember what his thoughts and feelings were himself."

"No doubt of it, Sarah Lambert," returned the Commodore, "and it is for that very reason that, if I was upon the jury, I should make a point of not listening to a single word you said. It must be a greenhorn, indeed, who would trust to a mother, or a nurse either, to pass judgment upon their darlings!"

While this angry dialogue was going on in a distant part of the room, Mr. Bolton and Mr. Foster, who were standing near the bed, conversed together in a whisper upon the steps that must be taken before the blackening corse which lay before them should be consigned to earth.

On this point, however, there was no longer any room for discussion. The indications of poison were too distinct to admit of any doubt, and Mr. Bolton hastened to announce this intelligence to his guest, in order to receive his sanction, without further delay, for summoning the coroner of the district.

But, before he reached his home, the result of Mr. Foster's examination had already been communicated to Helen, and he found his wife deeply lamenting her own want of firmness in not keeping it from her at any risk; for it was only too evident that no irritation produced by opposition to her wishes could have produced so terrible an effect as the compliance with them had done; for the unhappy Helen was already in a paroxysm of raving frenzy, which it was terrible to contemplate or listen to.

CHAPTER XXI.

It would be difficult to say which of the three friends who watched her, suffered the most. Her uncle, whose warm, though new born, affection for her seemed that of a fond father, rather than of a more distant relation, stood with his eyes fixed upon her vehemently agitated face till tears bedewed his own. Poor Mrs. Bolton grieved, not only with all the tender feelings of a woman's heart, but she grieved too with all the bitterness of repentance; for might not all this agony have been spared had Helen been sent away, as she ought to have been, before the violent manner of her father's death had been ascertained? But probably it was poor Mr. Bolton himself who suffered the most severely, for Helen was at least unconscious of her own misery; but he could not deny to himself, whatever he might do to others, that the pupil whom he had loved so affectionately, and of whose character and acquirements he had been so boastfully proud, had made himself liable to the suspicion of having murdered his own father, and that with so many fatal features of probability, as to render it almost impossible, even for a friend as partial as himself, to resist their influence.

But not even the unquestionable proof which had reached him of the desperate provocation he had received, nor yet the terribly strong coincidence of his absconding within a few hours probably, or even less, after the deed was done, not even this would have sufficed to conquer his persuasion that the boy was incapable of committing such a crime, had it not been for the desperate agony of his sister.

It was no longer possible to doubt that Helen believed him
guilty of it; every word she uttered in her delirium proved
that her mind was too fully possessed with this idea for her to
dwell for a moment on any other.

"Did I not hear him say the words?" she cried. "Did I not
hear him say that he could kill him? And now he has done
it; now he has brought the dreadful curse upon himself!"
Sometimes she shrieked aloud in utter madness, "William!
William! William! Where are you? Tell me where you are,
only tell me where you are, and I will come to you!"

Meanwhile the necessary steps were taken, and the proper
legal routine followed, by which it was speedily declared that,
"the late George Rixley Beauchamp, Esquire, of Beauchamp
Park, in the County of Surrey, had been found in his bed dead
from the effects of poison; the same having been detected in
the intestines in amply sufficient quantity to cause death, and a
portion thereof having likewise been discovered mixed with the
liquid remaining in a glass tumbler placed beside the deceased,
and within reach of his hand; but whether wilfully administered
by himself, or surreptitiously by another, there was no evidence
to show."

Such was the verdict recorded by the coroner, and such was
the conscientious belief of those who delivered the verdict; but
there were others who maintained a different opinion, and who
scrupled not to declare their conviction that the drug had been
administered by the son of the deceased.

The warfare between John Cummings and Sarah Lambert on
this point did not cease, both remaining as firm in their respective opinions as they had shown themselves during the scene
which had taken place in the dead man's room, when the cause
of his death had been ascertained by Mr. Foster.

Sarah Lambert had declared, before the people assembled in
the room on that occasion had separated, that those who were
wicked enough to accuse an innocent boy of such a dreadful
crime, would assuredly be made to blush for their folly, and
their sin; for though it was likely enough that the poor lad had
been out of the way of hearing what was going on at Crumpton, they would be sure to hear of him before it was long, and
then he should come forward, and speak for himself, and put his
vile accusers to shame!

Her deep sense of her own degraded position, now known
not only to Mr. and Mrs. Bolton, but doubtless to Helen's uncle
also, rendering the idea of presenting herself at the parsonage

intolerable to her, and her longing wish to see the suffering sister being thus rendered abortive, she determined, either from a miserable feeling of restlessness, or else from the real hope of finding him, to set off herself in search of the brother.

After quietly sitting in deep meditation for some minutes in the sad and solitary school-room, she determined to go at once to Falmouth, still thinking it probable that if he had really run off, in the hope of finding some means of existence less distasteful to him than what his father had proposed, he would be more likely to seek it there, than by wandering far and wide among villages where he was utterly unknown.

That she, at least, believed him innocent of the crime that had been laid to his charge, was fully proved by the earnest zeal with which she set out to find him; for had it been otherwise, she would most assuredly have done everything in her power to facilitate his escape instead of impeding it.

To Falmouth therefore she went, and had not been much above half an hour in the town before she learnt from perfectly good authority, that William Rixley had sailed in a little cruising vessel, strongly suspected by some of its captain's most intimate friends, of doing quite as much business in the smuggling line, as in any other.

"And to what port was the vessel bound?" demanded Mrs. Lambert, anxiously.

"Why as to that," replied the old nautical acquaintance to whom she had addressed herself, "we don't none of us make any particular inquiries when the 'Beautiful Polly' sets off upon a cruise, as to what port she intends to make, because it is not always maybe, that the captain is quite certain upon that point himself."

Mrs. Lambert paid for this confidential hint by the tolerant smile that was expected from her; and then, somehow or other, made her way back again to the Warren House, weary enough in limb, for she had walked a great part of the way, but apparently more calm in spirit than when she set out.

She must have felt indeed that she had done all she could do to find the unfortunate son of a most guilty father, in the hope that his own testimony might suffice to clear him of all suspicion of the crime of which he had been accused, and though she had failed in this, she had at least the consolation of feeling, that in all human probability he was beyond the reach of any present annoyance from the dreadful suspicion that attached to him.

There was now but one thing left in the place where she had passed the last twelve years of her life to which her affections clung; the thought of Helen being taken away to the distant spot which was to be her future home without her once more seeing her was dreadful, and yet there were moments when the idea that this dearly loved child would enter upon life as the wealthy heiress of her false, her cruel, her unnatural father, produced a degree of happiness at her heart's core which seemed to console her for everything she had suffered, or could suffer.

Any one who had watched the bright flashing of her beautiful and triumphant eye during these moments, would have fancied they were contemplating a proud woman who had accomplished the first and dearest object of her life.

But might she not see her at once? Doubtless her own disgraceful story was already known to the uncle whose task it would be to watch henceforward over the beautiful and wealthy orphan who had no other protector left; and ought not the very first act of his protecting care be to remove her for ever from the degradation of associating with her father's mistress?

"Shall I ask and be refused? Or shall I let her go without making any effort to press her once more to my heart?" Such were the questionings in which she passed a great portion of the night that followed her return from Falmouth; but the news which greeted her the next morning was of a nature to make her forget all other misery, for she was told that Helen was in a frenzy fever, and not expected to survive the day.

There was no room for any further doubt as to what she should do. Mrs. Lambert, pale and haggard, rushed to the parsonage, entered it by the door which led to the kitchen, and spared the guardian friends of poor Helen the difficult task of deciding whether she should be admitted, or not, by making her way to the room in which she had already seen her, without speaking a word to any one.

On first entering the room it appeared to her to be perfectly dark, and she only guessed she had not blundered by hearing a low moaning sound that proceeded from the bed. But Almeria Lambert was not a person to endure suspense of any kind. She approached the glimmering light which proceeded from the nearly closed window shutters, and threw them open.

A terrible foreboding made her feel that she was about to behold a dreadful spectacle; she thought that she might see her darling lying in the pangs of death before her; but even this could scarcely have been felt as more piteously sad than the reality that met her eye.

It was Helen! It *must* be Helen, for it could be no one else, who lay stretched before her; but it is difficult to do justice by description to the change between what she was, and what she had been.

She was lying on her back, with a wet napkin bound round her forehead, but neither napkin, nor pillow, were more completely colourless than her face. She had been bled so copiously that she had no longer strength to rave with the vehemence which had preceded her present state, but there was no trace of reason in the quick movement of her vacant eye, nor in the ceaseless moanings which she uttered, sometimes articulately, and sometimes not. Her dark brown hair lay scattered round her in dishevelled curls, that hung down over the bed-clothes to the very tips of her pale fingers, round which she incessantly kept twisting it. The tone of her voice was completely altered, and had a piteous trembling in it which gave the idea of excessive weakness.

Mrs. Lambert stood for a moment at the bottom of the bed as if transfixed, and then bending over her, she whispered, in a voice almost as tremulous as her own, "And is this all that is left of my child? Is this my beauteous Helen? Is this my peerless heiress?" And then covering her face with her hands, she fell on her knees and rather groaned, than distinctly uttered the words, "My God! I have sinned, and I am punished!"

There was by the side of the bed which was furthest from the door of entrance, a silent, motionless figure, which, in the vehement agitation of Mrs. Lambert, had been perfectly invisible, or, at any rate, perfectly unnoticed by her. It was the quiet, suffering, sympathising Mrs. Bolton, who, fully persuaded that poor Helen was dying, had herself undertaken to watch beside her, in preference to permitting any servant to listen to her ravings, in which she uniformly declared her conviction that her father had died by the hand of her brother.

Whether the fact were so, or not, there was as yet no certain evidence to show; and Mrs. Bolton humanely, and wisely, determined that the unfortunate young man should not be robbed of the benefit of this doubt by the delirious accusations of his wretched sister.

Mrs. Bolton now came forward, and, gently approaching the unhappy intruder, begged her, in a whisper, to rise, and compose herself. "Though we have little or no hope of saving her," she said, "we are still enjoined by Mr. Foster to keep her perfectly quiet, that being, he assures us, the only possible chance we can give her in aid of her youth, and fine constitution."

Mrs. Lambert said nothing in reply, but she rose from her knees, and fixing her eyes upon Helen, stood silently and motionless before her.

Whether it were from seeing this figure suddenly placed before her, or from being roused by the strong light, which the opening of the shutters had let in upon the room, it would be impossible to say; but certain it is, that the eyes of Helen, now stedfastly fixed upon Mrs. Lambert, had more appearance of consciousness of what was before them than had been perceptible since her delirium began.

Yet still it was evident that she by no means very clearly understood who it was who was looking at her so earnestly; but, by degrees, the vacant expression of her countenance seemed to give way before a touch of memory, for the unmeaning look of idiot indifference gradually became changed into a contracted brow, and an expression of great suffering. And presently she spoke, but it was in so weak a whisper, that it required an eagerly attentive ear to understand what she said.

"He told me so himself, Sarah Lambert, he did! he did!" were the first words distinctly audible, and Mrs. Lambert, perceiving she was recognised, changed her position, and placing herself at the bedside, bent down and took her hand.

But though the action caused poor Helen to raise her eyes to the face which hung over her, their vacant stare showed but too plainly that the awakened intelligence, which had seemed to beam from them for a moment, had passed away.

"I believe it is better not to speak to her," whispered Mrs. Bolton; to which the nurse of many years made no other reply, than again placing herself on her knees, and, though still retaining the hand she had taken, remaining as motionless as a statue.

But not so the poor patient. She presently gave symptoms of being restless, and uneasy, still remaining stretched upon her back, but turning her head from side to side upon the pillow with a movement every moment increasing in rapidity. "We have been wrong to disturb her," again whispered Mrs. Bolton, "it is just what the doctor told us to avoid! Let me beg of you to go down stairs, Mrs. Lambert! 1

promise you faithfully, that you shall be sent to, if there is the least change."

Mrs. Lambert felt that she dared not disobey, and gently disengaging her hand from the burning fingers which were now grasping it tightly, she rose and noiselessly approached the door. But this sufficed again to awaken the attention of the poor sufferer, and with a sudden effort she raised herself in the bed, and, stretching out her arms towards her nurse, exclaimed distinctly, "That is Sarah Lambert! and she is going away from me again! Cruel, cruel, Sarah! I should not have been ill, and obliged to lie here both night and day if you had stayed with me! You ought to have stayed with me, Sarah Lambert! You know that you ought not to have gone away from me!"

This plaintive and almost sobbing remonstrance immediately arrested Mrs. Lambert's steps, but it was to Mrs. Bolton that she addressed herself, and not to Helen.

"She has recovered her senses," she said, in a low whisper. "You cannot wish, madam, that I should leave her now?"

"I know not what to think!" replied poor Mrs. Bolton. "Her seeing and knowing you may make her worse than ever!"

"Surely, Mrs. Bolton, when she opposes my going, you would not insist upon it?"

"I know not what to do!" reiterated the poor lady, "his last words were, 'let her be kept perfectly quiet.'"

"Let Mr. Foster be instantly sent for," returned Mrs. Lambert, almost in a voice of authority. "Trust me she will not be the less quiet because I am near her. Send at once for Mr. Foster, and let us have the assistance of his judgment. I will stay with her the while, as she wishes me to do, but I will not converse with her."

And so saying, Mrs. Lambert, without waiting for any reply, placed a chair close beside the bed, and seated herself in it.

While these few words were passing between her ill-matched attendants, the eyes of Helen were again closed, and she remained for a moment perfectly still, upon observing which, Mrs. Bolton said, "Perhaps if we leave her quite to herself she will go to sleep."

It was immediately evident that these words were heard, and understood by Helen, for her eyes were again opened, and, after looking about her vaguely for a moment, she again fixed them on Mrs. Lambert, and made an effort to reach her with her hand; nor was the effort vain. The watchful nurse gently took possession of that hand, and having given it a gentle pressure, almost fancied that she felt a gentle pressure in return.

Mrs. Bolton had already left the room to dispatch a messenger for the doctor, whose advise she felt was more than ever needed; and then, Helen, after giving one lingering languid glance at the face of her nurse, closed her eyes, and presently gave evidence by her breathing, that she really had fallen asleep.

CHAPTER XXII.

HELEN RIXLEY, or, begging the heiress's pardon, Helen Beauchamp, like many another young creature, who has terrified the hearts that cling to them by appearing at the point of death, rallied at the very moment when it appeared most certain that all hope was gone, and very speedily made it evident that whatever other perils might threaten, her death was not just at present of the number.

Mr. Foster knew a great deal too well what he was about not to take advantage of Mrs. Lambert's very evident influence over his patient; but Mr. Bolton, who very plainly perceived that her attendance upon Helen was extremely distasteful to her uncle, had thought it right to hint this to Mr. Foster; but his only reply was, "I should have given up the case, Mr. Bolton, had you said this two days ago. The cause of Miss Beauchamp's malady was mental; and had not this favourite nurse come forward to help me, I sincerely believe we should have lost her."

"It is most unfortunate," returned Mr. Bolton, "that such powerful reasons should exist to render her attendance objectionable!"

"Certainly it is unfortunate," replied the doctor; "and I have been for years pretty nearly as well aware of this as I am at present. Had the same suspicion been awakened in your mind, Mr. Bolton," he continued, "I imagine that it would have been your duty to interfere, with counsel at least, though you might not have had authority, in order to get rid of her; but my vocation was different. Moreover, I had abundant oppor-

tunity for studying the real state of affairs at the Warren
House; and the result of this was, my feeling morally certain
that, though I might have power to do mischief, I had none to
do good, as far at least as getting rid of this decidedly objectionable attendant upon the young lady. But if I thought it
right to abstain from any such attempt, then, of course I must
think a contrary line of conduct infinitely more injudicious now;
for, in the first place, Helen is happily now so well protected as
to satisfy her most anxious friends as to her safety; and, in
the next, the question has been, in my opinion, one of life or
death; so that I only conceived myself free to act in my
medical capacity."

"Assuredly, Mr. Foster," replied the curate of Crumpton;
"and I should have blamed you greatly had you acted otherwise. But now that, thank God, this desperate state of things
no longer continues, we may certainly, without scruple, comply
with the wish of her uncle, that the attendance of Mrs. Lambert
should be dispensed with."

"Well, Sir," rejoined Mr. Foster, "I thank God, as you do,
that the question is no longer a medical one; and, therefore,
of course, I have nothing to do with it."

It was, in short, very evident that the office of dismissing
Mrs. Lambert was one which the village doctor did not wish
to take upon himself; neither did it appear that the clergyman of the parish was at all inclined to perform it personally,
for he asked his gentle little wife if she did not think it would
be more suitable and less offensive for her to hint that their
small house, being rather more than full, her departure would
be convenient? But his gentle little wife demurred; she did
not like the commission; but she suggested that Mr. Rixley
might make it known that he wished to hasten his departure:
and she promised that if he did this, she would undertake
to tell Mrs. Lambert that they all thought her separation
from Helen ought not to be put off till the very last
moment, lest the agitation arising from it might render her
less able to undertake the journey.

This device answered completely; Mrs. Lambert adopted
the proposal quite as eagerly as it was made. It was very
evident that she, too, dreaded the moment, and that, too, for
herself as well as for Helen, for her lip trembled as she
talked of it.

"Yes!" she said, "it is a trial—a trial for us both! For
me, it matters not. But for her, it must be made as easy as

possible. She shall not know that she is seeing me for the last time."

"Indeed, Mrs. Lambert, if you can manage that," replied Mrs. Bolton, "it will be saving her from great suffering. I never saw a young person so strongly attached to a nurse, as she is to you."

"Yes. There has been for a good many years a strong attachment between us," returned the other, with dry and forced composure. "It is not probable," she added, "that any one should even guess how much I have loved her; and as to their knowing it, that is a good deal less likely still."

She sat silent for a few minutes, covering her face with both her hands; and when she looked up again, the whole expression of her features was changed. It was almost impossible that any face could display less of tenderness, or speak more intelligibly of unconquerable firmness of purpose, than hers did at that moment.

Had she objected to parting with Helen, instead of so readily agreeing to it, Mrs. Bolton could not have looked at her at that moment without alarm, for the least observant eye could not fail in perceiving that *to will* and *to do* were not in her case very likely to be separated.

This conversation took place in the room in which Helen slept; and the moment had been selected by Mrs. Bolton as being safe from any interruption from her, because she had left it to accept her uncle's invitation to take a short airing upon the lawn, supported by his arm. She had done this twice before, and had seemed the better for it.

And now Mrs. Bolton rose, very greatly comforted at having performed her task so effectually.

"We must not let her walk too long," said she, looking out of the window.

"Is she there?" said the discarded nurse, in a voice so strange, that it made Mrs. Bolton start, as if she had suddenly heard that of an interloper, whom she did not know.

"Yes," replied she, "Helen is walking on the lawn. Her uncle is very kind and thoughtful; but women make the best nurses, Mrs. Lambert." And with these words she left the room.

For half a moment the suffering being she left in it remained stationary between the door and the window; but she trembled, as she stood, from head to foot—and then, with what seemed a desperate effort, she approached that open window, and, concealing herself behind its curtain, looked out upon the lawn.

Mrs. Bolton had reported truly. Helen was there, her arm resting upon that of her uncle, with the air of one who wanted support; but she was looking up at him affectionately, and there was a smile upon her countenance.

"Helen! my beautiful Helen! my lovely, gifted, high-born, wealthy heiress! you shall be the honoured bride of the rich and the noble! No tyrant voice, no tyrant glance, shall ever crush thee more!"

As she murmured these words she clasped her hands together, letting the curtain she had held before her fall aside. The moving drapery caught the eye of Helen, and she looked up, smiled, and nodded affectionately, and then passed on. "It is over!" whispered Almeria Lambert to her heart. "The rest will be very easy!"

<center>~~~~~~~~~~~~~~~~</center>

CHAPTER XXIII.

On re-entering the house Helen declared that her walk had done her much good, that she felt a great deal better, and that she should like very much to take her tea in the parlour—an announcement which was received with great satisfaction by both host and hostess, who met her at the door. There was a general protest, however, against her mounting to her room to deposit her bonnet and shawl; and she, therefore, passed on into the parlour, and was carefully placed on the sofa by her watchful friends. It was declared on all sides, however, that, notwithstanding her evident improvement, she must retire early to rest; to which she dutifully agreed, though declaring at the same time that she really felt "almost quite well again."

When the servant removed the tea-tray, she whispered a few words in the ear of her mistress, who immediately got up, and followed her out of the room. In the hall, she found Mrs. Lambert, in her bonnet and shawl, waiting for her.

"Are you going out, Mrs. Lambert?" said she; "Miss Helen will be going to bed immediately."

"May I speak to you for one moment in the library, madam?" returned the nurse.

Mrs. Bolton, remembering what had passed between them a few hours before, immediately guessed her purpose; and though half-frightened by its sudddenness, and by her fears as to its effect upon Helen, she still experienced a feeling of relief, from her conviction that the task she had so much dreaded was very nearly accomplished. Her only reply to the request of Mrs. Lambert was opening the door of the library, and entering the room.

Mrs. Lambert followed her, and closed the door. "I have thought it best, madam," she said, "to act at once upon your suggestion. The sooner Miss Beauchamp leaves this place, the better. She has a pang to suffer, but it must be borne; and the sooner it comes, the sooner it will be over. I have taken the liberty of using the writing materials which I found in Miss Beauchamp's room; and after you left me there, I wrote this letter to her. You are perfectly at liberty to read it, madam, and to show it to her uncle, and to Mr. Bolton, before it is delivered to her. I should recommend her not receiving it till to-morrow morning; but when she goes to bed, and expresses surprise, perhaps, at not finding me in her room to undress her, I think it will be best to tell her that I had received a message from a person I wanted to see on business, and that I should probably be detained too late to return to the parsonage to-night. This will send her to bed without any suspicion that she has seen me for the last time; and the longer the possibility of our meeting again is permitted to remain with her, the better; at least, till her health and strength are completely restored.—And in my judgment," added the unhappy woman, with a faltering accent, strangely unlike her usual manner of speaking, "in my judgment, it would be much better for her if she could be permitted to live and die without knowing that she had ever suffered the degradation of loving, and being loved by one unworthy to approach her."

"Your judgment respecting everything connected with Helen ought to be listened to with great attention," replied Mrs. Bolton, with all the quick, kind sympathy of a woman's heart; nor ought it to be recorded against the spotless wife and happy mother, as a sin, though she laid her hand with a friendly pressure on the arm of the trembling woman before her as she said it.

Had there been less of desperate sternness in the condition into which Mrs. Lambert had screwed her own spirit, she might have been tempted to kneel before the gentle being, who so evidently pitied sufferings which she never had, nor ever could feel; but, as it was, she only turned her head aside, and remained silent for a moment, and then said, "Here is the letter, madam. If you think it will assist the purpose which her friends have in view, you will give it to her: if not, destroy it, if you please, and say to her on the subject of my disappearance whatever may appear most judicious to yourself, and to those who act with you."

Having said this, she bowed her head, and left the room with a rapid step, as if to escape further parley.

Mrs. Bolton's first act of obedience to her wishes, was putting the unread letter in her pocket, and returning with an air of so much composure to the parlour, that Helen, who was listening smilingly to her uncle's description of what he called his rather ugly daughter and his very ill-behaved son, did not even perceive her entrance.

But she was not permitted to amuse herself in this manner long, before it was voted, in a committee of the whole tea-table, that it was high time for her to go to bed. Her very docile compliance was a proof, perhaps, that she thought so too; and, leaning on the arm of her uncle, preceded by a candle in the hand of her kind hostess, she mounted the stairs to her room.

"Where is Sarah Lambert?" were the first words she uttered on entering it.

"We must do without her to-night, my dear Helen," replied Mrs. Bolton, "for she has been sent for from the Warren House by some person who wished to speak to her on business. We shall be able to do without her; shall we not, dearest?"

"Indeed, my dear Mrs. Bolton," replied Helen, "everybody in your house is so very kind to me, that I must be a very whimsical girl if I fancied that I wanted anybody out of it." And in truth, all the little thoughtful attentions which she had of late received from her faithful nurse were now very ably performed by good Mrs. Bolton herself, and the 'Good nights!' exchanged between them at parting were equally cordial on both sides.

This more than hospitable attention was repeated on the following morning, and then poor Helen, despite a strong

wish not to betray any such feeling, certainly did look as if
she wondered why Sarah Lambert did not present herself.

"I am sure you are wondering, Helen, that your nurse is not
come back again to look after you; but I suspect that something unexpected has happened, which has detained her, for
she has written to you instead of coming."

Helen took the letter from the hand of Mrs. Bolton, but
looked more surprised than alarmed at receiving it.

"Will you read it now, dear, or after breakfast?" said
Mrs. Bolton. "The two gentlemen are waiting for us at the
breakfast-table, but it will not hurt them to wait a little
longer, if you wish to read your letter before you go down."

"Let me follow you, dearest Mrs. Bolton; may I?"
returned Helen. "Perhaps she may have heard something
about William."

Though this explanation for her wishing to read the letter
in private was neither very explicit nor very satisfactory, it
was listened to as if it were both, and Mrs. Bolton left her.

Scarcely had she closed the door behind her, before the
letter was opened. It was as follows:—

"I hope, my dearest child, that your judgment will accord
with mine in approving what I am about to do. We need
not tell each other, Helen, that William is the great object that
occupies our thoughts, and, therefore, you will not think any
apology necessary for my running away from you—(even at
the moment previous to your departure)—when I tell you
that I *think* I may be able to trace him, if I set about the
task in person. But, if I decide on doing this, I have not a
moment to lose. It is not very likely that I should be able to
give you constant, or even frequent information of my expedition, for I do not intend to confine my search to one country
only; but, whenever it is possible for me to write to you, I will
do so; and, should a longer interval occur than such an enterprise may reasonably account for, why then, my dearest child,
you may mourn for your faithful nurse as for one no longer to
be counted among the living. But let us hope that I may still
be useful to you, and that, through my means, the brother so
justly dear to you may be induced to return to the land of his
birth, where I know, as well as you do, my dear child, that he
will never want a friend as long as you remain alive in it. And
now, dearest Helen, I must say farewell. I have undertaken a
difficult enterprise, but my courage is strengthened by my con-

viction that you will be often with me in spirit, and that, whether
I live or die, you will still continue to love your affectionate and
faithful nurse,

"SARAH LAMBERT."

This letter, temperately and carefully as it was written, was
not read by Helen without strong emotion—much stronger,
certainly, than was desirable for an invalid, whose nerves had
been already so severely shaken; but, nevertheless, the three
friends to whom she communicated its contents, congratulated
themselves, and each other, that the strangely-situated young
creature, for whom they were so deeply interested, had passed
so well through one of the difficult and very trying moments from
which all their tender care could not entirely protect her; nor
could they, either of them, refuse to acknowledge a sentiment
in which a strange mixture of gratitude, and even of esteem,
was mixed with the feeling of earnest reprobation which led
them to hope that they might never hear of Sarah Lambert
again.

As to Helen herself, she suffered infinitely less than she would
have done, had not an almost superstitious feeling of confidence
in the wisdom and perseverance of her nurse led her to
anticipate the happiest results from the efforts she was about
to make for the recovery of William.

CHAPTER XXIV.

How far this statement of Mrs. Lambert's intentions contained
the record of her real projects, or how far it might have been
made for the purpose of satisfactorily accounting to Helen for
her absence, may be seen hereafter; at any rate, it had the
happiest effect on the spirits of the invalid, for not only did it
completely tranquillize her mind under the heavy affliction of
parting with her nurse, but it created more cheering hopes
respecting her brother than she had felt since she had first
heard of his absence.

Her confidence in the judgment and the firm affection of
Sarah Lambert, was unbounded; and she could scarcely be said

to feel any doubt either as to her success in finding him, or in
her power of assisting him afterwards. "Her first object will
be to bring us together again," thought Helen. "But yet—if
it would be best not—if it would be dangerous for my poor
William to come to me, why then she will watch over him till
the danger is over."

This was her next thought; and dreadful as was the pain
occasioned by the dark suspicion which led to this after thought,
it was immeasurably softened by the idea that he would soon
have Sarah with him. So healing, in truth, was this hope,
that though it could not chase away the feeling that the frightful accusation uttered by Cummings *might* be true, it gave birth
to a whole host of reasons for believing that it was false; and
one of the brightest blessings of Helen's age is the strong propensity to believe pretty nearly everything that we wish should
be true.

In this state of things the departure of Helen with her uncle
was robbed of almost all the melancholy features which must
have attended it, had no such hope as that suggested by the
letter of Mrs. Lambert reached her. As it was, there was,
despite all the painful and agitating circumstances through
which she had recently passed, a considerable mixture of that
delightful buoyancy, made up of present novelty and future
hope, which in early youth gives brightness to almost everything we look upon.

The result of this upon her companion was most happy also,
for more than once it had happened to him, when gazing with
newly-awakened affection upon her lovely face, to feel a painful
doubt as to the probability of her feeling unhappy, and ill at
ease, from being so suddenly removed from all that was familiar
and dear to her, and placed amidst a family of strangers.

But there was nothing now in the manner of Helen to justify
such misgivings. She had been ill, and now she felt well
again; she had been desperately terrified, and now her terrors
were soothed; her life had hitherto been as destitute of anything like real freedom as that of a squirrel, whose abounding
activity can take it no inch beyond the unvaried routine of its
unmeaning scamper; and now every glance showed her something new, and every word spoken by her kind companion made
her look forward to future scenes more new and more interesting still.

In short, instead of being fatigued or in any way injured by
her rapid journey to London, she was very greatly the better for

it, and when she entered the little drawing-room of her uncle in Davies Street, the family group she found there were almost startled at seeing the tall and lovely girl who entered among them, instead of the sickly, melancholy-looking child they expected.

This family group consisted of the still lovely Mrs. Rixley, her son Henry, and her daughter Anne.

There were certainly many circumstances connected with this newly-found relative, which tended to give a feeling of restraint and awkwardness to their meeting. In the first place she was the child of a near relative who had never been known to the two younger Rixleys, and scarcely to their mother either, but as a declared and inveterate enemy. In the next, the fact was patent among them that had this stranger young lady been out of the way, the noble property, of which she, poor child, had never heard till within the last miserable few weeks, but of which they had certainly been accustomed to hear a good deal, would have been their own.

It cannot be denied that these facts, well established, and clearly remembered, were not calculated to make them feel quite as affectionate, as they were curious concerning her. But a lovely young face is decidedly a very fascinating object. There is no denying it, and in this case, as in a million more upon record, all foregone conclusions were forgotten as they looked at her; and a very few seconds sufficed to make her reception all that her kind uncle wished it to be.

As to the impressions produced on Helen herself, they were quite as favourable towards the wished-for result of mutually kind feeling as those of her newly-found relatives; nay, perhaps, young as she was, there was more of wisdom as to the source of their formation than could be easily pointed out in those she had inspired. For it was not beauty that had captivated her. Not, indeed, that her cousin Anne at all deserved the epithet of "ugly," which had been bestowed on her by her father.

Anne Rixley was not ugly, but neither was she beautiful; nor was her brother handsome. Their mother, indeed, might still fairly be described as both, or either; but the beauty of forty-five is not so lovely in the eyes of fourteen, as it may appear to those of riper judgment.

No! It was not the beauty of her kinsfolk which had captivated Helen; but nevertheless she was captivated.

In the countenance of Mrs. Rixley there was as charming a mixture of goodness, and intelligence, as could well be expressed by human features; nobody who had eyes capable of detecting either, could feel a doubt upon the subject. In the young, fresh, guileless physiognomy of Anne might be read with equal facility all that makes youth and innocence most lovable, while there was something in the fine broad forehead that gave goodly promise of what was ripening within. And as to Henry, although a grave old Don might have been likely to detect rather a superabundant quantity of latent sauciness, Helen only saw a look of animation and light-heartedness that seemed to promise very pleasant companionship. In short, within a very few minutes after these very near relations, but very perfect strangers, had been introduced to each other, they were in a fair way of becoming excellent friends.

❋ ❋ ❋ ❋ ❋ ❋

There was of course a great deal of business to be got through before Helen's present manner of life could be decided on ; but though many things were to be attended to, there was no difficulty in the arrangement of any of them, nor is it necessary to rehearse the details of these arrangements. Mr. Rixley was appointed personal guardian to the young heiress, and as his small London house could not accommodate her, and the male and female servant appointed to attend her, it was finally settled that her uncle should give up his London curacy, and, very greatly to the delight of the country-bred Helen, that the whole family should take up their residence at Beauchamp Park. The chief, perhaps the only objection to this arrangement, arose from the difficulty of obtaining *finishing* masters for the heiress at the distance of forty miles from London.

If the conversation by which this knotty point was finally settled, be given to the reader, it may enlighten him a little as to the terms on which Helen and her newly-found family lived together. This conversation took place the morning after she had been taken to make a first visit to the noble mansion which was to be her future home.

"I am very glad, dear Helen," said her uncle kindly, " that the house and grounds of Beauchamp Park please you so greatly. I should have been sadly disappointed, if you had not liked the place."

"Like it, Uncle Rixley !" returned Helen, throwing up both hands and eyes in astonishment at his phrase. "Did you really think it possible in your heart that I should *not* like it ? "

"Possible ? Yes certainly, Helen, I thought it was possible.

You have seemed to be so much amused by all the fine sights we have been showing you in London, that I should have been but little surprised to hear you say that you should not like living at Beauchamp Park at all," replied her uncle.

"But I don't want to live in the sight-seeing places, Uncle Rixley," returned Helen, laughing; "should you really think it a good plan for us all to take a house next door to the Museum, so that we might conveniently run in and out there three or four times a day?"

"Not exactly that, Helen," he replied with great good humour, "but there is a long interval between living next door to one favourite exhibition, and being at forty miles distant from all. However, there may be greater objections than that. How are we to get proper finishing masters for you, young lady?"

"Oh uncle! uncle! don't finish me!" she exclaimed, clasping her hands, and looking beseechingly in his face. "I do assure you beforehand, that it would never answer! I know that I am not a sort of person that can ever be finished. I have read a great deal about a finished education, and I am quite certain that it would not do for me."

"But you draw so well, Helen, and are so very fond of it," said her aunt, "that I should have thought you would have liked nothing so well as having a good master."

"Perhaps Helen thinks that she has been too well taught already to require any new master," said Henry, smiling.

"I do not know whether you say that as a joke, Cousin Henry," she replied, "but if you say it in earnest, I can tell you that you are quite right. If I were to live a thousand years I should never like to remember that I ever had draw-ing lessons from anybody, except my mamma. I know that I was not very old when she died, very little more than twelve, but that does not signify. I am quite certain that nobody can ever teach me as well as she taught me. You look as if you were ready to laugh again, Cousin Henry, and I dare say you think me a very conceited girl for boasting so much about my mother. But my mamma really was quite out of the common way as to the power of teaching. It was not only draw-ing, but music, and French, and Italian, and everything. My mamma was brought up as a governess, or a teacher at a school, whichever came in her way first. She has told me all about it over and over again. Dear, dear mamma! She thought it might be useful to me in case I might ever be obliged to main-

tain myself in the same way! I don't believe she ever heard
of Beauchamp Park in her life, and sure I am that she never
thought it would belong to me. But as things have turned out,
I really don't think there is any good reason for my trying to
make myself into a little girl again. I don't think I should
learn anything but naughtiness. I should hate my masters, and
try, very likely, to make Henry laugh at them, instead of
laughing at me, for you may be very sure I should not think
them so clever as my mamma."

Mr. Rixley very patiently, and very willingly, let her run on
thus, for he wished to know her thoroughly before he decided
the important question, whether it would be best to use the
authority that was vested in him, in order that the next year or
two might be so employed, as to supply the educational defi-
ciencies of those which had intervened since her mother's death,
or to yield to her wishes, which it was easy to see would be
somewhat peremptorily pronounced, and suffer her to be happy
her own way.

He was determined, however, that, if possible, he would
decide on nothing hastily, for he felt that the duty he had to
discharge was an important one.

After the silence of a moment he said, "How then, my dear
Helen, would you propose, yourself, to occupy the time that has
yet to elapse before you can take your place in society as a
woman?"

Helen's bright eye was raised to his face with sudden quickness, and she replied, "I would read, read, read!"

"Bravo, Helen!" exclaimed her Cousin Henry, clapping his
hands, "I don't think she is quite a fool, after all. I have a
great notion myself that if the younger part of the divine sex
were, either from whim, or wisdom, to read a little more, and
study accomplishments a little less, it might be better for all
parties concerned."

"If you have such a notion, Cousin Henry," she replied, with
a good deal of comic solemnity, "I presume that my uncle will
feel no further doubt upon the subject. The question is settled;
is it not? dear uncle! dear aunt! say that the question is
settled, and that we shall all go and live together at
Beauchamp Park." The pair she addressed looked at her,
and looked at each other in a way that certainly did not seem
to threaten any very vehement opposition to her wishes; but as
the answer was delayed, probably because each was waiting for
the other to speak first, Helen rose from her chair, and bound-

ing across the room to her uncle, put her arms around his neck, and whispered in his ear, " Was not my grandmamma Rixley, whose maiden name was Beauchamp, born and bred there ? "

" She has gained her cause, ladies and gentlemen," said her uncle, returning her caress. " You may all pack up your properties. Beauchamp Park must be our home till this self-willed young lady bestows it with her own hand upon a master."

" Thank you! oh, thank you! thank you!" cried the delighted girl. " Shall we not, all of us, feel more happy in that beautiful large place, than jammed into this narrow little street ? You and I, Anne, will have one whole garden entirely to ourselves. Won't we have flowers by the bushel ? "

Upon being thus appealed to, Anne, who had sat profoundly silent, while profoundly listening, stood up to meet her cousin, who she saw was approaching her, and receiving on her fair rosy cheek the cordial kiss that was offered her, exclaimed in accents of the most cordial delight, " Oh, Helen, dear! you have made me so very happy! To live at Beauchamp Park! To live there for years, perhaps! I feel as if I were dreaming, and that it was all too wild and delightful to be true."

" Charming," cried Helen, gaily repeating her kiss. " But what says my dear gentle aunt to it? " she added, playfully approaching Mrs. Rixley, with her hands joined, beseechingly.

" I must answer like my happy-looking girl here, I think," returned her aunt. " The scheme would appear to me perfect, were it not a little too splendid to seem true."

" Ay, there's the rub," said Mr. Rixley, gently shaking his head. " The allowance made for you by the Court of Chancery, Helen, is two thousand a year, and a very noble allowance it is. But I greatly doubt if it will be found sufficient to support such an establishment as would be suitable for Beauchamp Park."

" Then let us all make up our minds, dear uncle, to live at Beauchamp Park with an establishment not suitable to it. I am quite sure that we should not be one bit the less happy for doing so. An establishment means servants, and carriages, and horses, does it not ? "

" Exactly so, Helen," he replied.

" Well then, we must do without horses and carriages, and manage so cleverly as not to want many servants. I will be your lady's maid, Anne, if you will be mine. Shall we ? "

" I can dress hair," returned Anne, joyfully clapping her hands.

" And I can iron beautifully," returned Helen, with equal

glee, " and as to my dear aunt," she continued in a more grave and business-like tone, " she can take her own factotum Martha with her, and her own cook too, and her own nice neat footman, and so you see, we shall not want anything but a housemaid to dust and sweep the rooms a little, for to be sure it is a very large house."

" Yes, it certainly is a large house," returned Mr. Rixley, smiling. "But you have not provided for your equipage, Miss Beauchamp. What sort of carriage do you propose to have?"

" Why, Mr. Rixley, as far as I myself am concerned, I should prefer a donkey for the present ; and as I know that donkeys are neither very troublesome nor expensive, I think we may afford to keep another for Anne; and then I think that we two should be as independent, and as well able to explore all the country round us, quite as much as prudent young ladies ought to desire. As to my aunt, and you, uncle, if I might have my own way, and that we should not find it too extravagant, I should like to have ·a comfortable little open carriage, so light that it might be drawn by a pony, like Mr. Bolton's, you know, uncle. And as to my Cousin Henry, if he will be very agreeable and very obedient, Anne and I will give him leave to follow our donkeys with a stick in his hand, to keep them in order."

" Upon my word, Helen," said her uncle, who had listened to her smilingly, but with a good deal of attention—" upon my word, I think you seem to have a very fair notion of good management; and if you are pretty tolerably in earnest in your little sketch, I really think this rather startling scheme may be put in execution without much danger of our disgracing ourselves by running in debt; but young as you are, my dear girl, I am mistaken in you if you cannot perceive, as clearly as I do myself, that there would be something lamentably disgraceful in an elderly clergyman, who, living very quietly, and with the most strict economy, during his past life, should suddenly place himself at the head of a splendid establish-ment as the guardian of a wealthy ward, and then run her into debt and difficulties in order to indulge his family by letting them live in a fine house."

To which Helen, who, in her turn, had listened with great attention, replied, " I do not believe, Uncle Rixley, that you could yourself shrink from such a scandal as this with more terror and abhorrence than I should do." And then she paused. The colour had mounted to her cheeks, and she had uttered the words with something more than gravity; the term solemnity would describe her manner better.

"Heaven forbid," she resumed, "that I should ever bring disgrace or difficulty upon you in any way."

The effect which the words of Mr. Rixley had produced was certainly greater than he intended; and he resumed, in a lighter tone, "Nay, dearest Helen, do not look so frightened! I really believe that we may do all you propose, and a little more, perhaps, without any risk of outrunning the income allowed you. I am but a poor man in comparison to my late brother; but the income we spent in Davies Street will come in aid of your allowance at Beauchamp Park. But remember that there must be no mistake. It is your establishment, my dear, and not mine, which is about to be *monté* there. It must be Miss Beauchamp's house, remember, and not Mr. Rixley's."

"Nay! do not burden my young head so heavily!" replied Helen, laughing. "Let there be no division between thy house and my house. Let it be for all of us, 'our house at home.'"

"So it shall, my dear child!" said Mrs. Rixley, justly appreciating the feeling which had brought a tear to the eye and a flush to the cheek of Helen; "and I am very sanguine in my belief that 'our house at home' will be a very happy one."

"May I," said Henry, suddenly starting up, and placing himself immediately before Helen, with a solemn reverence—"may I say one little word for myself at this propitious moment? May I venture to petition for permission to fish and to shoot occasionally within your domain?"

Helen returned his salute with a very dignified bow, and replied gracefully, extending her hand towards his father, "That gentleman, Sir, is my man-of-business: it is his permission you must seek for, and not mine. Nor can you be offended by this reference, young gentleman, when I tell you that it is my intention never to do anything without obtaining it myself.

CHAPTER XXV.

No further discussion was necessary to confirm the decision arrived at in this half-playful conversation. Had all those who had assisted at it been as grave in their demeanour as the Council of the Propaganda, they could not have been more in earnest in wishing to change their residence from Davies Street to Beauchamp Park.

Nor, in sober earnest, was there the least imprudence in their doing so. An establishment prepared conscientiously for a girl of fourteen, is a very different affair from what the same individual might reasonably require some half-dozen years afterwards; and not only her guardian, but her guardian's family, were so perfectly well aware of this, that while greatly enjoying the idea of a long sojourn in so agreeable a residence, there was not one of them who would not have shrunk from, and rejected, any project for placing themselves *pro tempore* in a station and style which was not properly their own.

Helen's programme, however, was considerably improved upon and enlarged.

Instead of the one-horse chair, "like Mr. Bolton's," they had a one-horse car, which, in very pleasant Irish fashion, could contain them all. Beyond the allowance entrusted to her guardian for maintenance of the heiress, a very sufficient sum was allotted for keeping up the place in general, and the beautiful gardens in particular—an arrangement which very happily enabled the ladies of the party to indulge themselves with a safe conscience in all the luxury that lawns and shrubberies, fruits and flowers, could give.

There had been so much of common sense, and of something more than common decision, in the manner in which Helen had put her veto upon the pursuit of accomplishments, that Mr. Rixley, after discussing the question with his wife, decided that it would be better to let her have her own way in this matter, illustrating his opinion by a parody, showing that—

> Those who are taught against their will,
> Remain in native ignorance still.

To which his wife had replied, "I believe so;" adding, more-

over, that the native ignorance of Helen seemed of a quality that
might be preferred by many to all the artistic accomplishments
that could be taught her. "Her sketches," continued Mrs.
Rixley, "are more like pictures left upon her memory, than
drawings made according to rule; and as to her music, both
in singing and playing, there is something much more like inspiration than art. So that, on the whole, I am very decidedly
of your opinion, that we had better let her have her own way."

So, from that time forward, Helen Beauchamp heard no more
about masters.

But there were other points of her education, concerning
which her guardian uncle felt a good deal of interest. Her
own definition of the system she thought necessary, contained in
the words, "read, read, read," had struck him as not precisely
devoid of reason, but as being, nevertheless, rather too indefinite
to be quite satisfactory. He accordingly took an opportunity,
when they were *tête-à-tête* together, of asking her (after he had
quoted her own words to her) whether her "*read, read, read,*"
was meant to be indiscriminately applied to every book that
came in her way.

"Not exactly that, uncle," she replied; "for I would avoid, if
I could, ever reading anything that was very silly or very
wicked. It would be such loss of time."

"It might be worse than that, Helen," replied Mr. Rixley.
"You might read what would be injurious to you."

"Perhaps; but I don't think it very likely," she replied.

"Why not?" said he. "I assure you, my dear child, that
people who read indiscriminately every book that comes in their
way, run a great risk of meeting with what they had better
avoid."

"In the way of silliness, or of wickedness, uncle?" asked
Helen.

"Both, my dear, both," was the reply.

"I don't feel afraid of it," she replied; "for I don't think, if
the reading silly books would make me silly, there could be
much mischief in that, for there must be a sympathising silliness here," touching her forehead, "already .And as to wicked
books, I think that in the first place they are not very likely to
come in my way; and if they did, I think I should put them
out of it."

"Yes, I am sure you would, if they were of that species which
carries evil legibly marked upon it. Danger to you from such
as these, I can easily believe would not be great. It is where

the mischief is more concealed that danger lies. Very persevering and very promiscuous readers can scarcely hope to escape occasionally getting hold of reasonings that may be more specious than sound."

"Yes, Uncle Rixley," replied Helen, while an expression of deep thoughtfulness took possession of her beautiful young features, "I think so too. But then I cannot help thinking, also, that our own opinions, and our own feelings about what is right or wrong, would be of little worth, and little utility to us, if we adopted them only because we had found the like in a book that we have been told by our friends is a good book. It would be very easy for us, certainly, to learn by rote the pages upon which these thoughts and opinions are inscribed; but having done so, I do not feel that I should have any right to call such thoughts and opinions my own. It seems to me, that one must think, and think, and think, a great deal before we can honestly say that we have got an opinion about anything."

"Then why do you conceive it to be so necessary to read, read, read, my dear Helen, if you believe that it is only by the process of thinking that you can arrive at the truth ? " inquired her uncle.

"I hav'n't said *that*, Uncle Rixley," replied Helen with quickness. "Our thoughts would be in the state of the sleeping beauty in the fairy tale, if they were never awakened. Every book one reads, if it be worth reading at all, awakens our thoughts, and sets them busily to work. If it be a statement of facts, we weigh, as it were, the value of them, and pass judgment upon the actors, and in doing this, you know, we actually *do* form opinions—we actually may be said to think. If our book gives us theories, of course we begin thinking again directly, to find out whether we can receive them as true. And if the book be imaginative, oh! then do we not enjoy ourselves, and feel as if we were born into another new world, perhaps almost as beautiful as that in which we live, and in some respects more beautiful still."

Her uncle looked at her beautiful animated face with a great deal of affection and some little surprise, and said to her, but by no means in a tone offensively inquisitorial, " Will you tell me, Helen, how it has happened that, living so much out of the reach of educated society as you must have done, you should at an unusually early age have acquired, as you evidently have done, habits of reading and of thinking by no means very common among young ladies, even when they have all appliances and means to boot? Tell me, dear child, how you contrived to learn all that you seem to know?"

"Dear, dear, Uncle Rixley," returned Helen, colouring violently, "do not let me take you in, by telling you that I am bold enough to think of countless thousands of things that I know nothing about. I believe in my heart that I *know* less than almost any body in the world; and the chief thing that has convinced me of my own ignorance has been the reading every sort of book that I could get hold of. Now, you know, uncle, that one cannot read any books at all without finding out that the people who wrote them understood all the things, however difficult or mysterious, about which they wrote, or at least, that they honestly believe in their own hearts that they do; while I only feel as I read and read, that as yet I know nothing! But I don't suppose that my mind is old enough to have got all its strength yet; and I hope the time will come when I may in my turn honestly be able to say to myself I know *this*, or I know *that*. The only people that I think I should ever be inclined to envy are those who know, *really know*, more than others; and that is my great notion about being in heaven, Uncle Rixley."

"And my notion about you, my dear Helen," he replied, "is that you have been in the habit of thinking too largely, if I may so use the word, for your age. I suspect that you have spent too many hours alone, my dear child."

"I don't know, uncle. I have been often very happy when alone," she answered. "Since mamma died," she continued, "I should have been very badly off, if I could not have amused myself with my books and my thoughts. My dear good Sarah Lambert was almost always very busy about the house, and my only other companion"—and here she stopped abruptly; the bright blood mounted to her cheeks, she fixed her eyes upon the ground, and an air of stiff reserve seemed to take possession of her, as different as possible from her usual manner when conversing with her uncle.

He looked at her for a moment, both with surprise and pain; but during that moment it suddenly occurred to him, that although several weeks had elapsed since she first became a member of his family, the name of *William* had never been mentioned in her hearing. This silence had arisen on his part, and on that of his family also, entirely from consideration for her feelings. He knew how tremendously she had suffered from his sudden disappearance, and had taught his family to be as cautious as himself in avoiding every allusion to a subject which, notwithstanding the rapid recovery of her health, might, he feared, be still too agitating for her to enter upon without suffering.

But he now fancied that he saw in her manner a sudden air of restraint, when thus evidently about to allude to her brother, which seemed to proceed from a fear least his name might not be freely spoken before him.

Determined at once to remove this impression, if indeed it really existed, he said, affectionately taking her hand, "your only other companion, dear Helen, was your brother William, of whom we all earnestly hope that we shall soon hear tidings—he must, indeed, have been your best companion, then—what were you going to say about him, Helen?" "My dear, dear uncle," sobbed the poor girl, throwing her arms around his neck, "I thought you meant that I was never to hear his name, and that I was never to speak of him again!"

"How greatly then have you mistaken us all!" he eagerly replied. "Believe me, Helen, our only reason for not naming him was the fear least your spirits were not yet sufficiently recovered from all the agitation you underwent at Crumpton to make it prudent to allude to it as yet."

"Your speaking to me as you do now, Uncle Rixley," said Helen, holding his hand caressingly between hers, "will do more towards restoring me to all my former health and strength than anything else in the world! You have been so very kind to me from the first moment I saw you—and you have all, every one of you, been so very kind to me, that I should like to live with you without having a single secret from you in the world! But this could never be if I might not talk to you about William. I will not do it very much either, that is, before you have seen and know him yourselves, because it is impossible that anything I could say could make you understand what sort of a person he is, and without that, all I could say about him would only sound like nonsense to you. For I do not believe there is any body in the world like him. My mamma had a great collection of beautiful engravings, portraits of all sorts of distinguished people, but not one of the whole set could be compared to my brother William, either for handsomeness, or for that noble air of pride and courage, that made him look so much like one of the famous heroes one reads of in history. I do assure you, Uncle Rixley," she added, after a short pause, during which she closed her eyes as if turning their speculating power inwards, " that he was the handsomest and cleverest person I ever saw, and I should say that he was the kindest and the best too, were it not that I have sometimes seen him, at least I saw him *once*, give way to very violent passion. That moment was very terrible. I cannot forget it. I am afraid I never shall forget it! But though his temper was certainly very quick and fiery, I never was really frightened at his violence but once."

In saying this Helen became extremely pale, and her uncle felt that, notwithstanding her rapid recovery from the frightful fever that had seemed to threaten her life, her nerves were still in much too excitable a state to make it prudent to continue a conversation which affected her so deeply.

"Your strong affection for your brother goes further towards convincing me that he must have great and good qualities, Helen, than any description of him could do. But we can neither of us do him any good by recurring to the painful scene to which you have just alluded, and let us therefore be wise enough to avoid discussing it. You may be very sure, my dear love, that as soon as any intelligence respecting his movements reaches Mrs. Lambert, it will be forwarded immediately to you; and from all I have heard of her, she is not a person likely to relax in her efforts to discover him. It strikes me, Helen, that the most reasonable interpretation to put upon his absence is, that being conscious himself of the unseemly violence which he manifested upon the painful occasion you have mentioned, he thought it better to withdraw himself for a time, trusting to his talents, of which he must be conscious, for support, than to run the risk of being again irritated beyond his patience. And, perhaps, my dear child, he was right. If this be so, and it certainly is very reasonable to hope it, we may some day have the pleasure of seeing him return, to look for his dear sister; and the position in which he will find you, Helen, will speedily turn all his sorrow into joy. But, for the present, let us all resolve not to torment ourselves by idle conjecture."

Helen listened to him as if her life hung upon the words he uttered. But these words, though both reasonable and soothing, did not reach the point to which all her thoughts were directed. She would have given a finger, could she

13

have conveyed to her uncle's mind all the thoughts which, for the last six or seven weeks, had been incessantly at work within her own, provided only that, having done so, she might have heard him declare decidedly, and without restraint, whether he thought it within the reach of moral possibility that her brother William could be guilty of the crime that had been imputed to him.

But upon this occasion, and at one or two subsequent opportunities that she had met, or made, when she employed all the skill she possessed in order to make her uncle talk freely to her about him, she so completely failed, that at length she resolutely determined never to make the same attempt again, till some event had occurred or some information had reached them, which must of necessity prevent her uncle, so kindly and flatteringly confidential to her on all other subjects, from being so mysteriously silent on this.

Her keeping this resolution—and she did keep it strictly, including every member of the family in her reserve—was so far beneficial, both to herself and to them, that it spared her the painful embarrassment of inventing opportunities of recurring to the painful theme, and it spared them the equally-painful task of seeking to avoid it.

To the Rixley family, this was really an unmixed good; for, as far as they knew, there was no disadvantage of any kind to set against it. But the case was different with Helen. It is true, indeed, that her constant intercourse with the family into which she was so affectionately adopted was no longer embarrassed by her perpetually looking out for opportunities to make them talk on the only subject they wished to avoid. But this advantage did not come unmixed to Helen; for the finding that she could not talk about William, and the dreadful accusation that had been brought against him, only made her think of him, and of it, the more: and the consequence of this was, that the recollection of him, and everything connected with him, and with her early life, frequently made a melancholy theme for her secret meditations, and in the midst of all the cheerful hilarity inevitably produced by her very happy position, as well as by her age and natural disposition, she was often seen musing, with an expression of painful anxiety upon her beautiful features, which distressed, as much as it puzzled, those around her.

Of Mrs. Lambert, she, for many months, heard nothing; but

at length, a letter arrived from her, addressed to Mr. Rixley, which was as follows:—

"REVEREND AND HONOURED SIR,

"I have faithfully kept the promise I gave to seek tidings of William, commonly called Rixley (the natural son of your late brother, Mr. Rixley Beauchamp), by every means in my power; but my success has been very limited. I know not where he actually is, nor where he is at all likely to be; but I have ascertained, beyond a doubt, that he had sailed from the coast of England before it was possible that tidings of any of the events which followed his departure from the Warren House could have reached him; and this perfectly accounts for his lengthened absence. Knowing, as I do, the estimable character, and the great abilities of this unfortunate young man, I cannot doubt but that he will, without difficulty, be able to maintain himself, let him go where he will; and those who best love him will not only find comfort from this consideration, but from remembering that his leaving home in the sudden and clandestine manner that we know he did, was *more* than excusable in him. Few people, in fact, if they knew what he had really suffered in that home, could doubt the wisdom and propriety of his leaving it.—And as to the cruel accusation that was made against him, no reasonable person could give credit to what is thus wildly asserted without a shadow of proof. I address myself to you, reverend and honoured Sir, in preference to the ever-dear young lady, your niece and ward, because, after much thinking on the subject, I have convinced myself that, had I the power of renewing my former familiar intercourse with her, it would be my duty not to avail myself of it, inasmuch, as it would be more advantageous to her that I should not do it. Had my former intercourse with her been merely that of a servant, I should be proud and happy to wait upon her in that capacity still. But many circumstances rendered this impossible in the house of her father; and were I again near her, I might find it difficult, if not impossible, to behave to Miss Beauchamp in the way that her servants ought to behave to her. I shall serve her better at a distance, by endeavouring to find her brother. Have the kindness, Sir, to present my duty to her, and tell her that the great object of my life shall be to bring back her noble-hearted brother to his country. Have the kindness, Sir, to tell her, also, to make her generous heart quite easy as to my means of living. The small house and garden left to me by my mother has been purchased, at a great price, by the shipping interest at Falmouth, in consequence of its vicinity to the harbour. I remain, with profound duty and respect, both your and her obedient servant,

" SARAH LAMBERT."

The first perusal of this letter produced torrents of tears from Helen ; but, after allowing them to flow without interruption for some minutes, her uncle checked them, by saying, "You should not weep so bitterly, dear Helen, because a person whom you love has acted from a sense of duty, instead of being influenced by any other motive. Mrs. Lambert is right, Helen, and I feel both respect and gratitude towards her for pursuing a line of conduct that, I am quite sure, must be painful to her, solely because her good, clear judgment tells her that it is right. I honour her for her conduct."

"Then I am quite sure that I ought to honour her too," said poor Helen, hanging her head and looking as if it were easier to say what ought to be done, than to do it.

"It would be scarcely reasonable at this moment to expect that you should approve her conduct," resumed her uncle, " because it must of necessity give you pain. But you will judge her more reasonably when you are older. She says most truly that the terms upon which you have hitherto lived together, are not such as could be adopted with propriety by Miss Beauchamp. Your relations have claims upon you as well as your old servant, dear Helen, and a little sober reflection will soon make you understand that Mrs. Lambert is right."

"If you say it, and if she thinks it too, uncle, I am already quite sure of it—I only wish that doing right was not so very painful!" she replied.

Mr. Rixley was too wise to lead her into any further discussion on the subject; and Helen was too wise to let him, or anyone else, perceive how difficult she found it to convert Helen Rixley, into Miss Beauchamp.

CHAPTER XXVI.

On the whole, however, it would have been well nigh impossible to have devised a better course than that taken by Mrs. Lambert to complete the transition of Helen Rixley of the Warren House, to Helen Beauchamp of Beauchamp Park. That it was painful was certain, but there was no mixture either of reproach, or repentance in her feelings, and moreover there was a vague hope at the bottom of her young heart, that the time might come when her situation would be sufficiently independent of circumstances and usages, to enable her once again to press Sarah Lambert to her heart without feeling that she was doing an injury to herself, or to anybody else.

The wound made by her separation from William was of a very different kind; but she never alluded to it in any way, for she was, somehow or other, quite aware that it would not be healed by family discussion, for that the subject was one of the very few upon which those around her could not sympathise with her feelings.

And thus it came to pass that neither Mrs. Lambert, nor William were any more mentioned among them, but nevertheless they were not forgotten by Helen. Her meditations respecting them, however, were, so to speak, of a different quality. The image of Mrs. Lambert never rose to her memory without creating a feeling of affectionate childlike tenderness, and had the object of this very natural feeling not withdrawn herself, it might for ever have been kept alive in the heart of her nursling, and would have been a source of great pleasure to her, had she been permitted to prove her grateful and affectionate feelings by such acts of liberality as her generous temper, and ample means would have led her to perform. But as it was, the recollection of this dearly beloved nurse gradually melted as it were into the mass of all other childish memories of things past, and if Sarah Lambert was no longer a source of happiness to her, the recollection of her did not become a source of suffering.

But far different was the impression left upon her mind by the loss of William. He alone of all the human beings she had ever known had ever been, properly speaking, her companion.

They had discoursed together of things vastly beyond the comprehension of either, but nevertheless this converse had been the most precious recreation that Helen had ever known, and though she had of late heard it perpetually proclaimed, either overtly or covertly, that she was beautiful, intelligent and charming, in all manner of ways, the only thing that really awakened a feeling of vanity within her, was the recollection of having seen her brother William close many a volume in which he was interested in order to converse with her.

Had this been all that remained upon her memory of the days that were gone, her thoughts might have dwelt upon it both with pride and pleasure. But unfortunately that was not all. She remembered the agony she had so often seen him suffer, not from the unkindness of his brutal father—for from his babyhood he had been too much accustomed to this, to heed it—but from the insulting tone of degradation in which it was his custom, and evidently his pleasure, to address him. She remembered how she had seen the warm young blood rush to his cheek upon these occasions, and then forsake it till he looked both ghastly pale, and fearfully indignant.

And even had this been all it would not have mattered much, for it might only have served to remind her that their being orphans was a dispensation of providence which could not reasonably in their case be lamented as a misfortune.

But it was in vain that she endeavoured to remember this, and this alone. Her father's violent death, and the great improbability of its being the consequence of his own act, as far at least as she had the power of judging, forced upon her the horrible belief that he had been murdered. But beyond this, it would be in vain to attempt to follow her reasonings. Everything was vague, nay, everything was contradictory.

She felt at her heart's core that the base and cruel insults which had been heaped upon William, and upon William's mother, in the hearing both of herself and Sarah Lambert, were such as might explain, though they could not justify a degree of indignation, and of rage, which might have led to horrible results; but just as her reasonings had reached this point, she remembered, also, with a rush of compunction and remorse, that wrung torturing tears from her eyes, that of every human being she had ever known, heard, or read of, her brother William was the last whose noble nature was likely to be so overpowered by rage as to make him capable of the most awful crime of which human nature could be guilty.

These painful reveries lasted longer than any one domesticated
with Helen could have believed possible, for from a very early
period of her domestication in her uncle's family she had, as if
by instinct, become aware that, notwithstanding the gentle and
even cautious manner with which they listened to her expressions of wonder and regret at not receiving any letter from
Sarah Lambert, they did not share her regret upon the subject.

Having once made this remark, everything which followed
strengthened it; and though she could not, from her total
ignorance of the facts, do them anything at all approaching
to justice while meditating upon the causes of this seemingly
cold indifference, she immediately resolved that she would not
make herself troublesome by alluding to feelings in which they
did not share.

This deficiency in sympathy was very nearly as visible on the
subject of her brother, as in the case of her nurse, and the same
resolution on her part was the result. Helen, for her age, had
very great command of herself, and therefore not any one of her
new family, notwithstanding their constantly affectionate communion with her, had any notion how many of her night
thoughts were occupied by meditations concerning this lost
brother; yet nevertheless her health, her beauty, her intelligence, went on improving, and at seventeen, the eventful
period to which we must now transport her, it would have
been difficult to trace either in her appearance or manners, any
trace of either objectionable associations, or defective education.

And yet on this latter point she had had some very strange
notions of her own, for though when transplanted into her
uncle's family she was still young enough to have profited
by the attendance of masters, if she would have submitted to
it, she so resolutely resisted all the arguments used to induce
her to do so, that the attempt was soon given up as hopeless,
and Helen remained to the end of her days without receiving
any more instructions in the shape of lessons, than she had
brought with her from the Warren House.

However, she read largely, and thought much; and this
prevented her being quite as much behindhand in mental de-
velopment as many persons acquainted with her early history
might have expected.

Neither were the advantages which she gained in respect to
society by her exchanging Crumpton Warren House for
Beauchamp Park at all lost upon her, either as a matter of
pleasure or profit.

Nothing could be more kind or more judicious than the conduct of her uncle and aunt towards her. She was certainly not one of those admirable young ladies who have no will of their own—Helen very decidedly had a will of her own—but as she was not at all obstinate, and by no means very unreasonable, everything went on smoothly, and nothing in the least degree approaching a dispute ever occurred between them. On the whole, therefore, my heroine was a very happy girl, although, at the bottom of her heart, she had a sorrow, which, if it did not actually rankle and torment her, was never quite forgotten.

CHAPTER XXVII.

It happened on a certain morning in the springtide of the year, that Helen, who was ever the earliest riser of the family, was returning from one of her long solitary morning walks, which had taken her considerably beyond the boundaries of her own beautiful park, when she saw her Cousin Henry sitting in very melancholy and Jaques-like fashion on the root of a venerable thorn, which spread its silver awning over the only bit of open brierless turf to be found within the shelter of the thick copse through which she was passing.

Her light step had brought her very near him befor he perceived her, but when he did, he started as violently as if he had seen a ghost.

"Have I frightened you, Henry?" said she, laughing.

"I suppose it would disgrace my noble courage did I say yes," he replied; "but I should disgrace my sincerity if I said no."

"I have frightened you, actually frightened you then, have I?" said she. "This will be something to boast of."

"Not much, Helen. I believe a mouse might easily have achieved as much," said he.

"Shall I guess what you were thinking of," she returned, as he rose up, and joined her.

"You may, an if you will, cousin," returned Henry, with a very melancholy smile.

"Very well, then, so I will. You were thinking of your

pony, and your fishing, and your waltzing with Mary Jackson; while, in the midst of all these beautiful visions, the spectre of your Oxford gown and cap to be put on next week, so completely appalled your spirit as to throw you very nearly into a state of insensibility, from which my approach aroused you with very startling, not to say terrifying, effect."

"Yes, that was it, Cousin Helen," said he, gravely.

"But why should this produce a more painful effect upon you now, dear Henry, than it has ever done before?"

"As you seem determined to bring me to confession, I will answer this question, too, though it is a searching one," he replied. "The reason is this, Helen, I have hitherto lived a very happy, because a very thoughtless life. I have enjoyed going to College, and I have enjoyed returning home—to our '*happy house at home*,' dear Helen. But now the case is altered. Thought will come—must come—sooner or latter, to us all. I suppose you do not know, for I dare say my faithful Anne has never told you, that I very greatly dislike the profession which my good father tells me is the only one that is open to me. I dislike, for many reasons, the idea of going into the church. I do not think I am fitted for it in any way, and I do think I am fitted for other things. I would rather a thousand times be sent on the most dangerous mission that they could find for me in India, than take holy orders. I am fit for the one, and if I should be shot, there would be no great harm done, and poor Anne would be a few thousand pounds the richer, but to be a clergyman I am not fit; and yet, you know, I am to set off on Monday expressly for the purpose of taking my degree, and, after that, a very few weeks more will see me a clergyman."

Helen was pained. It was evident that he was very much in earnest, and the misfortune of which he complained was not one for which it was very easy to find a remedy. She walked on beside him in silence for a minute or two after he had ceased to speak, and then she said, "Have you ever confessed to your father, Henry, how much you dislike the plan he has laid down for you?"

"Yes, Helen. I have done so as earnestly as it was in my power to do it."

"And how did he receive your remonstrance?"

"With a look of despair that it is painful to me to remember," he replied. "He implored me not to make him feel that he had been guilty of a crime in marrying without having sufficient means to provide for his children according to their wishes. In

short, I had rather do the deed at once than offer any further
opposition to his wishes."

" You are a dear good fellow, Henry! It would be a sin to
try to shake such a resolution as that," replied Helen. " But
though opposition to so excellent a father would be very painful, and might perhaps be very wrong, I can see no mischief, nor
any danger of it from delay. Take my advice in this, Henry, as
you often have done in lesser matters. Return to Oxford and
take your degree, and exert all your faculties to make it a
creditable one. The doing this cannot fail of being advantageous
to you, let your future walk be what it may. When you have
achieved this, ask your father frankly to give you a little breathing time before you take orders."

Henry took a deep breath. "Even that," he said, " would be
a great relief."

" Then I am very glad I suggested it to you," said Helen,
kindly. "I am quite sure that I can have done no harm by
that. But tell me," she added, " have you never spoken as
freely to dear Anne as you have now done to me on this subject ?"

" Oh! yes. A hundred times, I am afraid, or rather more,"
he replied.

"Then how comes it that you have neither of you ever alluded
to the subject when talking to me ? You may have been right
in abstaining from it with your father, but surely there could
have been no harm in your confiding your troubles to me."

"I am not sure of that, dear Helen," he replied, "nor is
Anne, either, for we have often discussed the point together;
and, at last, we both agreed that it would be a bad return for
all the happiness we have owed to you, if we took it into our
heads to prove our friendship by pouring forth all our miseries
upon you. No, dear Helen, if you had not cross-examined me
so cleverly, you would never have learnt what a rebellious heart
was hid under my seeming conformity."

"Do not say so, Henry!" she replied, affectionately. " I
would much rather owe my knowledge of your position, which I
certainly never understood before—I would much rather owe it
to your confidence in my discretion than to my own skill in
cross-examination."

" And in sober earnest, Helen, you do owe it to my confidence
in you," he replied; "nor would you have been so long without knowing all that I have now told you, but for the reason I
have already stated to you. Anne has repeatedly asked me to

let her tell you all our troubles, but I have always ended such discussions by convincing her that it was very wanton cruelty to make you uncomfortable about it, as it was totally out of your power to do us any good. However, I honestly confess that I have changed my mind upon the subject, for I think it will be a great comfort to Anne, when I am gone, to know that she *may* converse with you on this subject, as on all others, without restraint. And see! Here she comes as if on purpose to meet us. I should not be much surprised if she were to guess what we were talking about so very earnestly."

"We are waiting breakfast for you Helen," said Anne, as she approached them. "But what are you two in such solemn conversation about?"

"I have followed your advice at last, Anne," replied her brother. "Helen knows all the disobedient struggles of my rebellious spirit, and when I am gone back to Oxford she will listen as kindly and as patiently to your lamentations over me, as she has now been doing to mine."

"That I am sure she will, if you have been really explaining everything to her, and it will be the greatest possible comfort to me to have a dear friendly ear open to receive my moans and groans—for I really am very miserable about you, Henry."

"It is possible, young as she is," replied he, "that she may do something more than listen to your moans and groans, for she has been already giving me counsel that has brought an immensity of comfort with it. But there stands my father at the breakfast-room window, not looking impatient, for that is not in his nature, but decidedly looking very hungry."

Anne was quite right in prognosticating great comfort and consolation from the removal of all restraint from her intercourse with her young cousin, but this could not put off the melancholy day of Henry's departure, or prevent the sad impression left upon her heart by the parting look he gave her, while listening to the gay expression of his father's hope, that the next time he left them would be to receive ordination from their good friend the Bishop.

* * * * *

* * * * *

CHAPTER XXVIII.

It must not be supposed, though nothing has been hitherto said on the subject, that the beautiful heiress of Beauchamp Park had been permitted to attain the age of seventeen years without having made some acquaintance with her neighbours.

During the first year or two of her residence on the domain she had so strangely inherited, her guardian uncle, who was really conscientious almost to excess, avoided the hospitable advances of the neighbourhood; not from an unsocial temper, but because he felt that he should not like to receive hospitality without returning it, and that this return could only be made at the expense of Helen, who was as yet too young either to make or receive dinner visits.

But Miss Beauchamp was rather a precocious, and rather a self-willed young lady, and by the time she had reached her sixteenth birthday she had not only made up her mind upon the subject of family visiting in general, but very resolutely determined to take the management of the business into her own hands.

Not all her little efforts, and they had not been sparingly repeated, could prevent her uncle from betraying in various ways, that he had not forgotten that neither the house nor the revenue which supported it were his own. The consciousness that such were his feelings was a great annoyance to Helen, but she quietly made up her mind to endure it till she should be *as tall as her aunt*; nor had she very long to wait for this much-coveted dignity of appearance, and when her sixteenth birthday arrived, she took care to make this evident, by requesting that they might both be measured against the library door, when the fact of her not only having reached, but surpassed this desired standard, was most satisfactorily proved to the whole family.

"Then, now, I suppose, I can no longer be accounted a child?" said Helen, addressing herself to her aunt.

"No, truly, Helen, I think you look almost as old as your grown-up cousin Anne," replied Mrs. Rixley, with great sincerity.

"And you, uncle? Do you think I look like a child?" she

said, addressing Mr. Rixley, in a tone that had more of earnest than jest in it.

"No, Helen," he answered, with equal gravity, "you certainly do not."

"Nor do I any longer feel like a child. The last few years of my life, have, I think, produced the effect of many years upon me," returned Helen, thoughtfully.

"I doubt it not," replied her uncle. "The changes which have happened to you during that interval, have been quite enough to produce this effect; and moreover, Helen, you are, I suspect, rather addicted to meditation, and this is a temperament which makes us feel old."

"That accounts for it, uncle! That accounts for all the busy thoughts that I feel working within me," returned Helen, laughing. "Do not be frightened if I tell you that these busy thoughts suggest to me the idea that I should like for us all to see a little more of our neighbours. They all, as far as I have been able to judge, appear inclined to be very civil to us, but as you do not choose to dine out anywhere, it is of course impossible for me to know much about it. I do not mean to say that I wish to dine out myself just yet, I should be quite contented to wait another whole year before I do that; but if you would ask some of those we like best to dine here, we should soon become better acquainted with them, you know, and they would begin again to ask you to dine with them in return; and then all sorts of sociable meetings would be set going among us, and if I am to live here always, I think I shall find it very dull if I don't know any of my neighbours.

Mr. and Mrs. Rixley looked at each other with something a little like dismay. There was just enough of truth and reason in the young lady's remonstrance to make it difficult to answer her. Her uncle, however, like a sensible man as he was, took the right way, for he immediately told the truth.

"We are not rich enough, Helen," said he, "to visit the principal families within visiting distance, upon terms of equality. Have you forgotten the discussion we had together on this subject before we finally decided that we might all venture to live here together during your minority? Have you forgotten the style of establishment which you recommended in order to enable us to do so without imprudence?"

"No, Uncle Rixley, I have not forgotten one word of that discussion; nor shall I ever forget the kindness which induced you to yield to my wishes, though the doing so was in so great a degree to banish you from society. But the state of the case is different now, and I begin to know you so well, that I feel certain that you will feel many more scruples about my having no society than about your all being deprived of it yourselves."

He looked furtively at his wife, and smiled. "There might be something in that," he said, "were it not that the friendly attentions of our neighbours have by no means relaxed so much as we had reason to expect they might have done upon discovery that we were not diners out."

"But I do not like that their attentions should relax at all," said Helen, "and I think it would be bad management on my part were I to begin my career by living as a stranger among those whom I ought to make my friends."

"But how is it to be avoided, Helen? Everything in the way of expenditure goes smoothly now, but it would be very much the reverse if you entered upon a system of receiving dinner company," returned her uncle.

"I know it, Uncle Rixley," she replied. "But I know also that an additional thousand a year would enable us to do this without any imprudence at all; and this thousand a year, if added to my savings, could never be of such advantage, or such pleasure to me, as the spending it now, in the manner I propose, nor do I think it at all likely that this addition would not be made to my allowance, if the reason for its being asked for were explained."

Whether it were the wisdom or the wilfulness of this remonstrance which did most in obtaining its success may be doubtful, but it is certain that no further opposition was offered to the hospitable wishes of the young heiress. The increased allowance was asked for, and immediately granted, and very little time was lost before her sociable projects were in full activity; the car was changed for a very respectable barouche, which, either as an open carriage or a close one, could convey the whole party. A butler, too, worthy of Beauchamp Park, was added to their establishment, together with sundry other minor appurtenances necessary to the projected alteration in the family proceedings.

The prognostic of Helen respecting the facility of speedily increasing the frequency of their intercourse with their neighbours proved perfectly correct; and this was doubtless rendered more easy by the explicit avowal of the motives which led the Beauchamp Park family to wish for it.

The beautiful girl, who had hitherto only been occasionally

seen during a morning visit, now always took her place on her uncle's right hand at table, and her manner of assisting her aunt in receiving their guests in the drawing-room was soon spoken of in the neighbourhood as the perfection of youthful grace, and lady-like demeanour.

But Helen was quite as self-willed in the limits she placed to her own share of these neighbourly sociabilities, as she had been in establishing them. She positively, absolutely, and stedfastly, refused to dine in company anywhere but at home; and though this resolution was almost clamorously combated by every family in the neighbourhood, and with especially earnest eloquence where there were grown-up sons, the pretty heiress only gave a smiling " no " in return; but all this might have been fairly recorded by the well-known line:—

" Oft she rejects, but never once offends."

Few themes are more fertile to memorialists of my stamp than a well varied set of " country neighbours," but I do not mean to indulge in it now. There was to be found in a circle of about fourteen miles diameter round Beauchamp Park about the usual proportion of talent and inanity, warm hearts and cold ones, sense and nonsense, worth and worthlessness, and though the individual specimens of each class might be easily sketched, so as not to mimic humanity too abominably, I do not mean to indulge myself by making the attempt. I may indeed have occasion to allude to some of them subsequently, but as there was only one family who were of any real importance to my narrative at this time, I shall for the present restrict my descriptions to them.

The name of this family was Harrington, and it consisted of father, mother, two daughters, and one son, or more correctly of one son, and two daughters, for the young man was not only the only son, and the heir expectant of a splendid property known by the name of Speedhurst Abbey, but he was also the senior of his sisters by several years.

It was with this family—and this family only—that Helen had already, by means of pretty frequent morning visitings, and an occasional pony car excursion, formed something like an intimate acquaintance.

But it must not be taken for granted, that the above mentioned only son had much to do with all this, for the fact is, that at the time at which we have arrived, George Harrington scarcely knew any of the Beauchamp Park family by sight.

It was not only as being the son of his father that this young man was heir to Speedhurst Abbey, and its acres, but as the eldest, and indeed the only nephew of his father's elder brother. This uncle had been a childless widower for the last twenty years, and it was at a time when the father of George was the happy father of three sons, instead of one, that he had consented to the earnest and not unreasonable petition of his brother to make over to his care the boy who was to inherit his property.

For fifteen years after this transfer was made, not one of all the individuals concerned in it had ever been permitted to feel a regret on the subject, for a more amiable, reasonable, or considerate old man than the owner of Speedhurt Abbey never existed, and if the first object of his life was to make his future heir all that an English gentleman ought to be, and the very happiest boy in the world besides, the second very evidently was, to arrange the intercourse between the two families in such a manner as to prevent the parents of George from ever feeling, or fancying, that they had given away their son.

But within six months after George had taken a very brilliant degree at Cambridge, and set off, with a celebrated geologist for his companion, to make his first tour upon the continent, the two fine lads who had prevented his being painfully missed at home became the heroes of one of the most appalling calamities on record, having been both drowned when bathing, within sight of their father.

The eldest son returned to England immediately, and it was to his father's house he then went, as to his future home. It was a tremendous sacrifice that the venerable owner of Speedhurst then offered to make, for no father ever loved a son more devotedly than he loved his heir; but George's father would not hear of it, and so truly was he in earnest in wishing that the Abbey should still be his son's home, that he was permitted to have his way, and it was still only as a visitor that George occasionally passed a few days with his family.

But it had so happened that some of their intimate morning meetings with the Beauchamp Park family had taken place when he was with them, and though he had once been in his mother's drawing-room when the Rixley family, accompanied by Helen, entered it, he felt himself at liberty, being a total stranger to them all, to leave the room as they came into it, for his horse had been for some time pawing the gravel at the door.

The only observation he made upon them amounted to two questions which he asked his mother on returning from his ride.

"My groom told me that those were the Beauchamp Park people who were coming in, as I went out. That girl in the straw bonnet is pretty-looking, isn't she? Is that the heiress, mother?" said he.

"Yes, and yes," replied his mother. "The first of your questions you would have been able to answer for yourself, if you had not been in such a violent hurry."

"Don't scold, dear mammy! It was my horse who was in a hurry, and not I. I thought she looked very pretty," he replied.

"Pretty, George!" exclaimed his eldest sister. "I should think you must be the first person who ever applied such an epithet to such a face. Helen Beauchamp is by far the most beautiful person that I ever saw."

"Really Jane? Then I flatter myself that I shall ere long have an opportunity of atoning for my abrupt departure by being permitted to look at her at my leisure."

"You have not much chance of being able to perform this act of penance," said his sister Agnes, "for she never has dined out yet, and she is not to begin till she is seventeen."

"You don't mean to tell me that the tall, graceful creature who passed by me this morning when I was stationed at the door in act to fly, you don't mean to to tell me, Agnes, that she is still in the school-room?" he replied.

"I will not answer for her being always in the school-room, for I do not think her education is conducted at all in a tyrannical style, moreover I doubt if she ever had a governess in her life," returned his sister; "but nevertheless it is a certain fact that she is still so far treated as a child, as not to dine out with the family. However, I don't suppose this will last for ever, for it is evident that they are preparing to be more sociable than they were on first coming here, and this is doubtless the preparation for her coming out."

"Which coming out, I presume, you all consider as an event of immense importance to the neighbourhood," said the young man, laughing. "The letting loose a beauty and an heiress in such a quiet little neighbourhood as this, will be something worth watching."

"The Beauchamp Park family will never choose to make themselves very conspicuous, I think, in any way," said Mrs. Harrington. "They are all of them rational, and perfectly

14

unaffected, and the more they mix with the neighbourhood, the better will it be for us all."

This was all that George Harrington had ever seen or known of the family at Beauchamp Park at the period when Helen completed her seventeenth year.

This birth day was an epoch which she herself had fixed upon as one that was to be very important to her, and so it was; for with the same quiet steadiness with which she had, in fact, regulated the movements of the Rixley family from the time she first became a member of it, she succeeded in obtaining the position and the influence in the household which for some time past it had been her especial object to gain.

I am quite aware that I am not presenting my heroine in a very flattering light to my readers, but if I have not disguised the fact of her being self-willed, I must observe that there were many excuses for her.

Her situation was, in many respects, very peculiar. She was quite conscious that she was well-born (in the common meaning of the phrase), and very wealthy. She was also perfectly aware that she had a fair chance of becoming as well-looking as young ladies in general; nor had she any misgivings, notwithstanding the irregular style of her education, concerning her having also a fair proportion, both of intellect and information. But she was conscious, too, that, notwithstanding all these advantages, her position was, in many respects, a false and a painful one. She knew, for the circumstance had been more than once discussed before her, that her existence had been perfectly unknown to her uncle's family till the dreadful catastrophe arrived which had made them personally acquainted, and she could not, therefore, but be conscious, that when Mr. Rixley came to attend his brother's funeral, he came, presuming himself to be his heir.

She appeared amongst them, therefore, not only as a stranger, but as one who had blighted all their hopes.

The manner in which she had been received among them was such as, under any circumstances, must have won her affection, but the peculiar state of the case made this conduct justly appear to her as noble as it was kind.

This statement may not at first sight seem to account very satisfactorily for her so speedily determining to have her own way among them; but, for so young an observer, she showed considerable acuteness in the rapidity with which she discovered that if she wished that they should be benefited in any pecuniary way by her remaining with them, it must be achieved by her having *her* way, and not by the Rixley family having *theirs*. Having made this discovery, and by degrees also the more painful one, that their circumstances were such as to render attention to this point of great importance to them, she very soon determined what her line of conduct should be; and the excellent judgment with which she arranged her plans, and the steady perseverance with which she adhered to them, must be received in atonement for the unbending pertinacity with which she refused to listen to the occasional remonstrances of her uncle when he fancied that she was in danger of exceeding the liberal allowance of the Court of Chancery. But, in point of fact, Helen knew what she was about a great deal better than her uncle did.

CHAPTER XXIX.

A few days after Henry Rixley's departure for College, which happened at no great distance from the eventful day on which Helen completed her seventeenth year, she once again lingered in the breakfast-room after the morning meal was concluded, and upon her Cousin Anne's making a movement as if to leave the room, she stopped her, saying, "Wait for me one moment, Anne, and we will go to my room together, but I want first to say a few words to my uncle and aunt upon business."

On hearing these words, Mr. Rixley, who had also risen to leave the room, resumed his chair, saying, "At your orders, fair niece. What have you to say to us?"

"Very little, dear uncle, if you approve my proposal, but a good deal by way of convincing you that I am right, if you should happen to think that I am wrong," said Helen.

"Then I shall certainly contradict you at first setting out, for I like to hear you plead," replied her uncle, laughing.

"I shall bless you very heartily if upon this particular occasion you will dispense with all pleading, and yield to my wishes. It is not at all an imaginative theme, and if we talk about it all day we shall find no amusement in it, dear uncle," replied Helen, gravely, "but I mean that my project shall contain something better, for I flatter myself that it will be useful

—useful to me, dear aunt—yes, very useful, as part of my education. In short, I greatly wish that you would permit me to be my own housekeeper."

The silence of a moment followed this unexpected proposal. Had Helen's auditors been less convinced of her rectitude of principle, and steadiness of conduct, this silence might have lasted longer, or have ended differently ; but as it was, the voices of both her uncle and aunt were heard at the same moment uttering nearly the same words, for they were both equally eager to assure her that they saw no objection whatever to her proposal, and that they perfectly agreed with her in thinking that the sooner she learnt the value, and the use of money, the better would be her chance of subsequently managing her own affairs judiciously.

"Ever the same ; ever indulgent, and confiding," exclaimed Helen, and thereupon she kissed them both with the playful eagerness of a happy child ; but tears came into her eyes the moment after, as she added, "God forbid that I should ever give you cause to repent your confidence in me !"

The day on which Helen completed her seventeenth year was the fourth birthday which she had had to celebrate since she had taken up her residence at Beauchamp Park. On occasion of the three first a very modest little *fête* had been given, at the suggestion of Mr. Rixley, to the half dozen servants which constituted their little household, and the something was repeated on the present, which afforded, as Mr. Rixley observed, a very convenient opportunity for announcing that the young mistress of the mansion was, from that time forward, to assume the executive reins of management herself; an announcement which would probably have been received with more surprise, had not the beautiful features of Helen already assumed a cast of more thoughtfulness than is common at her age.

In truth, poor Helen had long ago begun to feel too acutely, and to think too deeply, not to have lost that airy gaiety of aspect which constitutes so large a portion of what is called, strangely enough, "*La beauté du Diable.*" Her *beauté* was of a different order, and had she been seven-and-twenty, instead of seventeen, she could not have received the dutiful bows and courtesies of her household with more sober, though gentle dignity, than she did on this occasion ; and never probably did a young creature so early and so suddenly assume the management of a family with so little apparent assumption of authority or so much efficient exercise of it.

Fortunately for Helen's comfort, and for Helen's projects, her Uncle Rixley was not a man to adhere to an engagement to the sound and break it to the sense. She had taken care to make it very clearly understood that the portion of their joint income which had come from him should make no part of the sum over which she desired to have control. At first, he had objected to this, telling her that in that case she might find it after all impossible to be, as she wished, her own housekeeper, for that a part of their joint expenses had hitherto been paid by him.

"Of that," she replied, "I am quite aware, my dear uncle, and a part of the expenses may be paid by you still. You must not forget that my allowance has been increased on the plea of my going into company more. But after all, Uncle Rixley, I think we are essentially a very domestic family, and the increase which you have asked for, and obtained, will suffice, if I mistake not, for all the increased visitings we shall wish for; that is, provided my aunt and you will make no objection to paying the wages of Amy, who has belonged to you all so long that I am quite certain she would accept wages from nobody else."

"Very well, my dear, that is very kindly thought of, and may be easily managed. But what sum do you propose I should pay you for the maintenance of myself and my family?"

Helen coloured a little, and looked somewhat embarrassed, but after the silence of a moment she recovered herself, and said, "I had hoped, dear uncle, that you would kindly have consented to become my guests till some reason should arise which might cause us to be separated."

"I will not say I thank you for such a wish, my dear Helen, because I believe we are on both sides too thoroughly convinced that we all mutually love each other for it to be necessary for either party to return thanks for a proof of it. But, on the contrary, I must reproach you with a want of judgment, Helen, and a deficiency of common sense, that rather surprises me."

"Yes, yes! I see it all!" exclaimed Helen, quickly, and colouring more vividly than before. "You are quite right, and I was quite wrong. Forgive me, Uncle Rixley! It was a blunder, and I beg your pardon for my want of thoughtfulness. You shall pay each of you, if you approve it, at the rate of one hundred a-year; and the pony that you ride, and that Henry rides when he is at home, shall be kept entirely at your expense, if you approve it."

Mr. Rixley paused for a little while before he answered, and then he said, "That will be leaving me a very rich man, Helen.

However, so let it be. We must all look forward to the time, probably at no very distant date, when you will have a partner to assist you in the disposal of your superfluous wealth; and, meanwhile, I consent to the terms you have dictated, because I feel quite certain that no way of spending your present income would give you more pleasure."

This was the last financial conversation which ever took place between the uncle and niece, as long as the young lady continued a minor; one reason for which was, that it would have been extremely difficult for either party to have found anything very interesting to say on the subject to the other. It was, indeed, impossible that any housekeeping, on any scale, could have gone on with more satisfactory regularity : no one ever heard of any bills; no people were ever served by more obsequious tradesmen. The servants were alert, obedient, and attentive ; and the whole establishment went on with the regularity of a well-ordered machine, the springs of which were both out of sight and out of hearing.

But with all this excellent good management, the enlarged hospitalities of Beauchamp Park did not display themselves with quite as much splendour as the Rixley family had expected. Whether this was, or was not, a disappointment to the gay-hearted Anne may be doubtful; but to her father and mother it unquestionably came in the shape of a very agreeable surprise. They had now been domesticated with Helen for some years, and they had become sufficiently acquainted with her character during that time, to have convinced themselves that she was a girl of no ordinary ability; but, nevertheless, they were very far from understanding the peculiarities of her disposition.

They had by no means suspected her of being likely to fall into any very objectionable expenses for the sake of indulging a taste for dissipation, or a taste for parade; but they certainly did think that her anxiety to become the mistress of her own house arose from a wish to receive more company, and accept more invitations, than her careful guardian had hitherto thought it prudent to do.

But they speedily found that they were mistaken, and that her proceedings had much more the appearance of increased economy than of increased extravagance. This increased economy, however, was not displayed in any branch of expenditure which could affect the comfort of the family, or of the household; in all such respects her only object seemed to be to follow scrupulously the example which her aunt had set her.

But Helen was vastly more enterprising and speculative than they suspected in her management of the acres reserved as the home farm, and which consisted of some rich and highly-conditioned pastures, besides the park, which surrounded the house, and which park, almost from time immemorial, as her grey-headed bailiff assured her, had been kept pretty nearly sacred to the fine herd of deer for which it was celebrated. This grey-headed bailiff had held his office too long to be dismissed without reluctance, and too long to be retained with utility. But Helen found means to settle this difficulty greatly to the satisfaction, as well as to the benefit, of all parties, for she settled the pretty cottage, in which he and his old wife had long resided, upon them as long as both or either should live, together with an annuity equal in amount to his yearly wages; and then she dismissed him with no more harshness than was contained in the observation that he had worked long enough to deserve a comfortable provision without working any more.

This arrangement was really too reasonable not to be approved of by all parties; but when it was followed by the announcement that the deer were to be sold, and the land let for grazing, a vast variety of observations followed: and, moreover, the promptitude with which this measure was carried into effect, caused a good many people to suspect that either the young heiress herself, or some of her friends for her, were determined to turn the place to profit.

But all this was done with such a systematic avoidance of discussion about it on the part of Helen, that, notwithstanding the very delightful and very perfect harmony which existed between them all, there was not any one of the Rixley family who had any knowledge of what her motive could be for robbing the place both of dignity and beauty, and that for the sake of gaining money, which it was very evident she could not want, and which it was very evident she did not spend.

It was, however, almost impossible for the Rixley family not to suppose, however little their previous knowledge of her had led to such a conclusion, that Helen was avaricious; and they certainly did suppose it, though there was so much in her general conduct and apparent disposition to make them think otherwise. But facts, as we all know, are stubborn things; and unquestionably there were many facts which led to this conclusion.

In the first place, her wish to become her own housekeeper

showed a decided inclination to obtain the control of money;
and although at first it might have been supposed that this wish
was created rather by the desire of spending money, than of
saving it, the results showed very clearly that this was not the
case. It is true, indeed, that she contrived, somehow or other,
that they should mix more freely with the neighbours, whose
society they really liked, than they had ever done before; but
this was not achieved by means of giving costly entertainments;
for although Helen very frequently invited two or three favourite
neighbours to dine with her, nearly a year had elapsed since she
had become mistress of her house, without her ever having
received what among country neighbours is called a " dinner
party."

There was another symptom of Helen's dislike to costly expenditure in her dress. Upon their first taking up their abode
at the Park, it had been agreed between Mr. Rixley and his
wife, that Helen should receive a yearly stipend of one hundred
pounds for her dress. She had appeared somewhat startled at
the large amount; however, she made no objection to receiving
it, but, on the contrary, seemed to enjoy the power it gave her
of buying pretty things exceedingly. Moreover, it very rarely
happened that she bought one pretty thing without buying two,
for it was only by this contrivance that she could make her
friend Anne look as smart as herself—a point upon which she
appeared at that time to be very particular.

But all this was altered now; she very rarely gave her Cousin
Anne anything that was much worth having; and as to her
own dress, if it had not been that the marked simplicity of her
attire seemed to become her so particularly that she might have
been suspected of coquetry for adopting it, she might have been
said to be the most economically dressed heiress in the world.

There was yet another point upon which her tender care of
money became evident, exactly at the time when she first began
to have considerable power over that variously valued article.
When Helen first took up her residence at Beauchamp Park,
there was no feature in her new neighbourhood which seemed
to inspire her with so much interest as the condition of the
poor, and often did she deny to herself, and perhaps to Anne
too, the indulgence of a new bonnet, in order to purchase a new
blanket for a poor neighbour.

Now, although this had never been done ostentatiously, it had
never been done mysteriously, and everybody, therefore, said
that "pretty Miss Beauchamp seemed likely to be very free

with her money," but nobody could say this any longer now; for pretty Miss Beauchamp, very decidedly, was not free with her money. Yet nevertheless she could never be said either to forget her poor neighbours; on the contrary, she seemed to keep them in her memory in a way which was too constant, and too resolutely active, to be at all agreeable to her servants.

Her alms, before she became her own housekeeper, had consisted chiefly of donations from her own private purse; but now the privy purse was spared, and the hungry part of the village population were invited to appear in the servants' hall twice a-week, where she very punctually gave them the meeting, and presented them such a proportion of well-prepared soup, or well-preserved fragments, as might be spared without any sin against economy.

Now certainly all this did look as if the heiress was learning to love money, and this love of money is not a species of affection which is contemplated with any very tender feelings by lookers on, even when they feel within themselves something like sympathy with it.

But, somehow or other, Helen, though she used but little caution in the manifestation of this weakness, seemed to escape the feeling of dislike which it generally inspires; for, to say the truth, nobody seemed to dislike her, notwithstanding her peculiarities; and considering the limited number of her acquaintance, a good many people really appeared to be very fond of her.

As to her own relations they were probably partial, for notwithstanding their having such excellent opportunities for seeing all her faults, it would have been difficult to make any one of them confess that she had any.

Neither did her " standing " in the neighbourhood appear to suffer in any important degree from her pertinacious averseness to dinner parties, handsome carriages, fine dresses, or stately deer.

The intercourse between the Beauchamp Park and the Harrington families had become not only frequent, but intimate in no common degree; for the elders of the two houses suited each other particularly well, and the two young ladies at Beauchamp Park, and the two young ladies at The Oaks (the residence of Mr. Harrington), might almost have been quoted as two pair of double cherries, so closely affectionate was the union between them.

Nor were these the only neighbours with whom the Rixley

family, and Helen, had contracted a degree of intimacy which had ripened into friendship. Sir William and Lady Knighton, who lived at the distance only of a mile from the park gates, though not in the same parish, together with their numerous progeny, were among those who lived with them on terms more resembling a friendship of long standing than an almost new acquaintance; moreover, there was a rather antiquated bachelor of the name of Phelps, who was nearer to them still, and who from various causes, one doubtless being the convenient vicinity of his residence, was more frequently a guest at the Park than any other individual.

No great dinners, nor costly receptions of any kind, were found necessary to keep up a constant intercourse between these friendly neighbours; and the Beauchamp Park family were, for the present, perfectly well contented without extending their intimacies any further.

It may seem, perhaps, a little strange, but so it was, that of all these intimacies, notwithstanding my double-cherry simile, the most intimate was that which existed between old Mr. Phelps and my young heroine. How this came to pass it might be tedious to relate in detail, for the circumstances which led to it were very trivial. Mr. Phelps dined exactly at the same rather early hour as the family at the Park, and during the fair weather months of the year this led to a long afternoon walk, or a long afternoon lounge on the garden seats of the Beauchamp shrubberies, for those who had nothing else to do that they liked better.

Now Mr. Rixley liked an after dinner nap better; and Mrs. Rixley had for years set this portion of her existence apart (when not very particularly engaged) to the reading a daily news-paper.

Anne Rixley, though not a distinguished musician by nature, was greatly desirous to become one by practice, and this was the interval which, whenever it was in her power, she liked to devote to this object; and thus Helen was left at perfect liberty to dispose of herself as she liked, a privilege which she valued greatly, and that she did so value it was not a secret to any-body.

Many of these precious hours were spent, as may easily be imagined, in reading; for much of Helen's very miscellaneous reading was of a kind that could best be enjoyed alone. During the short days of the year this luxury was indulged in within the shelter of her own dressing-room; but in the longer and warmer days of the year, her study was chosen from among the quietest and prettiest retreats of her ample gardens.

It was once, twice, and again, that while thus enjoying herself, her greatly valued old neighbour, Mr. Phelps, had found her out, and very decidedly disturbed her in her favourite occupation. And for the once or twice, perhaps, she was not only disturbed, but in a small degree vexed at the interruption; for she had loved to think herself alone, when she looked round upon the fair and tranquil spot she had chosen, and as quite beyond the reach of interruption.

Fortunately for her, however, her temper was too sweet, and her manner too gentle, for the intruder to discover that she was annoyed by his approach, and therefore the third time came. And then their conversation began by the seemingly commonplace question, " What are you reading ? "

But her answer did more towards converting them from neighbours into friends than it was probably any other answer of the same length could have done, and yet it only consisted in her telling him the title of the book she held in her hand. The book was a newly-published work on electricity, and its probable influence in many cases where no such influence is suspected.

Now in these blessed latter days there is nothing very extraordinary in a young girl getting hold of a book upon electricity, and reading it; so it could not be this fact which so much struck Mr. Phelps. The fact that did strike him was, that in all his pleasant intimate intercourse with the family at the Park, he had never heard a single word drop from Mr. Rixley, or from any member of the family, which had led him to guess that natural science was among the subjects to which their reading hours were devoted.

And this remark was neither hastily made, nor ill-founded. Mr. Rixley was not only an accomplished classical scholar, he was also a deeply-read historian; but accident, or inclination, or both, had led him throughout his life much more to literature than to science; and the consequence of this naturally was, that his family also were more literary than scientific.

Exactly the contrary of this was the case with Mr. Bolton; and, as great part of Helen's education, such as it was, had been received from him, it naturally followed that she had, in some degree, acquired his opinions respecting what is the most interesting occupation for the human intellect.

But she had sufficient quickness to perceive that her ideas on this subject differed essentially from those of her uncle and his family, and sufficient tact not to obtrude her love for scientific nibbling upon those who had no appetite for it; a sort of forbearance which it was the more easy for her to practise, because she had vastly more sympathy with their favourite studies than they had with hers.

With her new old friend, Mr. Phelps, the case was very similar. He half worshipped, half idolized, good poetry, as a sort of inspiration that was "light from Heaven;" but he dived and delved into the depths of science with the devoted and the hopeful industry of an Australian digger; feeling deeply convinced the while, that if any means exists by which man can improve his condition here below, or learn to guess what might await him in ages yet to come, we must look for them in the direction of natural science.

Now Mr. Phelps, being one of the most kind-hearted and social-tempered old bachelors in the world, had thought himself exceedingly fortunate in the acquisition of such very near, and such very agreeable neighbours as those at Beauchamp Park. The absence of all pretence and affectation among them delighted him, and he was much too wise a man to run the risk of weakening the cordial liking which so evidently existed between them, by endeavouring to lead the conversation to subjects which it was evident to him could not be interesting to them.

But, nevertheless, he would have dearly liked to cultivate a taste for his own favourite pursuits among them, could he have discerned the least germ of inclination for it in any of them.

The hope of this, however, he had long abandoned; for the only one of the party to whom nature had given a propensity to peep into her mysteries was one of the last in the world to obtrude her own speculations upon companions whose speculations were evidently directed elsewhere.

But this little adventure of the title-page led to sundry discoveries, that were exceedingly interesting to both the parties concerned in it; and it required a wonderfully short time to establish between the old gentleman and the young lady a sort of sympathetic cordiality, which soon ripened into a friendship that truly deserved the epithet of confidential; and the consequence of this was, that poor Helen soon found herself pouring out all the secrets of her heart to old Mr. Phelps, with a degree of *abandon* greater than she had ever indulged in since she had lost the companionship of her brother.

There were, doubtless, other reasons for this, besides the fact that they both loved to talk, and to think, of things in Heaven,

and things on earth, and things under the earth ; and amongst
these other reasons may be counted the fact, that the subject
upon which her heart was most deeply interested, namely,
the fate of her brother, and all the mysteries concerning him,
was one upon which, for a multitude of reasons, she never could
converse freely, either with her uncle or any of his family.

All this, however, was arrived at with a little less rapidity
than I have used in recounting it; but the friendship of Mr
Phelps was so soon to be resorted to by Helen, in an affair in
which the most confidential secrecy was required, that it was
necessary to explain to the reader how it came to pass that such
a feeling had so speedily been brought into existence between
my young heroine and her aged neighbour.

<hr>

CHAPTER XXX

Henry Rixley, though probably without any very sanguine
hope of an ultimate change in his destiny, had eagerly welcomed the temporary relief afforded by following his friend
Helen's advice to delay the ceremony of ordination as long as
possible.

The taking any step that led irretrievably towards his
devoting himself to a profession for which he felt himself
both unfitted and disinclined, was terrible to him.

There was so much of genuine truth, and of sound common
sense, in the judgment that he thus passsed upon himself, that
Helen, who was the only member of his own family to whom
he had opened his heart on the subject, felt no scruples of conscience in continuing her counsel in favour of delay ; but it
would have been difficult for Henry to have persevered in it,
without at once confessing his own hope of ultimate escape
from what he so greatly wished to avoid, had it not been for
the lucky accident of his having been proposed by his tutor as
the travelling companion of a young man of high rank, who
had, like Henry himself, just taken a very respectable degree.

This well-timed proposal was, in every respect, too advantageous to be declined, and the plotting cousins were, for the present at least, very pleasantly relieved from the painful task of

endeavouring to avoid an event which was pressing onwards
towards them too rapidly for any very reasonable hope that
temporary delay might enable them to escape it.

But now, everything seemed going on well. Very few young
ladies under eighteen have ever suffered more from anxiety to
achieve an important piece of business, in which love had no
concern, than Helen had done, in order to discover some means
of 'saving her Cousin Henry from a destiny which he dreaded,
and which, she was fully persuaded, would never have threatened
him, had she herself never been born!

This, certainly, was a painful situation, and it was made more
so by her conviction—and a very well-founded conviction it was
—that no argument which it was in her power to use would
induce her uncle to consent to her pledging herself to purchase
a commission for her cousin, as soon as she should come of
age.

It was under these circumstances that she had asked for an
increase of income, and for permission to regulate the expenditure of it herself; and it was with the very sanguine, but not
very reasonable hope of being able to save from this income the
sum necessary to the purchase of a commission for him, that the
young heiress made a *début* as a housekeeper with such extreme
economy.

It can hardly be said that she was disappointed at the result
of her economical contrivances; for, what with the profits of
her careful farming, together with the fruits of her strict economy, she found herself in possession of a sum that almost startled
her by the largeness of its amount; but yet it was not enough;
for Henry had despairingly told her what the price of a desirable commission might be, and the time now peremptorily fixed
by his father for his ordination was drawing very near, and she
was on the very eve of proposing to him that an *un*desirable
commission should be bought, rather than that he should take
the irrevocable step, when all her anxieties were suddenly brought
to a most happy conclusion by the appointment of her delighted
cousin as a travelling tutor.

The news of this appointment was very joyfully hailed by
the whole family, but not either of them had the least idea how
very much the joy of Helen exceeded theirs; had they guessed
it, they would probably have guessed also that some very tender
sentiment must have been at work within her to cause such
strong emotion; but, if they had, their guessing then would
have been most egregiously wrong, for the feelings and anxieties

of the young Helen concerning her Cousin Henry were infinitely
more like those of an affectionate mother, than of an enamoured
maid; and so full was her heart of the joy which this appointment occasioned her, that she at length indulged herself, by
confiding the weighty secret of all her plots and plans to Mr.
Phelps.

"And why did you not tell me of all this before?" said the
old gentleman, who perfectly well knew that he was more in her
confidence than any other person.

"Because I knew that if I did tell, you would offer to
help me with money," replied Helen, with unflinching sincerity.

"And if I had done so, Miss Nelly," replied the old man,
looking reproachfully at her, "what harm would it have done
you?"

"The very great harm of obliging me to refuse an offered
kindness from you," she replied.

"And wherefore should you have thought it necessary to
refuse such an accommodation from me?" returned Mr. Phelps,
somewhat sternly.

"Because I feel that in requesting permission as I have
done, to take into my own young hands, the management of the
money allowed for my maintenance, and for the keeping in
proper order the house and grounds where we are permitted to
reside, I have pledged myself to my most dear and confiding
uncle to act with the most careful discretion, and to the very best
of my poor judgment, so as to prevent his ever having cause to
repent the confidence he has placed in me."

"Perfectly right, Miss Beauchamp! I doubt if any minor
could have answered more discreetly. But I must beg you to
answer another question. Why should my being permitted to
assist you in a very praiseworthy object, be considered by you as
objectionable?" returned Mr. Phelps.

"It would have appeared objectionable to me," replied Helen,
demurely, "because my borrowing money from a neighbour,
before I could legally give any security for the repayment of it,
even though it was for the purpose of buying a commission
for a young gentleman, would not, according to the best
of my poor judgment, have been acting with careful discretion."

Mr. Phelps could not conceal a smile, but he held up a
threatening finger and he shook his head.

"Mark my words, Helen Beauchamp!" said he, "if you turn

out a lawyer upon my hands, it is not your boasting the dignity of the gown, or the coif either, that shall prevent my giving you up altogether. A pretty account I should have to give of myself did I, like other great men, keep a conscientiously true diary of my thoughts, and feelings! After making a touching statement of my joy and thankfulness at having found an unsophisticated young mind, full of energy and industry in the pursuit of the stupendously vast—and stupendously minute—truths of nature, I must go on to tell that the said young mind had, nevertheless, a deplorable propensity towards special pleading! Fie upon you, Helen! Fie upon you for having thought all those business-like thoughts and then acting upon them!"

"And in my private diary," replied Helen, "I should have to confess, that upon one occasion, when I thought I had found the most devoted lover of truth in the world, I subsequently discovered that the most striking feature in this candid indi-vidual, was a tyrannical love of scolding, which led him to find fault with people, even when he knew they were perfectly right. No doubt of it, Mr. Phelps, we are both of us *very* obstinate tempers, so I think that for the preservation of our friendship, which is really very pleasant, the best plan will be for us to agree to differ now and then, without quarrelling about it."

"Well! Miss Nelly! I believe you are right, so let us shake hands, and agree to endure each other as long as we can."

The compact thus entered into was a lasting one, and one effect of it was that Mr. Phelps was very soon in possession of all Helen's secrets; and the comfort and relief she found from being able to express, at last, with perfect unreserve, all her love, all her fears, and all her regrets about her brother, was very great. She had the certainty too that she was not giving pain to the patient listener, to whom she now, for the first time, described all the fine qualities of her brother, just as they ap-peared to her, and most assuredly the portrait she drew of him was one well calculated to create a very strong interest for him in the heart of such a man as Mr. Phelps.

There was one, and only one secret which she did not reveal to him. She did not tell him that there were moments when, remembering the warm, the vehement, the ardent temper of her brother, together with the fearful treatment which he had received,—she did not tell Mr. Phelps that there were dreadful moments, both by day and night, during which, the horrible idea that he might have been guilty of his father's death recurred to her!

And Helen was very wise in this, for herein Mr. Phelps could have brought her neither help nor comfort. It would have been much more easy for her to have imparted the vague suspicion which so often tormented her existence, than to have infused into the mind of her old friend, the species of antidote which was always, more or less, producing a neutralizing effect on her own heart, either in the shape of doubt of the fact itself, or of a feeling which she would not have recognised as justification, but which was somewhat allied to it, and which arose as she recalled the scene (never forgotten) in which he had proclaimed to the boy the infamy of the mother whose memory he so wished to reverence.

As to the other mystery which attached to Helen, namely, that of having a fondly remembered, and devoted old servant, who, for some reason or other, kept herself too completely concealed for it to be possible for any inquiry to discover her retreat, she said nothing to her friend, Mr. Phelps, for she felt that it would be difficult, if not impossible, to make him understand how well she deserved the tender recollection she cherished of her, while appearing so completely to forget her existence. As to the real explanation of this mystery it was not in Helen's power to give it, for she was herself as ignorant of it, as it was possible Mr. Phelps could be.

CHAPTER XXXI.

The economy of our young housekeeper was suffered to relax a little after her cousin's appointment was finally settled, and, by gentle degrees, she began to see a good deal more of her neighbours. This was not done, however, without a good deal of prudent forethought, Mr. Phelps quietly assisting her in all her schemes, though keeping himself as completely out of sight, and as carefully, as if their plotting together were for the purpose of affecting some treason against the state.

But the old gentleman plainly perceived, that with all her lawyer-like cleverness, she could not easily attain the object she

15

had in view without assistance; and that assistance he determined to give her, though not at the cost of being, or seeming to be a meddling busybody, which would in truth have been acting a part very particularly foreign to his nature. But, between them, they managed too well for there to be any danger of this, and her excellent uncle, his admirable wife, and amiable daughter, had no more suspicion that their well-beloved Helen was every now and then buying a little three per cent. consol-stock in the name of her cousin, Henry Rixley, than that when she set out upon one of her *tête-à-tête* rambles with old Mr. Phelps, she discoursed with him on subjects which led them to discuss a good many of those recondite things in heaven and earth, which, as Hamlet very just observed to his friend Horatio, were not dreamed of in their philosophy. But, nevertheless, notwithstanding all this very decided eccentricity on the part of my heroine, her neighbours seemed to take very kindly to her, and to welcome her progressive steps towards majority, and party-giving, with great satisfaction.

This increased sociability did not, however, bring the family at Beauchamp Park into intimacy with any neighbours likely to rival their friends the Harringtons in their affection; and by gentle degrees it certainly became evident that the heir of Speedhurst Abbey was not the individual of that family who was the least likely to declare that Helen Beauchamp was "made up of every creature's best."

The person who first discovered this was his sister Agnes, and as her opinion of Helen, allowing for the natural difference between a young gentleman and a young lady on such a subject, was in very excellent sympathy with his own, she watched all the symptoms of his rapidly growing attachment with very great satisfaction.

But she thought her own satisfaction in contemplating the probable result of this, would be infinitely greater still, could she bring him honestly to confess the fact that he was in love, and in order to procure herself this greatly desired satisfaction, she determined to invite him to a *tête-à-tête* ramble in search of a wild flower, indigenous to the neighbourhood, which she wished to transplant into her garden, and in the course of such an expedition she thought she might easily lead the conversation in such a direction as would produce the result she desired.

Nothing could be more easy than to obtain the companionship of her brother upon such an expedition; for he, too, was a gardener, and loved to make experiments.

Their talk, as they set forth, was on the marvellous effects of culture, and of the power granted to man not only of using, but of improving the natural productions with which we are so liberally surrounded.

"I often think," said George Harrington, "when I watch, year after year, the improvements, nay, even the variations which it is in the power of art to produce on vegetation, that we are not yet aware of all the power that has been bestowed on us, or, at any rate, that we do not use it." "Quite true!" replied his sister. "Your gardener at Speedhurst has shown me flowers in the conservatory there that were as unlike any I ever saw before, as if they were new creations. And yet they were all old acquaintances that had been subjected to a little clever discipline."

"Does it never come into your head, Agnes," returned her brother, "that if we took as much pains with education, and ventured to be as experimental, we might do a good deal towards eradicating some of our worst failings? It would be a good thing, wouldn't it, if we could weed out original sin?"

"Doubtless, but I suspect that we have no such power," replied Agnes. "It would be like attempting to revise creation, and improve the work by our contrivances."

"Not more so than when we graft a peach upon an almond, or a pippin upon a crab," returned George.

"I have often thought," he continued, "that the very puzzling question about the origin of evil might be solved by my theory. The labours of the human brain, and their effect upon the condition of man, are becoming more stupendous every day, and it would be an impious, as well as a bold man, who should fix a limit to them. It would have appeared quite as absurd a hundred years ago to talk of sending a message under the water from Dover to Calais, as it does now to talk of finding out a way of making human beings understand that it would be more for their interest, and gratification also, to do what was right, than to do what was wrong."

"When you contrive to do that, brother George," replied Agnes, laughing, "I shall be quite ready to allow that we may toll the knell over original sin." And having said this, she skipped off to climb the bank under which they were walking, apparently for the purpose of examining some plants growing on it, but in reality for the more important purpose of putting an end to her brother's discussion; for if she let him pursue the speculation upon which he was entering, she saw but little chance of her discovering before they got home again, whether he were in love with Helen Beauchamp or not.

After lingering, therefore, for a minute or two among the brambles and weeds, amidst which she had placed herself, she returned to the path by another active spring, and passing her arm under that of her brother she contrived cleverly enough to open the theme on which she was intent, without appearing too suddenly to abandon that which had occupied them before, by saying, "You never will persuade me, George, that any power, but that of God direct, could make such a faultless creature as my friend Helen Beauchamp. Education has had very little to do, I think, in making her what she is."

The name of Helen Beauchamp being at that moment perfectly unexpected, it made the young man start so vehemently that Agnes felt as if the question she was so anxious to ask was already answered. And this was fortunate, for it did not appear that she was likely to get any other answer, for they walked on for several minutes in very perfect silence. But Agnes was not quite satisfied, and renewed the attack by saying, "Why do you not answer me, George? Do you think that education could have made Helen what she is? I don't mean in beauty, but in intellect."

"I hardly remember what I said, Agnes," he replied, gravely; "I was half jesting, I believe; but if you must have a serious answer to your strange question, I must certainly confess, then, in the instance you have named, Nature has had more to do than education."

"I thought you could not deny that," rejoined his sister; "Helen is an extraordinary sort of girl, isn't she?"

"Yes, very," he replied, and again became silent.

"How can you be so very disagreeable, George?" said his sister. "You must know how very much I love and admire her, and unless you have some particularly good reason for it, I really think it rather unkind that you will not indulge me by hearing you talk a little about her. You must know perfectly well that your opinion has great weight with me, and I should not wish to select any one as my particular friend of whom you had not a good opinion."

"I have not at all a bad opinion of Miss Beauchamp," replied the young man, thrusting his hand into his coat-pocket, and drawing forth his pocket-handkerchief, in consequence of which manœuvre his sister's arm, which rested upon his, fell unsupported by her side,

"A bad opinion! You have not at all a bad opinion of Helen Beauchamp!" repeated Agnes, very slowly.

"It is impossible to misunderstand such a phrase as that, George!" she added, after the pause of a moment, "and I am very glad that we have had this conversation together before I put in practice the thousand and one little schemes which I had in my head for enabling us to see a great deal more of her. As to your having a bad opinion of her, I should not suppose there was much chance of that, because it would be so difficult to fix upon any thing upon which a bad opinion could be founded, and you are not a person to found either a bad or a good opinion upon nothing. But that may not be enough to prevent your disliking her. Liking and disliking are almost always involuntary, I believe, and have very little to do with the judgment."

"And what have I said, Agnes, to make you suppose I dislike her?" said her brother, speaking as distinctly as the necessity of blowing his nose enabled him to do.

"Oh, quite enough," she replied, rather petulantly. "However it is quite right that you should make yourself understood, because, Heaven knows, that we have not too much of your company as it is, and I suppose we should have less still if we were to gratify our own predilections by perpetually bringing into your society a person you do not like. Jane likes Helen Beauchamp quite as well as I do, but you may depend upon it, dear George, we will neither of us indulge our liking at your expense. You shall not be bored, when you are with us, by meeting our favourites, instead of your own."

The wily young lady's device answered perfectly. This promise of clearing the premises from the approach of Miss Beauchamp, for the especial purpose of gratifying him, was more than he could stand, and his next speech, beginning with,

"Oh, Agnes, Agnes! How can you torture me so!" was not brought to a conclusion till the well pleased sister had received the agreeable assurance that if he did not marry Helen Beauchamp, he should never marry at all.

The rest of their walk was exceedingly agreeable to them both, for their conversation was wholly and solely on the subject of Helen, her perfections, and their hopes; these delightful hopes, being uttered with very comfortable confidence by the sister, and with grateful diffidence by the brother, sufficed to make them utterly forget the flight of time, nor might they have either of them recollected such grovelling occupations as dining and dressing, had not the warning note of Helen's own sonorous turret clock given them a hint that they had better turn round and walk home.

"I wish," said George Harrington, as he threw a tender glance towards the splendid abode of his beloved, "I wish that Helen was not such a rich heiress. Girls with small portions, or with none at all, must look upon a declaration of love, and an offer of marriage, in a very different light from an heiress. There is no great compliment in a man's expressing a wish to marry a girl possessed of a magnificent mansion, and lots of thousands a year—is there, Agnes?"

"When a poor man expresses such a wish I grant that your observation may have some weight," she replied, "nay, so truly do I think so, that if you were a poor man, George, instead of a rich one, I should not desire to see this marriage take place as ardently as I do now."

"I truly believe it, Agnes," said he. "But cannot you fancy," he added, musingly, "how much more delightful it would be for me to propose to Helen if she had not a farthing? She could not doubt the sincerity of my love, then, you know."

"Nor is she at all more likely to doubt it now," said his sister. "The owner of Speedhurst Abbey, and its acres, is as little likely to sell himself to a wife he does not like as a rich girl is likely to accept him if he is disagreeable to her. In a well-assorted marriage, brother George, a tolerable equality of condition precludes the fear of interested motives on either side."

"True, dearest! Most true!" he gaily replied. "I should be sorry to spend my good uncle's property in the purchase of a wife, so if I get her, my Agnes, I will promise to take the good the gods provide without grumbling."

But although George Harrington had thus candidly confessed his tender passion to his sister Agnes, it was still some months before he ventured to confess it to the fair Helen herself. She was still very young, too young for it to be right for him to make her a proposal, without having first obtained her uncle's permission to do so; and George Harrington preferred waiting and watching with doubtful joy for occasional symptoms of partiality on her part, to the offering her his hand with the formal sanction of her guardian, which at her age would seem almost like a command to her to accept it. Moreover, as yet, George Harrington had no home of his own to offer her, and though nothing could be more convenient and proper than that if he married a woman who was mistress of a splendid residence, he should occupy it till he was in possession of his own, he still felt a repugnance to asking for the immediate use of her property while she was still so young as to render her granting it more the act of her guardian than of herself.

Meanwhile, the hours and days they passed together were becoming more and more delightful to them both, and not even the lover himself could feel an interval to be long which was passed with so much hopeful happiness.

During the whole of this time, however, it must be remembered that Miss Beauchamp had received no offer of marriage from Mr. George Harrington. But she was in no way surprised at this; she felt very perfectly sure that he was not only devotedly attached to her, but also that it was his intention to offer her his hand as soon as he considered her old enough to become his wife. And most thankful and happy did she feel as she silently meditated on the destiny which awaited her.

It is certain that the early years of Helen had passed in a manner to make her prematurely thoughtful, and it was with no light childish transitory feeling that she contemplated the happy prospects which now seemed opening before her.

She still clung with devoted love and admiration to the remembrance of what her brother was, before the last dreaded scene which preceded her father's death; but even while in the very act of recalling all the high ability and all the noble qualities he had manifested before the atrocious conduct and base reproaches of his father had lashed him into the terrible state of mind which she had witnessed, even while thinking of all he had been to her then, she could not help feeling conscious that the dreadful manner in which they had been separated formed an epoch in her early history which it would be painful to relate to George Harrington.

Nevertheless, she was fully determined that nothing should be concealed from him, and that she never would become his wife till every particular of her early position, so widely different from that in which he now saw her, should have been made known to him.

It would have been a pleasure, or, at least, a comfort, to Helen, could this disclosure have been made immediately; but she fancied that her volunteering this confidential narrative, before he had given her any positive right to believe that it was her duty to make it, would be exactly the reverse of the line of conduct which she wished to pursue towards him; for it would at once show him that she considered him as her future husband, though he had never yet formally declared his hope of being so.

She might have spared herself a good deal of suffering had she decided otherwise.

CHAPTER XXXII.

It chanced one fine summer evening, when Helen, her friend Agnes, and young Harrington were sitting together on a garden bench in Mr. Harrington's garden, that Agnes took it into her head to amuse herself by relating to Helen the conversation, or rather a part of the conversation, which she had held with her brother about a year before, concerning the great drawback which a large fortune, on the part of a young lady, offered to the perfect happines of a love match.

"As how ?" demanded Helen, slightly colouring.

"Oh! for a deeply romantic reason," replied her friend. "George says," continued Agnes, "that no man who falls in love with a girl of large fortune can ever have the delight of proving to her beyond the reach of doubt that he loves her for herself alone."

"I do not agree with him," said Helen. "If indeed the lover were in a station of life so much below that of his beloved as to render a marriage between them incongruous, or in any way degrading to the lady, I should then think that the best and most honourable thing he could do would be to conquer his tender passion as speedily as possible, for I do not think that persons in different situations of life, or disproportioned and ill-matched in any way, are at all likely to do well together as man and wife."

"You are wrong, fair lady! You are wrong!" returned George, very earnestly, "I can conceive nothing on earth so delightful—so perfectly enviable—as the situation of a young man possessed of a large fortune, falling in love with an adorable girl who has none. There must be something so very delightful in giving this unquestionable proof of love—this indisputable assurance that she is dearer than all the world beside! I can imagine no happiness superior to that. No man asking a rich woman to marry him can feel it!"

"Oh yes! I comprehend you perfectly," returned Helen, the "celestial rosy red" still deepening on her cheek. "It is clear that you are longing to enact the classic drama of the king and the beggar girl, or the dairy-maid, or whatever she was. But I think your theory very unphilosophical, Mr. Harrington. There is more of discord than of harmony in your notion."

"You would not say so if you perfectly understood me, Miss Beauchamp," returned George, eagerly. "My portionless angel may have all the advantages your imagination can heap upon her, save money. So far am I, indeed, from differing from you as to the absolute necessity that there should be no striking incongruity of position in marriage, that I don't believe there is a man in the world who would shrink from forming a really unsuitable connection more than I should do. I would far rather remain single all my life than give my children a mother who should in any way disgrace them. My theory, Miss Beauchamp, about wishing for poverty in a wife may, perhaps, have something fanciful in it, and I certainly can imagine the possibility of my getting over it. But Heaven keep me from falling in love with a woman who should bring dishonour with her. I really believe that if I were the hero of a romance, having a discovery of that sort as its catastrophe, I should lose my senses."

This tirade being uttered to the lineal descendant of the fine old race of Beauchamps, and the heir of its wide-spreading acres, as well as of its ancient name, was uttered as fearlessly, as it was vehemently; and when Helen got up and walked away with the air of a person who had listened to a discussion till it had become wearisome, he might, perhaps, feel a little vexed at himself for riding one of his hobbies to death; but he little guessed that he had sent a poisoned arrow to the heart of one whom he would have died to protect from injury.

And yet a poisoned arrow could scarcely have given a sharper pang to the heart of the unfortunate Helen than the words he had spoken.

That the brother she so dearly loved was the offspring of shame, would have, of itself, sufficed to make the words she had listened to, sound like a note of warning, giving her notice to beware before she permitted herself to love too well one who might shrink from all affinity with the being who, with the exception of her mother, she had hitherto loved better than any other in the world. But, alas! this was not all. Perhaps it was, now, as she hung over a rose-bush, appearing to admire its redundant blossoms, that Helen felt, for the first time, ALL the horror of believing it *possible* that this dear—this most fondly-loved—brother had been guilty of a crime more terrible, if it were possible, than that of the first murder.

Poor George Harrington, blushing like a school-boy at the idea of having wearied his lady love by his prosing, approached her, laughingly, and seizing playfully upon her hand, which she had extended as if to gather a flower, he exclaimed, "No, Helen! no! *Point de rose sans épines*; that is an established fact, we all know. But you have already had your share of *épines* while listening to my confession of faith about matrimony, and now you shall have a rose without any. All the other thorns shall be for me."

And so saying, he gathered one or two of the very loveliest buds he could find, and having at the imminent risk of excoriating his fingers, ran them resolutely up and down every stem, he presented them to her.

She received them mechanically, and mechanically, too, turned towards him as she did so.

Helen was not aware of the ghastly paleness of her own cheek as she did this, but the sudden start he gave, and the frightened expression of his eye as he looked at her, made her at once feel conscious that her looks were betraying a portion of the misery she was feeling at her heart.

"Helen! you are suffering! you are ill!" he exclaimed, in an agony of alarm. "You must sit down, Helen. You must let me place you on the sofa. And without waiting for an answer, which in truth she was in no state to give, he threw his arm round her and almost carried her through the open window by which they had passed from the drawing-room to the lawn.

Agnes, who had remained sitting on the garden-bench when the unfortunate conversation had began, plainly perceiving that her brother was supporting Helen in a manner which he would not have done had she been able to support herself, rushed into the room after them, and was as much shocked as surprised at finding her friend alarmingly pale, and evidently suffering, though protesting, in a not very audible voice, that she was now quite well again.

"No, Helen! you are not well," exclaimed Agnes, as she pressed the clay-cold hand of her friend. "And yet a few, a very few minutes ago I thought I had never seen you looking so well. You must have been very near fainting, dearest, or

you could not have looked so ghastly pale as you did when I
entered the room. Are you subject to fainting, Helen? You
never told me of it."

"No, no, I am not subject to it," replied Helen, attempting
to smile, "but I certainly did feel very unwell just now. It is
quite gone off, however, and I shall be perfectly well when I
get into the open carriage again, for my drive home. Will you
have the kindness to order it for me?"

"What! won't you stay till the evening with us, Helen, as
you promised?" said her friend Agnes, looking greatly disappointed. "Oh! I had so much to say to you, and about such a
multitude of things! Why should you not stay and get well
here, dearest?"

"Oblige me, my dearest Agnes," said Helen, languidly. "I
know so perfectly well how to manage my little nervous in-
firmities! I had a very bad nervous fever once, and though I
have been getting better and stronger every year since I came
to the Park, I am not yet quite so strong a person as I hope to
be when I am older. But you must trust me to my own
management, Agnes. And if you will come and see me to-
morrow, you may depend upon it you will find me quite well."

George Harrington had stood anxiously looking at her while
this discussion was taking place, and notwithstanding her pallid
cheek and shaking hand, he felt strongly tempted to think that
the malady which had seized upon her, was not caused by any
physical ailment, but was the result of some painful feeling
occasioned by the conversation in which they had been engaged.

It might be difficult to say whether this idea lessened or
increased his anxiety.

His first object, however, was to indulge her in her wish of
returning home, and that without harassing her by any explanations. The result of this feeling was his immediately leaving
the room into which they had entered, for the purpose of causing
her carriage to drive to the door with as little delay as possible.

Helen was, in truth, very much in earnest in her wish to get
home, and she blessed the kindness and the sympathy which so
promptly enabled her to do so; but the first hour that she
passed in the undisturbed solitude of her own chamber was a
very dreadful one.

It may very often happen, without any harshness on the part
of the commentator, that the first love of a young lady under
twenty may be treated as a whim, a fancy that is not likely to
produce any very important consequence upon her future life.

But it was not so with Helen Beauchamp. She loved George Harrington, and she knew she loved him; and, moreover, young as she was, she knew herself too well to believe, to think, or to hope, that she should ever live to conquer the feeling, or to substitute any other in the place of it.

The result of her first hour's meditation, therefore, was a deep conviction that her destiny was blighted for life. Never before had the terrible suspicion which lay half smothered at the bottom of her own heart appeared to her so fearfully well-founded as it did during that miserable hour. But, nevertheless, in the midst of this misery, she was true to the first affection of her heart, and could she by a wish have summoned the unfortunate Willian Rixley to her side, she would have done it; and when she had got him there, neither love, nor fear, would, for a single moment, have caused her to turn away from him.

As the consciousness of this rushed warmly to her heart whilst she thought of him, she thanked God for saving her from the baseness of loving any other better than she loved him.

"George Harrington has so much to make him happy besides my love!" thought she. "But what has William got? He is, and ever shall be, first, and dearest! But that is not now the question before me," murmured poor Helen, as she remembered all the recent scenes of her late happy life. "The worst of my condition is that I can never again utter one single word of truth to poor George Harrington! And he is so true himself! So very, very true! Here is my greatest misery. Were I to tell him the frightful story exactly as it is, I can easily believe that he would make light of it, and endeavour to persuade me that he loves me well enough to wish to become my husband, despite the sin and shame to which I am so nearly allied. And so he does!" thought the miserable Helen, as the tears rolled down her burning cheeks. "But is that a reason for my beguiling him into close alliance with what his nature shrinks from?"

The answer which her heart and conscience deliberately gave to this question, may be easily imagined, but it might not be so easy for anyone to guess with what admirable self devotion she finally resolved to lead him by gentle degrees far away from the belief, which she could not doubt he now cherished, of one day becoming her husband.

As to her ever marrying herself, she felt *that*, in her very heart of hearts, to be impossible; and the greatest comfort she

had, was from believing that when he discovered this to be her
determination respecting all others, he would be more easily
reconciled to his own disappointment.

The continued silence of Mrs. Lambert had suggested to Helen
the real truth, namely, that this faithful servant had actually set
off upon a wildly roving expedition in search of William ; and
the length of time that had elapsed since their parting, rather
tended to persuade her that she had not abandoned all hope of
finding him, than that she had given up the search in despair.

But whether this conjecture were correct, or not, the terrible
fact that if George Harrington knew all the circumstances connected with her, he would not select her as his wife, remained
the same, and the poor heiress felt, notwithstanding all the
wealth that had fallen upon her, that her lot was not a happy
one.

CHAPTER XXXIII.

No two heads ever plotted together with more perfect sympathy, and more perfect success, than those of Helen Beauchamp, and her friend and counsellor Mr. Phelps. Not only
was the sum of money necessary for the purchase of the commission, which was the object of her cousin's ambition, provided,
and safely lodged where it could be got at, on the shortest
possible notice, but the two plotters contrived between them, to
bring the subject of choosing a profession, on more than one
occasion, before the family conclave; and it was amusing to
both of them to observe how skilfully the other contrived in the
most easy unpremeditated manner imaginable, to find an opportunity of remarking on the great advantage in every way,
of a man's being able to devote his talents and his energies
in the direction that his inclination pointed out to him.

Mr. Phelps in particular, was exceedingly eloquent on the
subject, so much so, indeed, as to cause good Mr. Rixley to sigh
deeply as he replied, " Very true, Sir! Very true! There can
be no doubt of it. But it is unfortunately a point upon which it
but rarely happens, I suspect, that the person most deeply
concerned finds himself in a position which enables him to con-

sult his own inclination, instead of the means and convenience of those who have to provide for him."

"I am afraid so," replied Mr. Phelps. "But you agree with me, Rixley, don't you, that where circumstances permit the choice, it is a great blessing to the young aspirant for success of some kind, when the direction in which it is to be sought can be of his own selection."

"Certainly, certainly," was the cordial reply of Mr. Rixley; and it was not forgotten by those who heard him utter it.

And now, the great and important object of Helen's careful economy being acheived, she very gently and quietly began to relax in the practice of it. Anne, who from improving health had grown into a fine, tall, handsome young woman, found her wardrobe gradually improving from day to day, and what was, if possible, still more agreeable, the occasions for displaying her pretty things were multiplying almost as fast as the pretty things themselves.

But it was all done so quietly, and with such a total absence of everything like ostentation, or display, that it appeared almost like the result of accident.

The effect of this change was very pleasantly felt throughout the neighbourhood; but somehow or other it was Anne Rixley, and not Miss Beauchamp, who now seemed to be the favourite belle of the neighbourhood, for although in real grace of form, and beauty of feature, she was immeasurably inferior to her cousin, the sort of clever system by which the young mistress of the park contrived both at home and abroad, to put her forward as the *belle par excellence* of the neighbourhood was very skilful, and very effective.

She was really a very charming, animated, and perfectly unaffected girl, and being an unwearied dancer, waltz player, and charade performer, she speedily became a celebrated personage in the neighbourhood, and, with the exception of poor George Harrington's vote, would have been unanimously declared the most captivating girl in it.

On the subject of the beautiful heiress herself, opinions varied greatly. Everybody, old and young, male and female, would have agreed in declaring that she was very handsome, and very elegant, and very obliging; but one person would have said, perhaps, that she was proud, and another might have hinted a suspicion that she was not in good health. Some might have confessed that they thought her over-studious for so young a lady; and many, if they had been quite sincere, would have confessed that they liked her cousin best, because she was more like other people.

But of all the various individuals who, to say the truth, were puzzled because they could not make out why it was that she was not like other girls of her age, none were so painfully puzzled as George Harrington, and his sister Agnes. Till that unfortunate conversation took place upon the lawn, which left Helen with the dreadful persuasion that an insurmountable obstacle existed to her ever becoming the wife of the only man whom to her fancy it was possible for her to love, both the brother and sister had found especial delight in believing that they knew, and understood her character thoroughly; and often when Agnes had espied some particularly strong proof of her brother's devoted attachment to her friend, she had congratulated both herself and him upon the perfect safety with which he might rest all his hopes of happiness upon one whose beautiful "transparency of character," made it so very easy a task to guess what sort of wife she would make to a man to whom she was attached.

There was such a total absence, in the character of Helen, of everything resembling affectation, or pretence of any kind, that it seemed utterly impossible they could mistake, when they ventured to believe that she was conscious that George loved her, and conscious too, sweet soul, that she herself loved him.

But oh! the heavy change? Where was all their happy confidence now?

The rapidly failing health of his uncle had long led him to postpone the declaration of his attachment, and more than one reason had contributed to confirm his opinion that this delay was desirable.

The kind old man was, in truth, too evidently and too painfully declining, to make it desirable that any event so full of joy as his marriage with Helen, should be projected and decided on, when every month, every day, and almost every hour might be expected to be the last of his adopted father's life.

It was, indeed, less difficult than it had been, for him to leave Speedhurst Abbey without feeling that his society was wished for by its master, for the old man's memory, and almost his consciousness, was failing him. But although this made it more easy for him to be in her immediate neighbourhood, it was not a fitting time to ask her to be his wife.

Moreover, Helen was now very nearly of age; and George

Harrington greatly preferred the idea of proposing himself to her, instead of having to perform that ceremony to her uncle; not to mention his great repugnance, which has been alluded to before, to the idea of proposing himself to a wealthy heiress, while he was himself only an heir expectant.

All these reasons combined, made a short delay very evidently desirable, and, till the fatal conversation related in the last chapter, this delay was no drawback to their happiness. Each party seemed to understand the other perfectly well, and each was conscious that, happy as they were already, they were only waiting for a favourable opportunity to be more happy still.

It would really have been difficult for even an acute observer to point out any two persons less likely to wreck their happiness by a *misunderstanding*; but, nevertheless, it was a misunderstanding that now came and placed such a bar between them, as it was, in truth, very unlikely should be ever removed.

For what reasonable chance was there that Helen, who was herself so greatly in earnest when she listened to the high-flown language of George, should ever arrive at the conclusion that, in the first place, he was more than half in jest when he burst into magnanimous quotation, exclaiming, "And if it be a sin to covet honour, I am the most offending soul alive?" or that, in the next, if he had been ten times as much in earnest as she supposed him to be, yet still that his earnestness would have melted before his love like wax before the sun, if he had conceived the very slightest idea of the untold mystery, the remembrance of which now made her so miserable?

For a considerable time after the unlucky morning when she had met him with so much happiness, and left him with a feeling so very like despair, nothing worse occurred to the imagination, either of George Harrington or his sister, than that Helen had over-fatigued herself the day before, which they had spent at Beauchamp Park, and in the course of it had all walked together to make some purchase at the neighbouring village, the want of which had occurred to them while rambling along the path which led to it, though the distance was somewhat beyond the length of their usual walks.

But this interpretation did not last them long, for not all the efforts of poor Helen could prevent their perceiving that she was either seriously ill, or seriously unhappy, or both. There was, too, an alteration in the tone of her manner towards George, which, though so slight as to have been, perhaps, imperceptible to one less interested, was to him more painful than it would be easy to describe; and infinitely the more so, because there was nothing in it which could justify the idea of her being offended—for never, from the time they had first become acquainted, had she shown herself so assiduous in her attentions to his family, or so demonstrative of tender attention to his sisters; while there was a sort of deferential gentleness in her manner to him, that seemed to indicate a higher degree of esteem and respect than a man so young could often be expected to inspire. It was, therefore, evident that Helen was not offended. There was, in truth, no ground either to hope or fear it. No; it was very clear that she was not offended, but it was equally so that she was changed. Where was the bright glance which was wont to beam upon him as he approached, and which told him, even while her lips were silent, that he was dear to her heart, and welcome to her eyes? Where was that bright glance now? It was gone, put out, extinguished! Had there been, in any direction, the very slightest reason to suppose she was offended with him, the condition of his mind would have been very different. Conscious that every possible cause of offence could be but imaginary, his heart and his hope would have been sustained by the reasonable assurance that he should sooner or later discover where the blunder lay, and the removing it would be a task so delightful as to overpay him for all he had suffered.

But no grandmother, no venerable maiden aunt, ever bestowed more thoughtful care upon the object of her affectionate partiality than Helen did to prove to the whole family of Harrington, and to the unhappy George in particular, that there was no family in the whole country side that she valued so highly as she did theirs; and, most decidedly, that there was no individual who could compete, in her opinion, with him, in all the best and highest qualities which give one man superiority over another.

Yet, despite all this, she perfectly well managed to make him understand that if he said, "Helen Beauchamp, will you marry me?" her answer would have been, "No, George Harrington, I will not."

The poor young man was very wretched, and his sister Agnes was very wretched, too; for she felt that she had deceived him, or, at least, that she had been the means of leading him to deceive himself. But the subject was too difficult, as well as too delicate, for her to enter upon; and it was decidedly a relief, both to her and to Helen, when an express arrived from Speedhurst Abbey, bringing the startling intelligence that his venerable uncle had perfectly recovered his intelligence, and had expressed an earnest wish to see him.

Under no circumstances could compliance with this summons have been delayed for an hour; and in less than half that time both his father and himself were in the carriage which was to convey them to Speedhurst.

It was consolatory to them both to find, on arriving there, that they were not too late. Their venerable relative was not only still alive, but still retained a much clearer use of his mental faculties than he had manifested during many months past. But it is needless to dwell on the melancholy scene, for melancholy it was, and certainly not the less so because the farewell which both father and son received from the dying man manifested all the tender affection which had marked his character through life.

The death of the venerable owner of Speedhurst Abbey took place within twenty-four hours of the arrival of his heir, who was almost immediately left alone in the large and noble mansion which was now become his own, for his father had promised to return to his family as soon as the expected event, and the melancholy ceremony which must follow it, had taken place.

CHAPTER XXXIV.

No man can enter upon the possession of a large property, however long he may have been familiar with the idea that the said property was some day to be his, without feeling that his position is changed. He feels immediately that he has new duties to perform, new occupations to employ him, and, if not a new, a more pungent interest in almost every object that surrounds him. And so it was, now, in the case of George Harrington.

If he had been in other respects a happier man, he would very probably have felt the solitude in which he was left by his father's departure, immediately after the funeral, more painfully than he now did. But he was conscious that there was nothing of which he stood so much in need as solitary meditation on his own very singular position.

Though as far removed as it was well possible for a man to be from the danger of believing himself beloved, when " there was no such thing," and though during the last few agitating weeks of his existence he had never been in the company of Helen without feeling convinced when he left her that, notwithstanding all the gentle kindness of her manner towards him, she was fixedly determined never to become his wife, he had still a strong, and, as it seemed, an involuntary persuasion at the bottom of his heart, that she loved him.

But not even to his sister Agnes had he dared to dwell on this belief ; for when he had once hinted it, she had shook her head, saying, " I thought so once, George, nay, at the moment I would have said that I was sure of it. But I can honestly say so no longer. No woman, who loved, would so cautiously—so very cautiously—avoid every possible chance of being for a moment alone with the object of her choice, as Helen Beauchamp does, to avoid being alone with you."

And as the unfortunate young man could by no possible interpretation of signs and symptoms impugn the correctness of this statement, he could only determine not to allude to any such hope again ; but, nevertheless, he did not abandon it, or rather he could not make it abandon him, for, to do him justice, he really did endeavour to convince himself that he was mistaken. But in this he could not altogether succeed.

On this point, perhaps, as well as on many others, he had ample time to meditate, during several weeks of solitary residence at Speedhurst Abbey ; for though well known and well beloved in the neighbourhood, he was still enough alone to think, and think, and think, quite as much as was good for him.

At length, during one of the long reveries in which he was wont to indulge under the shadows of his noble elms, it occurred to him that although he had believed, and, in fact, did still believe that Helen had been fully aware of his attachment to her, he had never yet addressed a formal proposal for her hand, either to herself, or her uncle. It was possible, therefore—just possible—that she had not fully understood all his motives for the delay.

The time had been, indeed, before the fatal change in her manner towards him, when he felt persuaded that they had understood each other perfectly ; but it was certainly possible—

16—2

just possible—that he might have been mistaken in thinking so, and that Helen might have been offended by his seeming to take it for granted that because " of all the world he loved but her alone," she must, as a matter of course, love him.

This hope, slight as it was, produced a feeling more nearly akin to happiness than any he had known for many weeks, and it rendered him so gay and light-hearted that he positively laughed at himself for having contrived to produce a predicament wherein he should find himself rejoicing at the idea that Helen Beauchamp was displeased with him.

Under these circumstances it took him not long to decide what he should do. The post-bag, which left the Abbey that night, contained the following letter :—

" To Miss Beauchamp.

" In sitting down to address you, my beloved Helen, I feel that although I have much that is important to say to you, yet still that I have nothing to say which is not well known to you already. For, is it new to you, Helen, that you are dearer to me than the breath of life ? Or is it unknown to you that my only hope of happiness on earth is founded on the belief that you have not been blind to the love you have inspired, and that having seen it, you have not driven me from you in displeasure ?

" The melancholy state between death and life, in which my poor uncle lingered during the last months of his existence, made me feel that it was better to trust to our hearts to make their feelings understood to each other, than seemingly to forget the death-bed of my second father, while seeking to embellish and to bless my own young life by asking the hand of the only woman I can ever love.

" But the last sad scene of my dear uncle's life is closed, and well I know that if he could look back on those he has left behind him, his gentle spirit would rejoice to know that I was seeking my happiness from one who, if she will accept the heart and life I offer her, is so sure to bring goodness and happiness to both. Not even Agnes shall know that I have thus written till I have received your answer.

" O! Helen! the power of a woman, truly loved, is very great! Perhaps, dearest, you remember, as well as I do, ' the hours that we have spent when we have chid the hasty-footed time for parting us;' and if so, may you not laugh at me when I tell you, that, till I receive your answer to this letter, I shall live in doubt and dread lest it may not be all my devoted love leads me to wish for.

" Yours, Helen,

" Through life till death,

" GEORGE HARRINGTON."

Mr. Harrington did not exaggerate his feelings when he said, that he should live in doubt and dread till he received Helen's answer to the above letter. He did not wait for it long. The return of the post brought him the following reply from Miss Beauchamp :—

" MY VALUED FRIEND!—Permit me in this manner to address you, even though my letter should not prove either what you wish for, or expect. But I could address you in no other manner, George Harrington, without falsifying my feelings. I do, indeed, believe you to be my friend ; and I do, indeed, value your friendship, and repay it with my own. And yet, I cannot consent to become your wife. You know, in part, the history of my past life ; but there is much concerning it, which you do *not* know, nor is it well possible, my good friend, that you ever should ; for the knowledge you lack consists, for the most part, in such an acquaintance with the effect produced upon me by the sudden and violent change in my circumstances, as it is quite impossible should ever reach any heart and understanding but my own. It must very rarely happen that two persons whose juxtaposition is such as ours appears to be at present, should have passed the earlier years of their lives in a manner so strikingly dissimilar! *You* have always enjoyed the same happy associations, and the same favourable influences that you do at present ; my position was very decidedly the reverse of this ; and, depend upon it, that however truly and cordially we have liked each other, we are very likely to have deep-seated and out-of-sight differences of feeling and opinion on many essential points, which, although they might never happen to come forth and display themselves in any way which should militate against all the sympathy and all the attachment necessary for the foundation of very sincere friendship, might, nevertheless, go far towards destroying the perfect harmony which ought to subsist between man and wife. Nay, I will go further, my good friend, and confess to you that, though I have never heard you utter a sentiment which I did not think becoming and laudable in you, I have heard you express

thoughts and feelings which, to my own judgment, would be
very greatly the reverse in me. In a word, then, dear George
Harrington, I cannot consent to unite myself to you, because my
opinion is that such a marriage would be unsuitable; and this
opinion of mine is so deeply rooted in my mind, and partakes so
much of the stubborn and immutable nature of *matter of fact*,
that any attempt on your part to change it could produce pain,
and pain only, but it never could produce conviction. Nevertheless, I would earnestly ask for the continuance of your good
opinion and friendship. Your present position is such as must,
of necessity, occupy too much of your time at your own home to
permit your presence as much as heretofore at that of your
father. This must, of course, be submitted to by all your friends,
and myself among the number; but, I trust that nothing will
interfere to prevent my continuing to enjoy the society of your
family. Agnes and I have indulged in such constant walkings
and talkings together, that I do not think we could either of us
easily give up the habit.

> "Believe me, gratefully and sincerely,
> "Your Friend,
> "HELEN BEAUCHAMP."

The degree of suffering which it cost poor Helen to write this
letter could not easily be described in temperate language; but
it would have cost her more still could she have guessed the
degree of misery into which it plunged George Harrington.
The more he studied it, the more pitiable did his state of mind
become; for while the refusal of his hand was so vague as to
suggest positively nothing which could be considered as a
reasonable cause for it, the tone of resolute firmness in which
it was announced, seemed to forbid all reasonable hope that a
purpose so expressed could ever be changed.

For a short—a very short—interval, his profound sorrow
seemed to feel relief from a sentiment of anger, which suddenly
arose within him. He was so deeply conscious, poor young
man, of the fulness and the sincerity of his love, and the perfect
devotion with which he would joyfully have been guided by her
on every point whereon it was possible they could differ, that he
felt there was as much injustice as cruelty, in refusing this love,
because she deemed it possible they might some day differ in
opinion.

What cause had he ever given her for believing that she
might destroy her happiness if she trusted it to him, because

he might, perchance, contradict some of the theories she had learned in her nursery at the Warren House? What cause had he ever given to justify her fearing his authority more than she trusted his love? While this very reasonable view of the question which tortured him, held possession of his mind, his drooping spirits were roused to anger, though not cheered into hope; and then, for a few short moments of passionate indignation, he assured himself that it was a very lucky chance which had led the lady to proclaim her intolerance of all opposition, before it was too late for him to profit by it.

But this state of mind was more reasonable than lasting; for, as he started up from the desponding attitude into which he had thrown himself on a sofa in his library, in order to sally forth with renewed energy, to superintend some improvements which were going on in the garden, he suddenly recollected for whose sake it was that these improvements had been projected, and such a sickly feeling of indifference came over him concerning the embellishment of his garden, or of anything else belonging to him, that he reseated himself with a feeling of discouragement that was most truly pitiable, and which might have gone far towards convincing the over-scrupulous Helen that she had better think twice before she sacrificed herself, and her lover, to an over-wrought sense of honour, could his condition at that moment have been made known to her! But, as no mesmeric agent was at hand to set in action the spiritual electric telegraph of which we have heard such wonders, my unfortunate lovers were doomed to be tormented by the existence of a phantom which might have been easily laid at rest by one or two simple words of truth, uttered in due season. Instead of this, however, the daily post brought, in due season, the following letter from Agnes Harrington, at the Oaks, to her brother, George Harrington, at Speedhurst Abbey.

CHAPTER XXXV.

"My Dearest George,

"I have been earnestly endeavouring for some time to convince myself that both you and I should be acting with much more common sense if we separately and conjointly made up our

minds to believe that we had both been mistaken in fancying
that Helen Beauchamp ever, for a moment, conceived the idea
of becoming your wife. As far as I am myself concerned, I had,
as I believe you know, pretty nearly reached this point of
wisdom before your last melancholy departure for the Abbey;
and I have never, as you can testify, named her in any of the
letters I have written to you since. Nay, so far has my opinion
concerning her indifference towards you been in any degree
changed or weakened, by what I have remarked since you left
us, that, had I never come to this decision before, I think I
should have reached it since. It is not that she has ever alluded
to you in any way that could either have created, or confirmed
such an idea, for, in truth, as far as I know, she has never
alluded to you at all; but since she became of age she seems to
be perpetually occupied by business; and by what she says when
I laugh at her for paying so much attention herself to what
might easily be managed by her steward; she never replies to
me jestingly, but defends herself in good set terms, pointing out
very reasonably the decided advantage of understanding something of one's own affairs. Now this is much more like being a
sensible young woman, who knows when she is well off, and
wants nobody to help, than like being a young lady in love,
ready to make over her goods and chattels to her beloved. Nor
was this all. There were many other symptoms which all
tended to convince me that we were *wrong* in months long gone
by, when we flattered ourselves that in loving her, you was not
in any danger of loving in vain; and *right* when, during the
painful weeks which followed, we thought differently. It would,
however, be almost as difficult, as useless, were I to attempt
recording all the trifling circumstances which have, one after
another, led me to feel certain that love and marriage had no
share in her meditations. She had no such stuff in her thoughts.
But this assurance doubly sure, despite the disagreeable conclusion to which it had brought me, was greatly less tormenting
than the state of mind in which I find myself now.

"Perhaps I am wrong to appeal to you on the subject; yet I
cannot think so, for have we not shared together both the joy
and the sorrow, which this most mysterious subject has brought
with it? Why, then, should it be right for the confidence
between us to cease now? Certain it is, indeed, that you have
written to her without telling me of it; but that is no reason, I
think, why I should conceal from you what has happened to me
since.

"I have never, as you well know, my dear George, in any way changed my conduct towards Helen, in consequence of her mysterious change of manner towards you. From a very early period of our acquaintance, I have loved her, and I love her still. I have never ceased my visits to the Park, nor in any way changed the manner of them. My habit has been to ask for nobody but Helen, and very often I have not even asked for her, but when the hall-door has been open, which is often the case in fine weather, I have boldy made my way to her own snuggery, without any inquiry at all, and never have failed to be received with a kind welcome. I performed this same exploit yesterday, but the result was greatly unlike anything which had happened to me before. Helen was, as usual, alone; and, as usual, seated at her pretty little study-table, beside the window. She must have been deeply occupied when I entered, for she evidently did not hear the opening of the door behind her. She was sitting with her elbow resting on the table, and supporting her head with her hand. She was aware of my approach, however, before I reached her, and turning suddenly round upon me, exhibited a face as pale as a snowdrop, and eyes which had very evidently been recently employed in weeping. There was, moreover, in the whole aspect of her sweet face, an expression which I cannot recal even now, without feeling strongly disposed to weep myself, for it spoke a whole volume of mental suffering! But this was not all that I saw, my good brother. On the desk before her lay a letter from you. It was open, and so placed as to have been evidently the object upon which her eyes had been fixed when I entered the room. She made a strong effort to recover herself, and might have succeeded better, had she been less anxious to succeed. She threw her arms round my neck, and embraced me most affectionately, but I felt that she trembled from head to food as she did so! I am certain that she immediately recollected that your letter was lying very conspicuously displayed upon her desk, for instead of installing me as usual on the seat beside her, on the sofa, which she always occupies, she threw her arm round me, and led me back towards the door. 'Let us go into the east parlour, my dearest Agnes,' said she, 'I know that my aunt and Anne are sitting there, and they are longing to see you.'

"To resist this movement on her part was, of course, impossible, and, accordingly, I accompanied her to the east parlour, and there I certainly found her aunt and cousin, who were, as usual, extremely kind, and gave me a very cordial welcome;

but as to the *longing* that Miss Beauchamp talked of, I certainly
saw no symptoms of it.   I speedily saw symptoms, however, on
the face of my beautiful friend, that she was not quite at ease in
her mind concerning the state in which she had left her writing-
desk, and the black-edged epistle so conspicuously exposed upon
it; for, before we had been in the room two minutes, she slid
out of it again, but returned after an interval just about long
enough to permit of her locking up her letter and bathing her
beautiful eyes; and, during the remainder of my visit, though
still very pale, she contrived, in a great degree, to recover her
usual manner, and talked of Lady this, and Miss that, and their
seedling geraniums, almost as gaily as if nothing had happened
to her.

"But something *has* happened to her, George Harrington!
Something that has shaken her self-possessed soul to the very
centre; and I expect you to tell me immediately what it is.
Why have you suddenly become so reserved towards me? Why
have you written to her, when, in your very last letter to me,
you declare yourself to be devoted to your rural occupations, and
determined to think of nothing else? Or why, if anything has
happened to make you change your mind, have you kept it secret
from me? I should be less anxious on the subject, had it not
been made so very evident to me that, whatever has passed
between you, has been of a most painful nature. It is no light
thing that could have made Helen Beauchamp look as pale as a
marble statue, and tremble when she embraced me, as if she had
been caught in some act of high treason, that not only put her
own life in peril, but the lives of all that are dearest to her into
peril also. What can you have written that should produce
such effects as these? As you love me, brother, let not this
letter remain many hours unanswered!

"Ever your loving sister,
"AGNES HARRINGTON."

George Harrington did not obey this earnest injunction; he
did not answer his sister's letter; but, as rapidly as railroad
speed could do it, he conveyed himself to the Oaks.

Whether he set forth upon this journey more in hope than in
fear, or more in fear than in hope, it would be difficult to say.
The letter which Helen had addressed to him, and which had
reached him the day before that of his sister, had rendered him
as miserable as it was well possible for a man to be who has
nothing in his destiny to complain of, save the having become

practically convinced of the fact, that " the course of true love never does run smooth." But, in sober truth, this was quite enough to make him very miserable—and very miserable, accordingly, he was.

For there was, with all its gentleness, a tone of such decided firmness in this cruel letter, as to make him feel that the doom it announced was immutable; and at the moment when the above epistle from his sister was brought to him, he had a map of Southern Europe before him, and Murray in his left hand, while he traced out a tour of some few thousands of very beautiful circuitous miles with his right, being fully determined to leave England, and not return to it till he had in some degree conquered the attachment which made him feel all the blessings with which he was surrounded to be either indifferent or distasteful to him.

But, utterly unintelligible as his sister's account of Helen seemed to be, and utterly irreconcilable as it certainly was with the calm and resolute tone of her letter, its immediate effect was to overthrow all his foregone conclusions, and to make him decide upon deferring his tour through the south of Europe, till he had made one more attempt to solve the mysteries of Helen Beauchamp's heart.

Notwithstanding her earnest entreaty for a *tête-à-tête*, the personal appearance of her brother in the drawing-room at the Oaks, surprised Agnes much less than it pleased her.

After recalling, with the most scrupulous accuracy, all that had passed between herself and Helen, from the time that George first began to pay her any marked attention, she became convinced that Miss Beauchamp had either voluntarily deceived her, and her brother also; or that she had involuntarily deceived herself, and blighted all the happy prospects that seemed opening before them by some misconstruction or blundering, which might perhaps be easily set right, if the subject matter of the blunder could only be discovered, and brought to a fair examination.

That Agnes was quite right in so believing, the reader, who has been let into the secret, is aware; but it was not so easy a matter, to make this truth evident to the parties most nearly concerned.

The first thing that George heard, when, the cordial family greetings being over, he at length got Agnes to himself, was that the Beauchamp Park family had just sent out cards throughout the whole neighbourhood, for a fancy ball, at the distance of a fortnight from the present time.

"A ball!" exclaimed George. "Oh, Agnes! Agnes! How cruelly have you deceived me! Do you remember the portrait you sent me in your last letter? The marble paleness! the trembling limbs! How can this be reconciled with the sending out cards for a universal fancy ball?"

"Upon which part of my intelligence do you mean to throw a doubt, George?" returned Agnes, quietly.

"I know not!" he exclaimed, impatiently. "Of course I know nothing, and must believe whatever you tell me with un-doubting faith, because you desire that I should do so. But, nevertheless, my common sense revolts against both your state-ments being correct at one and the same time."

"It is not quite one and the same time," returned his sister. "It is two days and a half since I sent off my letter to you, and the card, inviting us to the fancy ball, only reached us this morning."

"Are you laughing at me, Agnes?" said her miserable look-ing brother. "You are either very cruel, or very injudicious if you are."

"I am quite as well aware of that, as you can be, George, and quite as little inclined to try such an experiment, in order to mend matters. In no case, I think, should I feel any propensity to laugh at the strangely mysterious conduct of Helen Beau-champ. Even if your happiness were not concerned in it, the affection which I still retain for her is too sincere to permit my making a jest at her inconsistencies."

This was said by Agnes in a way to prove that she was very much in earnest, and not at all in jest, and it was with an air of vexed repentance that her brother replied, "Forgive me! I did not mean it, Agnes, but I am almost too miserable to know what I say!"

"Perhaps, George, I might be more able to guess what has been passing in her mind, if you would tell me the nature of the letter that I saw on her writing-desk, when I found her in the terrible state of agitation which I described to you," said Agnes.

"I will do more than that," he replied, "I will not only tell you the nature of the letter, but show you both the letter itself, and her answer to it."

And so saying, he drew both the epistles from his pocket-book, and put them into her hand.

" May I ask you, George, before I read *either*, what circumstance, or what new train of reasoning, it was, which led you to
alter the resolution you had made to accept her marked change
of manner towards you, as a sign and signal that the intimacy
which had gradually grown up between us, was not intended by
Helen to pass the limit of friendship ? "

" Indeed you have a very fair right to ask the question,
Agnes, and I will answer you with perfect frankness. When
canvassing together all circumstances concerning the marked
change which we had both perceived in Miss Beauchamp's
manner to me, we both perfectly agreed in thinking that it
was intended to indicate an important and friendly caution to
me, for it said, as plainly as manner could say, ' So far shalt
thou go, and no further.' I need not recal to you that
wretched period, or remind you of all the misery I suffered. I
am quite sure you have not forgotten it. But in the solitude of
Speedhurst, Agnes, I went over all the old ground again, and
my memory was not good-natured enough to cheat me of any
single circumstance which went to prove that Helen Beauchamp
had no intention of becoming my wife. But in the midst of
these long and sad meditations, a very strange idea suggested
itself. In going over all the scenes which had passed between
us, both hopeful, and hopeless, it occurred to me that I had
never yet positively and explicitly proposed marriage to her."

" Nonsense! George," exclaimed Agnes, suddenly interrupting him. " Are you not creating a distinction where there is
no difference? Do you mean to tell me that you think Helen
had any doubt about your wish to marry her ?"

" I did not think so before her manner changed towards me,"
replied her brother, " but, nevertheless, it is a certain fact that I
never did explicitly propose to her. We used to talk of the
future, but never explicitly alluded to our being married ; the
reason for which was, as I thought she understood as well as
myself, that my poor dear uncle must die before this *future* could
be reached."

" To be sure that was the reason !" cried Agnes, again interrupting him, " and I feel not the slightest doubt that Helen at
that time understood it to be so as well as we did ourselves."

" It may be so," returned George, mournfully, " but I was
mad enough to hope that it was otherwise, when left alone,
Agnes, to my own imaginings, and I wrote to her accordingly,
making an explicit avowal of my love, and offer of my hand.
Her answer will show you, I think, why it was that I felt as I

read it, that it extinguished every hope for ever. And so it ought to have done, as you will say when you have perused it; yet, nevertheless, I am here again with a feeling of renewed uncertainty. Why should my letter have thrown her into the state you describe? This was, of course, the question which immediately suggested itself, and the fact is, Agnes, that I am come here solely in the hope of discovering why it was that she looked so pale and so wretched while my letter lay before her."

"Nor can I blame you for taking this step; and still less can I wonder at your being puzzled," replied Agnes. "But how are we to understand this last commentary? How are we to interpret this fancy ball invitation? It cannot possibly appear one half so extraordinary to you as it does to me, because you did not see her as I saw her, when I so rashly broke in upon her, and no description of mine can do justice to her manner and appearance then! But let me see her answer, George. Let me read it at once. It must have been written immediately upon the receipt of that which I saw lying upon her desk, and surely I must be able to find some trace in it of the suffering that was so terribly visible on her features when she was in the act of contemplating that to which it was an answer."

George waited not to reply, but instantly put the letter of Helen in her hand.

"Shall I read it to you?" he said.

"No, George, no!" she replied. "Let me read it myself!"

Her brother left the painful document in her hands, and silently watched her countenance as she perused it.

Having very deliberately gone through it once, she began again at the beginning, and read it through a second time before she uttered a word. She then replaced it in her brother's hands, saying, "And I asked for this in the full hope that it would throw some light upon the mystery!"

"And you are disappointed, Agnes?" returned her brother, with a melancholy smile.

"Disappointed!" she repeated. "Why before I read that letter everything was clear and plain, compared to what it is now! You offered your hand and she refused it, and though it was not very easy to understand why she should do so, and at the same time look so miserable about it, yet still, you know, it was possible that she might be very sorry for old friendship's sake that she did not feel inclined to marry, and, therefore, was obliged to disappoint you. This was *possible*, though it might have seemed to us more capricious than reasonable. But this explanation of her motives for refusing you has much more of mystery than of caprice in it. What on earth can she mean by saying that she has heard you express thoughts and feelings which though laudable in you, would be the reverse in her? And to what mysterious secrets can she allude, when she talks of the associations of her former years? My dearest George, you must think no more of her! There *must* be some painful history connected with her early years, and, perhaps, she is only doing her duty when she refuses to become your wife. If this be so, it is easy enough to account for the suffering which this refusal has cost her, and she deserves our admiration and affection more than ever. But let us not be less reasonable than she is, my dear brother! Absent yourself from us all, for a time. Finish your continental travels, my dear George, and change of scene, and your own good sense, will enable you to forget this disappointment, and to look elsewhere for a wife. There is not much chance, I should think, of your being equally unfortunate a second time."

"It is possible I might be more so," he replied, with something like a bitter smile; "I might offer myself, sister Agnes, to another, and I might be accepted."

"Very good, George. And now you are beginning to be witty, I have good hopes that you will not break your heart. But what say you to my travelling project?"

"The project certainly has its attractions, Agnes, and I may think further of it; but not just at present, for I am doing a good deal to the gardens at the Abbey, and I should not like to leave England till I have accomplished the object I have in view. Meanwhile, however, you will not be annoyed by any symptoms of love-sickness on my part. Do you think, Agnes, that I shall be included in the Beauchamp Park invitation?"

"Of course you will, if you are still here," was her reply.

"And that I certainly will be," he returned, gaily. "I have an immensity of curiosity on the subject."

"I am glad to hear you say so, for sorry indeed should I be if this strange conduct on the part of Helen were to break up the intercourse between the families. I love Helen dearly," continued Agnes, with feeling, "and the being convinced, as from her letter I think we must be, that her early years were passed under very disadvantageous circumstances, will never lead me to love her less. Whatever her former companionships may have been, I know what she herself is now; and she must hint at something worse than even vulgar relations, before I shall give her up."

George Harrington listened to this with great satisfaction. He, too, as well as his sister, was of opinion that when Helen alluded to the disadvantages of her early years, she meant to confess that she had lived among low-born relatives; but, unlike Agnes, he saw nothing sufficiently important in this to form a lasting barrier between them; on the contrary, indeed, from the moment his sister suggested it, he devoutly prayed the gods that it might be true, feeling something very like a comfortable assurance at his heart that no such cause could keep them asunder long. And yet George Harrington was far from being indifferent to such considerations as had brought his sister to the conclusion that, charming as Helen was in person, intellect, and demeanour, and highly as she was placed by fortune, she might be, and doubtless was, unhappily situated with respect to the connections with whom she had passed her early life.

This solution certainly appeared to him the most obvious, amidst the darkness in which Helen's conduct had involved him; and he very naturally determined to receive it as the true one, and to act accordingly; unless he subsequently saw reason to believe that he and his sister also had failed to interpret her mysterious letter aright.

Had he avowed this determination to Agnes in the same words in which I have now expressed it, she would have agreed with him most cordially as to the propriety of doing so; and yet nothing could be much less alike than the result which they respectively contemplated. Agnes paused not a moment in coming to the conclusion that if such were the fitting inter-pretation to be put upon Helen's letter, the obvious, and inevit-able consequence was, that she never ought to become the wife of her brother; while her brother, with equal distinctness and rapidity, arrived at a conclusion which was precisely the re-verse.

But here let me do George Harrington the justice to say that it was not the influence of Helen's personal beauty which bribed him to this decision; neither was it by any means from either ignorance, or indifference, concerning the importance which ought to be attached to the character, as well as the position, of those with whom we are brought into connection by marriage. He understood, and felt all this very sufficiently; as much so, perhaps, as even Agnes herself; but he thought, and he was quite right in thinking so, that he knew more of Helen than she did; he knew her temper, heart, and intellect better, It was not that Agnes was either a careless or a dull observer. But "the sweet passion of love" is made up of a multitude of susceptibilities, some more, and some less sublime, but forming altogether a sort of spiritual electricity, which enables one human mind to detect, and combine with, the occult qualities of another, with a force that is often stronger than reason, though in no wise contrary to it.

But at the same moment that he discovered this essential difference of opinion between himself and his sister, he very stedfastly determined not to communicate the discovery to her; and here again he was very right.

There was, for the present at least, no chance whatever that either party would be able to convict, or convince the other of error; and discussion, therefore, must be worse than idle. So there was no discussion between them on this point at all; and they both, fortunately, agreed in thinking, that in the interval which was likely to take place before the young master of Speedhurst Abbey set off to finish his continental tour, their best course would be to alter nothing in their outward demeanour towards Helen; to keep the secret of the offer, and its refusal, entirely to their own hearts, and to reconcile themselves as speedily as possible to taking the good the gods had provided, without making themselves miserable about what was denied.

Perhaps George did not deserve quite all the credit his sister gave him for the air of genuine resignation with which he listened to this edict, and submitted to it; perhaps she was in no degree aware of the pleasant effect she had produced on his mind, by explaining so clearly and cleverly the probable cause of Helen's refusal. It was with the most perfect sincerity that he had acknowledged his conviction that her interpretation was correct; but he did not feel himself called upon to say how much consolation he found from her description of poor Helen's suffering under the performance of the terrible duty she had imposed upon herself.

<hr>

CHAPTER XXXVI.

No disappointment awaited George Harrington concerning his invitation to the fancy ball about to be given at Beauchamp

17

Park. But, though very well pleased to receive it, he fell into a very deep fit of very grave musing, upon the style and manner in which he should make his appearance there.

His meditations were not confined to the style in which he should decorate his person, or to that by which he should regulate his manner. The first question was not without its difficulties, but the second, as may easily be believed, was infinitely more puzzling still.

George was no coxcomb, but, nevertheless, he was not wholly ignorant of the fact that he was rather a handsome fellow, and then visions of sundry very becoming costumes did certainly come into his head, and even shot from thence to the point of his pencil, causing the implement to sketch, with very brilliant rapidity, Greeks, Turks, Figaros, and Hamlets.

But he suddenly stopped short in this agreeable occupation, and tore the paper into atoms. "What an idiot I am!" he exclaimed, bitterly. "Do I hope to win her by the aid of my tailor? If I go at all, it shall be in my ordinary attire."

But the moment after, he found that there would be something very particularly marked, and, therefore, very particularly wrong in this, and then, having manfully resolved that he would wear the livery of Folly, in some form or other, but without giving a thought to his looking well or ill in it, he began to fix his thoughts with a good deal of anxiety upon the degree of familiarity with which it would be proper that he should addres her, either in his own character, or in any other that he might take it into his head to assume. But, on this point, at least, he had sufficient common sense, and sufficient consciousness of not being altogether sure of keeping a resolution if he made it, to induce him to bring this particular cogitation to a conclusion, by deciding that he would not make any resolution at all, but be guided by his own feelings at the moment, inspired as they were sure to be by her manner of receiving him.

But then came the important question as to whether he ought or ought not to call at Beauchamp, after the correspondence which had taken place between himself and its fair mistress. But, fortunately, this was a point upon which he could still call his faithful Agnes to council, notwithstanding her perfectly unsuspicious ignorance of the ultimate hope which lay nestling at the bottom of his heart.

After the meditation of a minute or two, she gave it as her opinion that if he intended to accept the invitation to the ball, he ought to call upon the Beauchamp Park family before it took place. George discreetly fixed his eyes upon the carpet when this wished-for decision was pronounced; but the flush which mounted to his forehead told his sister plainly enough, that her opinion on the subject had not been listened to without considerable emotion, which, she doubted not, was of a very painful kind.

"I have vexed you, my dearest George!" said she, with true sisterly feeling, though certainly with no great sympathy. "But you must pass the ordeal of a first meeting, at some time or other; that is, if you accept her offered friendship. The question, in my opinion is, not whether you should make a morning visit at the Park, before you present yourself at the ball, for if you decide upon doing the last, you cannot in common civility avoid the former. The real question is, whether you have courage enough to meet Helen in society without suffering more than she ought to see you suffer; or whether it would not be better for you to go abroad at once, and remain beyond the reach of danger from meeting her again, till time and your own good sense shall have enabled you to conquer your unfortunate attachment."

George continued to keep his eyes fixed on the carpet as she spoke, and when she had finished, he drew out his pocket handkerchief, and blew his nose, which produced a painful and compunctious feeling on the heart of his sister, for she fancied that he was either weeping, or about to weep.

However, he almost immediately answered in a tolerably cheerful voice, "Yes, Agnes, you are quite right. That is, in truth, the real question. But there is, I think, always something cowardly and contemptible in moving away under any circumstance, and though quite aware that I may have some disagreeable scenes to encounter, I had rather endure whatever may happen to me, than positively take to flight.—So I will ride over to the Park to morrow morning, I think, and get the first awkward meeting over as soon as possible."

"Shall I go with you, George?" said Agnes, in a tone that showed plainly enough that she most sincerely pitied him.

"No, my dear Agnes," he replied, "I will get through it as well as I can; but I suspect that my part of the performance will not be graceful enough for me to be anxious to exhibit it."

Nothing more passed between them on the subject, nor did Agnes even know when it was his purpose to perform this painful but necessary ceremony; she saw plainly enough that he had

17—2

no inclination to talk about it, and though she was a little surprised at this reserve, she was determined to indulge him, for she felt persuaded that such an interview could not fail of being intensely painful, and she pitied him most sincerely.

Yes, Agnes did pity her brother exceedingly; but though she would willingly have stood courageously beside him in more perilous encounters, she was, at the bottom of her heart, very sincerely glad to escape this; one reason for which assuredly was, that she knew she could do him no good, and could only have brought with her to the meeting an additional element of embarrassment.

George prepared himself for the interview by very attentively reading the letter of Helen which he had received in answer to his own. Having fully accepted the rational interpretation of Agnes as to the latent meaning of this letter, it no longer appeared to him such a desperate document as it had done when he first perused it; yet still there was enough of stedfast purpose in its tone to make his heart quail as he meditated on the possibility of her fancying that it was her duty to adhere to the resolution she had announced.

This sinking of the heart as he meditated on her taking such a view of the question, was the strongest possible proof that he did justice both to the rectitude, and the strength of Helen's character. His best chance lay in the possibility of making her feel that in her case, as in many others, there might be conflicting duties, and that the sending him to an early grave, with a broken heart, might be a heavier sin, than permitting him to ally himself, through her, with some individual, or individuals, less perfect than herself.

During his leisurely *pas-à-pas* ride to Beauchamp Park, he came very decidedly to the conclusion, however, that nothing could be so injurious to his cause as any attempt at present to shake her resolution. Something, indeed, whispered to him that the day might come (if the tone of their former intercourse could be restored) when she, too, might think that she had overrated the importance of her early associations, for if they had really produced any effect that could reasonably keep them asunder, he must have made the discovery ere now; and to this he was determined to trust.

As to the precise arrangement concerning the time and place for their first meeting, his former familiar knowledge of her daily routine of occupation enabled him to settle it very skilfully. He knew perfectly well that when the family separated after breakfast, Mr. Rixley invariably retired to enjoy a peaceful perusal of the daily paper in the library ; and as invariably did Mrs. Rixley take her station in a peculiarly pleasant morning sitting-room, wherein she was sure to find, not only her favourite sofa, her worsted work, and some half-dozen or so of the last-arrived new books, but her daughter, also, who pretty constantly employed the first hour or two after breakfast in practising all the intricate new polkas and waltzes, by the bewitching influence of which, she contrived to convert every party given in the neighbourhood into a dance.

Anne Rixley's style of playing these German fascinations was really admirable, and her mother so well loved to listen to her, that it must have been some very remarkable occurrence which could have tempted her to give it up.

All this was perfectly well known to George Harrington, and, therefore, without letting anybody into his confidence, besides his groom, he found his horse precisely at ten o'clock in the morning, not pawing the gravel before the door, but waiting for him, both out of sight and out of hearing, just beyond the precincts of the oak-sheltered paddock which surrounded the house.

A very few minutes of sharp riding brought him to Beauchamp Park, and having reached it unattended, he rode, as he had often done before, into the stable-yard, and gave his horse to one of the stable servants. He asked no questions concerning the whereabouts of the family, but turned with neighbourly license through a small door which led into the shrubberies.

Harrington knew perfectly well that Helen, in all human probability, was in the conservatory, and, accordingly, it was there he sought, and there he found her. She had heard his step, and it may be that she knew it, too, before he became visible, for when he entered and first caught sight of her, instead of being as pale as Agnes had described her, the fair face was blooming with as radiant a blush as ever dyed a virgin cheek.

The first moment of meeting was doubtless one of pretty severe trial to both of them ; but this first emotion was got through very well, and very quietly, as far as outward appearances could be trusted, on both sides ; this very desirable result being the more easily obtained, because it was the stedfast purpose of both that so it should be.

As far as this went, it mattered little how wide might be the difference between the ultimate object of the lady and that of the

gentleman; and it must be confessed that this ultimate difference was considerable; that of the lady being to remain
unchangeably within the line of single blessedness which she
had marked out for herself; while that of the gentleman was to
" bide his time " with all the appearance of the most submissive
obedience, but never to abandon the hope of making her his wife
as long as they both should live, and live single.

Fortunately, however, there was no occasion for either of them
just then to enter upon the subject of their future intentions;
each thought, and thought very properly, that they had been
sufficiently explicit upon the subject already, and all embarrassment, therefore, upon that score, was spared them.

After the usual mutual inquiries for their respective families
had been exchanged, the attention of George Harrington was
called to sundry alterations and improvements in the gardens, of
which, as he truly said, he had heard nothing, but which
appeared, as far as he could judge, to be very ingenious in the
conception, and very promising as to the general effect of the
result.

" I am glad you think so," she replied, " for some of my
manœuvres have been rather bold, and as I have consulted no
one but my uncle and the gardener, your approval is very satisfactory.   But we are not sufficiently advanced as yet to talk
much about it.   If you were not something of a gardener yourself, Mr. Harrington, you would not have understood what we
are about so much as you appear to do.   But do not talk of my
winter garden scheme to Agnes, I mean to surprise."

George promised to be very discreet on the subject, and then
the conversation went on in the question and answer style very
glibly, till, at length, Helen said, " And now, Mr. Harrington, I
think I have told you all that I know about my plans, myself;
so I will take you to see my aunt and Anne."

" I shall be truly glad to see them, and your good uncle,
also," he replied.   " It seems an age since I have had that
pleasure."

And so saying, he followed her through a labyrinth of newly
marked-out walks, and flower-beds.   But just as they were
about to leave the precincts of Helen's magnificent innovations,
which were divided from the lawn behind the house by a thick
shrubbery, he made a hasty step in advance, which brought him
before her as she walked on, when suddenly turning round, and
facing her, he gently laid two fingers on her arm, as if to make
her pause, and then said, " Helen ! Your will is law.   It ought

to be so, and it shall be so! Fear not that you will be tormented by me. I will teach myself to rejoice as being permitted to be your friend."

She started when he first stopped her, but recovered herself immediately, and said, cheerfully, "I thank you, George Harrington; I thank you sincerely."

"And we are then to be as good friends, Helen, as if I never had written you that letter?" said he, looking at her, earnestly.

"Yes, yes!" was her reply, uttered rapidly, and turning aside her head, as if fearing to meet his eyes.

He ventured, however, to hold out his hand, and she put hers into it; upon which, with the friendly and familiar action of a brother, he drew her arm under his own, as he had often done in days of yore, and walked, neither very slowly nor very rapidly, towards the house, while he very demurely descanted the while on the very extensive alterations she appeared to be making in her gardens.

CHAPTER XXXVII.

WHILE these very important, but very unguessed-at, occurrences were passing over Helen, her sincere liking and friendship for Mr. Phelps continued without the slightest diminution; neither had his sincere affection for her been in any degree lessened, though he was very nearly as conscious as she was herself that he was no longer fully in possession of her confidence. But there does sometimes exist between human beings a degree of sturdy obstinate esteem which nothing less weighty than obvious matter of fact testimony can suffice to destroy, and the esteem which old Mr. Phelps felt for Helen Beauchamp, was of this quality. He was quite sure that she had something on her mind which affected her happiness, and weighed upon her spirits, but as she evidently wished to conceal the cause from him, he immediately came to the conclusion that the secret, whatever it was, was not her own secret only, and this not only exonerated her from all blame in his eyes, but gave him an additional reason for thinking that she certainly was " made up of every woman's best."

But Mr. Phelps, when left in the dark, very naturally, like all other sharp-witted people, felt a strong inclination to grope his way out, and he soon fancied that he saw a glimmer of light in the direction in which probably most people would have looked for it, namely, that in which the tender passion of love was most likely to appear.

Now, whatever love passages had hitherto passed between George Harrington and Helen Beauchamp, they had been, more perhaps from the character of the individual than from any systematic purpose on the part of either of them, entirely invisible to all eyes save those of Agnes.

Mr. Phelps, in short, had no more idea that Helen was in love with George Harrington, than that she was in love with him. But still he thought she must be in love with some one, for how else could he account for the change that had taken place in her? Not, indeed, that she was in any material respect changed towards him; no! There was the same unmistakable expression of pleasure in her sweet face every time that he unexpectedly appeared before her; but there was not that fresh and brightly sustained interest while engaged with him, either in literary or philosophical discussion, that used to make this long *tête-à-tête* so delightful.

More than once he had found it necessary to restate a dogma, or repeat an argument, before she looked as if she fully understood him. Now this was quite new in their intercourse, and by no means agreeable. But what was worse still, was the fact that when, at length, she *did* appear to comprehend what he was talking about, she did *not* appear to take much interest in it. And so at last the rational old gentleman came to the conclusion that Helen was in love.

Having reached this point, it was not very long before he arrived at another, for he discovered, or fancied he had discovered, that her Cousin Henry was the happy man. This discovery certainly took off in his estimation a little of the beautiful disinterestedness which he had so warmly admired in all her economical efforts before she became of age, in order to procure for this highly favoured youth, the object of his first ambition. But good Mr. Phelps soon felt ashamed of himself for thinking she could have acted upon any motive more amiable than that of gratifying this honourable ambition of the man she loved, and he determined to atone for this injustice by taking an early oppor-

tunity of delicately hinting to her that he had discovered her
secret, and greatly approved her choice.

An opportunity for doing this soon occurred, for a letter from
Henry, who had now been nearly a year abroad, arrived very
soon after the philosopher had made this acute discovery,
announcing his return to England, and his hope of being at
Beauchamp Park in a few days.

This pleasant news was speedily circulated throughout the
neighbourhood, and the lucky chance which brought him back
in time for the fancy ball was welcomed most cordially, especially
by all the young ladies, for Henry Rixley was acknowledged to
be the best dancer in the county, and was on that, as well as on
many other accounts, so great a favourite, that the delightful
invitation itself had scarcely given more pleasure than did the
sudden announcement that he was to be a sharer in the
fête.

It so chanced that on the same day on which Henry's letter
announcing his arrival in England reached Beauchamp Park,
one of the large dinner parties, which were now very frequent
there, took place. Mr. Phelps was one of the guests, and having heard the general burst of cordial satisfaction with which
Mr. Rixley's announcement of this news was received at the
dinner-table, he took an opportunity, when rambling tête-à-tête
with Helen on the following morning, through her new flower-
garden, to revert to this circumstance, as a means of leading to
the subject upon which he was so anxious to speak to her
without reserve.

"What a very popular individual your Cousin Henry seems
to be!" said the old gentleman, looking at her rather earnestly.
"He certainly was proclaimed by acclamation at your dinner-
table yesterday as the one thing needful to make a fancy ball
an epitome of perfect felicity."

If Mr. Phelps expected to see his companion blush upon
hearing this abrupt mention of her cousin's name, he was not
disappointed, for her beautiful face was instantly suffused with
the celestial rosy-red which has been, rather arbitrarily, termed
"Love's proper hue."

"Dearest Henry!" she eagerly exclaimed. "I thought you
would remark it, Mr. Phelps. Oh! If you knew what a
pleasure it is to me to think that he may still be prosperous
and happy, notwithstanding the heavy misfortune of my having
been born! But nobody can ever know—can ever understand
this! Not even you, Mr. Phelps."

Mr. Phelps smiled aside, as he marked the ingenious manner in which she contrived to confess the tender interest which she took in his prosperity, without compromising her maiden dignity by pleading guilty to the " soft impeachment." He remained silent for a moment, and then replied, taking her arm and passing it, in a confidential sort of manner, under his own, " Come, come, Helen ! It is too late in the day for you and I, when we are talking to each other *tête-à-tête*, to say one thing, when we mean another. I know that you love Henry Rixley, and that you mean to marry him when he shall have tamed his vehement military ardour by serving for a campaign or two; I know this, Helen, quite as well as if you had informed me of it with all the solemnity of a most important avowal—so do not be foolish enough to say NO about it, my dear child, for I tell you frankly that I shall not believe you."

Helen Beauchamp loved truth dearly. She loved it conscientiously, she loved it philosophically, and she loved it habitually. But never was an untruth offered in a more tempting form than that which was now presented for her acceptance. She could not but fear, for she had very good and sufficient reason for fearing it, that many of her friends and acquaintances had shrewdly suspected that the marked intimacy between the Harrington family and her own would end by a union between Speedhurst Abbey, and Beauchamp Park; and the gossip, the wondering, and all the imaginative explanations, likely to follow upon the discovery that everybody had been mistaken, or at any rate that the affair was very mysteriously broken off, formed no trifling addition to the suffering which weighed so heavily upon her during this portion of her existence. The possibility of getting clear of all this by permitting the circulation of a different fable was a desperately strong temptation offered to her integrity; but, nevertheless, she would probably have had courage to resist it, had her old friend remained with her only one moment longer; but perceiving that she hesitated how to answer him, and believing he had put her in a painful position by his abruptness, he suffered her arm to drop as suddenly as he had taken it, and gaily saying, " I will not torment you any more with my discoveries just at present, dear Helen," he bustled off into the shrubberies, and left her to meditate upon the comparative value of truth and its opposite at her leisure.

CHAPTER XXXVIII.

Two days after the dinner-party mentioned in the last chapter, Henry Rixley reached Beauchamp Park ; and, short of the species of reception which Mr. Phelps had predicted for him, it was pretty nearly impossible that he could have been more affectionately welcomed. The first hour or two that they all passed together was occupied by such a deluge of questions and answers concerning where he had been since he left one place, and what he had liked best when he got to another, that nothing approaching grave and confidential talk had taken place amongst them ; but early the next morning, very nearly at the same hour at which Henry had communicated the heaviest sorrow of his heart to his Cousin Helen some twenty months before, they met again under the greenwood tree, and being again *tête-à-tête*, the grateful young traveller eagerly seized the opportunity of expressing all the gratitude he felt for her kindness to him.

For Helen had not trusted to the regularity with which his salary might be paid in order to satisfy herself that this very happy interlude in his life's history was not dimmed by the want of a little " needfu' cash."

"Had you been my own dear mother, Helen, you could not have been more thoughtful about my enjoyments ; and how you could manage to time your generous gifts so happily must ever be a mystery, for I do positively declare that I never once particularly wished for a little extra cash, that I did not speedily afterwards get a polite intimation that if I would be pleased to draw on Messrs. So-and-So, I should be sure to get it. How can I thank you as I ought to do for all your generous kindness to me?"

"By not calling anything I have done by such a name, dear Henry," she very gravely replied. "Though no great lawyer, I sufficiently understand the omnipotent power of the law to be aware that it is right and proper for me to possess this place, and all the thousands a year that it brings with it, instead of you, or your good father either. But this need not, and cannot prevent my remembering, that had I never existed, all the

wealth I now enjoy must have been yours, for my father had no
other heir. Such being the facts, Cousin Henry, it cannot be
very difficult for you to understand that I do not feel entitled to
many thanks, merely because I find pleasure in now and then
preventing your being inconvenienced by the want of a little
money. Besides, you must observe, if you please, that I run no
risk of doing mischief by permitting myself this indulgence, for
I happen to know, from the best possible authority, namely,
that of your father, that though your allowance has been a
small one, you have never run in debt at College. So no more
about gratitude—no more of that, Hal, if thou lovest me!"

"I do love you, Helen, and I will not plague you with any
more thanks; but you will not scold me for telling you how
greatly I have enjoyed myself? I suppose," he added, with a
sigh, "I suppose that everything in this world is a mixture of
good and evil. For instance, I greatly doubt if any man could
have enjoyed the pleasure and excitement of travelling so keenly
as I have done, unless, like me, he knew that his future years
were to be spent in a way that must render the recurrence of
such delightful excitement impossible. But the pleasure is not
over for me. I shall never forget what I have seen.—There is
a great comfort in that. What a beautiful world this is, Helen!
You have no idea of the magnificence, the variety, the intense
loveliness of the various scenery and the various climates,
through which I have passed since I left England; you don't
know what *blue* means, when it is used to describe the colour of
an Italian sky; you don't, indeed, Helen! Claude himself does
not dare to give it in all its splendour. Or perhaps his unguents
failed him."

Helen looked at him, and smiled.

"Don't laugh at me, Helen! Don't fancy that I am trying
to cram you with travellers' tales, as full of lies as of wonders.
I will exaggerate nothing when I am talking to you of what I
have seen, but it will be a great pleasure to describe it all.
Besides, the doing so will impress it on my memory, and hence-
forth, you know, that is the treasury on which I must draw for
the pleasure of enjoying fine scenery."

"And do you think the remembrance of what you have seen
will suffice to gratify this passionate love of scenery for the rest
of your life?" said Helen, again looking at him with a smile.

An expression of painful feeling passed across the young
man's features for a moment; but whatever might be its cause
he evidently made an effort to get rid of it, for he returned his

cousin's smile, as he replied, "I take the good the gods provide me, and do not mean now to quarrel with my destiny, even if I have never again the good fortune to pass the 'Herring Pond.' Has my father been talking much since I went away about my ordination? Has he got his eye upon any particular curacy for me, Helen?"

"No, dear Henry, I am pretty sure he has not. We ought all of us to do him the justice of believing that if he had the power of placing you in a profession that you felt more suited to, he would be very glad to do it. He acknowledged this to Mr. Phelps, the other day, when they were discussing the subject together. No! It is I who have fixed my mind on a particular cure, and not my uncle," returned Helen.

"You!" exclaimed Henry, in an accent of surprise. "Of course I ought to feel greatly flattered by your thinking of me at all, but fixing upon a curacy for me, was one of the very last ways in which I should have expected you to show it."

Helen did more than smile now; she laughed outright.

Henry stared at her.

"My dear cousin," she said, endeavouring to recover her gravity, "I fear you never will be a correct speaker, for it is evident to me that you have no very clear idea of the nature of the English language. If you were already in orders I should be dreadfully alarmed at the idea of your preaching, inasmuch as you have just made it clearly evident that you do not know the difference between *curacy*, and *cure*. I should say, particularly in your case, that not even *rectory* and *cure* were synonymous, and surely curacy and cure must be wider apart still. No, dear Henry, I have not been looking out for a curacy, but I think I have found a cure for the malady that seemed to threaten you, namely, that of endeavouring to force your faculties into the performance of a task for which nature has not fitted you. The remedy I prescribe for this, my dear cousin, is your preparing yourself with all convenient dispatch to join your regiment, which I am told is destined for service at the Cape at no very distant period."

"My regiment!—Join my regiment! What can you mean, Helen Beauchamp? It is impossible you can be laughing at me! It is not like you."

"I hope not, Henry. No, dearest cousin, I am very greatly in earnest in telling you, that, by and with the assistance of our most kind friend Mr. Phelps, a commission has been secured for you in one of the regiments which I remember your having named as the most desirable. If you had come home at the time you first talked of, which was six months ago, and before I became of age, you would have found the commission ready for you; for I beg to observe, friend Harry, that I am an excellent manager—a little in the miser line now and then, perhaps, but nobody has a right to complain of that, you know, if it amuses me, and some of my saving tricks certainly did amuse me, after you went away. It really is almost a pity, as far as I am concerned, that the necessity for them is over. However, this full-blown majority of mine is convenient in some respects, because it has enabled me to deposit sufficient money in the proper quarter to purchase on as rapidly as maybe, till I have fairly made you major as well as myself. And now tell me, does this please you, my dear disinherited cousin?"

Henry Rixley looked absolutely bewildered by this intelligence. He gazed with a puzzled expression of countenance into the fair face of his smiling companion, not exactly as if he thought she was in jest, but yet as if he were afraid of permitting himself to be too sure that she was in earnest. After standing immovably still, with his eyes fixed upon her, for about a minute, he drew a long sigh, which really sounded as if he were gasping a little for want of breath, and pronounced the words, "And my father?"

"Fear nothing from that quarter, Henry," she replied, affectionately pressing the arm upon which she was leaning. "Everything is exactly as you would wish it there. Mr. Phelps and I took good care to ascertain that, before we proceeded too far in the business to involve ourselves in any domestic troubles on that score. Everything is right in the home department. Father, mother, sister, are all of one mind on the subject as completely as heart can wish. If you are pleased, dearest Henry, you will not find a single doubting, or dissentient voice at home."

"Pleased! If I am pleased!" exclaimed poor Henry, in almost uncontrollable agitation. "Oh, Helen! Helen! I wish now that I had not taken so much pains to conceal from you all I suffered at the idea of sitting down as a country curate for life! If I had let you see only a tenth part of what I suffered then, you would be more able to understand how great is the happiness you have bestowed upon me now! Shall I thank you? No! The fullest, the most glowing expression of thanks ever uttered by man would fall so short, so very short of what I would wish to express at this moment, that I am positively

determined to make no attempt of the kind ! There is, however, one little remark which I will venture to make, though I
am sadly afraid that your woman's wit is not of a calibre to
enable you to comprehend it. You have once, and again, Cousin
Helen, hinted at the desperate wrong you did me when you took
the liberty of coming into the world. Now, setting aside the
fact, which has been repeatedly hinted to you, but to which you
have never appeared to pay any attention, that if you had never
been born, your father's estate would never have been mine,
setting aside this fact, I do implore you to believe me when I
declare that I would not give up the position in which you have
placed me, to become a *landed gentleman* with an estate ten times
the value of yours. For then it would have been my *duty* to
stay at home, and look after my acres, and my tenants; and
upon my word and honour, I think I would rather be a red
Indian. While now ! But I will not describe this glorious *now*
further, than to say that it gives me everything that I most
coveted on earth."

Helen had spoken very truly, when she said that her little
saving tricks had amused her; but had she suffered, and pretty
severely, too, in the performance of them, she would have
thought herself most amply repaid for all she had done, by contemplating the changed aspect of Henry Rixley, and listening to
his own energetic description of his happiness.

<hr>

CHAPTER XXXIX.

Nothing could have been better timed than this return of
Henry, and the bright demonstration of his exceeding happiness
which followed it; for though Helen's high toned character
kept her from sinking into the degradation of pining sorrow,
because one precious hope had been disappointed, she did in
truth suffer from the disappointment more deeply than it would
have been easy for anyone to believe who only saw her in
society.

But Helen was not a person who lived for herself, and herself
only; the watching the gay spirits of Henry, the satisfaction of

his father, the gratified ambition of his mother, and the over-
flowing joy of his gay-hearted sister, seemed to restore her
again to happiness, and the delightful consciousness that she
had the power of thus embellishing the existence of those she
loved, taught her to feel the value of her wealth and her
independence greatly more than she had ever done before.

With the sort of healthy strength of mind which made so
essential a feature of her character, she welcomed this feeling
of satisfaction as an especial blessing, and wisely determined
to keep it in useful activity. She had long ago made up her
mind as to the degree of retribution she should make to her
cousins by the disposal of her property in case she never found
her brother; but as she felt herself quite sure that she should
cling to the hope of his being restored to her to the last hour
of her own existence, it was obvious to her common sense that
this resolution in their favour might be of little or no advantage to them, whatever it might be to their heirs. The only
method, therefore, by which she could hope effectually to benefit
them, was by disposing of her noble income in such a way as
might be most likely to be advantageous to them.

She meditated on this matter for a long time before she
finally decided upon the system she should pursue. The
question stated broadly, might be divided into two propositions :
should she economize her income, by contracting her style of
living, for the purpose of bestowing upon her cousins the
money so saved? Or should she give them the advantages of
a splendid home as long as they remained with her, together
with all the other benefits, more easily understood than enumer-
ated, arising from the associations to which such a style of
living gives easy access? She finally decided (taking the
whole family, herself included into the account), that the latter
method would be the best; a decision which was rendered the
more reasonable by the obvious fact that if indeed her brother
were ever restored to her, the having regularly spent every
shilling of her income in the interval, would be no impediment
to her providing very nobly for her cousins afterwards, without
depriving herself of the dear power of providing very nobly for
him likewise.

All these business-like meditations did her good. Few occupations perhaps are more hostile to the growth of green and
yellow melancholy, than a practical attention to the material
interests of life, especially when, as in the case of our fair
Helen, this practical attention is to be bestowed upon the expen-

diture of a large income, instead of the thrifty management of a small one.

Moreover it cannot be denied that Helen loved splendour. She would, however, most certainly have conquered that love with the same characteristic steadiness of purpose with which she had done battle with another species of love of a more insidious kind, had she not been very conscientiously persuaded that it was the duty of every one possessed of a large income, to spend it freely; and therefore in deciding upon being as sumptuous in her manner of living as her income would allow her to be, she was acting perfectly in accordance with her sense of duty.

She had read and thought too much on the subject of gratuitous alms-giving to trust to that for the utility to her fellow creatures which she was fully aware it was her duty to exercise; and where this feeling is one of the main springs which regulate expenditure, there is very little danger of such a degree of profuseness, as shall open a road to ruin.

From the day that Helen had first become her own housekeeper, she had never upon any occasion made the subject of her domestic finances a matter of discussion in the family. For the first few months of this period, both her uncle and aunt had felt a little anxious least her systematic avoidance of the subject arose from her feeling it to be a painful one. But the very particularly quiet, and orderly way in which all things proceeded under her rule, very soon set their kind hearts at ease on this subject; though until the carefully preserved secret of the purchase of Henry's commission was disclosed, some few little incongruities in her system were thought to be discernible; when it was discovered, however, that all these had their beginning and ending in the generous project of providing for him in a way so happily accordant with his wishes, and his character, her affectionate anxiety for his welfare was, if anything, a less remarkable trait in their estimation, or at any rate a less unexpected one, than the skilful and steady generalship by which she had enabled herself to accomplish it.

When, therefore, upon her coming of age, she assumed the management of her large income, with the assistance only of one honest man who was both bailiff and steward, without making a single observation to any one, either on the pains or the pleasures which this important epoch of her life brought with it, no sympton of alarm or anxiety of any sort was felt either by her uncle or her aunt, although they had themselves

18

endured no small share of pecuniary embarrassment during great part of their marriage life, and were both of them, probably in consequence of this, of a somewhat nervous temperament respecting money affairs; but the great *à plomb* of the young heiress seemed to have cured all this, and they marked her well-regulated —but often rather sumptuous—proceedings without fear or blame of any kind. Mrs. Rixley indeed seemed to think that she very satisfactorily summed up all the observations that could rationally be made on the subject, by saying that "it was pretty Helen's way."

Now in order to do "pretty Helen" full justice on this subject, it is necessary to remember that had she made it her habit to have recourse to family conclaves and consultations, upon all her projects, either of saving or of spending money, the result would have inevitably been to bring an unceasing tax of grateful thanks, and modest remonstrances, upon every member of the Rixley family; for most certain it is, that their interest, or their pleasure, was, in some shape or other, the real object of all her most important manœuvrings.

Had no dear trembling hope of the return of her brother been ever, and always alive in her heart (though never named, or hinted at to any human being), she would have managed all her affairs much more simply; or rather, she would have let them manage themselves; which they would have done in a very satisfactory manner, had no such hope existed.

But Helen's loving thoughtfulness for the family into which she had been so affectionately grafted, did not confine itself to the simple process of taking care that her pecuniary affairs were always in a healthy condition. Though the junior of her cousin Anne by a year or two, she felt a watchful sort of anxiety about all her little personal affairs, which she often used to say herself had a very maternal character.

Those "fable not" who declare that many a celebrated beauty owes as much of her renown to her *name*, and her *modiste*, as to Nature. Anne Rixley certainly never deserved the epithet of "*ugly*," which her father a little in sport, had bestowed upon her; neither did she, strictly speaking, deserve that of beautiful, which was now freely bestowed upon her by a large proportion of the Beauchamp Park neighbourhood.

Now to this delusion, if it must be so called, Helen had very greatly contributed in many ways, and if she had been ten times the young lady's mamma, she could not more thoroughly have enjoyed this result of her clever manœuvrings.

Anne Rixley was, however, in very sober truth, a charming girl; well-grown, with bright laughing eyes, dark hair that curled naturally, a soft smooth skin, neither too pink nor too pale, and a beautiful set of teeth, which she displayed exactly enough, and no more. In addition to all this, she was sweet-tempered, light hearted, clever and animated, and with a flow of good spirits which not only enlivened her own family, but seemed to carry cheerfulness and enjoyment into every circle she entered.

No wonder, then, that Anne Rixley was declared to be a lovely girl, although her features were neither regular, nor strictly handsome. Helen Beauchamp was not altogether ignorant of the fact that her cousin was less likely to be called beautiful by an artist, than herself; but she was most sincerely persuaded that beyond all comparison she was more attractive: in fact, Helen herself admired her so greatly, that the seeing her dressed to perfection, and shown off in every way to the greatest possible advantage, was one of her favourite occupations, and an unceasing source of pleasure and amusement to her.

Now it so happened that in the immediate neighbourhood of Beauchamp Park there was but one mansion which could compete in splendour with itself, but this one in some respects decidedly excelled it. This rival mansion was honoured with the aristocratic appellation of Rothewell Castle, and was the autumn and early winter residence of its noble owner Lord Rothewell. The family of this nobleman consisted of himself, his lady, one daughter, and one only son; and as such the young man was, of course, considered as a person of considerable importance, not only in his family, but in the neighbourhood, where he had been known and loved from a child, and to which he was recently returned after a long absence, which had been spent in wandering through pretty nearly every country in Europe.

Previous to the return of this young man from the continent, a great degree of intimacy had sprung up between Anne Rixley and his sister, the Lady Honoria Curtis. The young ladies were very nearly the same age, and had many points of character in common, which very easily, and very naturally led to their becoming great friends.

Another circumstance which assisted to bring about this result was, that the two Harrington girls, who were also very near for country neighbours, had neither of them the same joyous tone of character which belonged to Anne Rixley and her noble friend, so that they naturally, and inevitably as it were, formed two pair of Helena and Hermia-like confidants among them—Lady Honoria and Anne forming one pair, Agnes and Helen the other, while the reasonable Jane contentedly submitted to be very happy without belonging to either, while perpetually appealed to for her superior judgment by both.

The only daughter of a noble house can never be quite so important a personage as the only son, nevertheless, Lady Honoria Curtis was a very dearly beloved, and a very influential individual, and during the long absence of her brother, Lord Lympton, swayed the councils of Rothewell Castle with as little opposition as he could himself have done.

The consequence of this was, that Rothewell Castle was decidedly the gayest mansion in the country. Their dinner parties, perhaps, were neither so frequent, nor so *recherché*, as those at Beauchamp Park; but their *impromptu* dances were at least three to one, and they acted charades, and indulged in *petits jeux*, with a degree of unwearied vivacity which never could have been achieved had any one, save Lady Honoria, been mistress of the ceremonies, or, more properly speaking, of the sports and pastimes of Rothewell Castle.

The return of a gay young heir to such a home as this, was naturally the signal for a multitude of *fêtes* to be both given and received by his family; and, indeed, if he had been eaten up by a shark while bathing in the Mediterranean, or buried in an avalanche while crossing Mont Cenis, it is very probable that our sober-minded Helen would never have sent out cards for a fancy ball at Beauchamp Park.

Had the Rixley family not lost the inheritance which Helen had persuaded herself would have descended to them had she never came in their way to prevent it, she would very probably never have become the plotting young schemer which she has already shown herself; and this—far from unjust—imputation was still further confirmed by the circumstances which I have now to relate.

The intimate friendship which existed between Lady Honoria Curtis and Anne Rixley, led to very frequent visits of a week or ten days' duration of Anne at Rothewell Castle, and it was no " malignant fate " which ordained that one of these visitations was in progress when Lord Lympton returned to the castle from his two years' ramble on the continent.

It had been arranged before this visit took place, that Miss

Beauchamp was to call for her cousin on a day fixed among them for her return. This engagement, very punctually kept by Helen, brought her to Rothewell Castle precisely at the moment when this newly-arrived Lord Lympton was in the act of teaching her cousin Anne (and his own sister, of course, into the bargain) some particularly beautiful new polka step.

It would be a useless, as well as perfectly vain attempt, were I to endeavour to make my readers exactly comprehend every-thing that Helen saw, or fancied she saw, during this, her own first interview with the handsome young heir of Rothewell Castle. Let it suffice that I assure them she did not think the young Lord Lympton in the least danger of falling in love with herself.

Her drive home with her cousin was not a very talkative one. Anne said but little, and seemed to take an unaccountable degree of pleasure in looking out of the carriage window; and this of course gave Helen time to think.

And she did think. She thought a little then—and she thought a good deal in the course of the next week or two—and the consequence of all she thought and of all she saw was, that she sent out invitations for the fancy ball which has been already mentioned so repeatedly.

This plotting and scheming, like several other traits of character which I have faithfully set down concerning Helen, are, I am perfectly well aware, by no means befitting a heroine; but I cannot help it. The Helen I speak of was exactly such a person as I describe, and my reader must judge her as leniently as he can.

Certain it is, that from the time this said ball was decided upon, Helen's thoughts had been fixed on the subject of Anne Rixley's costume with a degree of interest which it could hardly have excited in her, had no object beyond her looking pretty while she wore it been in her head.

I will not take upon me to decide whether a young lady is justified in endeavouring to make her friend look beautiful with all her milliner's might, for the express purpose of turning a young gentleman's head thereby. Justified or not, however, Helen certainly attained her object; for not only did her cousin look more attractively bewitching than she had ever done in her life before, but the young Lord Lympton thought so, quite as much as Helen.

Au reste, the ball was a very brilliant one in all respects, Miss Beauchamp herself was not dressed in costume, and notwith-

standing her faultless face and form she was decidedly one of the
least remarkable figures that could have been pointed out among
the young and the fair who adorned the assembly; neither did
the elaborate studies of costume produce any very satisfactory
result for George Harrington; for though nothing could have
set off his handsome person to greater advantage than the dark
green and black chasseur's dress which he had chosen, Helen
Beauchamp was not at all more in love with him at the end of
the evening, than she was at the beginning of it.

CHAPTER XL.

My narrative must now return to those with whom it began,
but from whom it has long been parted.

When the unfortunate Mrs. Lambert told Helen that it was
her purpose to seek William, and not to rest until she found
him, she very strictly spoke the truth ; and, moreover, she
adhered afterwards very faithfully to her promise. It has been
already stated that her inquiries among the sailors at Falmouth,
many of whom were of long standing acquaintance, had enabled
her to ascertain that William Rixley had sailed from that port,
on board a large boat which called itself a fishing smack, but
which was strongly suspected by the intimate associates of its
owner, of occasionally-doing a little business in the more profitable line of smuggling.

As to the probable destination of the little vessel she could
learn absolutely nothing, but her captain had been long known
to her as the brother of a woman who had once lived as servant
with herself and her mother, while they were maintaining themselves by letting lodgings in Falmouth. After a few moments'
reflection, therefore, she determined on returning to the Warren
House for the purpose of removing from thence the trunks containing her wearing apparel, and on establishing herself in a
lodging at Falmouth, till such time as the boat should return
thither, on board of which William Rixley had taken his
departure. Nor had she very long to wait before this happened
—the " Pretty Polly " again showing her saucy head in the
offing within about ten days after she had left it. Her old
acquaintance appeared rather shy, however, of answering her

questions; but whether this reserve was the result of caution on
his own account, or on that of his late passenger, she could not
for some time discover. It probably was the latter, for the
report of the young man's having murdered his father, had been
loudly and widely circulated through Falmouth, and its neighbourhood; and it was, therefore, to remove this that she exerted
herself.

It was probably the deep sincerity with which she expressed
both her own attachment to the unfortunate young man, and
her firm conviction that he was innocent of the dreadful crime of
which he was accused, that at length gained her point, and led
the friendly smuggler to describe to her exactly the point at
which he had parted from William. This was an out-of-the
way spot on the coast of Holland, and when, while thanking
him for his information, she gave him to understand that it was
her purpose immediately to follow him. the blunt tar told her
that she did not know what she was talking about, and that
nobody but a downright raving mad woman would ever take
such a wild notion into her head.

But Almeria Lambert was as well capable of proving herself
to be in her right senses as most people, and, moreover, she had
little or no difficulty in convincing her old acquaintance that it
was in her power very amply to reward anyone who would
promptly and effectually assist her in the search she was upon.

Having achieved thus much, her subsequent steps were comparatively easy.

Her smuggling friend soon made her very plainly perceive
that if she had enough ready money at hand to prosecute the
search she was upon, her best plan would be to remain where
she was, and commission him, whose profession it was to
embrace from day to day whatever employment presented itself,
to set about the task for her.

That the man meant to do her errand fairly was sufficiently
proved by the terms which he himself proposed, and which
stipulated that not one farthing of the fifty pounds, which she
proposed to give for the recovery of her lost darling, should be
paid before he had been found.

This bargain was very quickly concluded; the only objection
made to it by Mrs. Lambert being, that it might prove a very
unprofitable one to Joe Burton, the smuggler, if the search
lasted longer than he expected, or if it finally failed altogether.

But this scruple was removed in a spirit as honest as that by
which it was dictated, by Joe Burton's assurance that he knew

perfectly well what he was about. "There is not a sea-coast in Europe that I don't know as well as you do your sampler, Mrs. Lambert," said Joe, with the tone and manner of a man who was by no means ashamed of his profession; "and, moreover," he added, with a good deal of self-complacency, "there is not a nook nor a corner where I have not had dealings, and where I have not got friends; and so it would be, you may take my word for it, if we were to go to war to-morrow, from one end of Europe to the other."

This assurance perfectly satisfied Mrs. Lambert, whose information respecting human affairs extended considerably beyond her sampler.

Within two days after this bargain was concluded, the "Pretty Polly" was again upon the high seas, and Mrs. Lambert established in the occupation of a garret, in her own house, in the town of Falmouth.

Her manner of life was very retired and quiet; but she affected nothing like concealment as to the object she had in view, distinctly declaring that her purpose in practising a greater degree of economy than her circumstances rendered necessary, was to save money enough to enable her to prosecute a search for the basely-maligned William Rixley, which search she would never abandon so long as she remained alive, and that there was the least shadow of a hope that it might eventually prove successful.

No great time was lost after this compact was concluded before the wanderer was traced, by the sagacious and indefatigable Joe Burton, till he finally discovered that he had enlisted in a foot regiment on the very eve of its starting for the Cape of Good Hope.

When this perfectly-correct information was reported to his employer, Joe Burton received and pocketed the stipulated reward with a well-pleased smile and an approving conscience; for he naturally enough supposed that it was as well calculated to set the good woman's mind at rest respecting William Rixley, as it was well possible any intelligence could do; for, whether innocent or guilty of the dreadful crime of which he stood accused, it clearly proved that he was very satisfactorily out of reach of pursuit, and safe from all the painful consequences which must have followed if he had been arrested.

Nor did Almeria Lambert give him reason to suppose, either by look or word, that she was less completely satisfied by his intelligence than he supposed her to be; and so they parted on the very best terms possible; the contented smuggler whistling as he went, and the stedfast-purposed Almeria remaining alone in her garret, and instantly becoming occupied with all the practical details necessary to be taken into consideration before she set out upon the expedition which was to enable her, with as little delay as might, to follow the — Regiment of Infantry to the Cape of Good Hope. Nor did she lose an hour in setting about it. But, notwithstanding all her eagerness to depart, she would not have done so, even if a vessel had that hour been ready to receive her, without first giving instructions to Mr. Lucas, respecting his being left in charge of the will which was to bequeath her little wealth; and, moreover, taking leave of Mr. Bolton, whose pitying gentleness had left a deeper impression of compunction, as well as of gratitude, on the conscious sinner's mind than could have been produced by the most indignant reprobation that human lips ever uttered.

CHAPTER XLI.

MRS. LAMBERT had never entered Crumpton Parsonage since the day Helen left it. Two months had elapsed between that day and the one she now selected for her farewell visit to it; and, much as she had silently and secretly suffered during those two months, she felt that the penance she was about to inflict upon herself, by now going there, was harder to endure than all the rest.

It happens, oftener than we think for, that the passion of PRIDE makes as wild work in the human heart, and rules it with as absolute a tyranny, as either love, hatred, or any other of the fiercest passions which roar most loud, and thunder in the index. Anyone who has often visited asylums for the insane, in company with a professional guide, able and willing to answer questions concerning the causes of the various hallucinations which have peopled the sad abode, must, I think, have been surprised by the frequency with which the word "*pride*" is uttered in reply to such questions.

Mrs. Lambert was certainly not insane, according to the ordinary meaning of the word; but yet, from a very early period of her life, there had been little enough of sanity in her conduct whenever this master passion of her nature had been brought into action. That she had some fine qualities cannot be denied; and of these, the total absence of that detestable species of selfishness, which leads human beings to be too much occupied about themselves and their own little individual comforts to have any time or any interest left for those of others, was one. From this engrossing, hateful, paltry little sin, Almeria Lambert was wholly free. Moreover, had nature led her to be strongly and devotedly affectionate to those whom she loved, and who she believed loved her, and this to a degree which could lead her, as in the case of her fatal attachment to her late master, to forget even the dictates of her pride, as well as of her reason. She was, too, notwithstanding her criminal life, still capable of discerning, and of duly appreciating, the purity and the holiness of such beings as Mr. and Mrs. Bolton, and her conquering her feelings of torturing shame, when now presenting herself before them, ought not to be left out of the scanty catalogue of her merits, because her motive for doing so was a good one, being perfectly unselfish, and arising from her wish to give them all the information she possessed herself respecting the unfortunate young man on whom they had bestowed so much kindness, and for whom they had proved themselves so deeply interested.

Her painful task in thus presenting herself was, however, rewarded by hearing more particulars respecting the situation of Helen than she had dared to flatter herself she should ever hear again; for neither Mr. Bolton, nor his gentle-hearted wife either could resist the silent but unmistakable appeal made to them by the varying complexion and anxious eye of the unfortunate woman, upon hearing the name of Helen pronounced.

Both Mr. and Mrs. Bolton had received frequent letters from her, minutely detailing all the pleasant features of her present home; nor did they shrink from repeating to the painfully-abashed being before them, the affectionate terms in which she had been inquired for by the innocent girl whom she had so long loved, even as a mother loves her child. She was more cheered and soothed by this, than she would herself, an hour before, have believed possible, and so greatly did it tend to soften and to open her heart, that she not only told Mr. and Mrs. Bolton all the intelligence she had been able to gather respecting William, but explained to them, before she left the parsonage, what her own projects were respecting following him to the Cape.

Her auditors listened to her with great feeling and deep interest; but Mr. Bolton shook his head as he did so, and when she had finished the detail of what she intended to do, told her candidly, though not without reluctance, that he feared she over-rated her own strength, as well as the probabilities of ultimate success in the undertaking.

But on this point he had no influence; her resolution was not to be shaken; and this speedily became so evident, notwith-standing the extreme quietness of her manner while confessing that she did not think she could be induced to alter her mind, that Mr. Bolton changed his reasonable remonstrance into a most friendly and earnest expression of his good wishes for her success.

And so they parted; Mrs. Lambert returning to Falmouth by aid of the same fisherman's cart which had brought her to Crampton, and the good clergyman and his wife wandering down, arm in arm, to the sea-beach, moralizing on the strange mixture of good and evil so legible in the character of the unfortunate woman who had just left them.

Early on the following day Mrs. Lambert paid a visit to Mr. Lucas, the attorney. It did not appear, however, that she had any very particular business on which to consult him, as she had entrusted the care of her house, and the important business of letting it, to an old female friend, whom she well knew to be in all ways perfectly capable of executing the task to her satis-faction. It seemed, indeed, that she now sought Mr. Lucas rather to speak of past, than of present business, for what passed between them was on this wise:—

"Good morning, Mrs. Lambert," said the friendly attorney, upon her presenting herself in his office; "I hope you are better than when I saw you last. That terrible business at the Warren House almost killed you, I believe. I shall never forget your looks when I came to the house to take the inventory with you, and put seals on the property! And no wonder, I am sure! It was a most shocking affair altogether. Do walk in and sit down."

Mrs. Lambert accepted the invitation, and placed herself in the chair indicated, which was just in front of the desk at which the attorney himself was writing. "Have you heard of that sweet pretty girl, the daughter?" he continued.

"Yes, Sir," quietly replied Mrs. Lambert, "I have heard very excellent news of her. I have heard that she is well, and finds a very happy home in the family of her uncle."

"And is it true, Mrs. Lambert, that she is come into such a monstrous fine fortune by the death of her father?" said he.

"Yes, Sir, it is perfectly true," she replied, with a slight augmentation of colour, and a tone that seemed to have some touch of pride in it. "Miss Beauchamp, I am told, is one of the finest fortunes of any young lady in England."

"So I hear," rejoined the attorney. "It must have come upon you as a great surprise, Mrs. Lambert, after so many years of service, to find out that your master was of a different name, and in such a very different situation of life from what you supposed."

"Yes, indeed, Sir," she returned, "it was a great surprise to us all, and to no one more than to the dear young lady herself."

"I daresay," rejoined Mr. Lucas, "that it will not be very long before we hear of your joining her again. You have been a good and faithful servant to her, and her mother before her."

"If I had nothing but my own pleasure to consult, there would be no duty I could so gladly undertake as that of personal attendant upon Miss Beauchamp," said Mrs. Lambert, earnestly, but in a voice of perfect composure. "But I believe, Sir," she continued, "that it falls to the lot of very few to be able, without self-reproach, to do exactly the thing they like best. I am very strongly persuaded, Sir, that it is my duty to seek for my late master's unfortunate son, for the purpose of telling him of the vile and most false reports that have been circulated against him, and of inducing him to return to his native land. Never were a brother and sister more tenderly attached to each other than Master William and Miss Helen; and the fine fortune she has inherited will enable her to provide for him very handsomely without injuring herself."

"And you really mean to set out upon a voyage round the world in search of him, Mrs. Lambert?" said the attorney, looking at her with great astonishment.

"Yes, Sir, I do," was her succinct reply.

"But, my dear, good woman," he rejoined, "you ought to think a good deal about it, before you set out upon such an expedition as this. I have a great respect for you, Mrs. Lambert, for I believe you to be a very excellent person, and I should think I really committed a great sin if I saw you set out upon such a scheme as this without advising you against it. Think about it, Mrs. Lambert—think about it."

"I have done little or nothing else but think about it, Sir, from the time I found he was gone, to this present hour; and the more I have thought, the more entirely convinced I have become that it is my duty to follow him, and bring him back," she replied.

"But has it never occurred to you, in all this thinking, that you may do the unfortunate young man considerably more harm than good, if you succeed in finding him, and bringing him back to this country with you? The circumstantial evidence against him, is very strong, Mrs. Lambert."

"Is it possible, Sir, that you are one of those who suspect William Rixley of having murdered his father?" returned Mrs. Lambert, her eyes flashing, and her pale face suddenly becoming crimson, with what appeared to be a burst of uncontrollable passion.

"I have no wish to anger you, Mrs. Lambert," returned the lawyer, gently, "on the contrary, I do assure you that I feel very true respect for your warm attachment to these young people, to both of whom, I have heard, you have been a most faithful nurse, and useful friend in all ways. But I am sure you have good sense enough to be aware that I am much more likely to understand the degree of suspicion which rests against William Rixley than you are."

"No, Mr. Lucas. No, Sir," returned Mrs. Lambert, vehemently. "I am not, and never can be aware that anyone is so capable of forming a just opinion concerning William Rixley as I am. His sister, with all her love, and all her confidence in him, is much too young to have the power of judging character; and though, of course, she would turn with abhorrent disbelief from the wicked slander, she might not be able to give such reason for her disbelief as I could do. Have I not known the boy from his infancy? And do I not know this most wicked charge against him to be something so absolutely contrary to his nature as to render the belief of it impossible?"

"Who then do you suspect of this terrible deed?" said Mr. Lucas.

"Indeed, Sir, I suspect no one," she replied, "and, if I did, I should certainly be very reluctant to say so, after the proof just given by so reasonable a gentleman as yourself, of the ease with which a word may be received as truth, which rests upon nothing but the most vague suspicion."

"True! very true!" replied Mr. Lucas. "It is much easier to throw suspicion on an innocent individual than to remove it, for it sticks like birdlime. There is one suspicion, however, which I know has come into the heads of several of our town's people, who knew a good deal of your late master's odd ways," continued the attorney, with a look which seemed to show that he was meditating deep matters.

"And what is that, Sir, if I may be so bold as to ask ? " said Mrs. Lambert, respectfully.

"Yes, certainly, you may ask," replied Mr. Lucas, "and I see no reason why I should not answer you. I have heard more than one hint a pretty strong suspicion that it was the poisoned gentleman's own hand which administered the deadly draught. What is your opinion upon the likelihood of such a suggestion as that, Mrs. Lambert ? "

It was a minute or more before this question received an answer, yet it did not appear that the person to whom it was addressed, listened to it either with much emotion or surprise. Her eyes, however, which during the former part of the dialogue had been pretty constantly fixed on the face of Mr. Lucas, now changed their direction, and fixed themselves upon the ground.

"Why do you not answer me, Mrs. Lambert ? " said Mr. Lucas. "You can do no harm to anybody, you know, by throwing suspicion in that direction."

"Neither can I do any good, Sir," she replied.

"But, indeed, it *may* do good by removing it from the inno- cent," said the lawyer.

"If I really and positively knew that my late master had destroyed himself," she rejoined, "I own that I should not hesitate to throw the imputation on his memory; but I am very far from being able to say that I know it."

"Well ! well; for the present it certainly matters little to anybody whether you have any suspicion or not, for the poor boy William is not very likely to be found, I take it, even by you, my good woman, persevering as I doubt not you will be in your search for him."

"In that, Sir, I trust you will be mistaken," she replied; " and if I should be the happy means of restoring William to his sister and his country, I shall feel little, or rather no doubt as to his being able to prove his innocence. There is an old and a vulgar saying, Sir, which I daresay you have heard, '*Murder will out !*' And if my late master really was murdered, we may be very sure that God will make it known in his own good time; nor will I believe that the innocent will be made to suffer for the guilty."

"Altogether it certainly is a most mysterious business, and the chances in favour of its being his own work appear greatly more probable from the previous strangeness of his conduct in concealing his real name, and circumstances," said Mr. Lucas, rising from his own chair in order to give his visitor a hint that he was busy, and that it was time she should rise from hers.

This hint was immediately attended to. Mrs. Lambert was on her feet in a moment.

"Is there anything in the way of business that I can do for you before you leave the town?" said Mr. Lucas, cordially, as she was preparing to take her leave.

"Nothing more than what you have already kindly done," was her reply. "The will which I made, Sir, just before all this dreadful business happened, is in your hands," she continued, "and I will beg of you to take care of it for me. If you remember, Sir, it was sealed up in your presence as soon as it was executed, together with a letter addressed to our good clergyman, Mr. Bolton. If I return you will be pleased to restore this packet to me in the state in which I gave it to you; but should you hear that I am dead, I will beg of you, Sir, to break the seal of it immediately, and deliver the letter it contains according to the address, with as little delay as possible. And as to the will, Sir, you know that will speak for itself."

Mr. Lucas very cordially shook hands with her, uttering many friendly wishes for her safe return; but promising that her instructions should be carefully remembered, and faithfully attended to in any case. And Mrs. Lambert, took her leave with great respect, and many expressions of gratitude.

CHAPTER XLII.

It would not be easy to imagine a situation more miserably forlorn than that of Almeria Lambert, while thus preparing, utterly alone, and unsupported by any human spirit but her own, for a long and perilous voyage, the result of which was so wildly uncertain, and cheered by hopes so vague, as almost to defy her efforts to give them any form approaching probability.

But her stedfast purpose was not to be shaken by any such considerations as these; on the contrary, the call thus made upon her courage and endurance seemed to awaken her to new life, and to renew all the original energy of her character.

But desperately resolute as was the purpose which thus sent her forth in search of the unfortunate William Rixley, she could scarcely have undertaken it effectually had not a singularly well-timed piece of good fortune befallen her, which did, in fact, render an expedition *possible*, which without it must have been pretty evidently the reverse even to her excited and over-wrought mind.

The house in Falmouth, which she had inherited from her mother, had, contiguous to it, about half an acre of ground, which had hitherto been both pleasant and profitable as a garden, but which was now unexpectedly become a very valuable morsel of the earth's surface.

The quarter of the town in which the house was situated was by no means a particularly agreeable one, for it was at no great distance from the very busiest part of the sailors' quarter, and consequently noisily near the port.

It chanced that two speculating individuals happened at nearly one and the same time to conceive the idea, that, in consequence of the rapidly-increasing business, great profit might be realized by erecting warehouses on this rare bit of unoccupied freehold ground, and proposals for the purchase of it were made to Mrs. Lambert on a certain Monday morning about ten o'clock.

To these proposals she very discreetly replied that they should receive an answer on the following morning. Before mid-day, however, of the same eventful Monday, another proposal, precisely of a similar nature, reached her from another quarter, to which she returned a similar reply ; and then she tied on her bonnet and pinned on her shawl, and set forth to consult Mr. Ringwood, the banker, a kind-hearted and sharp-witted old gentleman, who had been a kind friend both to her and her mother upon more occasions than one, and who now, on hearing the proposal of the first applicant, nodded his head and rubbed his hands, with an air of very considerable satisfaction.

But when his visitor resumed her narrative, and proceeded to state that in the course of an hour or two she had received a similar proposal from a second speculator, Mr. Ringwood uttered a long whistle, which the intelligent Mrs. Lambert immediately felt must mean something more than met the ear.

"You must tell them both, my dear, good woman, that you do not intend to sell your garden by private contract to anybody," were the first words to which Mr. Ringwood gave utterance.

No one, when consulting another, could be more perfectly well-disposed to follow the advice they asked for, than was Mrs. Lambert upon this occasion, nevertheless, she ventured to say, "I am quite sure, Mr. Ringwood, that you will tell me to do what will be best for my interest; but I must not conceal from you that the sale of this unexpectedly available bit of property would be very convenient to me."

"Would it, indeed, Mrs. Lambert?" he replied, joyfully. "That's all the better, and I am heartily glad to hear it, because money that is wanted is worth ten times as much as money that is not. But you must not sell your garden by private contract for all that."

"But how then shall I be able to manage it?" she replied, anxiously.

"Write a short civil little note to both the parties," said Mr. Ringwood, "and tell them both exactly in the same words that the property is about to be sold by auction."

"But how shall I be able to manage that, Sir?" returned the eager Mrs. Lambert, looking a good deal annoyed. "I happen to want the money immediately, Mr. Ringwood, and I believe it takes a long time to get an auction over, and to settle everything."

"I am sorry you are in such a violent hurry, my good friend," replied the banker. "But will you give me three days? I don't mean, observe, to undertake that I will get an auction over in three days, but I will undertake within that time to obtain sufficient information to enable you to judge whether it would not be worth your while to wait a little."

This was spoken with so much earnest kindness, that Mrs. Lambert, though greatly annoyed at the idea of delay, could not refuse her compliance; and she was rewarded for her good behaviour by receiving a message from her old friend, early on the second day, desiring to see her.

His report was a very pleasant one, but it astonished, as much as it pleased her, for he told her that he had ascertained from sources that might be relied upon, that for sundry commercial reasons, into which it would be useless to enter at large, her garden, and her house, too, were likely to become a very valuable property. "Tell me," he added, "what are your reasons for wishing to have the money directly?"

Mrs. Lambert looked for a moment somewhat embarrassed,

for as yet she had made no mention of her projected voyage to
Mr. Ringwood.   She knew that he had much kind and friendly
feeling towards her, but she knew, also, that he was a very
sober-minded reasonable sort of man, and she thought, not,
perhaps, without some reason, that he might consider it his
duty to dissuade her from undertaking an enterprize, of which
all could see the dangers and difficulties, while none but herself
could comprehend the motives, and feelings, which led her to
undertake it.

Nor was she at all mistaken as to the result she anticipated
from her avowal.   Mr. Ringwood certainly did feel, and did
express a good deal of astonishment when she told him, in
answer to his question, that her reason for wishing to be put in
immediate possession of whatever money her little freehold property might produce, was, that she was immediately going to set
sail for the Cape of Good Hope.

No very long discussion, however, followed upon the wisdom
of this measure after he had listened to the announcement of it;
for Mr. Ringwood was a man of observation and discernment,
and he speedily perceived that, whether the resolution of his old
accquaintance were wise, or not, it was immutable.

It required, therefore, but little meditation on the subject to
make him aware, that with such a project firmly fixed upon,
Mrs. Lambert was quite right in wishing to be put in possession
of the money in question before she set out to execute it.   There
was a great deal of kindness shown in the zealous manner in
which, as soon as he felt her purpose to be a fixed one, he set
himself to think in what manner he could most effectually assist
her in the accomplishment of it.   Like everbody else in Falmouth,
and its neighbourhood, he had heard of the terrible suspicion
thrown upon William Rixley, and as he now listened to the
earnest, and almost passionate declaration of his being incapable
of the crime attributed to him, uttered by the person who,
perhaps, of all living, had most reason to believe herself capable
of forming a correct judgment of his character, he could not but
feel that if rash, she was decidedly righteous in seeking him
out, and bringing him forward to brave the charge, and to dis-
prove it.

Mr. Ringwood was too much a man of business to find any
difficulty in so arranging matters as to guard the enterprising
woman from any danger of being involved in pecuniary difficulties: but, nevertheless, he had become so fully aware of the
probable value of her property that he was determined not to

make the sale of it a hasty transaction. It was, therefore, finally arranged between them, that he should from time to time honour her drafts upon him, she leaving him full power to dispose of her property according to his own judgment and discretion; and having legally invested him with full powers to act for her, she lost not an hour more in preparing herself for her strangely adventurous expedition.

Notwithstanding all the desolate loneliness of her situation, notwithstanding the dangers, the fatigues, the anxiety of the enterprise she had undertaken, and all the miserable uncertainty as to its result—which she never for a moment permitted herself to forget—she was conscious of a feeling almost approaching to enjoyment as she seated herself as much apart as might be from all the bustle on the deck: and in silence, and alone, looked out upon that one of all the mysteries of creation which is the most distinctly divided from all the rest; and she felt as if she herself were now divided from all the scenes in which she had suffered.

"Is it not possible that I may in some degree FORGET?" thought she. "Is it not possible that the distinctness of all the torturing scenes I have passed through may in some degree wear away?" There was luxury, positive luxury, in the thought that this *might be possible*; and as she rolled her large camlet cloak around her, contriving so to place herself as to see nothing but the waves on which she floated, she felt a sensation infinitely more like calmness of spirit than any she had experienced since the hour in which her destroyer had first informed her that he had fallen in love with a beautiful young lady, and was about to marry her.

It is not my purpose, however, minutely to follow the progress of Mrs. Lambert from Falmouth Harbour to the Cape of Good Hope. It proved, on her arrival there, that the information she had received, respecting the regiment of infantry, was perfectly correct. The said regiment had arrived at the Cape only a few months before she reached it herself; but it was met by orders there which caused it to re-embark to India; and beyond this she could learn nothing, save that it was expected to be immediately engaged on very active service.

That this intelligence was a disappointment is most certain, though she was in some degree prepared for it, by the surmises, at least, if not by the positive information of the captain with whom she had sailed from Falmouth.

Her joy would, indeed, have been great, had she overtaken

the unfortunate fugitive at that point: but it was not so to be. She had the great satisfaction, however, of learning that the regiment, into which she knew from good authority that William had enlisted, had arrived at the Cape with a clean bill of health; and departed again for its ultimate destination, a few weeks only before her arrival there. She found, also, that the letter of credit which she brought with her from the Falmouth banker was not only available for the purpose of immediately replenishing her purse, but enabled her to obtain a very considerable sum of money, if she should need it, from a correspondent resident in the settlement to which the regiment she was pursuing was said to be destined.

Once again, therefore, the adventurous woman found herself on the high seas, with a still unconquered spirit, and with hopes of ultimate success in her quest, rather increased than lessened by the experience she had gained, and the information she had acquired, since her pilgrimage began.

CHAPTER XLIII.

THE second voyage was got over as resolutely as the first; but at the termination of it she again found, poor soul, that the object of her search was as much as ever beyond her reach. Yet, still, the tidings she received, though full of present disappointment, were by no means such as to suggest the abandonment of her enterprize; on the contrary, she again heard that William's regiment had completed its long voyage very satisfactorily, and had been marched, together with other troops, upon a very important expedition into the interior.

Had Mrs. Lambert's object been an ordinary object, and if the quest she was upon had been undertaken merely from the wish of being re-united to an object of affection, this delay in the accomplishment of her affectionate wish of meeting him would have been felt as a heavier misfortune than it was at present.

But her objects were, in truth, of a more important character, and the knowing that the regiment, in which it was so perfectly well ascertained that he had enlisted, had actually been ordered upon an expedition, which was. not likely to be very speedily terminated, sufficed to restore her to all the practical every-day steadiness of mind, which made so remarkable a feature in her character.

It may, perhaps, be doubted whether, after the first feeling of disappointment at not immediately seeing him was over, she did not almost rejoice at the delay, for it gave her time to revolve, at leisure, all the various schemes which had suggested themselves for the purpose of releasing the unfortunate young man from the engagement into which he had so rashly entered, and for restoring him to his sister, and his country.

The great improvement in the state of her own finances, made her feel very comfortably confidant that she should be easily able to purchase his discharge; but she felt, also, that even after this should have been accomplished, her difficulties would not be over. Had it not been for the frightful accusation which had been brought against him, her future plans would have arranged themselves readily enough, for all which would in that case have seemed necessary for his future well-doing, would have been easily within her power to achieve; it would only have been necessary to liberate him from his military thraldom, convey him back to Europe, and inform his sister of his arrival there, in order to secure to him the certainty of a happy destiny.

But how was this dreadful accusation to be met? Even presuming that he had at his command the most satisfactory proofs of his own innocence, the very fact of such a charge having been brought against him, would, as she very justly thought, be productive of so much pain, both to the brother and sister, as to render the success of her efforts to reunite them, almost a doubtful good.

After many very painful hours bestowed upon meditating upon these difficulties, Mrs. Lambert, at length, came to the conclusion at which sundry wise people have arrived before her, namely, that it would be best to spare herself the pain of debating the question as to what she would do, under circumstances which she could neither foresee, nor control; and having come to this conclusion she very quietly, rationally, and successfully set herself to arrange her affairs in such a manner as might enable her to act with promptitude whenever William should be sufficiently within her reach to benefit by her means of serving him.

She soon obtained all the necessary information respecting the purchase of his discharge, and found that on this point she was not likely to encounter any worse difficulty than a little delay. As to her money concerns, all was smooth and easy enough in that quarter, and all this being achieved, she established herself as an inmate in the family of a very respectable English settler, and screwed her courage to the task of waiting patiently.

But this waiting was a considerably longer business than she had calculated upon, yet, nevertheless, she bore it admirably. She had been long ago taught to endure resolutely, what she had brought upon herself wilfully, and these lessons were very useful to her now.

The expedition upon which the English troops were now engaged was not only important, but of a nature as tedious and uncertain, as it was dangerous. From week to week, and occasionally almost from day to day, intelligence arrived, sometimes good, sometimes bad, but for many months nothing at all definitive was known concerning the success of the expedition. The matter at issue was one of considerable importance, as on it depended either the acquisition, or the loss of territory, which was considered on all sides to be of great importance. At length, however, the doubtful affair arrived at the conclusion to which British arms are the most accustomed, and a complete and very important victory was announced to the English authorities, as the result of the struggle.

The news, of course, was received with all natural triumph, and becoming joy; but by degrees it was rumoured that the victory had not been obtained without heavy loss of life on both sides, and having long remained doubtful, had been achieved, at last, by one of those desperate displays of resolute valour which are never called for, and never put in action, without appalling loss on both sides.

The listening to all this was a process of fearful suffering to the unfortunate Almeria Lambert, and to render her agonising anxiety more acute still, she had to listen day by day to statements all tending to prove that the regiment into which William had enlisted had been distinguished both by its bravery and its heavy loss.

At length, however, this regiment, as well as several others, were re-called to head-quarters, and then followed the anxious business of obtaining a correct list of the names of those who had fallen. This list was a fearfully long one; but the name of William Rixley did not appear in it. This fact of itself seemed for a time to bring enough of comfort to atone for much

that she had suffered ; but she had still the difficult task before
her of ascertaining where and how a private of the name of
William Rixley could be found. In this difficult task she was
assisted by the friendly offices of an English family, with whom
she had become acquainted, and whose daughter, being on the
eve of marriage with an officer of the same regiment, was able
to make the necessary inquiries ; to please his beloved one, the
young man took the trouble of procuring a roll-call, such as it
was before the regiment went on this last service, and such as
it was afterwards.

It was with a trembling hand that poor Mrs. Lambert
received this proof of her young friend's influence, as well as of
her kindness ; and so conscious did she at that moment become
of her own weakness, that she begged permission to retain the
documents till she could examine them alone.

Great was her surprise, as well as her disappointment, upon
discovering that the name she sought was in neither of these
two lists. Was it possible, then, that she had been altogether
misinformed and deceived from the period of her earliest
inquiries ? Such obviously seemed to be the fact, for the
accuracy of these official papers could not be doubted. She
recurred to the quarter from whence she had received the
intelligence that William Rixley had enlisted, and it was one
that it would have been very difficult for her to doubt. It
might be, indeed, that he had died on the passage, or had
deserted either at the Cape of Good Hope or after his arrival in
India. But on both these points she obtained such satisfactory
assurances that no such event had happened, as to leave her
perfectly at a loss to conjecture the cause of the discrepancy
between actual facts and former evidence.

Her situation, poor woman, now became infinitely more painful to her feelings than she had ever felt it before since her
departure from England. All that was before her now was a
dark blank, without a ray of hope, or even the doubtful light of
a vague and feeble uncertainty to sustain her.

There was a moment when she was not very far from deciding
that the best course now left her was self-destruction ; but
despite her resolute temper and constitutional courage, she
shrunk from the " end-all" which has tempted so many miserable beings of a somewhat similar temperament.

For several weeks after her researches had brought her to
the miserable conclusion that all she had done, and all she had
suffered, in the hope of saving poor William from the con-

sequences of his ill-timed flight had been utterly useless to him, she remained in a state of such profound discouragement that all things future, and present, too, seemed matters of utter indifference to her. The results of the late splendid and most important victory, which was the theme of every tongue, were never dwelt upon in her hearing without causing her a feeling of desolate disappointment almost too painful to bear; and it was probably this consciousness, rather than any real longing for her native land, which made her suddenly resolve to take her passage in the next vessel that was bound to England.

Her preparations for this sad homeward voyage were not very elaborate, nor had she long to wait for a vessel bound to the land to which it was her purpose to go, though without the slightest hope, poor soul, of finding herself less miserable there than she was sure to be everywhere else. The idea, the hope, the confident expectation of serving and saving the friendless and penniless William Rixley, had been to her what the soul is to the body; and now she had lost it, the idea of dying, and being buried and forgotten, was the only one from which she did not turn with weariness and disgust.

Perhaps, if her feelings of apathy and discouragement had been less intense, she might not have shrunk, as she now did, from the idea of self-destruction. But as it was, she arranged all things for her homeward voyage, and heard the day fixed for her departure, with the consciousness of that sort of relief which is almost always found to attend a change of suffering.

The family which I have already mentioned as having, with friendly and active kindness, obtained for her the information she was so anxious to receive, and the result of which had so fatally blighted all her hopes, had never wearied in their kind attempts to soothe and comfort her. Her aspect, all faded as it was, could not easily be contemplated without interest; and the total absence of all querulous complainings under a disappointment which had so evidently destroyed every hope that made life valuable, could not be witnessed without pity.

This interest and this pity showed itself in many acts of friendly attention, all of which were proffered so quietly, that they were often accepted because there was less exertion necessary for the accepting than the refusing them. One of these habitual acts of kindness was the running up of the pretty young bride elect to the rooms which Mrs. Lambert inhabited in the neighbouring house, and taking her as a prisoner to their family tea-table.

This habit had for a long time been very precious to Mrs. Lambert, because it ensured her meeting the military adorer of her young friend, from whom she hoped to receive intelligence of William. Nor did the friendly habit cease when this long cherished hope was crushed by the intelligence that no one of the name of William Rixley had belonged to the corps since it had quitted England.

Only two or three days now remained before the vessel was to sail, on board of which she had secured her passage; and the gentle Lucy Wilmot failed not, though she left her lover in her mother's drawing-room, to go as usual for their evening guest.

As Lucy and her companion entered the room together, they found Captain Burney in the act of relating some anecdote with great animation, and it was, moreover, evidently listened to with great interest by her father and mother.

"What is that you are telling them, Captain Burney?" cried Lucy Wilmot, eagerly. "We must not lose that story, whatever it is, for I am sure it is something exceedingly interesting."

"Yes, it is," replied her mother, as she extended her hand to welcome her pale and silent guest; "and I think it will amuse Mrs. Lambert, too, for, as Burney relates the story, it is a perfect romance."

The little party then reseated themselves, and Captain Burney recommenced his narrative.

CHAPTER XLIV.

"Once upon a time the noblest country in the world, which I scarcely need tell you was called England, was engaged in a very long and difficult warfare with another mighty country at a very considerable distance from itself."

"Oh! goodness, Richard Burney, do not begin so!" exclaimed his betrothed, "or we shall have the whole history of England and its dependencies to listen to, before we come to the particular bit of romance that mamma has promised us."

"I am afraid you are a very impatient young lady!" said her lover, looking at her with an aspect of great alarm. "However, for the present, I suppose my wisest course will be to indulge you. I will, therefore, cashier my narrative of its very instructive preface, and state to you at once the dramatic anecdote for which you appear so impatient. When we all marched off in such violent haste, as you may perhaps remember, Miss Lucy, with the desperate determination of either thoroughly routing the confounded hordes which were rushing forward to overwhelm us, or to leave our bodies with them for booty, one part of our force consisted of the recently arrived — Regiment, concerning which our good Mrs. Lambert here, was at one time so much interested. They had a monstrous large lot of new recruits among them, and our most experienced officers were very far from being greatly delighted by the parade display of these new arrivals. No choice was left them, however, so off we set, bag and baggage, raw recruits and worn-out veterans, rather thankful than not upon the whole, upon having a line of marching men, of which we could not examine the accoutrements of the van and the rear at one and the same moment; an advantage which we have not always possessed, you know, in some of our *sorties*. You have heard enough, dearly beloved," added the young man, shaking his head, as if conscious of having already dilated sufficiently on the subject, " of our exploits on this occasion, but you could not have heard before this morning of the most gallant deed that has been recorded for many a day, for it was only late last night that the party concerned in it got back to head-quarters. There would be no use in my describing all the minor particulars to you, for unless you had seen a little fighting in the bush with your own eyes, it would be impossible to make you comprehend it. But the upshot of the affair is this :—our favourite old veteran, Captain Maclogan, one of the bravest fellows in the service, had been rash enough to follow a lot of rascally natives, who had got possession of the colours, right across a brook that would have swamped any fellow less like a giant than himself. His men, a score of them, at the very least, seemed ready to follow him, but not one of the set got half across the stream before their discretion sent them back again. The old hero, however, was not doomed to die in a ditch by himself, for in the very nick of time a stalwart young private of another company, seeing how the case stood, bethought him cleverly enough that there might be a better way of getting across a brook than wading through it, and thereupon, after pausing for an instant, as they say, to reconnoitre the ground, he took a vigorous run and cleared the stream at one noble leap. As to what happened after, it is absolutely necessary to hear Captain Maclogan himself describe it, in order either to understand or believe the dauntless courage displayed by the young fellow when he overtook the party. And it is certain that the said young fellow gives as fine an account of the old fellow, as the old fellow does of him, and the best proof that they both speak the truth is, that the colours have been marched back to the regiment in the highest style possible, being only a very little draggled, and a very little torn."

"And what have they done to reward the young soldier?" said Lucy.

"Why, there is some little doubt and difficulty about that," replied Captain Burney, "for the young man is wounded, and, therefore, the making him a corporal, or a sergeant, or anything of that sort is out of the question, because the brave veteran, whose life he has saved, will not permit his being taken to the hospital, and, therefore, instead of promotion, Captain Maclogan has obtained his discharge, and has taken him to his own lodgings, where he is nursing him as if he were his own son."

"And so he ought!" exclaimed Mrs. Wilmot, adding, "Your story really is a beautiful story, Captain Burney. Fancy a young fellow, with his musket to carry, too, taking such a leap as that, just for the slight hope of saving another man's life, and with such a terrible good chance of losing his own!"

"It was a fine action," said Lucy's father, "a very fine action. I hope the young man is not badly wounded?"

"No, not badly," was the reply; "it is only a flesh wound on the right arm, but he will not be able to draw his sword again for a week or two."

"Was this young man belonging to the — Regiment, which has recently arrived from Europe?" said Mrs. Lambert.

"Yes, ma'am," replied the young officer, "and if there were a few more in it like him, they would soon acquire a name that would make their raw recruits forgotten."

"Do you happen to have heard his name, Sir?" rejoined Mrs. Lambert.

"Do I happen to have heard it, my good lady! It would have been a very strange hap if I had not," replied Captain Burney, "for I don't believe that a single minute of the day passes in which it is not repeated by some one or other. His name is William Maurice."

Mrs. Lambert bowed very civilly in return for this information; and she sighed, too, poor soul, for there *was* a well-known name, which, if it had greeted her ear at that moment, would have almost seemed to repay her for all she had endured.

The next evening was the last she had to pass with her new, but kind-hearted, friends, before she was to embark upon her weary homeward voyage to England. When she entered the family sitting-room, she found them again engaged in listening to further particulars respecting the same adventure which had been discussed the evening before.

Captain Burney was now, however, recounting what he had heard at the mess, respecting the future prospects of the wounded soldier; and these prospects, as he stated them, appeared to be fully as romantic as the adventure which led to them.

Captain Maclogan, he said, was a bachelor, on the shady side of fifty, of good connections, and of easy fortune; and it was currently reported that he declared it to be his intention to purchase a commission for his preserver, with as little loss of time as possible.

This report had, of course, created great interest and curiosity for the fortunate individual whose youthful prowess had been exerted in the service of one who was able to requite it so nobly. " It is quite the fashion, I can assure you, among the officers to go and call upon the young fellow; and, of course, I have gone among the rest: and there he is, lying on Captain Maclogan's sofa, wrapped up in the old Scotchman's handsome dressing-gown, and looking no more like a common soldier than I to Hercules."

" What does he look like ? " said Lucy, laughing.

" Why, that is exactly the most curious thing of all," replied Burney ; " for I do assure you, without the slightest exaggeration, that he looks, and, what is more, that he speaks, too, exactly like a well-educated gentleman."

" That *is* very odd," said Lucy.

" Very odd, indeed," said her father, smiling; and adding, with an admonitory shake of the head, " Burney ! my dear fellow ! you are romantic."

" Not an atom of it, upon my life and honour !" returned the young man, eagerly. " If you will let me, Mr. Wilmot, I will bring him here some evening, when the doctor has dismissed him ; and when you see him, and converse with him, I feel certain that you will agree with me,"

"Ask him to describe his person," said Mrs. Lambert, in a low whisper, to Lucy.

The request was immediately complied with.

"Tell us exactly what he is like in appearance, Captain Burney," said the young lady, with the authority of a *fiancée*.

"He is like an extremely handsome young man, Miss Lucy— so handsome, that I will give you leave to declare, when you see him, which I am quite sure will be the truth, that you never saw any man so handsome before. He is under twenty; but he is very tall, and as athletic as any man of his age ought to be, though you would call him a slight young man at the first glance, on account of his great height. His features are perfectly well formed; his mouth and teeth peculiarly handsome; his complexion clear, but rather dark than florid; and his hair, which, though not black, is very near it, curls naturally, but so close to his head as not in any degree to conceal its very peculiarly beautful and intellectual formation. However, by far the handsomest, as well as the most peculiar features in his face, are his eyes, which, notwithstanding his dark complexion and hair, are of the very lightest blue, although the eye-lashes, which are very long, and completely black, give a general effect to his countenance, which might deceive one into thinking that he had dark eyes."

While Captain Burney was rapidly and eagerly giving this description, Mrs. Lambert kept her eyes immovably fixed upon him, with an expression that was perfectly indescribable; for it varied from moment to moment; at one time seeming to express the most vehement and concentrated anger, and in the next, beaming upon him with a look of such deep affection, that one might have fancied her first movement would be to enfold him in her arms, and press him to her heart.

The moment he had finished, she stood up, and, walking round the table to the chair he occupied, she stood before it, and fixing her large eyes sternly upon him, she said, "You have, either by some secret means, which I know not how to trace, obtained a description of his person, or else you have seen him yourself!"

"To be sure, I have seen him myself, my good lady!" returned the young man, laughing, and looking at her with an expression of drollery which seemed to indicate a considerable degree of amusement in contemplating her sublimely-tragic demeanour. "What is there so very extraordinary in my having seen him?"

"Nothing!" she replied, evidently endeavouring to compose

herself, " nothing!   If you could but tell me that his name was
Rixley!"

"But I can't tell you that, Mrs. Lambert," replied the young
man, "for he has told us all that his name is Maurice."

" May he not, from some motive or other, have changed his
name?" suggested Mr. Wilmot.

"Yes!" exclaimed Mrs. Lambert, vehemently; "for many,
many reasons he might have done it!"   And as she said this,
she trembled so violently from head to foot, that Lucy, springing from her chair, hastily pushed it towards her; while Captain
Burney, seizing her by the arm, placed her in it; a very well-
timed act of kindness; for, without it, the unfortunate Mrs.
Lambert would unquestionably have measured her length upon
the floor.

A few moments, however, sufficed not only to restore the
fainting woman to life and reason, but to suggest to the by-
standers a probable, and very satisfactory solution of the
mystery which had produced so vehement an effect upon her.

"I will bet anything you please that the young man *has*
changed his name," said one.

"It is the most likely thing in the world!" exclaimed
another.

"It is exactly what happens nine times out of ten," said
Captain Burney, " when a lad takes a freak for enlisting which
he thinks would not be approved at home."

And Lucy gently whispered in the ear of her *protégée*, " Do
not let your hopes overpower your strength, dear Mrs. Lambert,
after enduring despair so patiently."

"You are right, my dear child!" replied Mrs. Lambert, with
suddenly-recovered firmness; " I, at this moment, feel as sure as
if I had already seen him, that William Rixley is found!—You
do not know, you cannot guess, all the consolation which this
persuasion brings with it!"

She was silent for a few moments, and every one present was
too much occupied and interested in watching the effect of this
newly-born hope on the countenance and in the demeanour of
the altered being before them, to disturb her meditations.

At length, she said, with the propitiating smile which had so
rarely visited her features since she had been parted from her
nurslings, "It is to Captain Burney I must now look for procuring me the means of meeting William.   An unknown poor
woman might probably be refused admittance by the servants of
the gentleman who has afforded my dear boy an asylum.—Will

you contrive, Sir, to procure me admittance? Miss Lucy shall thank you for it, if you will."

"Yes, Mrs. Lambert, I will contrive it," replied Captain Burney, gaily. "The only difficulty that I see in the business being respecting the time at which your introduction shall take place. I don't think we can attempt it to-night, because I know that Captain Maclogan is to have one or two of the officers with him to-night, who were almost as anxious as you are to be introduced to our young hero, William Maurice."

"Well, then," returned Mrs. Lambert, with a sigh, "I must wait as patiently as I can for to-morrow!"

"And yet I am afraid that the delay may be very inconvenient to you, Mrs. Lambert," he replied, "on account of the early hour at which the English-bound vessel sails to-morrow. You will scarcely be able to satisfy yourself on the question of his identity before you ought to be on board."

"I do not mean to go on board at all, Captain Burney," replied Mrs. Lambert, in a tone of the most undoubting decision.

"Do you, indeed, trust so implicitly to my description?" said Burney, in a tone of mingled interest and surprise. "If I have in any way deceived you, Mrs. Lambert, I should never forgive myself."

"No, no, no, you have not deceived me," said she, looking at him with a very friendly smile, "neither have you been deceived yourself, my dear young gentleman. You saw him, such as he is, and you described him with admirable exactness, exactly as you saw him. I do not believe that anyone could paint in words such a portrait as you have given us of William from fancy. You have seen him, Captain Burney, and you have seen him here; and that is enough to make me lay my head upon my pillow, and sleep better than I have slept for many a weary month."

"But your passage-money, Mrs. Lambert? Will you not endeavour to get back your passage-money?"

"No, Captain Burney," she replied, "I do assure you, that my passage-money is of no consequence. Perhaps, Sir, I am richer than you think for—at any rate, I am a great deal richer than William will expect me to be; and I have so much to think of just at this moment, that I must beg of you not to mention the passage-money."

All this was said with a look and manner so perfectly unlike anything they had ever witnessed in her before, that there was not a single individual in the party who did not feel a sort of vague suspicion that she was seized with fever, and was already becoming light-headed.

Mrs. Wilmot came to her, and gently taking her hand, pressed her fingers upon her pulse.

Mrs. Lambert looked up into her face with a smile, but did not interrupt the operation. "You think I am delirious, my dear lady," said she, very quietly, "and it is very possible that my head may be very strongly affected by this sudden change from despair to something which I feel to be stronger than hope. But do not be alarmed for me. People never, I believe, suffer seriously in their health from being too happy."

"That is very true, Mrs. Lambert," said the good man of the house, in a voice that carried authority with it. "But if happiness is not likely to injure health, disappointment may. You must excuse me for being so peremptory, Burney, but I will not let Mrs. Lambert go to bed till this question of the young man's identity is settled upon surer evidence than your animated description. You must go immediately to Captain Maclogan, and state the case exactly as it stands, not forgetting this good lady's intended departure to-morrow; having done this, ask him, with my compliments, whether he will permit you to bring her to the room occupied by the wounded soldier. One glance will suffice to settle the question, so he will not be disturbed for more than a minute, if our poor friend's hopeful fancy has deluded her. And if she is right in her notion, Captain Maclogan will, doubtless, be as glad as any of us to procure for his *protégée* the great comfort of seeing an old acquaintance."

"I will do your errand without wasting a single moment in unnecessary formalities," replied the young man, springing towards the door, which was closed behind him before the trembling Mrs. Lambert appeared to be fully aware of the nature of his embassy.

"What is he gone to do?" said she, looking anxiously in the face of Lucy, who was affectionately hanging over her. "Is he going to tell him that they have found out his real name? Do not let him say that! If he choose to have his name known, he would have told it himself, you know."

"No, no, dear Mrs. Lambert," replied Lucy, "Burney is not going to say anything about his name. He is only going to ask leave for you to go there to satisfy yourself, by looking at him, whether you are right in fancying that he is the young man for whom you are so much interested."

"And you think it possible that I may see him to-night?" cried Mrs. Lambert, starting from her chair, and appearing, as if by magic, to recover all the strength and firmness of her character.

"I am not often so pitifully weak as I must have appeared to you to-night, Mrs. Wilmot," she continued. "It was the sickening feeling of uncertainty which overwhelmed me. Is the distance long?" she continued, fixing her eyes with a sort of resolute steadiness on the door, as if determined to seize the answer, which the messenger would bring, even before he could deliver it.

"Not ten steps," replied Mr. Wilmot, contemplating her tall figure, her firm demeanour, and her fine eager eye, with great interest.

"Burney will be here in a moment, and before five more have passed over you, all your doubts will be solved."

Mrs. Lambert was clad exactly as if sitting in her own apartment, save that she had a large shawl over her shoulders. She now prepared herself for her expedition, by wrapping this shawl over her head, while at the same moment she advanced towards the door, and stationed herself beside it in such a manner as not to impede its opening. "At least, sit down, Mrs. Lambert," said Lucy, kindly, and at the same time placing a chair for her beside the door.

But before she could either accept or decline it, Captain Burney, re-appeared, and upon her laying her hand upon his, while she raised her speaking eyes to his face, he replied to the perfectly intelligible inquiry by taking her arm, and passing it under his own, while he nodded to the rest of the party, exclaiming, "Old Maclogan is a trump! He says the good lady shall be as welcome as flowers in May."

CHAPTER XLV.

MRS. LAMBERT made no attempt to speak during the short and rapid walk, which took her from the dwelling of Mr. Wilmot to that of Captain Maclogan, and yet she felt as if one short question might enable her to learn all she sought to know; but she had literally no breath to utter it. And for some reason or other, Captain Burney was as silent as herself, so that when they stood before the door of the apartment, at which her companion stopped, and knocked, the words "COME IN!" which were uttered in return, causing the trembling woman as vehement an emotion as the word "FIRE!" might have done had she been tied at a stake to be shot.

The movement by which Captain Burney obeyed this command was not a slow one, for in the next instant Almeria Lambert stood within a few feet of a sofa upon which lay a lengthy individual, whose head was in such deep shadow, and the features so nearly concealed by the cushions, and by the hand on which he was leaning, that it was not the first glance which sufficed, as she had predicted, to satisfy all her doubts in a moment.

But if the recumbent figure was in a great degree concealed from sight, it was not prevented from seeing, and while Mrs. Lambert was bending forward to ascertain, if possible, who it was that thus lay stretched before her, she suddenly found herself very firmly encircled by the tight grasp of a stalwart *left* arm, and her name pronounced in accents which made it quite unnecessary that any further discovery should take place.

It would be both a difficult and unnecessary task, to attempt describing the feelings of either party at this recognition. To poor William it was scarcely less welcome than to the enterprizing woman, who had dared, and endured so much to obtain it.

The grateful, warm-hearted Captain Maclogan, who had been still in his dining-room, and alone, when Burney called upon him, not only granted the mysterious old lady's request for an interview, but determined to enjoy the discovery scene that was likely to follow upon it, without destroying the fine effect of it by giving his young guest any hint of what was about to happen. Had his well-beloved preserver been less safely advanced towards recovery from all inflammatory effects from his wound, the grateful veteran would not have thus indulged his taste for romance; but as it was, he knew there would be no danger, and thought there might be much interest from the scene. Nor was he disappointed, for it is rare that two human beings, not bound together by the ties of blood, or the tender passion, could meet with such evident symptoms of delight on both sides.

"It is your mother, William," said the old officer, advancing after the first accolades were over, to welcome his stately-looking guest with both his hands. "I am sure," he added, "that she *is* your mother, first, because she has found you out with such true maternal instinct; and, secondly, because she is just such a finely formed and commanding-looking mother as you ought to have."

William remained silent for a moment, as not knowing well how to answer; but Mrs. Lambert quickly spared him from all embarrassment on the subject, by saying, "No, Sir! I am not his mother, I am only his nurse; but circumstances have endeared us to each other with an affection which I cannot think would have been much stronger had the tie between us been such as you, Sir, imagined it to be."

"And I doubt not he deserved all your love, my good woman," replied Captain Maclogan, "and I don't find any difficulty in believing that the case is exactly as you say, and that you love the saucy fellow as well as if you were his mother, for to let you into a secret, by speaking a little honest truth, I am beginning to love him myself very much as if he were my own son."

When Captain Burney and Mrs. Lambert entered the room, they had found Captain Maclogan and William *tête-à-tête*; and, now, having so satisfactorily performed his mission, Lucy's lover seemed to think that his presence might be more welcome elsewhere; he, therefore, nodded a good-humoured farewell towards the sofa, where the nurse and nursling were now seated side by side, and left the room, saying, as he paused a moment to shake hands with its master, "They must have plenty to say to each other, I daresay."

This thoughtful hint was immediately seized, and acted upon by the kind-hearted Captain Maclogan, who instantly prepared to leave the room, saying, "You must both of you excuse my taking myself off, for I have an engagement down stairs, but I hope you will both make yourselves comfortable, and this good lady will make tea for you, William."

And in the next moment the long-revered Sarah Lambert, and her dear boy William, were once again in full and free communion together.

They had both of them much to say, and much to relate; but they were far from being equally unreserved in their communications. William, with the most perfect frankness, confessed that the rage into which his father's taunting and cruel treat-

20—2

ment had thrown him, led him to resolve that he would leave his home, and see whether the stranger world would treat him as harshly as his own father had done.

"The leaving my dear, dear Helen," said he, "was terrible to think of; but I felt afraid of myself, Sarah Lambert, and I thought that I might run the risk of giving her more pain by staying than by going. And the leaving you, too, my dear and always kind friend, was dreadful, too; but not both these sorrows together, nor yet the fear of all the destitute misery which lay before me, appeared so terrible in my eyes as the thought of living under the roof of a man who called himself my father, and who could speak in such terms of my unhappy mother! In short, Sarah Lambert, right or wrong, I suddenly made up my mind to endure my condition at the Warren House no longer. You know all the rest of my adventures, which, perhaps, you think may have ended better than I deserved. And now then, tell me how it comes to pass that I have the immense happiness of seeing you here? Where have you left my darling Helen? How comes it that you *have* left her, and . . . . her father?"

" I should keep you up all night, my dear boy, if I attempted to answer all these questions at full length, and you are looking a little too pale to make that a prudent measure," she replied. " And yet, William," she added, " I have much to tell that I am most anxious you should hear immediately, as it may be likely to influence your own projects very essentially. The event which I must first communicate is that which has led to all the rest. Your father is dead, William!"

"Dead! Mrs, Lambert? My father dead!" exclaimed the young man, the happy calm of his aspect being metamorphosed into a look of horror. "Why, I left him a few short months ago triumphant in health, and rampant in strength, and the uncontrolled power of using it! Dead! I cannot believe it. What could cause the death of such a man as that? I never saw a human being who in health and strength could be com-pared to him."

" Nevertheless, he is dead, William," she replied, in a tone of forced composure.

" But how did he die, Sarah Lambert?" reiterated William. " Tell me all the circumstances—all the particulars about it. I think it will be long before I shall bring myself to believe that this most unlikely event has come to pass. Dead! Sarah? Actually dead? If, indeed, this be really so, tell me how did it come to pass? Was it an accident? Had his wild boating anything to do with it?"

"I should have thought, William," replied Mrs. Lambert, quietly, "that your first anxiety would have been for Helen. Is not my having left her, as it should seem, *alone*, more extraordinary than the death of any mortal man, let him have been as healthy as he might?"

"True! Gracious heaven! What was he to me, compared to Helen? But as to my fancying that you left her alone, don't you know, Sarah Lambert, that it is as impossible for me to suspect it as for you to do it? No, no! I am not afraid of your having left Helen alone—moreover, I daresay I can guess where she is. It is the kindness of the dear good Boltons which left you at liberty to look after the runaway! Have I not guessed rightly, Sarah?"

"Quite rightly, in believing firmly in their constant kindness, my dear boy. But you have a strange tale to listen to, William. I will preface it, however, by telling you, at once, that you have no need to be anxious about your sister. She has inherited a very noble fortune from her father, and is living under the protection of an excellent family, who were her father's near relations."

"Was my father really very rich, Sarah Lambert?" said William, looking at her with an air of great surprise, and a little as if he doubted the correctness of her information.

"Do you call the having an income of above eight thousand a-year, being rich?" was her reply.

"Eight thousand a-year! Do you know, Sarah, that the seeing you sitting there, close before me, when I have been so lately thinking that we should never, never meet again—the seeing you there, and the hearing you make such very extraordinary statements, by way of giving me a narrative of facts, makes me feel very suspicious about the state of my head. I know I was delirious the night after I received my wound, for the surgeon told me so, and, upon my word, I am beginning to suspect that I am falling back into the same condition again."

"No, my dear boy! There is no delirium either on your side or mine. Your father's whole life was a wild and wicked romance, William, and his living in the humble style, which he did at the Warren House, was a part of it."

"But in his will, then, he disclosed his real condition, and confessed that Helen was his heiress?" said he.

"He did," she replied.

"And did he name me in his will, Mrs. Lambert?" demanded the young soldier, but in an accent which spoke more of scorn than of hope.

"No, William! he did not," was the reply.

"I rejoice to hear it! Truly and heartily do I rejoice," rejoined the young man, with a look and tone that most honestly proclaimed his sincerity. "It would have galled me," he added, "had it been my fate to go through life living upon a bequest from a man I had injured by thinking worse of him than he deserved. I shall have no such burden upon my conscience now; and, trust me, Sarah Lambert, I shall work my way through life with a lighter heart for it."

"I can easily believe that possible, my dear boy," was her reply.

"And you, Sarah? What did this rich man do for you, in return for your having so carefully watched over his neglected heiress."

"In that matter, William, my conscience may rest as tranquilly as yours," she replied, almost with a smile. "In truth," she added, after the pause of a moment, "I should have been by no means well pleased if I had found that he had provided liberally for me in his will."

"But how have you contrived to get here, my dear, faithful, tender-hearted Sarah Lambert?" he resumed. "I came here at the Queen's cost; but I believe those who come at their own, have a heavy sum to pay. How did you contrive to manage this, my dear old friend?"

"I did not make the voyage in a very expensive style, William," she replied. "Moreover, I am myself become, by a lucky chance, considerably more wealthy than I was when you ran away from me; I will explain how this happened when we are more at leisure. But before I bid you good night, my dear boy, you must tell me why it was that you took it into your head to change your name? You little guessed when you did it, my dear William, the miserable heart-breaking disappointment of which it would be the cause to your poor nurse."

"Had I guessed that it would have produced any such effect, I would not have done it," he replied, "but as no such objection suggested itself, my reason for it seemed a very good one. You know, I believe, that in the last interview which I ever had with my father, he informed me, in no very soothing terms, that I had no right to his name?"

"I know it! I know it!" returned Mrs. Lambert, her brow

contracted into a frown, which spoke more sympathy for the suffering produced by that scene than any words could have done.

"Then, can you wonder that in my very soul I swore I never would be known by it," he replied. "It was part of the temptation to the step I took."

"And why did you choose the name of Maurice, my dear William?"

"You do not know that it was the name of my poor mother, or you would scarcely ask that question," he replied.

"Indeed, I should not! I never heard her name. How did it become known to you?" said she.

The young man remained silent for a moment. His eyes were full of tears, and his heart of emotion, too strong to permit his answering immediately. At length, he said, "I have two little books, Mrs. Lambert; her name, 'Selina Maurice,' is written in both. They were put into my hands, and given to me, by that most angelic of human beings, Helen's mother. 'Keep these little books, dear William,' she said, 'and love them for your mother's sake. That is her name written by her own hand, and, of course, you will love it, my dear boy!' That angel woman, Mrs. Lambert, could not have been much more happy than my unfortunate mother! If I were wretch enough to forget all her tender, pitying kindness to myself, methinks I should still remember the tone of voice in which she said 'love them for your mother's sake!' I did not understand it then, but I do now; and can you wonder that at a moment when my unnatural father gave me so clearly to understand that I had no claim upon his protection, and no right to his name, I should deeply swear in my heart that I would no longer be supported by his niggard alms, nor ever acknowledge any other appellation than what I derived from my unfortunate mother?"

"No, dearest William!" she earnestly replied, "I neither blame nor wonder; nay, now that my sufferings in consequence of it are over, I go much further, for I very greatly approve and applaud the resolution you have taken. Adhere to it, my dear boy, firmly, and carefully, too. Let us both forget for the future that we have ever, in any way, been linked with a name which we can neither of us ever recal without pain."

"Agreed!" replied William, eagerly. "Were it not still borne by my darling Helen, I would hug myself in the hope that I should never hear it pronounced again."

"And you may hug yourself in that hope still, William,"

returned Mrs. Lambert, "for your dear Helen no longer bears
it. Among the other disclosures made by your father's will, we
learnt that his name was Beauchamp; and it is by that name
you will have to address your sister when you meet—till such
time, at least, as she shall have changed it by marriage."

"I will never address her by any name, Sarah Lambert, till
she shall have heard that which I now bear pronounced with
honour! Dearly as I love her, I would rather die without ever
beholding her sweet face again than appear before her as the
wretched refuse of her father's vices, with no claim upon her
affection and esteem save that of my abject poverty."

These words were uttered not with vehemence, but with a
stedfast sternness of purpose that made his old friend at once
aware that he would keep his word.

She did not immediately reply to him, but sat for a few
moments with her head bent down, and her face covered by her
hands, as if in deep meditation.

At length she said,—"Perhaps you are right, William
Maurice! And yet, only a few short minutes ago, the most
earnest wish of my heart was that I should find means to bring
you and your sister together with as little delay as possible!
But I honour your pride, for it is of a noble quality, and I
honour your self-reliance, which is fully justified by the opening
of your unaided career. So be it, then, dearest William! so
be it! Your meeting will be of more unmixed happiness if it
be waited for till she shall have heard you spoken of as I have
already heard you spoken of here."

"Alas! dear Sarah Lambert," replied the young man,
smiling, "how can I reasonably hope for such another happy
chance as that to which this lucky scratch is owing?"

"And I may say alas! also, my dear boy, as I think of the
perilous nature of the warfare in which you are engaged, and
the too frequent chances you are likely to have of proving that
your heart, and your arm, too, are more likely to be useful in
the strife than those of most men," she replied.

"That is only because there have been many moments in my
young life, though you knew it not, my dear Sarah, when I
would very gladly have risked its sudden termination against
a very slight glimmer of hope that I might change my miserably degraded condition! But if I should have the blessed luck
to get hits and honour, in consequence of the sudden fit of rage
which led to my escapade from the Warren House, what a
superlatively lucky fellow I ought to consider myself! If my

——, if Mr. Rixley, as he called himself, had happened to die the night before he insulted my mother's memory, instead of the night after, I should never have saved dear old Maclogan's life, but have remained to become a pensioner on the bounty of my rich sister!   I thank heaven for my well-timed fit of fury!"

"WELL-TIMED!" thought Mrs. Lambert, with a stifled groan. "So timed, thou poor unconscious boy, as to have brought upon thy innocent head the imputation of having murdered him!"

But her face was again covered with her hands, and William saw not its expression.

In the next moment, however, she had completely recovered herself, and it was with a perfectly tranquil accent that she said, as she rose from her chair, "We must be prudent, dearest! You have too much colour in your cheeks, now, instead of too little!   Good night! good night!   To-morrow we will contrive to meet again."

He wrung her hand affectionately—and so they parted.

<p style="text-align:center">~~~~~~~~~~~~~~~~~</p>

CHAPTER XLVI.

THAT such a youth as we have described William Maurice, in such a country as India, and under such circumstances as those in which we left him at the end of the last chapter—that such a one should speedily become not only an officer but a very distinguished one, can surprise no one.

The interest of his grateful, warm-hearted, and somewhat influential old friend, Captain Maclogan, was not without its use, for many a daring act, and many a brave deed, the fame of which might have reached the Horse Guards but slowly, without his zealous activity in assisting its transmission, were all made to tell very effectually in his favour.

No soldier of fortune could, indeed, have more in his favour than the hitherto seemingly ill-starred William Maurice. A frame of very remarkable strength and activity; health, which neither fatigue nor climate had apparently any power to affect; the dauntless courage, which is only found when constitutional fearlessness is united with great moral firmness; and that ardent desire for fame which, in his profession, at least, can scarcely be classed as 'that last infirmity of noble minds,' for which Milton bespeaks indulgence, rather than applause; all these qualities together, joined to brilliant intelligence, and an almost irresistible charm of person and manner, produced, during the next half-dozen years of his life, a result, the particulars of which must be given hereafter.

But, before we thus leave him to fight his way to fortune, one short conversation between himself and his umwhile nurse must be recorded.

Not many weeks had elapsed, after these strangely-paired friends had been re-united, before William was sufficiently recovered from his wound to permit his following Captain Maclogan upon another bush-fighting expedition, as a volunteer.

Almeria Lambert was not the sort of woman likely to dissuade him from such an enterprize; on the contrary, she felt quite as strongly as he himself could do, that danger must be the element through which alone he could hope to rise to distinction, and that if the ardent hope which glowed within him, of obliterating the disgrace of his birth, by the nobleness of his life, could ever be acheived, it was only to be done by his own individual efforts, for not all that his sister could bestow on him, if it amounted to the donation of half her estate, could place him before the eyes of his fellow-creatures in the position he wished to occupy.

This conviction was so equally strong in the minds of both, that nothing like argument, and scarcely anything like discussion, took place between them on the subject. Till she had seen William, as she now saw him, with the path to fame and honour visibly open before his eyes, the utmost extent of her hopes had seemed to be limited to finding and to keeping him in safety from the terrible dangers which threatened him in consequence of the suspicions thrown upon him by his father's death.

But now, her hope and her ambition went much further. No one living knew so well as herself what was really the quality of his mind, and the strength of his character; and this knowledge, joined to the circumstances in which she had found him, fully justified the opinion at which she speedily arrived, that she should be doing him better service by permitting him to pursue the career which happy accident had opened to him, than even by restoring him to the protection of his wealthy sister.

For a moment she thought there might be a middle course, and that the affection and assistance of Helen might be made to ease, without impeding his career; but the energy with which William pleaded for the privilege of entire freedom from all dependence upon his father's bequeathed wealth, even though it should reach him through the hands of his beloved Helen, obtained its object, and Almeria Lambert consented to indulge him by keeping his very existence a secret, on condition that he would promise that she herself should *never lose sight of him*.

To the giving this promise, he made no sort of objection, provided, as he told her, laughingly, that her phrase was not to be quite literally interpreted.

"For instance," said he, "I should be decidedly averse, my dearest Saran Lambert, to you being an eye-witness to my exploits, whenever it shall happen that I am engaged, sword in hand in slicing and slashing my way through the bush, and the red-skinnned defenders thereof."

This protest was uttered with a smile; and therefore it was with an effort to return the smile that Mrs. Lambert answered it.

"No! William; No. I do not mean to follow to the bush, but, nevertheless, my demand may be more literally interpreted than you may be inclined to think reasonable. Wherever it is possible I may be useful to you, I shall be more than ready, more than willing, to follow you in person. Nothing that life has left could make me feel so nearly happy as being near you, and with you, when my being so could be of use, or comfort. But the *never losing sight of you*, for which I petition, has a different meaning. For many reasons of interest, many worldly reasons, my dear William, it is very desirable, and very important that I should be made acquainted with every step that you may take in life, before it is absolutely made. I do not mean about your falling in love, or marrying, or anything of that kind. In all such cases, I think you would be the best judge; but what I particularly allude to is *change of residence*. Only promise me, that while I remain alive you will never return to Europe without me, and then I shall be fully satisfied."

"And is that really all that you want me to promise?" he replied. "Well then, I do promise it, my dear old nurse; but a pretty sort of fellow you must think me, to fancy I would run off, and leave you behind!"

"No, no, no!" she replied. "But the time may come William, when leave of absence might make your return to England the most natural thing possible, without your being accompanied by me. But this must never happen. *Remember! Never!*"

Such a promise was then gravely and affectionately given by the young soldier; and Mrs. Lambert declared herself perfectly satisfied, and sufficiently at ease in spirit concerning him to enable her to resume again her functions of attending to all his wishes, and forestaling all his wants, which she did with as much quiet thoughtfulness, and business-like regularity, as if she had still been the *bonne* of the Warren House.

It was not, however, quite without a feeling of repugnance, that William found himself altogether dependant for his daily bread upon the bounty of his *ci-devant* nurse; and this feeling would have been deeper, and more painful still, if he had been less capable of understanding the devoted affection of his bene-factress. Not many words, however, passed between them on the subject, before they both seemed to forget that there could be any mixture of pain in the circumstances of their union. Once, and once only, William uttered an exclamation, expressive of mortification and regret, upon seeing her return to the lodg-ings they occupied together, with the materials necessary for furnishing his rather defective wardrobe, with sundry articles of which he very desirably stood in need.

Her only answer at the moment was given by a few silent tears; and as this was not a weakness which often came upon her, it struck him the more forcibly. "My dearest Sarah Lam-bert!" he exclaimed, "I never saw you weep before. What have I said that could so pain you?"

"Nothing, William!" she replied, "nothing of which I have any right to complain. Nor do I complain, dearest! I only lament that I can never hope you to feel as if I were worthy of being your mother!"

This was the first and the last discussion that ever took place between them respecting the pecuniary relation in which they stood to each other, but it sufficed to remove all uneasy feelings on the subject from both.

CHAPTER XLVII.

WE must now return to Beauchamp Park, reminding our
readers that the narrative, since we left it, has been retrospective, and that an interval of rather more than six years had
elapsed between the period at which we left William Maurice,
at the end of the last chapter, and that at which we had arrived
when we dropped the thread of his sister's story, in order to
follow him in his bold effort to escape from a tyranny at home
too painful to be endured.

When we left Helen, in order to follow her brother, she had
nearly reached her twenty-second birthday, and had just given
a very brilliant fancy ball, partly to please her well-beloved
cousin Henry, but principally, it must be confessed, for the
purpose of dressing her cousin Anne to her heart's content, in
order to prove to the already captivated Lord Lympton that she
could look still more lovely, and still more irresistibly enchant-
ing, than he had ever yet seen her.

Nor had Helen any reason to doubt the successful effect of
this very feminine manoeuvre; for, considerably ere the waxen
tapers had began to fade before the light of day, the young
man had very explicitly declared to his fascinating partner, that
he neither would, nor could, live without her; and she, on her
part (being, to confess the truth, as heartily in love as himself)
had very sweetly assured him that she had not the least wish
that he should make the experiment; provided always, that the
papas and mammas on both sides made no particular objection to
the course he seemed to prefer.

Had the amiable young nobleman been somewhat less of a
spoiled son and heir, it is possible that the advantages attending
a more brilliant connection might have occurred to his parents;
but, as it was, his earnest assurances that he never could love
any other woman as much as he loved Anne Rixley, was
received as being so perfectly unanswerable a refutation to all
objections, that preparations for the marriage were set about
with as little delay as possible. Most certainly there can be no
instance on record in which the course of true love ran more
smooth, or was enlivened by a more brilliant atmosphere around
it; for not only Rothewell Castle and Beauchamp Park became
animated from garret to cellar with joyous preparations for the

wedding, but the whole neighbourhood became more or less enlivened by it; for all the party-giving portion of the population seemed to think it a duty incumbent upon them to give either a fine dinner or a fine dance, for the express purpose of giving the happy young couple an opportunity of making love before the eyes of their friends and acquaintance.

And then came the bright and brilliant wedding; and then the delightful little tour upon the Continent, and the happy return to dear, beautiful Rothewell Castle, where one wing had been splendidly fitted up for the young couple, who were to make it their home whenever it pleased them so to do.

All this happiness was not witnessed, even by my sober-minded heroine, without as much sympathy as sufficed to make her happy too; as happy, at least, as she thought she ever could be in this lower world of ours. And assuredly, notwithstanding the sorrow and disappointment which had fallen upon her, there was much in her situation to bring happiness to such a mind as hers.

She had learnt to be quietly and comfortably aware, that the untoward accident of her having been born had not proved of any very serious injury to her uncle's family, and this was a great comfort to her. She might even, perhaps, have taught herself to feel happy still, had it not been for the long and frequent visits of George Harrington at the house of his father. But these visits were very hostile to her peace. He always spoke of Speedhurst Abbey, indeed, as a residence he greatly admired, and for which he felt much partial attachment; nevertheless, it was clearly evident that he liked his father's little parsonage better; for it rarely happened that he ever came there with the avowed intention of staying one week, without remaining for three or four; nay, even when, as not unfrequently happened, either his mother or his father, accompanied by one of his sisters, had established themselves at Speedhurst, as his guests, their visit seldom came to an end without his galloping across the country in the interval, to inquire concerning the health and welfare of those who had been left at home.

Helen neither was, nor could be insensible to all this, any more than she was to the enduring sentiment in her own bosom which taught her to understand it; but she gravely schooled herself into the belief that time would cure them both of the weakness of wishing for an union against which there were obstacles insurmountable, and which, though they might be concealed, could never be removed.

Poor Helen! all this time she strove hard to be reasonable, and sometimes, though not always, enjoyed the consolation of believing that she was so; but yet she might very easily have been convinced of the reverse, had some happy accident led to a discussion of any subject approaching the bugbear vision which kept them asunder.

But months and months went on, without any such lucky accident occurring, and without their advancing a single inch on either side towards a better understanding of each other.

Her valued old friend, Mr. Phelps, too, found all his philosophical speculations completely at fault. He had quite abandoned his notion that she was in love with her Cousin Henry, from the time that he had witnessed the joyous sympathy with which she entered into his feelings when his regiment was ordered to Ireland; but he only gave up this idea to make room for another. If Helen was not in love with her cousin, she certainly must be in love with George Harrington. But, if so, why did she not marry him? As to George Harrington's being in love with her, he had long ago made up his mind on that point; for, in the first place, he considered this result of their frequent meetings as inevitable, and, in the next, he had seen with his eyes, and understood with his heart, quite enough to convince him that there was no room for doubt on that point.

But he was doomed, good man, to be puzzled for a while longer; for, though the frequent and very delightful companionship between himself and the fair mistress of Beauchamp Park continued to be enjoyed by them both as much as ever, there never was the least approach made on either side towards explaining the mystery.

This state of things tormented him considerably, and he had very nearly made up his mind to ask her in good set terms why she did not marry George Harrington, when several circumstances occurred which led him to think that it might be as well to delay this direct mode of examination a little longer.

Henry Rixley had not been many months quartered in Ireland when the regiment of Guards to which he was attached was recalled to England; and, soon afterwards, a short leave of absence was accorded him, for the purpose of paying a visit to his family.

One of the devices which George Harrington put in action, in order the more rationally to account for his so frequently forsaking his own splendid residence, while he occupied the identical little apartment in his father's house, which had been

allotted to him in his boyhood, was the mixing himself as much
as possible in all the visiting in his father's neighbourhood, and
promoting, by every means in his power, the frequency of these
neighbourly meetings.

The hope, nay, pretty nearly the certainty, of meeting Helen
upon these occasions was, of course, his primal motive for this;
but it was not the only one, as was made evident by the readiness
with which he accepted invitations for many dinner-parties to
which no ladies were admitted. The real state of the case was,
that his existence was so positively painful to him when he was
too far distant to feel that the passing day, or the coming
morrow, *might* be cheered by seeing her, if only during the
fast-fleeting moments of a morning visit, that the avoiding it
was the end and object of all he did.

The only individual of his family who had any suspicion of
this was his sister Agnes; but it was rarely that he indulged
himself in speaking of Helen even to her. The hearing her
repeat her conviction that her simple-mannered, but very puzzling, friend still loved him, disturbed his tranquillity more than
it consoled him, for his own heart perpetually told him that it
was so, notwithstanding the cruel steadiness with which she
checked every attempt he made to resume the tone of their
former intercourse.

His only source of steady hope lay in his persuasion, that if
she did not love him she loved no one else; and that time *might*
teach her to feel that she was not wise in sacrificing a well-
tried affection for such vague reasonings as she had given him
reason to believe had dictated her refusal of his hand.

Meanwhile he contrived to make his frequent abode at the
Parsonage assume a sort of systematic shape, which saved him
the trouble of periodically accounting for it. He hired stables
for coach and saddle-horses, and converted a *ci-devant* tithe-barn
into a coach-house: having achieved which, he discovered that
both his mother and sisters found so much comfort from the
arrangement, that he could not bear to think of depriving them
of it.

Helen saw all this, and understood it, too; but still the
miserable feeling rested heavily upon her heart, that no attachment could ever atone to such a man as George Harrington for
forming an alliance, any circumstance of which could be considered as degrading to him.

It is true that six long years had passed since her separation
from her dear unhappy brother; and that during that long

interval she had never even been comforted or terrified by hearing of him. She remembered, also, for her uncle had deemed it best to check her restless efforts to obtain tidings of him, by making her, in some degree, acquainted with the result of the inquest held on her father's body, and of the suspicions that the flight of her brother had fixed upon him, which, though she totally disbelieved, she still remembered;—but she felt in every fibre of her heart that he was her brother, her fondly-loved brother, still; nor could even the love of George Harrington tempt her to endure the idea of placing herself in a position which might teach her to dread receiving tidings of him.

CHAPTER XLVIII.

THINGS were in this state when Henry Rixley returned from Ireland to Beauchamp Park. He had always been a favourite in the neighbourhood; nor was he at all likely to be less so now, for every month that had passed over him since his destiny had been changed from what he greatly dreaded to what he greatly wished, had tended to improve him in many ways.

He was very nearly as tall in stature, and as stalwart in limb, as his uncle of the Warren House; and this, indeed, seemed to be the type of all the male descendants of the Rixley race. Nothing, therefore, was so favourable to their comeliness as a little military drilling and deportment; and Henry, who, when he had left his home, was only considered as a fine well-grown youth, returned to it with the aspect and carriage of a military-looking and distinguished gentleman.

His sister's noble marriage, too, had certainly helped to make him an important personage in the neighbourhood; and the hunting-parties, dinner-parties, and dancing-parties given in honour of his return were rather more numerous than could be conveniently accommodated within the space of the three weeks during which he was to remain at home.

Had Anne Rixley been Anne Rixley still, there can be no doubt that Helen Beauchamp would have seized this occasion, as joyfully as she had previously done all others of the same kind, to promote every opportunity of obtaining for her petted cousin the amusements which she was so well fitted both to

21

embellish and enjoy. But Lady Lympton wanted no such aid; she was herself become the autocratic *fête*-queen of the whole neighbourhood; and though she would joyfully have admitted her Cousin Helen as an ally, she had no want of her as a prime minister, the Lady Honoria Curtis being as capable as she was willing to fill the office.

And thus it happened that my sober-minded heroine was not unfrequently permitted to stay at home and read to her rheumatic aunt, without being accused of anything worse than excessive kindness and inconceivable self-denial.

Kind she certainly was, but self-denying she was not. Had she at this time learnt from good authority that George Harrington was about to leave the neighbourhood with no intention of returning to it, she might probably have felt a pang at her heart which she might have been puzzled to explain to herself satisfactorily, for she was scarcely aware, perhaps, how much of interest, if not of positive pleasure, was given to her existence by frequently seeing him. But the meeting him at a fine dinner-party, or at a crowded ball, gave her no pleasure whatever; for in such scenes she was often inclined to reproach herself for not feeling as happy as she ought to be.

When she remembered her childhood, and the many painful scenes and the many painful privations attending it, and compared her present brilliant position with what had preceded it, her heart reproached her with want of gratitude to heaven for the blessings she now enjoyed.

And yet it was the memory of this hard and comfortless childhood that furnished the images upon which her solitary thoughts were most apt to dwell: and even when her heart was aching from the conviction that she could never become the wife of George Harrington without forfeiting her own esteem, and deserving to forfeiting his also—even then, the bitterest pang which accompanied the thought of her brother arose from the idea that she might live and die without ever beholding him again!

And it was in such moments as these that she felt it was better for her, when her aunt had dismissed her for the night, to sit in her own room and weep alone, than to deck her face in smiles, and parade a ball-room.

Henry Rixley, however, was not the only gay recruit who contributed at this time to enliven the neighbourhood. Sir Richard Knighton, the son and successor of the late baronet of Knighton Hall, had recently fixed his bachelor residence there;

and at the time that Henry returned to Beauchamp Park his house was enlivened by a party of young men, whom its owner had brought down with him from London, to enjoy for a week or two the field-sports, for which the neighbourhood was celebrated.

Of course, wherever there was a ball or a hunt, Sir Richard Knighton and his three gay guests were sure to be present; but the dinners with which they were regaled were enjoyed at the mansion of their hospitable host, who declared his party too large to be led out on foraging expeditions, without risking the imputation of taking unfair advantage of their numbers, for the purpose of laying waste the country.

The bachelors dinners at Knighton Hall, however, were repeated often enough to bring his guests sufficiently well acquainted with the gentlemen of the neighbourhood, to prevent their being looked upon or treated as strangers by any of his friends.

The festivities of the neighbourhood, however, were by no means confined during this time to hunting, shooting, and dining; on the contrary, a sudden mania for dancing seemed to seize all the young ladies in the vicinity of Knighton Hall; and the male part of the population were well pleased to content the females by indulging them, while they propitiated the favour of the party at Knighton Hall at one and the same time.

It was on the morning after the first of these well-timed dancing-parties that a quiet *tête-à-tête* between Helen and her Aunt Rixley was interrupted by the arrival of the two Miss Harringtons and their brother, who had rode over, as Jane Harrington declared, for the express purpose of assuring Miss Beauchamp that she had lost by far the most agreeable party that had ever been given in the country by so foolishly choosing to stay at home the evening before.

" Has not your Cousin Henry told you what a perfect ball it was ?" demanded Jane Harrington, eagerly.

" Not yet, dear Jane," replied Helen, " for I have not seen him. He set off to Rothewell Castle before I was up, and as he is not returned yet, I presume he went to breakfast there."

" And very right, too," replied the young lady, joyously clapping her hands. " I will bet you what you like that he is gone there on purpose to make Lady Lympton give a ball before this glorious constellation has left our hemisphere. Just fancy four superbly handsome young unmarried men in one house! And all such divine dancers, too! Just fancy, dearest Mrs. Rixley,

21—2

the effect likely to be produced by such a phenomenon in a quiet neighbourhood like this!"

"Among the hearts of the young ladies, my dear?" said Mrs. Rixley, laughing. "Is that what you mean?"

"Yes, to be sure it is, my dear lady!" replied Jane, gaily, "and by way of a sign and symptom of the said effect, just look at Agnes. She began to blush, as I daresay you observed, the very first moment that I mentioned the Knighton Hall heroes, and her cheeks have been going on *crescendo* ever since. Just ask her, dear Helen, what she thinks of the magnificent Colonel somebody, that she danced with twice, besides the cotillon. Or of the exquisitely elegant and enchantingly languishing Captain what's-his-name, who not only honoured her by devoting himself throughout an interminable polka to her service, but did her the still greater honour of directing his *lorgnette* towards her to the infinite advantage of her complexion during the supper, for she blushed, then, very much, as she blushes now."

"Whatever happened to me at this famous ball must have been less overpowering in its effects than what happened there to you, Jane," replied her sister, rather gravely, "for it is evident that something or other has completely turned your head."

"Upon my word, young ladies," said Mrs. Rixley, laughing, "I begin very seriously to regret that I did not drive Helen away from me. My only complaint against her is, that she is rather too reasonable for her age, and this defect might, very probably, have been cured if she had accepted Mrs. Wilcox's invitation for last night. But do let me hear *your* opinion of these brilliant strangers, Mr. Harrington."

"I must understand what you require of me before I answer you, Mrs. Rixley," replied Mr. Harrington, assuming a look of profound meditation. "Do you ask my opinion of their intellects, their acquirements, their manners, their persons, or their dress?"

"Your catalogue of qualities reaches a climax, Mr. Harrington, and let me hear you answer to the last, and most important article first. How did you like their dress?" demanded the old lady, solemnly.

"Unimpeachable!" he replied, in the same tone.

"Now, then, go on to the rest," said she. "It does not matter so much, certainly, but, nevertheless, we must of course feel interested in every particular concerning those who have produced such conquering effects by their presence."

"Dear Mrs. Rixley! do not laugh at us so unmercifully!" said Jane Harrington, looking a little ashamed of her ecstasies, "but let George tell you in sober matter-of-fact style if the party assembled at Mrs. Wilcox's last night was not greatly enlivened by the presence of Sir Richard Knighton, and his three bachelor guests."

"The difficulty lies in treating such matters-of-fact with sobriety," replied George. "However," he added, "I will, in all my best, obey you, madam. Of Sir Richard Knighton himself I need say nothing, for you have the pleasure of knowing him already. Of the three guests that he has now brought down to enliven his bachelor solitude, I should say, speaking collectively, that they seem to have been selected for the purpose of displaying the striking effect of contrast. The least invidious way of classing them as first, second, and third, will be by taking the eldest as number one, and so on. I must begin, therefore, with the gentleman called Hackwood—Captain Hackwood, I think Knighton called him. He is still a young man, certainly not more than four or five and thirty, and is, I daresay, generally considered as handsome; but no one, I should imagine, could ever have thought him so handsome as he evidently thinks himself. This is a disadvantage to him; at least, it appeared so to me. What was your opinion upon this point, Agnes?"

"I do beg to assure you all, relatives and friends, that I did not consider Captain Hackwood's demeanour with sufficient attention to discover whether he thought himself handsome or not," replied Agnes, earnestly.

"Your attention, perhaps, was engaged elsewhere, my dear," said the old lady, looking rather mischievous.

The tell-tale cheeks of poor Agnes again excited a smile from her sister, but she only shook her head, and said nothing.

"The next in review," resumed Mr. Harrington, "was, if I mistake not, called Spencer, but I know nothing as to his rank or title, for I only heard Knighton call him 'Spencer,' and nothing more. Of him, I think, I may fairly say, that he neither was handsome nor thought himself so, but he seemed to be possessed of a degree of vivacity which knew no bounds. It repeatedly appeared to me that he was dancing with two or three ladies at once, and if I may judge from the smiles, or rather, I should say, the laughter, with which his various partners replied to all he said, his wit must have been as brisk as his heels."

"And now then for the third portrait, George," said his eldest sister, with a furtive glance at Agnes.

"Yes, Jane; I will endeavour to give the third portrait also, but it is by no means so easy a task as what has gone before it. The name of the third gentleman, ladies, is Maurice, Colonel Maurice, and most assuredly he is as little like the other two as it is well possible to imagine. I scarcely know why it is, that I feel persuaded of his being younger than either of the others, for his complexion, which must always have been rather the reverse of fair, is now evidently sunburnt, and not only has he the title of Colonel, but he decidedly looks like a man that has seen service. Nevertheless, I do not think he can be more than seven or eight and twenty. He is superbly tall, and, in my estimation, superbly handsome also. And here I feel that I must stop short, because I am quite at a loss to explain, or even to express, the sort of impression he has made upon me. I have a conviction, which is certainly anything but reasonable, considering that I know no more of him than I do of the man in the moon, but, nevertheless, I *have* a strong conviction that he is—to speak in plain prose—worth meeting again."

"And is that all you can say of him after so magnificent a preface?" said Jane.

"No," replied her brother. "I can say something more for him. I can say that I should like Miss Beauchamp to see him. I should like to hear her opinion of him."

These words produced a strangely different impression upon Helen herself, and upon her friend Agnes. The first thought of Agnes might be rendered thus—"Well! I suppose he is cured at last! If he were not, he could scarcely wish to set her upon a deliberate examination of the person and manners of Colonel Maurice!"

Whereas the first thought of Helen might be thus expressed. "Alas! Not all my reserve, not all my care has prevented him from knowing that I love him still!"

The visit did not last much longer, for both the sisters were fully bent upon making many other visits; partly for the purpose of learning what other people thought about all that had occupied their own thoughts so much, and partly in the hope of learning that the delightful party of the previous evening was likely to be assembled somewhere or other at no distant date, and at no distant spot.

CHAPTER XLIX.

THE two Miss Harringtons were not the only persons who admired the guests at Knighton Hall sufficiently to desire to see more of them; and the consequence of this was, as they had hoped, that many more very delightful balls followed that which had first introduced them to the neighbourhood.

Nor did Helen feel at all disposed to be less hospitable on this occasion than she was wont to be on all others; on the contrary, she did not listen to George Harrington's more than once repeated expressions of admiration respecting the much=talked-of Colonel Maurice, without feeling considerable curiosity to see him.

She had decided upon gratifying this very natural feeling at Rothewell Castle, where her Cousin Anne, as usual, had taken measures for the gayest entertainment which had as yet been given to the strangers. The *fête* was to begin by charades, in the arrangement of which Lady Lympton was considered as unrivalled, and to conclude with dancing; and so attractive was this programme, that not only Helen, but her invalid aunt also, decided upon being present on the occasion.

But destiny is stronger even than woman's will, and, therefore, they were not present, for on the morning of the festival Mr. Rixley broke his arm, by a fall from his horse, and though no alarming symptoms followed the accident, his faithful woman-kind would not leave him, and thus it happened that this bright constellation came, blazed, and passed away, without either Helen or her aunt having been present upon any single occasion when it was visible.

There was certainly something like a feeling of regret in the mind of my heroine when she heard that the party was broken up, and that George Harrington was gone to Speedhust Abbey, accompanied by Colonel Maurice.

George Harrington assuredly did not leave the neighbourhood without making a farewell call at Beauchamp Park, and he came, too, accompanied by this new friend; but as ill-luck would have it (as the familiar phrase expresses such mishaps), its fair but unlucky lady was wandering away with Mr. Phelps and her

Cousin Henry, at too great a distance from the house to be recalled by the messenger whom her aunt dispatched to look for her.

Helen had fully intended to see this Colonel Maurice before he left the neighbourhood, for the terms in which she had heard George Harrington speak of him had awakened a deeper feeling than mere curiosity. George Harrington was by no means apt to run into sudden intimacy with anyone, and she had already heard enough of the terms on which they appeared to be together, to make her feel very deeply persuaded that he must be an individual of no common stamp.

The hearing of their setting off *tête-à-tête* for Speedhurst Abbey added condiderably to this persuasion, as well as to her disappointment at not having seen him, and she felt, rather justly perhaps, angry with herself for giving way as she had done to her growing dislike of gay society, to which she very fairly attributed it.

It was with even more pleasure than usual that she welcomed a visit from Jane and Agnes, the morning after their brother's departure, for instead of feeling inclined to quiz them for their unceasing rhapsodies in praise of the marvellous stranger, who had created so unusual a sensation in the neighbourhood, she was now anxious to hear all they had to say about him, and, contrary to custom, led to the subject herself, by saying, " And so, dear friends, your brother has carried off captive this wondrous hero of whom I have heard so much."

But instead of replying in the same gay strain, Agnes only sighed, while Jane answered in a sort of matter-of-fact, and not very well pleased tone, " Do not let us talk any more about him, dear Helen! I, for one, have talked of him, I am afraid, a great deal too much."

" Then, at any rate, do not talk of him any more!" returned Agnes, with considerably less than her usual gentleness of manner.

" You need not alarm yourself, Agnes," said Jane, demurely. " I have not the least intention of talking of him at all. But we have agreed, you know, not to begin *now* having any secrets concealed from Helen, because we never have had any, so, if you please, you must not interrupt me while I tell her what has just happened."

" Upon condition that you never tell anybody else, I have no objection to your telling Helen," said Agnes: " I should have no more idea of keeping a secret from her than I should of keeping it from you, Jane, for I love her quite as well as if she were my own sister. Only she must promise not to teaze me about it afterwards."

"I do promise!" replied Helen, gaily, but blushing at the same time like a clove carnation at this allusion to sisterhood. "But pray make haste! I am all impatience. What is this secret about?"

"About love and marriage, of course, Helen," replied Jane Harrington, laughing. "How can girls have any other secrets?"

"*Halte-là!*" interrupted Agnes, holding up her finger, and shaking her head. "Your preface, Jane, is calculated to deceive Helen in a most important particular. This secret, as far as it concerns me, has no more to do with marriage than with murder."

"I should be sorry to deceive Helen in any way," returned Jane. "Nevertheless, my tale has much more to do with marriage than with murder. Captain Hackwood never proposed to murder you, Agnes. At least, I never heard that he had said anything about it as yet. But he did propose to marry you."

"After a fortnight's acquaintance!" cried Helen, with a gesture of astonishment.

"Yes, Helen, exactly so," replied her friend, in an accent which expressed very perfect sympathy with the feeling manifested by that gesture.

"Oh, yes, that is all very true," said Jane, with a look that seemed to express superior wisdom, "but nothing could be more evident than that he really was most devotedly attached—and it was evident from his proposals, too, that he would have been an excellent match."

"Excellent match! Fie upon you, Jane," exclaimed her sister, "I wonder how you would have liked to make an *excellent match* with a man of whom you knew absolutely nothing."

"Well, Agnes, nobody has blamed you for refusing him. Only, you know, it is impossible to deny that other people besides this unfortunate Captain Hackwood, may fall in love in a very short space of time."

"Yes, Jane, that is quite true. Only, in general, people do not venture to propose marriage after the acquaintance of a few days," said Helen.

"Pray do not think that I wanted Agnes to marry him!

Nothing could be further from my thoughts. I hope that if she ever marries at all, it will be some one that she really loves," returned Jane, "and in that case," she added, "I should not feel inclined to be at all severe upon her, even if I found out that she, too, had fallen in love before she had known the happy man for a fortnight."

"Let us look at your new garden, Helen!" said Agnes Harrington, suddenly starting up, and going to the window.

"You want to see my new garden?" replied Helen. "Well, then, I will take you to see it. But it does not lie in that direction, dear friend! I should have thought, Agnes, that you knew the geography of Beauchamp Park better, than to look for the flower-gardens in that direction."

"Agnes is very stupid sometimes, and not only forgets her geography, but her chronology, too, occasionally."

Helen had soon enveloped herself in her ever-ready garden costume, and the three young ladies set out to explore conservatories, and examine exotics. But the only person who, upon this occasion, seemed to take any real interest in the business, was Jane Harrington, and she speedily got into very earnest conversation with the head-gardener, who was an old acquaintance, and not unfrequently the generous bestower of half a dozen ultra-precious flower-seeds.

This left the two friends *par excellence*, to all intents and purposes, *tête-à-tête*, and they, neither of them, seemed disposed to lose the opportunity of exchanging a few words in a more serious tone than accorded with the temper of the lively Jane.

"Tell me, my dearest Agnes, what is it that Jane seems so bent upon tormenting you about?" said Helen. "Did this perfect stranger really and seriously propose to you?"

"Yes, indeed, did he," replied Agnes, "but it is very disagreeable to me to confess it, even to you; for it is next to impossible that you should not suppose me guilty of giving very extraordinary encouragement."

"Let it be *next* to impossible," replied Helen, affectionately, "provided you do not suspect its being so. I know you too well, Agnes," she added, "not to be quite aware that this Captain Hackwood's presumption was no fault of yours. But do tell me, dearest, did it not make your brother very angry?"

"Yes, truly, did it! I have rarely seen him look so gravely displeased at anything," replied Agnes, "and I strongly suspect that this very sudden fancy of his, for returning to Speedhurst, exactly at the time when we all so much desired to have him here, originated in his wish to avoid encountering Captain Hackwood again. When George dislikes a person, I know of old that he finds it a difficult task to be civil, and in this case, the difficulty must be increased, you know, by there not being any very ostensible cause of offence. *Entre nous*, I certainly love George all the better for being in a rage with any man who could suppose that I should be ready to accept him as my husband upon the acquaintance of a few days; but, nevertheless, I have no doubt in the world that the man thought he was paying me a prodigious compliment, instead of being impertinent. However, it is quite as well, perhaps, that George should take himself off."

"Perhaps it is," replied Helen. And after a moment's pause, she added, "But it seems that he did not go alone? He appears to have fallen into a fit of friendship as suddenly as the unfortunate Captain fell into a fit of love."

"You don't mean to blame George for inviting such a man as Colonel Maurice to visit him, do you, Helen?" returned Agnes, colouring.

"Blame him? Good heavens, Agnes, no!" responded Helen, in rather an indignant tone, and with a flushing cheek, which seemed to reflect that of her friend.

"If you had not shut yourself up, as you have done, since all our gaieties have been going on," said Agnes, "you might have had an opportunity of judging for yourself, as to Colonel Maurice's claims to the honour of an invitation, even to Speedhurst Abbey. I very much wish that you *had* seen him, Helen."

"I wish so, too, my dear," replied her friend, with a quiet smile, which had a little the air of quizzing her vehemence.

"If you think it extraordinary that George should have invited this gentleman to his house, you will find it still more so, I imagine, when I tell you that now, for the first time since he has been in possession of the property, George has made the notable discovery, that he has been over-negligent of the duties of hospitality towards his uncle's old friends and neighbours, and that he has invited my father, mother, sister, and myself, to come to him next week for a fortnight, in order to assist him in obliterating the character which he fears he has acquired, of being a churlish neighbour."

"I am very glad to hear it," said Helen, with great sincerity; for it had more than once occurred to her that he was not

exactly fulfilling the duties of his station, by so constantly
absenting himself from his property and his dependants; and if
something like a consciousness that she was herself the cause of
this, might bring with it a feeling that was not altogether painful, she, nevertheless, heard of his making this effort with
pleasure, and the accent with which she had spoken made this
so evident, that Agnes quite forgave the symptoms of quizzing
which had preceded it, and the farewell kiss that was exchanged
between them was as cordial on both sides as long years of
friendship could make it.

CHAPTER L.

There are probably but few human actions which may not
be traced to mixed motives, though one among them may
have settled a wavering balance, and been the final cause of the
act.   And so it was in the case of this sudden resolution on the
part of George Harrington.   He really did think that he had
not been sufficiently sociable in his intercourse with his Speedhurst neighbours; and he really did dislike the idea of again
encountering the consummate puppyism and audacity of Captain
Hackwood; moreover, he had never before met any man whose
acquaintance he so much wished to cultivate as he did that of
Colonel Maurice; but the final and immediate cause of the
resolution he had taken, was the having heard from Sir
Richard Knighton, that his friend Hackwood had promised to
remain with him for some weeks longer, for the purpose of
superintending the training of a young horse, preparatory to
his making his *debût* at the approaching races, which annually
took place in the neighbourhood.

Now, if anyone had hinted to George Harrington that it was
possible his sister Agnes might change her mind, and end by
accepting the man she had so promptly refused, he would have
been excessively indignant at such a supposition; yet, nevertheless, it is certain that he did not like her remaining where she
would, in all probability, meet him frequently, and it was this
which first suggested the idea of opening his own house in a
more hospitable style than he had yet done since he came into
possession of it.

It is not necessary that we should follow George Harrington and his party to Speedhurst Abbey, in order to assure ourselves that the honours of that handsome and well-conducted mansion were well performed; neither have we any pages to spare for a description of the quiet, if not very happy days which Helen passed during the absence of the whole Harrington family from her neighbourhood; but after the Speedhurst party was broken up, several circumstances occurred which must be related as essential to the progress of my narrative.

Helen and Agnes were not only sociable neighbours when within reach of each other, but very regular correspondents when they were separated, and there was no want, therefore, of many a pleasant document dispatched from Speedhurst Abbey to Beauchamp Park, redolent of gay doings, and of happy companionships.

The letters of my heroine, in return, were, it must be confessed, infinitely less amusing; for Helen had little or nothing to relate beyond the completion of some garden structure or the propitious birth of a seedling geranium.

It is certain that, from causes either well understood or misunderstood, the frequent near neighbourhood of George Harrington and Helen Beauchamp was a doubtful blessing to them both; nevertheless, it is certain, also, that the hours of my heroine passed with less of hope, and more of heaviness, when all possibility of her meeting the man whose hand she had refused was beyond her reach, than when every sun that rose brought with it the possibility that she *might* see him before it set.

It was not, therefore, without a sensation, which a good deal resembled pleasure, that she listened to her maid's news, while her long tresses were under the brush; for that news went the pleasant length of declaring that the family at the Oaks were expected to return on the morrow, and that the young squire of Speedhurst was coming with them.

It boots not to tell how many times Helen turned her head upon the pillow, before she went to sleep that night, but it is absolutely necessary to my narrative that I should mention, that Mr. George Harrington called at the Park at an unusually early hour on the following day, and omitting the ordinary ceremony of asking for Mrs. Rixley, inquired if Miss Beauchamp were at home, and upon being answered in the affirmative, sent in his name, with a request that he might see her immediately.

There was something sufficiently unusual in the form of this message to cause a slight palpitation of the heart to the lady of the mansion; she answered, however, with great apparent composure, that she should be glad to see him, and in the next moment he entered her morning sitting-room.

"You must forgive my want of ceremony, my dear Miss Beauchamp," he said; "but I have news to tell you that I feel sure will be interesting to you; and as my tidings are for the present to be kept secret from the world in general, I have ventured to make my way to you in the most direct manner possible."

She shook hands with him in the way she had carefully taught herself, and which was the very perfection of neighbourly friendliness, and nothing either less or more.

"I am quite sure that your tidings are pleasant tidings," she said, "by your manner of announcing them; so pray sit down, and tell me what they are."

"I know you love Agnes," he replied, "and the friendship between you is not of yesterday; you will not be greatly surprised, therefore, when I tell you that I come, commissioned by herself, to tell you that she is going to be married—but not to Captain Hackwood, Miss Beauchamp."

"Of that I am very sure, for reasons that shall be nameless," replied Helen; "but I will venture to go still further than that, Mr. Harrington;" she added, "I would venture a little bet, that I could guess, not only who it is not, but who it is."

"Indeed!" he exclaimed; "that surprises me a little, I confess; for when you last saw Agnes, I very much doubt if she could have told as much herself."

"Very likely not," said Helen, laughing; "but lookers-on, you know, sometimes—. The proverb is somewhat musty, but there is truth in it."

"Assuredly there is," he replied; "only in this case it does not apply, fair lady; for if I am not greatly mistaken, you never *were* a looker-on. I am tolerably sure, moreover, that you never saw the gentleman in question."

"That may be very true," returned Helen, "and yet I may be able to make good my boast. Eyes are not the only means by which we can become acquainted with individuals."

"Then, perhaps, Agnes was not so heart-whole as I fancied when I took her away?" rejoined Mr. Harrington. "Perhaps you heard her speak of the person to whom you allude?"

"Scarcely, Mr. Harrington," replied Helen, earnestly, fearful she should do her friend injustice; "but I have heard *you* speak of him."

"Yes, you have," he replied; "I remember it. I remember thinking that you would agree with me in my judgment of him. And I think so still, Miss Beauchamp; and it is for that reason that I think also that the news I bring you is good news. Yes, you are quite right. My sister Agnes is engaged to be married to Colonel Maurice."

"It *is* good news to me!" replied Helen, with deep feeling. "The heart of Agnes is no common heart; and it is more than mere pleasure, it is happiness to me to know that her choice has fallen upon a man that you can speak of as you did of this Colonel Maurice."

"And, believe me, it is a source of happiness to me, too, Miss Beauchamp," replied Mr. Harrington; "and I trust I do not flatter myself in believing that, when you shall have become acquainted with him, your own judgment will justify my opinion—my personal opinion of him. I am sure, it will," he added, with a slight augmentation of colour, which gave additional earnestness to his words; "but yet, Miss Beauchamp, your indulgence must go further still before you will be able fully to approve this marriage for my sister."

"I understand you," she replied, smiling. "The sister of Speedhurst Abbey ought, perhaps, (*ought* in one sense) to expect a larger settlement than this young soldier may have to offer. And yet the rank he has so early attained looks as if he had influential friends."

"No; that is not it. In the first place, he does not owe his rank to any influential friends, but solely, using his own modest phrase, to his own good luck in the service," replied Harrington; "and as to his power of making a settlement," he added, "that has nothing to do with it either. I know he told me that he was enabled, by a recent legacy from his earliest military friend, to offer a very respectable sum for that purpose. But no! the difficulty does not lie there, Helen; and I have a painful misgiving that, when I name it, you will consider it as a much more important objection than I do. I am a positive coward about it, for I declare to you that I dread the expression of your face upon hearing it."

"Nonsense, Mr Harrington! I am sure you cannot be in earnest," she replied, laughing. "You must be quite sure, I should think, that a man beloved by Agnes, and approved by you, cannot be in much danger of appearing objectionable to me."

"You are all kindness," said he, "and I listen with full confidence to the assurance of toleration which you so cordially
give. But, believe me, my kind friend, your phrase, *approved
by me*, goes but a litt'e way towards expressing what my feelings are respecting Colonel Maurice. You know Agnes well,
and, perhaps, I know her better still; but I suspect we shall
both agree in confessing, dearly as we love her, that she is not
quite perfect. She is much too fastidious in her likings, and in
her dislikings. She is nearly three years older than you are,
and yet it is a certain fact that, till she had the advantage of
knowing you, she never formed any intimacy out of her own
family. She has had repeated offers of marriage made in a less
objectionable style than that of Captain Hackwood; but though
upon former occasions she may have been less angry, she has
never been at all more inclined to accept any. In short, Colonel
Maurice is the first man she ever looked upon for a moment
with an eye of favour; and, knowing her as I do, I feel convinced that the impression he has made upon her heart will
never be obliterated. That this conviction has great weight
with me, is certain; but is far, very far, from being my only,
or even my chief, reason for wishing the connection; but the
real fact is, dear friend, that I have never met with any man
whom I could wish to call my brother till I met with him."

"Need I tell you that it is a pleasure to me to hear you say
so?" returned Helen, earnestly. "Dear Agnes!" she continued, while tears of tenderness started to her eyes, "with all
her fastidiousness, she could never be happy without loving,
and being loved; and now, thank Heaven! this destiny seems
assured to her."

"But you have not yet heard the ONE THING which I fear
will appear so much more terrible in your eyes than it does in
mine!" said he.

"I greatly doubt it," she replied, with a very cheering smile;
"I greatly doubt that anything you can have left to tell will
suffice to neutralize what I have heard already."

"Well! I will hope so too," replied he, starting up, and gaily
approaching her; "and I believe you ought to be angry with
me for doubting it: for, after all, it cannot be put in competition
for a moment for one-hundredth part of what is on the other
side of the balance. But the fact is, Helen Beauchamp, that the
man whom my heart thus joyfully welcomes as a brother is a
natural son."

George Harrington, as he uttered these words, was standing

immediately in front of Helen, and her eyes were earnestly fixed upon his face. He saw and felt this with the sort of trepidation which an earnest look from her always occasioned him : but he was totally unprepared for what followed. Her eyes, which were raised to his face with an expression of gentle, tranquil confidence and hope, closed for an instant, and when they opened again, all the tranquillity was gone, and they were raised to heaven with a look that spoke more of rapturous thanksgiving than of doubts and fears, reasonably satisfied. She rose from her chair, and extending both her hands, placed them for a moment in both his, which seemed to open instinctively to receive them, and then she as suddenly withdrew them, and sat down again ; and, finally, she burst into a passion of tears, laying her arms upon the little table which stood beside her, and hiding her face upon her hands while she continued to sob convulsively.

Notwithstanding the habitual sort of forbearance which the steady demeanour of Helen had taught him to understand was necessary to the continuance of their friendship, George Harrington now lost all command of himself, and dropped on his knees before her.

The movement might, however, be described as involuntary, as he knew not himself what he meant by it, for he was most completely at a loss how to interpret the cause or signification of her emotion. Neither did she seem at all disposed to elucidate the mystery, for having indulged herself in the luxury of weeping without ceremony or restraint for the space of about two minutes and a half, she gently raised her head again, and looked at him with a smile which, instead of being likely to explain the cause of her tears, expressed nothing but the fullest and most radiant satisfaction.

"Pray do not kneel, dear friend!" she exclaimed, playfully extending her hand in very regal style as a signal that he might change his posture for one less humble ; "pray do not kneel !" she repeated in a voice that had then nothing of playfulness in it. "It is I who ought rather to kneel to you, to implore your forgiveness for having so vilely misunderstood your noble heart!"

"Helen !" he replied, looking at her with astonishment, which was, however, strongly blended with delight, "Helen! dearest and best, ever best and dearest, though ever a mystery, you must long have seen that I am in your power. You may not have seen, perhaps, how sincerely I have struggled to escape. But this matters not; you know, you must know, that these said struggles have been of none effect, and that a word, a look, a gesture is enough—has been enough you see—to bring me to your feet again, with the confession on my lips, that I never can be happy without you. You say that you have misunderstood me, Helen. How can this be? What have I done or said that could be mistaken? But it matters not, dearest! It shall be enough for me to know that you misunderstand me no longer! Whatever the delusion was, I feel assured you were not to blame for it, and only confirm by one word the hope that those dear eyes now give me, and I will ask for no further explanation."

"But the explanation must be listened to," replied Helen, still vainly endeavouring to raise him from his kneeling posture, "and all I can say before you receive it is this, that if, after receiving it, you still persist in wishing me to become your wife, I shall no longer offer any opposition to that wish."

The animated delight likely to be experienced by a man both heartily and deliberately in love, upon listening to such words after having despaired of ever hearing them, is pretty nearly equal in its intensity to the dulness produced on the minds of others by all attempts at describing it. Not a word, therefore, shall be said about it. The interview, after all, was but a short one, for Helen sent him away by so very sincere an assurance that she longed to be alone, that he could neither doubt its truth nor resist it.

"Remember," she said, "that it is all very well for you, hotheaded and impetuous young man as you are, to make up your mind upon this most important question, without at all knowing what I may have to confess to you of a nature to make you alter your mind; but the case is different with me. My fate cannot be decided till you have been made acquainted with the motives of my past conduct. If after this you shall still wish me to be your wife, I know of no reason in the world which should prevent my being so.—And now leave me, George Harrington! It will not take me long to commit to paper the confession I have promised you, and if neither men nor horses fail me, you shall not wait long for the document."

Before she had ceased speaking, George Harrington was already on his feet, and having pressed his lips upon her hand as she uttered the last word, he sprang to the door, opened and closed it behind him, without the loss of a moment.

CHAPTER LI

Helen kept her word. She lost no time either in writing her dispatch, or in sending it, and the following letter reached the hands of George Harrington at least an hour before he dared to expect it.

"I know not," it began, " whether, after reading what I am about to write, you will consider it a self-accusation or a self-acquittal. All I can answer for is, that my statement shall be a true one. I presume that you have known, pretty nearly as long as you have known me, that the early part of my life, and as long as I was called Helen Rixley, was passed in a manner wholly unlike what it has been since I have been Helen Beauchamp. I know that I have talked to you in days of yore about my beloved mother, and made you understand, I think, that her having been educated with the object of her becoming a governess, was the reason why I was not as ignorant when Agnes first took a fancy to me as might have been expected, from the homely manner of life to which I had been accustomed in other respects. But I was still very young when I lost her, and I should probably have relapsed into lamentable ignorance, had it not happened that the clergyman of the parish was a poor, as well as a highly instructed man, and that he made no objection to receiving a very meagre salary for very persevering lessons. But these lessons were not alone for me. I had a brother, my dear friend, who was four or five years older than myself, I think, but whose faculties were of so exalted and so brilliant a kind, as to make him fitter for my master than my fellow-student. Nevertheless we studied together, and I can hardly tell you now whether I admired or loved him most. You have never heard of this dear brother, George Harrington, but although the mention of his name, if not absolutely forbidden, has been carefully avoided in my uncle's family, you would have heard of him ere now from me, had it not been for a certain conversation which took place between us upon the lawn at the Oaks, in the course of which you uttered sentiments and opinions which, according to my stupid judgment, rendered it impossible that you should ever hear his name and history without feeling deep re-

22—2

pugnance to the idea of being brought into any close relation with him.

"His history is this :—

"He is the natural son of my father, and if he could be said to have any name, save that of William, it was Rixley. But neither he nor I knew anything of his unhappy mother, or of his disgraceful birth, till during the last hour that we ever passed together—and this was the last evening of my father's life.

"We were in the parlour with my father, at table, if I remember rightly, and the good kind nurse who had ever had the care of us was either in attendance or sitting at the table likewise. My father became angry with William, for what cause I have no distinct recollection, but he became fearfully violent, and in his fury told my unhappy brother the disgraceful secret of his birth, and that, too, in language the most cruelly degrading to his innocent, but most unhappy son, and most insulting to his unfortunate mother.

"The faculties, the feelings, the affections, the temper of my poor brother, were all quick, impetuous, and vehement. I know not if he spoke in answer to the cruel taunt. I have no further recollection of anything that happened that evening till I was alone with my dearest William in the school-room, and the agony of indignation which he then expressed at the language my father had used to him, made an impression upon me which can never be effaced! On that same terrible night it was that my father died; and on that same night my dear and ever dear William left the Warren House, where we both were born, and from that dreadful day to this I have never heard of him!

"But I have not yet told you all.

"Mr. Bolton, the good clergyman, who had been our friend and tutor, would not suffer me to remain in the Warren House after my father's death; but he, and his kind wife, took me to their own home, and there I remained till the arrival of my good Uncle Rixley, and my father's will was opened; and then, somehow or other, it was made manifest that my name was not Rixley, but Beauchamp, and also that my father's will had left me in the possession of a large fortune.

."My kind uncle appeared inclined to be very fond of me, notwithstanding the estrangement which had existed between him and my father; and the happy home with him, and his dear family, which I have now enjoyed for years, was at once offered to me.

" But I was not destined to enjoy it without carrying there with me a thorn which has never ceased, more or less, to torture me. I have never from that hour to this heard any tidings of my brother William, and till I knew you, George Harrington, I did not think that I ever could have loved any one as I loved him. I tell you this in order that you may more fully understand the strength of the feeling which has caused me to act as I have done. Never, George, never have I seen nor heard tidings of this much-loved brother from the day he left our father's house to the present hour! But this has not been my only misery. Guess what I must have felt, young as I was, at accidentally overhearing a brutal sailor declare that he believed the sudden death of my father to have been the act of my unhappy brother! More than six long years have passed over me since I listened to those dreadful words, and yet I seem to remember the impression they made upon me as freshly as if the dreadful scene had occurred but yesterday! I was but little more than a child when it occurred, and I had neither sufficient strength of mind nor clearness of judgment to form a proper estimate either of the speaker or his words. I received them at the moment as the true statement of a known fact, and the effect they had upon me was to rob me for a time of my reason under the influence of a violent frenzy fever.

" But while recovering from this I had many long and reasonable conversations with the good and affectionate old servant who had nursed both him and me, and she, in a great degree, succeeded in removing from my mind the horrible impression which this frightful statement had made upon me. Her idea seemed to be that my father had died from the effect of vehement passion, and that the departure of my unhappy brother was the result of the very natural feeling of resentment towards one who could reproach him with the infamy which he had himself brought upon his unfortunate mother, and which might well lead him to prefer the precarious support of his own talents to dependence upon such a father! I have never ceased to have occasional intercourse, by letter, both with Mr. and Mrs. Bolton, and from them I have learnt that Mrs. Lambert, my nurse, left Cornwall within a few weeks after my uncle and I left it for London; and that her purpose was to follow some trace she had obtained of my brother, in the hope of persuading him to return to his native country, and to me.

" But the good Boltons have heard nothing of her since her departure, and I therefore presume that her courageous pilgrimage has proved abortive. You will not wonder, my dear friend, that, young as I was when these events occurred, they have left an impression which nothing can ever efface, and I certainly have suffered more, rather than less, from the sort of systematic silence which my good uncle has thought it right to preserve upon the subject.

"But when I became sufficiently acquainted with you to believe that I was still destined to be one of the very happiest women in the world, I began to indulge myself in speculations on the delight I should have in making you acquainted with the character of my noble-hearted brother, not only such as I remember it, but such as my good Mr. Belton always declared it to be; nay, there have been moments, dear George, when I have imagined it possible that you, too, as well as poor Sarah Lambert, might be seized by a desire to find him, and knowing how rich we should be with our two great fortunes put together, I will not deny that there were moments, too, when I was silly enough to build castles in the air, making my dear lost William the principal tenant of them all!

"But these bright day-dreams, and a great many others besides, were all scattered to the winds and destroyed by the never-to-be-forgotten conversation on your father's lawn.

"I wonder if you remember it as well as I do? You had been uttering some pretty flights of romantic eloquence upon the superior advantages of being in love with a poor girl instead of a rich one. I thought in my heart, perhaps, that you were a little personal, but I did not much mind it, for I remembered the immense power lodged in that eloquent French word *quoique*, and I felt that it might as fairly be used by you as an excuse for taking me, as by the coquettish French nation for taking a Bourbon. So I listened, and laughed, and did not mind it. But then, George Harrington—then followed a burst of enthusiasm from your lips which has rung in my ears, and rested heavily upon my heart, from that day to this! I will not deny to you, for why should I, since you know it as well as I do, that I was at that time fully aware that you were attached to me, and fully understood, also, that you were only waiting till I was perfectly my own mistress in order to tell me so; and I, on my side, was only waiting for this, in order to tell you the painful story which I now send you. Now that the mist, which then fell upon my understanding, is removed, and that I feel that your glowing tirade upon the subject of HONOUR did in no way justify my believing that your attachment to me could be affected by circumstances over which I had no control, it seems to me that the reasoning by which I destroyed your happiness, and my own, was little short of madness. Had I, at that time, asked myself how in a like case I should have felt towards you, the answer might have gone far towards making me see how greatly my excited feelings were leading me to exaggerate the strength of yours. My excuse can only be found in my utter ignorance of life, and all its intricacies. To no human being had I ever been able to speak of the strange events which I have now disclosed to you; and this solitary brooding over what I so darkly comprehended must, doubtless, have produced the morbid state of mind which has led me to act as I have done.

"But so firmly did I feel persuaded that the fact of my father's having a natural son, to whom I was attached with the tenderest and strongest sisterly devotion, would be felt by you as a misfortune and a DISGRACE, that I truly believe nothing could have removed the impression, short of my hearing you speak with pleasure and approval of your sister's approaching marriage with a man who, in respect to his birth, is in the same unfortunate situation as my dear brother.

"Shall I ever forget the overwhelming sensation of happiness with which I heard you state this fact? I hope not! That moment was, perhaps, the happiest of my life. And now, George Harrington, you know as much about me as I know myself, and the feeling this is, of itself, so great a pleasure to me, that I can only wonder at the strange delusion which has so long prevented my enjoying it.

"HELEN BEAUCHAMP."

CHAPTER LII.

HELEN kept her word, and lost no time in forwarding her dispatch. The above letter was written with great rapidity, but before she began it she allowed herself time to ring her bell, and order that a man and horse should be immediately prepared to take a note for her to the Oaks.

The visit of George Harrington had been made at an early hour; but as the said visit was not a short one, the letter of

Helen was not written, and sent off, before four o'clock. Nevertheless, she was destined to have another visit from the same gentleman, before that period of the day which fashionable people designate as the "morning," was over; that is to say, he was seen galloping at full speed towards the portico a few minutes before the six o'clock dinner-bell sounded from the venerable turret over the stables.

Helen had not yet left her dressing-room, but fortunately her maid had left her, and, therefore, the crimson blush, and the radiant smile with which his appearance was welcomed, did not furnish the servants' hall with a theme for their evening's amusement.

George Harrington did not dine at home that day; Mr. Rixley dozed a good deal over his "Quarterly Review," for the print was small; his son Henry was at Rothewell Castle, and nobody seemed inclined to enter into general conversation. But as for dear good Aunt Rixley, she became very anxious about Helen before their friendly neighbour, George Harrington, ceased his, as it seemed to her, interminable visit; for, as the young people sat together at the table, which was always covered with literary novelties, looking over a variety of books of beauty, and other interesting publications, she observed that her dearly-beloved niece was often flushed to a degree that looked extremely like the effects of a sudden attack of fever.

But "time and the hour," as usual, brought all this, as it does everythink else, to an end; Henry returned home; George Harrington wrung his hand very affectionately, and then, at last, wished them all good night, and departed.

Helen Beauchamp had been a young, beautiful, loved, admired, well-born, and rich heiress when she left her bed on that eventful morning; and she was a young, beautiful, loved, admired, well-born, and rich heiress when she returned to it at night; yet the change which had come upon her between that rising up and that lying down, involved all the difference between the most enviable happiness and the most hopeless reverse.

George Harrington and Miss Beauchamp had not turned over the leaves of half a dozen picture books without having found both time and opportunity to converse on subjects somewhat more interesting than the comparative beauty of rival eyes and noses; he contrived to tell her, during the three hours and a half which intervened between their leaving the dinner-table and the announcement of his pawing steed at the door, that it

was only since the sun rose that morning that he had become
fully aware of the perfect accord which existed between them in
their opinions on many important points; and that, now, he
felt almost ashamed of himself for having loved her so devotedly
while still ignorant of the noblest traits in her character. But
for this weakness on his part he declared himself to have been
sufficiently punished, by the miserable condition of heart and
spirit in which he had lived since the death of his uncle; and in
his manner during this part of his discourse, as he hung over
the volume which was before them, there was so much of
mournful truth, that tears streamed almost unconsciously from
Helen's eyes as she listened to him; and had it not been for
some very clever management on the part of the young man,
neither the gentle dose of Mr. Rixley, nor the pretty, steady
reading of his wife, could have sufficed to prevent her emotion
from being perceptible.

As it was, however, everything went well. The waning moon
was quite high enough in the heavens, by the time George
Harrington had finally made up his mind to depart, to afford
him light enough to make his ride agreeable; and in fact, this
light was so beautiful in its effect upon the park scenery, and
the state of the atmosphere altogether so delightful, that he
could not resist his inclination to run back into the drawing-
room for the purpose of making Helen and her uncle come out
to look at it.

The few moments they thus passed together in the portico
gave her an opportunity of telling him that she should greatly
like to receive an early visit from his sister Agnes on the
morrow.

"Is she to drive over in solitary state, alone?" whispered
George, rather piteously.

"Yes!" she replied, with inexorable firmness, after the
hesitation of a moment.

The well-behaved young man received this answer in perfect
silence, and turned submissively away, as if to set off immediately, in order to obey her commands; and it was probably,
because she was touched by this meek obedience, that she followed him with rather a hasty step, and laying a finger on his
arm, to arrest his retreat, said, rather kindly than otherwise,
"I shall like to keep her with me all day. We shall have much
to say to each other. But, perhaps, you will dine with us, and
escort her home at night."

This arrangement seemed, lover as he was, to content him

tolerably well, for his final good night was uttered cheerily; and so they parted, for the first time for nearly three long years, without each having left an aching pain in the heart of the other.

The family at the Oaks were, of course, all gone to bed before George Harrington reached his home; but it was at rather an early hour on the following morning that he made his way to his sister Agnes, and delivered the message he had brought to her from Helen.

Had the heart and head of Agnes been less full of her own concerns, it is highly probable that she would have perceived some symptom, in the eye, or the voice of her brother, which might have led her to think that he was not precisely in the same state of mind which he had been in when she conversed with him last. All she perceived, however, was, that this invitation was not quite an ordinary invitation. The early hour at which it was stated that she would be expected, and the circumstance of her being distinctly invited to come alone, fully justified her coming to this conclusion, and so much of the real state of the case suggested itself as to make her exclaim, with a blush which expressed more of happiness than of anger, "Then you have told her, George?"

"Yes, Agnes. I have told her," he replied, in a tone which she did not quite clearly understand. "Yes, I have told her; and she will tell you all I have said to her, I daresay, or at least a good deal of it."

"But what *did* you say to her, George?" returned his sister, rather anxiously. "Did she seem to think me wrong for accepting him?"

"No, Agnes; I did not perceive any feeling of that kind. However, you will be a better judge yourself of what she feels upon the subject when you talk to her about it, than you can possibly be by my repeating what she said."

"I don't know what to make of your report," said Agnes, looking at him earnestly. "If she has expressed herself to you as greatly shocked by the misfortune of his birth, I would rather not go to spend a long day with her."

"Do not torment yourself by idle fancies, my dear Agnes, your friend, Miss Beauchamp, is a very sensible young woman, and I really don't think that you have any reason to fear that she should lecture you disagreeably upon the choice you have made. May I go and order the carriage for you? Shall I say that you will be ready in an hour?"

"Yes, you may," she replied, cheerfully; "for I am quite
sure you would not propose my going so early if you thought
she had anything disagreeable to say to me. I shall be ready
in an hour, George."

"You are quite right, Agnes, not to suffer yourself to be
frightened. Miss Beauchamp certainly told me that she should
have a great deal to say to you; but she will take care, I am
sure, not to make herself really disagreeable."

And having make this rather equivocal speech, he quitted
the room, leaving the affianced bride of Colonel Maurice in
rather a nervous state of spirit; but fully determined that not
even her well-beloved and greatly-admired Helen should persuade her, for a single instant, to doubt that the choice she had
made was as much for her honour as her happiness, and that
no other human being could possibly be found so well calculated
to ensure both.

<hr>

CHAPTER LIII.

It was really a pity that the now gay and happy-hearted
George Harrington could not have witnessed the first meeting of
the two friends, for he would undoubtedly have found something
exceedingly comic in the doubting and inquiring expression of
both the fair faces, while each was endeavouring to guess how
much, or how little, the other had been enlightened by him as
to the exact state of the important affairs which at that moment
occupied the thoughts of each.

The sure remedy, however, against anything like really painful embarrassment between them for more than a few minutes,
was found in the fact that they really loved each other dearly;
and Agnes speedily remembered that, however aristocratic and
severe the notions of Miss Beauchamp might be on the subject
of good and legitimate birth, her friend, Helen, would be easily
led to forget them in her particular case; while Helen felt
with equally confiding faith, that however surprised, or however
puzzled, the sister of George might be at her sudden change of
conduct towards him, her friend Agnes would not fail to make

her feel that, great as her surprise might be, her satisfaction was greater still.

Nothing could be more correct than the conclusions thus arrived at on both sides, and before the two blushing girls had been half an hour together they had exchanged a tender kiss of mutual congratulation, and were both in the full enjoyment of giving, and receiving, a multitude of anecdotes and confessions, all tending to prove the happiness of each.

"Can anything be so strange," said Helen, "so unexpected, so improbable, as that your accidentally making acquaintance, and accidentally falling in love with this young soldier of fortune, Agnes, should pave the way to your brother's marrying me? I really cannot, with the exercise of all my ingenuity, imagine any other possible process which could have removed the mountain of adamant that stood between us!"

"Strange, indeed!" replied Agnes; "and delightful as it is strange! But were the finale of the romance less likely to be propitious, I should feel inclined to preach you a pretty long sermon, Miss Beauchamp, upon the grievous sin of doubting those we love. You ought to have known my high-minded, noble-hearted brother better, Helen, than to have permitted yourself to believe him capable of such feelings as you laid to his charge."

"I suppose I was very wrong, Agnes," said poor Helen, meekly. "In truth I do believe I was! I seem to see it all now in a totally different light. However, sister dear, you may take my word for it, that I have suffered enough to punish me sufficiently for a very heavy sin."

"But, Helen;" returned George Harrington's unforgiving sister, "though you did blunder so grievously about his opinions, I do not think that even this explains your so strongly miscalculating the power of his attachment to you. How could you doubt for a moment that his love for you was strong enough to swallow up and overcome every possible objection? Don't you think that you deserve a little more suffering on that score?"

"No, Agnes! No! There I was right, perfectly right. I was wrong in my estimate of the importance he would attach to the unfortunate situation of my beloved brother, but right in believing that if he thought it wrong so to connect himself, he would have shrunk from doing it. Trust me, I thought of all that before I finally decided upon my own line of conduct. I was not blind to the fact that there might have been a struggle in his mind between what he wished, and what his judgment would approve; and the idea of using my influence for the purpose of warping his sense of right, was more intolerable than the idea of losing him. No! No! You will bring me to no humble confessions on that point. With the notions I had conceived as to what his opinion would be, as to my position with respect to my unfortunate brother, I was quite right not to make any experiments as to the power I might possess over his feelings, in order to seduce him into acting in defiance of them. No! No! I was right there."

"You have stated the case so sublimely, Helen, and so clearly proved that it was your duty to make him as wretched as possible, that I have not a word to say against it," replied her friend. "All your fault, therefore, my poor dear, lies in the weakness of your intellectual capacity in forming so very monstrous a judgment concerning his notions of right and wrong, and for this I give you absolution, blended with pity. Poor dear Helen! I daresay you did feel very uncomfortable all the time that you were fancying yourself so very magnanimous."

"Well, Agnes! You may laugh at me, now, for I can afford to bear it. The happiness side of my account is so miraculously improved within the last twenty-four hours, that it would not be very easy to make me complain of anything," replied Helen. "And yet," she added, with a sigh, which was, however, scarcely audible, "and yet, dearest, when I see this marvellous man who has contrived to turn the heads of yourself and your brother both, it will be difficult for me not to contrast his fate with that of my poor William! I shall be surprised if, with all my inclination to love and admire all that you and George love and admire, I certainly shall be surprised if I find this happy soldier more admirable in any way than I was wont to think my beautiful brother!"

"Put all comparisons out of your head, Helen, and I shall feel no doubts or fears respecting your judgment of this new friend of ours," said Agnes, gaily. "But what a strange fatality there seems to have been about your having never seen him. If your aunt was not well enough to go out when he was here, I wonder your Cousin Henry never brought him to call on you. For nobody seemed more struck by his appearance than Henry Rixley did, the night that he was first shown off to the neighbourhood at Mrs. Wilcox's ball."

"Oh, yes, he quite raved about him," said Helen. "But you forget that Henry was obliged to go to London, on regimental business immediately afterwards. He never met him at any of Sir William Knighton's bachelor dinners, nor at Rothewell Castle either, where I know he dined more than once. Nay, do you know, I doubt, if Henry was ever introduced to him at all," she added.

"Well, then," returned the happy Agnes, gaily, "he will only burst upon you all with the more effect when he shall be at length presented—for will he not have, in addition to all other good gifts, the honour and glory of being proclaimed as the affianced husband of Agnes Harrington?"

"There will be something in that, Agnes," replied Helen, laughing, "we shall be too much afraid of you not to be ready to accord our suffrages to him. But when is he to appear again above our horizon? We are expecting Henry back to-morrow, and as, notwithstanding his lengthened leave, we shall have him, I fear, only for a day or two longer, I think I must screw my courage to giving a dinner-party myself."

Then, after the silence of a few moments, she added, "What an enormous, what an astounding difference, Agnes, can a few short hours, and a few gentle words, make in us! Do you not, in a hundred thousand ways, feel that you are no longer the same being that you were before you paid your brother that last visit at Speedhurst? And cannot you imagine that, in a hundred thousand ways, I feel myself a different being from what I was before your brother favoured me with his early morning visit yesterday?"

"Imagine! I can do more than imagine," returned Agnes, placing her hands before her eyes, "I see it, I know it, I feel it all! It is not a dream, is it, Helen? Good Heaven, my dear, how dreadful it would be to wake up, and find the vision gone! But pray don't tell Colonel Maurice that I said so, however much you may admire him, or however intimate you may become. I really and truly should not choose that he should know for an absolute certainly that I doubt if I could make up my mind to live without him."

"Do not let your brother hear you say that," said Helen, while tears started to her eyes, "for he knows that I had made up *my* mind to live without him."

"Very true, Helen! I think it would be quite as well to keep him in ignorance of the inferiority of your capacity in the loving

line. But even if he did know it, I don't think that it would
signify much. He is so infatuated, that I should not be at all
surprised to hear him declare that he loved you all the better
for your hard-heartedness. But let me learn a little more about
this dinner that you are going to give. I enjoy the idea excessively! Do not delay it, for if you do, I am quite sure it never
will take place at all. As a bit of useful information on the
subject, I may announce to you that Colonel Maurice will make
his first appearance at the Oaks, in the character of an acknowledged and accepted lover, on Saturday. That, you know, is
the day after to-morrow. Now he, you must know, has military
business to attend to, as well as Master Henry; and, therefore,
I strongly advise that you should fix Monday next as the day
for our dining, will you?"

"*Soit*," replied Helen, joyously, "I am, by no means, more
inclined for delay than you are. But what must we do about
the ceremony of a morning call upon the brave Colonel? My
uncle is knee-deep in flannel, for the purpose of giving a friendly
welcome to the gout, which he is expecting to visit him, for,
really and truly, it has not come yet. But I should not like to
propose a morning visit to him. And as to Henry, it is his
invariable custom to gallop over to Rothewell the moment
breakfast is over, and we may think ourselves highly favoured
if we see him again before the next morning. How, then, shall
we manage a call at the Oaks, which is exactly in the contrary
direction?"

"I will undertake that the omission shall cause no offence,"
replied Agnes. "But tell me, Helen, shall you think it a matter
of absolute necessity to invite Lady Lympton, and all the other
fine folks at the Castle?"

"No," replied Helen, thoughtfully, "my happiness, dear Agnes,
runs too freshly, and too suddenly come upon me to be worn
with all the calm composure which ought to accompany it. You
have long been a sister to me in heart, and now we are about to
be sisters indeed; and, therefore, I feel as if there were something strange and unnatural in my never having seen the man
you are about to marry! But were it not for this, dearest, the
'dinner party' we have been projecting would not take place
just yet. Of course, dear Jane will come to me, but my first
meeting with your father and mother must not be at a dinner-
party, Agnes! Perhaps they will have the kindness to call
upon me to-morrow, and if so, I could with confidence ask them
to join our truly family party on Monday."

And so it was definitively settled between the two happy girls,
who, after a morning visit of four hours' duration, during which
they had talked with unceasing energy and animation, parted,
at length, with infinite regret, because they had still, both of
them, so very much that they wanted to say to the other.

CHAPTER LIV.

Who is there that does not know and understand the sort of
accelerated movement and energetic activity communicated to a
family when one of its members is about to enter into the
honourable state of matrimony? It may easily be imagined,
therefore, that the two weddings, so unexpectedly settled, and
so speedily to be accomplished at the Oaks, must have thrown
the whole Harrington family into a very unusual state of
excitement and commotion.

As to the young squire of Speedhurst, indeed, he just at this
time passed so few of his hours in his father's house, that it
would be hardly fair to say that he added greatly to the commotion which reigned there.   In the larger field of the
Beauchamp Park establishment the awful notes of preparation
was not so easily detected ; yet still excitement reigned there,
though it was, for the most part, pretty well kept out of
sight.

That every hour and every occupation of its fair owner's life
was completely and altogether changed, is nevertheless quite
true ; for when she walked in her noble gardens, lately the
object of so much peaceful occupation to her, she now, with
George Harrington by her side, positively forgot that the
gardens *were* her gardens, or that they had any possible interest
for her, except, as did now and then happen, they seemed (probably because their beauty was the result of her taste) to have
some interest for him.

In her own pretty morning-room, too, where heretofore she
really had, in good earnest, devoted some hours in every day to
whatever her critical old friend, Mr. Phelps, dignified by the
name of study, the difference between past and present time was
very remarkable ; for there it was that all George Harrington's

morning visits (sometimes amounting to three in a day) were received; and it must, therefore, be obvious to the commonest capacity that it must have been difficult, not to say impossible, for her to have persevered in her by-gone literary habits.

But in sober truth, and quite apart from all the *idlesse* usually attributed to the social intercourse of lovers, Helen Beauchamp and George Harrington really had a great deal to say to each other, and a great deal that it was very essential to their future happiness should not remain unsaid. The systematic avoidance by Helen's uncle and his family of all allusion to her unfortunate brother, had taught, nay, almost enforced, such an habitual reserve on her part, respecting everything connected with him, that probably nothing less incompatible with such reserve than their approaching marriage would have led her to infringe it, even with him. But she now, for the first time since she had left Mr. Bolton's house, rather more than eight years ago, now for the first time she indulged herself in pouring forth all her young and fond recollections of her earliest days.

And it was, indeed, an indulgence; for the silence in which these recollections had been hoarded, had, in no degree, tended to obliterate, or even to lessen their effect; and it was long since the beautiful and richly-endowed girl had enjoyed anything so nearly approaching perfect happiness as she now did while watching the eager and pleased attention of her lover, as he listened to her animated description of the endearing character and noble qualities of this long-lost brother.

"We must find him, my Helen!" exclaimed George Harrington, after having heard her painful narrative to the end: "Yes, dearest, we must find him, even if the doing so should involve the necessity of our setting off for India in the same romantic style which that wonderful old woman seems to have done of whom your Mr. Bolton speaks with so much admiration, or I should rather say, with so much astonishment; for does it not strike you, Helen, that Mr. Bolton in that earliest of his letters there, which you have just read to me—does it not strike you that he does not speak of her affectionately, though he talks so much of her singular devotion, and unflinching resolution? It seems to me as if he did not quite approve her setting off with so much enthusiasm in pursuit of her lost nursling."

"You must be an acute critic, dear George," replied Helen, with rather a melancholy smile, "to discover this seeming want of sympathy with our dear nurse Lambert, for it is quite certain that among the multitude of recollections and impressions which

23

have been silently hoarded in my memory respecting everything connected with my childish life, there is one which completely justifies the observation you have now made. I seem to remember as freshly as if it all had happened yesterday, that when I had that dreadful illness at the Parsonage, I very often felt unhappy when I recovered my senses and was getting well again, because I thought that neither Mr. nor Mrs. Bolton loved my dear Sarah Lambert as I thought she ought to be loved. I perfectly well remember, too, that when this dear Sarah Lambert suddenly went away from me, and with the intention, as it proved, of never returning, I thought that it was because she had found out that they did not like her as well as she knew she deserved. Dear, dear Sarah Lambert!" continued poor Helen, as tears of which she did not seem conscious ran down her cheeks, "Oh! how I wish that you could see her at this moment, George, exactly as my memory paints her to me now! Trust me, she was no ordinary woman, although she was a servant. I never saw anybody like her, and I don't remember to have seen anyone so beautiful as I think she must have been when she was young. Her ways, too, were so lovingly gentle with us! But somehow or other, I am quite sure that you are right, and that Mr. Bolton did not like her, nor his wife either."

"How long is it, Helen, since you have heard anything about her, or her bold enterprize?" said Harrington.

"I have never heard her named at all since I left Cornwall," replied Helen, "nor have I found her name once mentioned in any letter of Mr. Bolton's since the one on which you made your critical remark."

Nor were the other pair of affianced lovers less fortunate in obtaining the wished-for privilege of a long and uninterrupted *tête-à-tête*; but to follow them through it would be to involve ourselves in a greater length of personal narrative on the part of the gentleman than we have now space for—for there were abundance of moving accidents by flood and field, and most literally true was it that "she loved him for the dangers he had passed, and he loved her that she did pity them."

And then, towards the conclusion of the precious interval between luncheon and dinner, during which they were pretty certain of being left in peace, Colonel Maurice ventured to ask a few questions respecting the estimable friends with whom, as he had been informed, they were doomed to dine on the coming Monday. "I wish it had happened otherwise, dearest Agnes!"

said he; "for I must be off to town on Tuesday, and I should so much better have liked to pass our last evening quietly at home."

"And were we going to any other house, I should say so, too," replied Agnes; "but you forget that it is not among strangers and aliens that we are going to take you. It is to the house of a very lovely girl, who is a wealthy heiress."

"But what care I how fair she be, or how rich either," returned Colonel Maurice, laughingly interrupting her. "I want to spend these last precious hours quietly with you, and not in the fine drawing-room of any beautiful young lady in the world, even if she were as rich as a Jew."

"If you had not interrupted me, impetuous soldier as you are, I was going on to state that Miss Beauchamp has other claims upon us than merely being a beauty, or heiress, or even a kind neighbour," said Agnes. "I have positively had no time to tell you any further particulars about your friend George than that he, too, like your own rash self, was speedily about to be married. I really don't believe that I have ever said a single word to you about the lady. But it is this identical Miss Beauchamp, with whom we are going to dine on Monday, who is to be his bride."

"No, fairest and best! Most certainly I never heard her name mentioned by any of you; but I am now quite willing to confess that you stand excused for taking me there; and as fellow-feeling, you know, generally makes us kind and considerate, I daresay that your fair sister elect will forgive us if we do happen to think of a good many things which we may possibly wish to say to each other before we part."

"Oh! You need have no fears on that score," replied Agnes, with an eloquent nod of the head, which was not only well calculated to reassure him, but to make him comprehend, also, that her brother's lady-love might be likely to require a little indulgence on that particular point as well as herself.

"And truly, truly," she added, in an accent which gave evidence that she was much in earnest, "I feel as if I had not time, either here or there, to hear you tell me one quarter of what I want to know about a hundred and fifty interesting points of your eventful history."

"Trust to my loquacity when we shall become man and wife," replied Colonel Maurice, laughing. "The love of spinning long yarns is by no means confined to the nautical branch of Her Majesty's service. Soldiers love the occupation quite as

well as sailors can do, and woe betide the tender-hearted bride
who has listened before marriage to all that an enamoured
husband would most particularly wish her to listen to respecting himself, for in that case she will run a great risk of having
to listen to a twice-told tale. What I want to talk to you about,
Agnes, and what I am pretty sure I shall want to continue
talking about as long as I stay here, is the inconvenient and
very unnecessary importance which your dear good mother, and
your dear, darling, fussy sister, attach to these horribly-lengthy
preparations for your wardrobe, which Jane very coolly told me
last night could not possibly be completed in less than six weeks
or two months. Now the real fact is, Agnes, that we must either
postpone our marriage or postpone the wardrobe."

"Postpone our marriage," repeated Agnes, gravely shaking
her head. "The talking of the wardrobe at all, Colonel
Maurice, is a very sufficient proof that matters have not been
unreasonably postponed. Remember, dear friend, how short
our acquaintance has been!"

"Has it been too short to enable us to love one another,
Agnes?" said the lover, reproachfully. "If it has, you are
quite right in asking, let me rather say, in *demanding*, some
further delay. But—"

"But nonsense, Maurice!" returned Agnes, interrupting him
with a very petulant, but not very solemn frown. "There is
no truth in you! For neither do you in your heart suspect me
of any want of love, nor do you believe the least in the world
that I wish to demand delay."

"Then you don't call to months *delay* two a man who was
hoping to be married in a fortnight?" returned the gallant
Colonel, with a good deal of vehemence.

"A fortnight!" exclaimed Agnes, almost with a shriek.
"You must be mad, Colonel Maurice! Completely and entirely
lunatic! Be quiet, if you can, I do entreat you! Now hear
me, then," she gravely continued, upon seeing him assume the
posture of a man in a strait waistcoat, "do pray listen to me
like a reasonable being! If we ever think of marrying at all—
there now! Would not anyone suppose that I had said something uncivil about *never* marrying at all? Hear me, I say,
Colonel Maurice! If we really are, both of us, seriously in
earnest about this very solemn business, we must take care not
to disgrace ourselves in the eyes of Miss Beauchamp, by proposing to do anything that may appear particularly shocking to
her—and to tell you the real truth at once, your friend George

has·made up his mind that the two weddings must take place on the same day."

"Where is George?" exclaimed Maurice, starting up, "I have no doubt that I shall get him to listen to reason, though it is so impossible to make you do it. Where is he, Agnes?"

"I have little doubt, my good friend," she replied, "that he is engaged very much in the same manner as you are. That is to say, that I think it highly probable that if you track him skilfully you will find him about the same distance from Miss Beauchamp that you are from me, scolding her heartily because she cannot contrive to make hours suffice to do the business of days."

My researches have furnished me with no record as to the exact manner in which this terrible interview ended; but as I purpose in the following chapter to give some account of what passed at Helen's dinner-party, at which none of the guests whom she expected failed to appear, it is obvious that the scene above described did not end in any positive quarrel between the parties.

CHAPTER LV.

It must not be considered on the part of my heroine as any indication of cold indifference concerning the destiny of her friend Agnes, if I confess that her own situation, so new to her as the affianced wife of George Harrington, prevented her dwelling with all the interest which she would otherwise have felt upon the idea of first seeing and judging the man upon whom the future happiness of that dear friend so greatly depended.

She, in some sort, took it for granted, indeed, that he must be both excellent and amiable; because George had said so; and it was, therefore, without any overpowering feelings of anxiety or emotion of any kind that she passed from her toilet to the drawing-room, in order to receive the guests, some of whom were already so dear to her, and to all and every of whom she was so soon to be allied to by the very closest ties which human beings have been able to invent to bind loving hearts together.

Her Aunt and Uncle Rixley were already in the drawing-room; and the few minutes which elapsed before their punctual guests arrived were passed in the expression of a little natural curiosity on the part of both respecting the utter stranger to whom they were about to be introduced in the character of very near connections.

"It does seem queer," said Mr. Rixley, "that we should all three of us have to receive this celebrated Colonel as something nearer and dearer than merely an intimate friend, without our either of us having ever beheld him before!"

"Queer, indeed!" said Mrs. Rixley, gravely shaking her head, "and I cannot but fear that our poor dear Helen must feel it to be very awkward for her, as mistress of the house, to receive a guest whom she has never beheld before, and then feel herself obliged to treat him as an intimate friend!"

"Why, now you mention it, aunt, I think there is something a little preposterous in the idea of welcoming a young man as a dearly beloved, of whom I know absolutely nothing, excepting that Agnes and George Harrington have both fallen in love with him! I certainly do wish that I had happened to see him before!"

"Of course you do, my dear child!" returned her aunt, in a very penitent tone, "and it is all owing to me, and my unfortunate rheumatism, that you did not become acquainted with him, like all the other people in the neighbourhood. I cannot forgive myself for having let you give up everything in order to stay at home, and take care of me."

"No, my dear wife, your conscience may be quite at rest on that score. The fault was her own. She chooses to pet us, and humour us, to such an excess at home, that it is next to impossible that old folks on the high road to three-score should ever like to go out; and having done this, I verily believe that she finds a great deal of amusement in staying at home, and watching our cat-like ways of enjoying ourselves. Is not that the fact, Helen?"

"Whatever the cause, dear uncle, my stay-at-home system during the last few months has been the result of my own will, and if blame there be, it must rest on me, and on me alone."

"But why does not Henry make his appearance?" said Mr. Rixley. "At any rate he has not been shut up at home; and as he must have made acquaintance with this newly-imported hero, the awkwardness of his reception here would be much less if there was one of the family who could shake hands with him

as an acquaintance. Do ring the bell, Helen, and let us send
for him."

Helen wrung the bell very obediently; but said, as she did
so, "He will not help us much, uncle! He is as much a
stranger to Colonel Maurice as we are."

"I beg your pardon, Helen dear," returned her uncle, "I can
testify to having heard Henry rave for an hour by Shrewsbury
clock concerning the excellences of this wonderful hero."

"And so have I, too, Uncle Rixley," replied Helen, "yet,
nevertheless, he cannot help us by welcoming him as an
acquaintance, for he has never been introduced to him. He
only saw him one evening, which was at Mrs. Wilcox's famous
ball. It was at breakfast the following morning that he amused
us by the tirade you speak of; and two days afterwards he was
off to London again, and so missed the dinner-party at Sir
William Knighton's, to which he was invited, and where he
would, doubtless, have been introduced to the stranger, like the
rest of the neighbourhood."

"Quite true!" said Mr. Rixley. "Henry is exactly in the
same predicament as we are; nevertheless, it is quite right
to send for him. It is better that we should all be introduced
at once, and then, you know, George Harrington can do it in
the words of the critic: 'And these are all my poor relations!'
while by a circular wave of the hand he can indicate us all."

Henry Rixley entered as she spoke, and being made
acquainted with the subject under discussion, he confirmed
the statement of his cousin, and his mother—declaring that no
introduction had taken place; but that he already felt that he
knew him better than half the people with whom he had gone
through that ceremony.

"His handsome and expressive countenance, his noble figure,
his general aspect and bearing, at once riveted my attention
upon him," said he, eagerly. "But it is a positive fact, mother,"
he added, "that though I am not in general celebrated for any
very superabundant degree of modest shyness, it was that, and
nothing else, which prevented my being introduced. You know
I went with the Lymptons, who are always late, and he was
talking so earnestly to the people about him, that really, and
truly, I had not sufficient audacity to be led up, as if on purpose
to interrupt him. But, decidedly, I never saw such a man in
my life. His height is—"

At this moment the two carriages which conveyed the party
from the Oaks drove up to the door; the eloquence of Henry

came to a sudden stop; and the group, who were all standing round Mrs. Rixley's chair near the fire, remained both stationary and silent.

It was, however, but a very short interval which intervened between the arrival of the carriages and the opening of the drawing-room door; and the party that entered were so animated, and so joyous, that a minute or two was devoted to the loving embraces of the ladies, before the introduction of the stranger could take place.

He stood meanwhile with as much gentlemanlike avoidance of staring at the individual whom he was most anxious to see, as he could contrive to do without positively shutting his eyes. But, nevertheless, he certainly did feel a good deal of curiosity about the young and beautiful heiress who was about to bestow herself upon George Harrington.

Many circumstances had contributed to excite and increase this curiosity, the most effectual of all, perhaps, being the fact that she was the only young lady in the neighbourhood whom he had not seen. Another circumstance, also, had doubtless contributed not a little to the frequency with which her name and distinguished position in the county were made to attract his notice—and this was the peculiarly conspicuous situation of her house and grounds.

It was difficult to walk or to ride in any direction throughout the whole neighbourhood without coming, in some way or other, within sight of Beauchamp Park, its noble mansion, and its magnificent woods; and the having been told whenever this happened to him, and however varied the different points of view might be, that all he saw and admired belonged, not to the odious Lord Marquis of Carabas, but to a beautiful young lady, owning the sonorous name which appertained to her splendid domain, could scarcely fail of exciting a certain degree of curiosity concerning the appearance and much vaunted beauty of this highly-favoured individual.

It is certain, indeed, that he was far too agreeably and too completely occupied while at Speedhurst Abbey, by the fascinating employment of falling in love, to retain any very distinct recollection of all he had heard about the beautiful lady of Beauchamp Park, but his interest upon the subject was effectually roused again by learning, upon his first visit as an accepted lover at the Oaks, that his future brother-in-law was the happy and envied individual upon whom she had determined to bestow her heart, hand, and acres.

It was, therefore, certainly not without some effort, and a determination to behave particularly well, that he respectfully bowed to the tall young lady to whom he was immediately presented, and who was, of course, named to him as the Miss Beauchamp, of whom he had heard so much, and then followed his friend George to the chair of her aunt, without pausing an instant to look at the beautiful face he had heard so enthusiastically extolled.

Mrs. Rixley was, at that time, too nearly being a cripple for her to rise from her chair to receive the party, but she very cordially extended her hand to him, even before he was named, as an evidence that, though unknown, he was not held to be a stranger.

The promptitude with which this friendly welcome was offered caused their hands to meet before George Harrington had pronounced her name; but, when he did so, the brave Colonel Maurice started as vehemently as if he had been a nervous young lady, who was listening to something that particularly affected her sensibility, and abruptly dropping the hand which the good lady had so kindly extended, he stood looking at her with an air which had much less of gentleman-like ease in it, than of eager, but embarrassed curiosity.

She looked up into his face for a moment in a manner which certainly seemed to indicate a doubt as to his being in a perfectly sane state of mind. And, perhaps, she was right, for the abruptness with which he turned away from her and approached the mistress of the house, to whom he had just paid his compliments with so much observant decorum, fully justified the persuasion, which immediately took possession of her, that there certainly was "something odd about him."

But it required little time to perceive that this oddness was either infectious, or that, at any rate, it was shared by one who had never heretofore shown any symptoms of eccentricity, for on fixing her eyes upon her niece, as Colonel Maurice turned round and approached her, Mrs. Rixley, with equal astonishment and alarm, perceived her to be as pale as death, and with her eyes fixed upon the gallant Colonel, with an expression which it was not very easy to interpret, but which certainly did not express either anger or aversion.

But thought, with all its rapidity, had barely time to suggest the question, "What can all this mean?" before Colonel Maurice had sprung forward, and, throwing his arms round her, held her in a close embrace, bending his lofty head upon

her shoulder, and vehemently exclaiming, " My Helen ! my
Helen ! It is my own Helen ! "

That the Rixley family were, all three of them, greatly
startled and astonished is very certain, for one from the dead
could scarcely have come among them more unexpectedly than
did this long-lost wanderer; yet, nevertheless, it took no great
time, and no great exertion of memory, before the truth suggested itself to them all; and they perceived, without a shadow
of doubt, as to the fact, that the magnificent-looking young
man, whom they saw before them supporting their precious
Helen in his arms, was no other than the natural son of her
father, upon whose name and existence an act of oblivion had
been so systematically passed by the whole of the Rixley family,
that the possibility of his being still among the living had for
years ceased to suggest itself to their minds.

But the case was different with respect to George Harrington; for though but a few hours, comparatively speaking, had
elapsed since Helen herself had narrated to him all the circumstances of her early history, and had, moreover, succeeded in
awakening a warm and affectionate feeling of interest in his
heart for the poor forlorn boy, whom she had only designated
as her "unhappy William," no thought for an instant suggested itself that the highly distinguished man whom he had
only seen in pride of place, and the honoured and admired of all
observers could be one and the same. Yet so it was; while so
unconscious was this umwhile "poor William" that there could
exist any doubt about his being Helen's brother, that, after again
and again kissing her, and perceiving at last that the close
embrace in which she had held him seemed to relax, and that in
the next moment she was sinking from his arms, he caught her
up as unceremoniously as if she had been an infant, and carried
her to the further extremity of the room, where stood a large
sofa against the wall, permitting him to lay her down at full
length, which was evidently the best thing to do; for she had
fainted, and was completely insensible.

All this had passed almost in less time than it can be told;
yet, nevertheless, the unfortunate George Harrington's brain
found leisure to fabricate a romance, which very nearly drove
him mad. In fact, at that moment he utterly forgot all Helen's
explanation respecting the fanciful obstacles which had so long
kept them asunder, and only remembered the manner in which,
for such a length of time, she had clearly given him to understand that she would not, or could not, receive his addresses.

Here, then, was the explanation! The man whom she had
so evidently loved had been waited for till she had ceased to
hope for his return! And then she had accepted HIM! Colonel
Maurice's exclamation, "*Helen! my own Helen!*" rung in his
ears; and it was with gestures, very like those of a maniac,
that, after gazing for a moment on the spectacle which mad-
dened him, he prepared to rush out of the room. The feelings of
his family were decidedly in very perfect sympathy with his
own. Not one of them had ever heard it hinted that the heiress
of Beauchamp Park had any brother belonging to her. What
inference, therefore, could they draw from the scene they had
witnessed, save that a long-lost lover had been restored to her
in the person of Colonel Maurice? Both Jane Harrington and
her mother were so deeply shocked and outraged by the sight of
the endearments so audaciously displayed before them, that they
indignantly turned away, each taking possession of a distant
window; while the unhappy Agnes, quite as miserable, though
not so vehemently distracted, as her brother, supported herself
as she could by placing her trembling hands upon the back of a
chair, and endeavouring to soothe her indignant father, who
stood beside her, muttering something that did not sound at all
like a blessing, either upon her quondam lover or her quondam
friend, or it might be upon both!

Meanwhile there was one, and but one, individual present who
understood what had happened. The only individual capable of
interpreting the whole scene was the reverend Mr. Rixley; and,
to do him justice, he felt, as he contemplated the various systems
of unhappiness before him, that he had been greatly to blame,
for that he had, in a very great measure, been the cause of it
all! Nor was he altogether wrong in this severe self-judg-
ment.

He perfectly remembered the repugnance, for it was more
than indifference, with which he had turned from Mr. Bolton
when he had endeavoured to excite some degree of interest in
his heart for the friendless boy whom his unprincipled brother
had left in a state of such utter destitution; he remembered
keenly, too, at that moment, all the noble qualities, and brilliant
talents for which the good clergyman of Crumpton had given him
credit, and of which his subsequent success in his profession had
now given ample and unanswerable proof. Neither could he
forget, in that moment of disagreeable self-examination, how
many a time and oft poor Helen had endeavoured, during the
first few months of her residence with him, to awaken some

feeling of kindness towards her unhappy brother, and he now felt, what he had never felt before, that he had been wrong, very wrong, in hating the son for the sins of his father.

Of the facts, which would have made it impossible for any feelings, however kind on his part, to have assisted the desolate boy, he knew nothing. Had he been better informed on that point, he might have felt less dissatisfied with himself at the present moment. As it was, however, the very obvious truth suggested itself that the best way to atone for his past blunders would be by correcting the effect of them; and this he immediately began to do in the most judicious and gentlemanlike manner possible.

He had been standing on the hearth-rug at the moment when the sound of his name had produced so startling an affect on the nerves of the distinguished officer, who, after having been *fêted* throughout the whole neighbourhood, had now honoured Beauchamp Park with a visit for the first time. And it was from this same post on the hearth-rug that he had looked on upon the scene that has been described.

From the moment that the "Helen! my own Helen!" had reached the ears of Mr. Rixley, he comprehended the whole of the mystery, which was doubtless less a mystery than it would have been if he had not remembered the many vehement encomiums so vainly uttered by poor Helen upon her lost brother, to all of which he had thought it discreetest and best to turn a deaf ear.

Perceiving that George Harrington, upon hearing these words, was about to leave the room in a very demented state, Mr. Rixley stepped hastily towards him, and laying a gentle hand upon his arm, said, in the most quiet manner possible, " I must request you, my good friend, not to leave the room till you have listened to me for half a moment! You must excuse our dear Helen for suffering herself to be overcome by this most joyful surprise. Colonel Maurice is my nephew, Mr. Harrington, and the brother of Helen."

Then lowering his voice, he added, in a whisper, "Her natural brother, Mr. Harrington, and it is probable, I think, that he has preferred taking another name, perhaps that of his mother, to retaining that of Rixley; for I am sorry to say that my brother did not leave any provision for him by his will; and, as we have entirely lost sight of him since his father's death, and now find him again, so highly placed in the profession upon which he must have entered entirely without patronage or assistance of any kind, we have every reason to suppose that his conduct has been all that his best friends could have wished it to be."

It was evidently with some difficulty that the impetuous George Harrington permitted himself to be detained by the gentle voice and gentle hand of Helen's uncle till he had finished speaking ; for, before one-half of his explanation was uttered, the penitent young man was ready to accuse himself of more base ingratitude and vile suspicion than was ever before exhibited by mortal man.

He restrained himself, however, with exemplary respect and deference, till Mr. Rixley paused, and removed his hand, and then bounded, in defiance of chairs and tables, to the sofa on which Helen was still lying, with her eyes closed, but with cheeks and lips less deadly pale than they had been.

Her brother was kneeling beside her, with her hand locked in his, and his eyes fixed upon her, with an expression which seemed very eloquently to tell how dearly and unchangeably he had loved her since they parted last.

Agnes Harrington, almost as penitent as her brother, was already stationed at the sofa, scarcely venturing to look at Colonel Maurice—for had she not dared to believe him capable of all sorts of sin and iniquity for the space of several seconds?

A word in good season is always good, and rarely have more seasonable words been uttered than those which Mr. Rixley had spoken, and continued to speak. The cloud of suspicion and distrust which had seemed to lower around Colonel Maurice suddenly assumed the very brightest hues, and his being welcomed to Beauchamp Park as the beloved and honoured brother of its mistress, appeared likely to strengthen his pretensions to the hand of Agnes much more than the blot on his escutcheon had ever tended to weaken it. Such being the feeling produced by the scene I have described, it is scarcely necessary to add, that Helen opened her fair eyes upon a scene of much more perfect happiness than she had ever, in her most sanguine moments, dared to hope for ; and, indeed, it might be difficult to find anywhere a party of more well-pleased, hopeful, and warmly-attached human beings, than those which sat down to dinner at Beauchamp Park on that eventful day.

CHAPTER LVI.

THERE are some sorts of contentment which seem to soothe people to sleep, and there are other sorts which are calculated to keep them waking. The recovery of her long-lost brother was not an event which produced anything like a tendency to sleep in Helen. A sense of happiness seemed to accompany every throb of her heart and every thought of her head; but neither the one nor the other suggested any idea of dreaming inactivity. On the contrary, she felt that her situation was greatly changed by the events of this important day, and that her first duty was to meditate upon this change in all its bearings, and then to decide according to her own best and most deliberate judgment upon what she ought to do in the perfectly new situation in which she found herself placed.

Perhaps the first thought which presented itself to her mind, as she sat herself before the fire in the midnight solitude of her dressing-room, was, that whatever she did must be done by her own judgment, and be dictated by her own heart, for that it was quite impossible that anyone—no, not even George Harrington himself—could share, or even understand, her life-long feelings for her brother.

And the thought which followed this came in the shape of a feeling of thankfulness that William had been restored to her before she had become the wife of any man. It is very possible that her lover might have been pained, had he been cognizant of this thought; but, if so, he would have been wrong, and blundering. The love which Helen bore to him, and which she had pledged to him with equal truth and devotion, was in no way affected by the thoughts which caused her to rejoice that she was not yet his wife.

She knew, with a feeling of the most undoubting certainty, that had the ceremony passed which would make his will her law, that will would have taken the colour of hers, in all that she might wish to do for her brother; but *then* he would have complied with her wishes, *because* she was his wife, and might have felt that no alternative was left him.

But now the case would be different. Perhaps she felt a little conscious, too, that her own idea of the claims which her brother had upon her might not precisely assimilate with the ideas of others, a discrepancy of judgment which she very fairly accounted for, by remembering that nobody but herself could know what William had been to her during the first fourteen years of her checquered life. Sarah Lambert, indeed, if she still existed, might remember how the boy would, day after day, give up his favourite pastimes, to cheer and comfort her. But not even Sarah Lambert could tell how much his mind had been the parent of her own, or how deep was the influence which his generous and noble spirit, and his bold clear intellect, had left upon her.

"I should have been a drone, a very clod, an animal with nothing of humanity but its weakness, had it not been for him! Shall I forget the hours, ay, the years during which he made our dreary school-room at the Warren House the dearest spot on earth to me?" Such was the sort of soliloquy in which Helen Beauchamp indulged, during more than one long hour of that sleepless night, and most assuredly she was right in the conclusion to which she came, namely, that as nobody in the whole wide world, except herself, knew how much she owed to him, or how much she loved him, so nobody but herself could know with how good a right her heart claimed the privilege of dictating the manner in which he ought to be treated by her.

If she were wrong in thus thinking, she erred without guilt, for most conscientiously did she believe that she was right. The result of all this meditation may be gathered from the following letter, which she wrote the night after she had recovered her brother, before she laid her head upon her pillow.

"My Dearest George Harrington,

"I need not tell you that I am happy, for you know it already. But what I would tell you, if I had the power, is the nature and species of the happiness which has been to-day added to the large stock I had before, by finding again the precious treasure I had lost. But I must have patience, my dearest friend. There is but one way by which you can be made to understand the value of this treasure, and that is by learning to know William as well as I know him. Then, and then only, will you be able to comprehend what it is you have bestowed upon me, by bringing us together, and what it is you have bestowed upon Agnes, instead of choosing her a husband by the assistance of the 'peerage,' or the 'landed gentry.'

"But 'for a' that, and for a' that,' George Harrington, there is still a *discovery scene* to be opened to you, which most women as old as I am might consider as a tremendous touchstone to be applied to your affection; but I tell you very frankly, that I have not the very slightest shadow of alarm or trepidation in applying it to you. And yet I am quite aware that I might not perhaps feel quite so indifferent about making the disclosure if either my dear good uncle or your dear good father were to be the recipient of it.

"Not that I think that they would either of them eventually oppose me, but just at first they might neither of them receive it exactly as I should wish them to do.

"It will not be feeling like a good-for-nothing Pharisee, will it George, if I always go on thinking, as I do at present, that *you* are not as other men are? I really do think so, however, whether it be pharisaical or not, and it is for that reason that I now venture so fearlessly to remind you that I am no longer the wealthy heiress that I appeared to be when you offered me your hand.

"I refused your hand then, George, because I thought that if you knew the whole truth about me, and my singular position, your pride might receive the wound too deep for even love to heal. You know how this fancy was cured, and since I recovered from its baleful influence, my happiness has acquired a sort of healthy robustness which it will require something stronger than fancy to destroy.

"It is, therefore, without any mixture of doubt or fear as to the result that I now announce to you a fact which I certainly believe would greatly shock many men, though I am very comfortably persuaded that it will not very greatly shock you. This redoubtable fact is, that the property which you believed me to possess has become only half as much as it has been represented to you, for it will have to be divided equally between my brother and myself.

"For reasons which it is not necessary that I should dwell upon, the whole of what may be strictly called the *Beauchamp property* will form my portion; but a large sum in the funds, together with the rents of three large out-standing farms, which have been purchased long since the Beauchamp property and the Beauchamp name have been united, will produce an income fully equal to that which I retain for myself.

"This epistle, dear George, would, I believe, be considered by most gentlemen as but a queer sort of love letter; nevertheless, I feel that nothing but my very perfect love for you could have inspired the feeling of happiness with which it is written, or the feeling of approval and happiness, too, with which I know it will be received. So, after all, you see, it is a very perfect love-letter and nothing else.

"And now, dearest, 'good night,' or rather 'good morning,' for the turret-clock has long ago rung, in twelve sonorous strokes, the knell of yesterday. I daresay it will not be many hours before we meet again, and then we will talk over in proper business-like style the subject upon which I have opened in this midnight scrawl. Though I go to bed late, I think I shall get up early enough to dispatch this in time to reach you before your lazily late breakfast.   ·

"Yours now and ever,
"HELEN BEAUCHAMP.

"P.S.—Tell William to leave Agnes, and come to me as soon as he can get permission to do so." ·

Having finished and sealed this letter, the happy Helen crept noiselessly to bed, and fell into a most delicious sleep almost as soon as she laid her head upon the pillow. But habit was stronger than fatigue, and she waked early as usual, and, accordingly, as she had predicted, her letter reached George Harrington before the family had assembled for breakfast.

If the spirit of Helen could have been put "*en rapport*," as the mesmerists call it, with the spirit of George Harrington, while he read this letter, she would have enjoyed another moment of that very perfect species of happiness which arises from feeling that we are loved even as we love, and understood even as we would be understood. The postscript produced its expected effect, and Colonel Maurice arrived at Beauchamp quite as soon as his sister expected him, which is equivalent to saying that he arrived as speedily as George Harrington's fleetest horse could bring him. The feelings produced in the hearts of these long-severed children of the Warren House by this meeting needs no description. A reunion under almost any circumstances would have gratified what had certainly been the first wish of both their hearts for many long years; but under the circumstances in which they found each other now it required, as Helen said, a strong intellectual effort to enable them to believe that it was not a dream, but a reality. A few laughing moments were actually spent in what they both called improving their personal acquaintance, and when this was accomplished so effectually as to enable them both to declare that they should know each other again let them meet where they would, the eagerly anticipated delight of listening to each other's adventures began.

"You shall begin, Helen," said Colonel Maurice, placing himself, not on the seat she offered him beside herself upon the sofa, but on a chair on the opposite side of the little table which stood before it. And he was right in so placing himself, for her countenance was indeed one of those in which feeling—

"So divinely wrought,
That one might almost say her body thought."

"Where must I begin, William?" said she.

"At the very beginning, Helen," he replied, "and that is the moment when I wished you good night, after that dreadful scene with my father in the parlour!"

Something like a shudder passed over her at the mention of that scene, but she raised her eyes to the dear face opposite to her, and inwardly breathed the words, "Thank God!"

"Yes, I must begin there," said she, with a happy smile, though tears were in her eyes at the same moment. "You wished me good night, William, and poor Sarah Lambert told me I must go to-bed, and to-bed I went, and, child-like, went to sleep, too; though, even then, my heart, as I well remember, was very, very sad. But, oh! the dreadful waking, William! Shall I ever forget it?"

"Because you heard I was gone, dearest?" said Colonel Maurice, tenderly.

"No, no, that came after!" and again poor Helen shuddered, in spite of all her happiness. "No! I was waked by Sarah Lambert, and, when I opened my eyes, I saw her hanging over me with a face as white as the sheet. I well remember that my first words were, 'What's the matter, Sarah?' and that her answer, spoken very gently and soothingly, was, 'Compose yourself, my dear! I have strange news to tell you—your father is dead!' I scarcely know what I did, or what I said. I suppose I uttered some cry, for I know that she told me to be reasonable, for that the house was in confusion, and that I must not make myself troublesome. And then I said, '*Where is William?*' Poor Sarah! I well remember that she did not answer me immediately; for she knew what her answer would be to me! But on my saying again, '*Where is William?*' she replied, 'He is gone away, Helen. He is gone somewhere—I know not where;' but then she added, 'Of course, my dear, he won't stay long. Get up, Helen, get up! Perhaps he will come back, and want his breakfast.' But she did not speak as if you would come back; and when I went down-stairs and saw Rebecca Watkins, she told me that you had gone away in the night, and got out of your window."

"Gracious Heaven!" exclaimed Colonel Maurice, greatly agitated, "what a frightful coincidence!—What did my father die of, Helen?"

"They say he died from poison," she replied.

"And I let myself down from my window by the help of my sheets during the night he died! Everybody must have thought I had poisoned him! Did not people say so, Helen?"

"My dearest William I hardly know what they said," she replied, her lips trembling, and her complexion varying from pale to red, "for I became very, very ill, and for a time I lost my senses."

"And she never told me of this! She never told me a single word of it!"

"Who are you speaking of?" said Helen. "Who is it could have told you of it?"

"Sarah Lambert," he replied, with strong agitation.

"Did she find you, then? Did Sarah Lambert really find you, William?"

"To be sure she did, Helen; but her conduct seems to have been most mysterious! You know, then, that she left England to seek me?"

"Yes, and that is all I know," returned his sister. "Mr. Bolton wrote, to tell me that our old servant had left England, declaring to everybody she knew in Fa'mouth, that she would never return till she had found you."

"And she did find me, Helen," said Colonel Maurice, "notwithstanding the immense distance to which I had wandered, and the further impediment of my having dropped the name, to which, as I had been so cruelly told, *I had no right*, and taken that of my unfortunate mother. But she found me, a poor soldier, just launched on my career in India, and from that time she never left me till she died!"

"She is dead, then!" cried Helen, mournfully. "Our poor Sarah Lambert is dead! I thought it must be so; I thought that she would have let me hear something of her, had she been alive."

"No, Helen," replied her brother. "Her death is of very recent date; it only happened a week or two before I quitted the country. She seemed to have a strong and a strange repugnance to the idea of recalling herself to the memory of anyone whom she had known while in the service of my father. It seems hardly consistent with the tone of her character in other respects, but I think it must have been some species of pride which dictated this reserve, for her feelings towards you were evidently as tenderly affectionate as ever. But she had come into the possession of some property before she joined me, and was in perfectly independent circumstances, and I presume that this must have been her reason for not wishing to preserve any intercourse with those who knew her only as a servant."

"If this be so," replied Helen, "her character must have been one of very extraordinary inconsistency, for, to the best of my recollection, she was the most perfectly indifferent to everything approaching pride of place, as far as it concerned herself, at least, of anyone I ever knew. I am quite sure that she would not have cared a farthing whether she had been looked upon as the confidential housekeeper, which she certainly was, or as one of the hardest-working of kitchen-maids."

"I should have thought so, too," returned her brother; "but, nevertheless, it would be very difficult to find any other theory by which her conduct to you can be accounted for. She seemed to remember the kindness of dear good Mr. Bolton, however, very gratefully, and but a few days before she died, she employed herself for an hour or two in writing to him."

"Did you forward that letter to him immediately, William?" said Helen. "I do not think he could have received it," she added, "for I am almost sure that if he had got such a letter he would have told me of it."

"He never has had it as yet, Helen," returned Colonel Maurice, "for poor Sarah's dying request was, that I should deliver it to him myself. And I would have done so long ere this, notwithstanding the many things which have detained me in London, had it not been for an accident which has occasioned some months' delay in the arrival of the package containing the writing-desk which contained it. In fact, my baggage got mixed with that of another officer when we changed our sailing-vessel for a steamer at the Cape, and as he did not come on with us, my very important packing-case was left behind. However, I got a letter from him the other day explaining the blunder, and telling me that he was about to forward the case immediately, consigned to my own agent in London, and you may depend upon it, dearest, that I will not unnecessarily delay the delivery of it, though in all probability it contains nothing more important than her grateful thanks for all the kindness he had shown her."

"I suppose so, poor thing! And, indeed, I well remember that he and his sweet wife, also, were very, very kind to us both!" replied Helen. "But now, dearest William, tell me, I entreat you, how it happens that after having heard all that Sarah Lambert must have been able to tell you, you could have been at any loss where to seek for me?"

"You are now touching upon a theme, Helen," he replied, "which is indeed most strangely full of mystery. For some reason or other which I could never get her to explain, she never ceased repeating to me that if I knew my own interest I should avoid returning to England for some time to come. She more than hinted that I had enemies, and, at length, named your Uncle Rixley as one very likely to treat me with the same indignity that my father had done. I was, from many fortunate accidents, rising rapidly in my profession; and I imagine that it was *this* she alluded to when she repeated, as she did almost every time that I had leisure to converse with her, '*The time will come, dear William, when you may venture to return, and be afraid of no man. Only wait patiently for a year or two; it will not be very long, I think.*'

"Once I understood her to say that if she were dead, nobody would be able to annoy me afterwards, but when I pressed her to explain what she meant by this, she prevaricated strangely, and ended by saying that she did not mean it."

"But why did you never write to me, William," said Helen, in a tone of very gentle reproach. "I can easily imagine," she added, "that it would have been impossible for you to come to Europe without cutting short the brilliant career on which you had entered. But surely you might have written to me!"

"Surely I could have done no such thing, dear Helen," returned her brother, "for she positively assured me that she knew not to what part of the world your uncle had carried you; but she constantly added that she was sure all this mystery would be over in a year or two. 'Wait till you are still higher in rank, dearest William!' was her invariable reply to all my questionings about you; and I will confess to you, my Helen, that I did in some degree share in this feeling myself. It would have been otherwise had I not known you were in the hands, as she called it, of my father's brother, and as the higher rank she prophesied did certainly seem to be coming upon me very rapidly, I could not help thinking that she knew what she was talking about. Moreover, her advice was the more likely to be listened to, from the fact that I could not have run counter to it if I would, for at no moment up to the time of her death, could I ever have quitted my regiment without such a dereliction of duty as must have rendered my doing it impossible under any circumstances; and as to writing, it was of course vain to think of it, since I knew not where to address my letters."

Helen remained silent, and her expressive features showed that she was in deep meditation. "What are you thinking of, dear one?" said her brother, taking her hand. "Are you still reproaching me in your heart for not coming back to look for you?"

"No, dearest William, no," she replied, endeavouring to return his smile. "I was only meditating on the singular manner in which poor Sarah Lambert seems to have conducted herself."

"I marvel not that it puzzles you, my Helen," he returned, "for it has never ceased to be a puzzle to me. But I must leave you now, sweet sister, or my termagant wife that is to be, will accuse me of abusing her confidence. You are all to dine with us to-day, are you not? And then I must absolutely and positively tear myself away from you both, and hasten to London, or else, instead of being made a K.C.B., I shall probably be sent to the right about."

He shook hands with her as he spoke, then gave a parting kiss, and left the room.

<div style="text-align:center">~~~~~~~~~~~~~~~~</div>

CHAPTER LVII.

HELEN saw him go without making any effort to detain him, though she had still much to say which was important for him to hear; for it was her purpose to tell of the division which she intended to make of her property, which she was quite aware that it was necessary he should know directly, on account of the difference it would doubtless make in the settlements upon which the lawyers were already employed, and she was aware also, that as he had delayed his departure for a day, for the sake of being with her for a few tranquil hours before they were again parted, she ought to have put it in his power to have written to his lawyer by that day's post.

But poor Helen felt her troubles were not over yet, and at that moment she wished for nothing so ardently as to be left alone. Though she had spoken of the conduct of Mrs. Lambert as mysterious, and though she had felt it to be so as she listened to him, a dark memory of the past recurred to her. The dreadful scene which she had witnessed in Mr. Bolton's hall (the immediate effect of which had been to throw her into a frenzy fever) had never been forgotten, though it long rested upon her mind more like the recollection of a painful dream than of a reality; but as Colonel Maurice described to her the strange perseverance with which Sarah Lambert had reiterated her advice to him *not* to return to England till many years had passed, it occurred to her as highly probable that she also had remembered it, and that her advice was dictated by the fear that should it be discovered, notwithstanding his change of name, that he was again in England, and, as would probably happen, paying a grateful visit to Mr. Bolton, the Crumpton sailors, with Commodore Jack at their head, would be very likely to receive him in a mannner which, to say the least of it, would be exceedingly disagreeable.

What Sarah Lambert could have meant by stating that a few years would suffice to remove the obstacles to his return, it was difficult to say; but it was not on this point that Helen was pondering when her brother took his hasty departure from her dressing-room; she was, in truth, weighing the pros and cons respecting the wisdom of communicating to him the suspicions to which his departure had given rise.

It is probable that she would have decided against repeating what it must have given him so much pain to hear; but he had vanished before she had reached a final decision on the subject; and no sooner was he gone than these vague memories of the past vanished before the positive importance of the present, and she immediately sat down to her writing-desk, and indited a letter to him, in which without preface or circumlocution of any sort, she briefly stated to him the fact, that property which she believed to be of the value of about ninety thousand pounds, was about to be made over to him, and stating also, with great sincerity, that her reason for sending after him in such haste was, that if he wished to make any alteration in his marriage-settlements he might have the advantage of that day's post to announce it to his lawyer. She added, also, that George Harrington had already been made perfectly aware of this division of their father's property, and that he highly approved it.

On this point, indeed, George Harrington did not leave it to the man who was to be doubly his brother-in-law to enter upon the subject with him; but even before Helen's letter had reached the hands of her brother, the Squire of Speedhurst, having waylaid him as he returned from Beauchamp Park, had stated to him in the simplest and most business-like manner possible, that such and such farms, in the neighbourhood, and such and such sums in the funds, were his. In short, the manner in which this announcement was made, both by his sister and his sister's affianced husband, was such as to render the whole transaction as soothing to his heart as it was advantageous to his fortune.

The hours of that busy, happy day soon made themselves wings, and flew away; and the following morning left the two affianced brides at full leisure to console themselves as well as they might for the absence of their departed lovers, for they agreed to pass the whole morning *tête-à-tête* together, because both Jane and Henry were so exceedingly tiresome and disagreeable.

And what with this soothing *tête-à-tête* for the present, and the prospect of all sorts of happiness for the future, tempers of worse texture than could be found either at Beauchamp Park or the Oaks, might have contrived to endure without any very grave grumbling, the tediousness even of lawyers and coach-makers, had these been all the evils which threatened to intervene between them and their bright future.

But such smooth sailing as this was not long destined to be their lot; and the fearful disappointment which awaited them was made the more bitter by its coming at the very moment when the arrival of those so eagerly and so gaily looked for was expected.

It had been settled that Beauchamp Park should be the scene of the happy reunion. Colonel Maurice was, of course, to take up his residence there till the day fixed for the double wedding, after which it was arranged that George Harrington and his bride should go at once to Speedhurst Abbey, but that Colonel Maurice and his Agnes should make a short tour upon the Continent, while a very charming mansion, which they had been lucky enough to find wanting a tenant, near Speedhurst, was being made ready for them, under the superintending care of their neighbours at the Abbey.

The train which was to bring the two gentlemen to the station, which was at no very great distance from the residence of either, was to arrive about an hour before the usual dinner-hour at Beauchamp Park, and under the superintending care of his sister Jane, who, as she said, was more in possession of her senses than Agnes could be expected to be, all things necessary for the toilet of George Harrington were laid ready for him there.

Colonel Maurice, as poor Helen delighted to say, was " coming home," and never did any home look more smilingly ready than the apartment prepared for his use.

Helen herself, as may be easily imagined, was lingering at no great distance from the hall door, that she might be in readiness to meet them ; nay, as she had on both her bonnet and shawl, it might be that she had some thoughts of taking a little stroll with her Cousin Henry towards the Lodge.

But for some reason or other the train was upon this occasion rather before than after its time, and she was still waiting for Henry at the door of the billiard-room, when she heard steps in the hall, and rushing eagerly forward, she found herself in the next moment almost in the arms of George Harrington, who hurried forward upon seeing her in a state of very perceptible agitation, and in answer to her quick inquiry, "Where is William?" replied in a voice which he vainly attempted to render tranquil, "He is well, Helen! But I am alone. I could not bring him with me. Business has prevented his coming." "Business!" echoed Helen, with cheeks and lips as white as marble. "What business could prevent his coming now?" "It was impossible he could come, my dearest love!" replied the greatly agitated young man. Take me to your dressing-room, Helen! I have much, very much, to tell you."

Nevertheless, George Harrington could not tell all which I wish my reader to know, for many circumstances respecting the events which he wished to narrate were as yet unknown to him. The narrative of them must be given more fully than Helen got it from him at that moment.

CHAPTER LVIII

The circumstances which followed upon Colonel Maurice's arrival in London shall be given as briefly as possible.

His first call, as in duty bound, was made at the Horse Guards, and though it was not his first visit there since his return to Europe, he had the gratification of being received in a manner highly flattering to all his military feelings and military hopes.

Of course, he had a lawyer to visit, the construction of a travelling carriage to superintend, no trifling amount of shopping commissions to attend to, and some few friendly calls to old acquaintance known in India, to pay.

But he managed to do it all; for he carried an active mind, and a willing spirit to the work, and before three weeks had passed, both he and his friend Harrington had the gratification of wishing each other joy upon the probability of their being able to leave town before the end of the following week.

Colonel Maurice had accepted an invitation to dine with an old Indian acquaintance upon one of the five remaining days. The party, which consisted wholly of gentlemen, was a large one, and the first among the guests upon whom he happened to cast his eyes as he looked round the drawing-room, was the Captain Hackwood who had some months before been his fellow guest at Knighton Hall.

They were men so utterly dissimilar, both in intellect and character, that it was nearly impossible they should ever have become really intimate, even as companions, and the circumstance of their having passed a week or two together in the same house had tended to make them enemies rather than friends. On the part of Colonel Maurice, however, there was a stronger feeling of contempt than of dislike, and had he never again heard Hackwood's name mentioned, it is possible that he might have lived long, and died late, without ever recalling the accident of having met him to his recollection.

But the case was widely different on the part of Captain Hackwood. Not many weeks had elapsed after his own coldly civil rejection by Agnes Harrington, before the disagreeable news reached him that she was about to be married to Colonel Maurice.

It happened that the sister of Captain Hackwood had recently married a young barrister of the name of Bingley, whose father resided in Cornwall, at no great distance from the village of Crumpton, in which was situated the Warren House, where the earlier scenes of my narrative were laid.

It might have been for the purpose of diverting his thoughts from the disappointment of finding that his handsome person was not quite irresistible, that Captain Hackwood, immediately upon leaving the hospitable mansion of Sir Richard Knighton, announced his intention to his sister of accepting the invitation of her father-in-law, Mr. Bingley, to meet her at his house near Crumpton.

Captain Hackwood was one of that numerous class of individuals whose principal intellectual resource in conversation is the discussing the persons, characters, and circumstances of the last set of people he had left, for the edification of those who were present. The neighbourhood of Knighton Hall furnished an excellent opportunity for the exercise of this species of eloquence, for it boasted of more than one well-known name among its notabilities.

Among many other mansions which he named, was Beauchamp Park, which he declared was one of the finest places he had ever seen, "positively an ornament to the whole neighbourhood."

"It really is a fine place, is it, Captain Hackwood?" said Mr. Bingley, the father-in-law of Hackwood's sister. "Whom does it belong to now? The young heiress, I suppose, is married by this time."

"No, Sir, I don't think she is, but I do not know much about her, for some of the family were ill when I was staying with Knighton, and I did not go there; but I heard them talk of *Miss* Beauchamp. She is living there in very dashing style with an uncle of the name of Rixley. Old Rixley's daughter had made a very fine match, and she deserved it, too, for she is a most fascinating creature. She married Lord Lympton, the son of the Earl of Rothewell, of Rothewell Castle, I met her brother, young Rixley, there, and a capital fellow he is."

"Whose brother did you meet?" said Mr. Bingley, addressing his talkative guest with an air of considerable interest. "Do you say that you met the brother of Miss Beauchamp?"

"No Sir, it was Henry Rixley, her cousin.   Miss Beauchamp has got no brother."

"So much the better for her, Captain Hackwood," said Mr. Bingley; "but she had a brother once, and certainly the best thing that could happen for her, or for him either, perhaps, is that he should be dead and buried."

"Indeed, Sir!" replied Captain Hackwood, with the interest which a constitutional gossip, whether male or female is sure to feel in everything that has the appearance of *secret history.*

"I can easily understand," he continued, "why the heiress should be worse off for having a brother, because you know it might prevent her being an heiress at all; but I don't understand why the brother would be the better for being buried."

"Here comes a fresh bottle of claret, Captain Hackwood," said the host, and if you can resist following the ladies for ten minutes longer, I'll tell you a romantic story about these Rixleys, or Beauchamps, as the owners of the estate are called. Many years ago, Captain Hackwood, when I was not much older than my son is now, though I was already in possession of this place (for my poor father died early), it may be some twenty-six or twenty-seven years ago, an old tumble down sort of a mansion, known by the name of the Warren House, was purchased in this neighbourhood by a person of the name of Rixley. I should be sorry to say anything uncivil of any person connected with friends of yours, but I cannot say that this Mr. Rixley, of the Warren House, was fortunate enough to make himself much respected in the neighbourhood. In the first place, he was as rude as a bear to us all, and as it was speedily circulated among the quidnuncs that the woman, who lived with him, was his mistress, and not his wife, he was very speedily left to follow his own devices without anyone taking much heed of him. But in a few years the poor young woman died, leaving a little boy of two or three years old behind her; and the next thing we heard of our Warren House neighbour was; that he had brought home a wife to comfort him for the loss of his mistress. She was a very beautiful creature, was this wife, and everything we heard of her was to her credit. Her conduct to the poor motherless child she found on coming to her home, was most admirable, and the worthy parson of the parish, who, by the way, is our worthy parson still, could not speak of her without enthusiasm. His own newly-married wife, too, described her as being very highly accomplished, and charming in every way; so, by degrees, several ladies of the neighbourhood called upon her; but, greatly as she was approved and admired by them all, it was quite impossible to live upon anything like sociable terms with Rixley himself, for it was evident that the more we wished to be civil to him and his sweet wife, the more heartily he wished us all at the devil. In fact, there was but one amuse-ment—but one occupation—that he cared for, and that was boating. He seemed to delight in making himself a sort of king among the sailors of our little fishing town, but to feel the most sovereign contempt for every other human being. His wife added a daughter to his domestic treasures, but, by all accounts, neither son, daughter, nor wife had any great attractions for him, for he often left his house for months together, and when he returned to it, his days, and I believe his nights, too, were passed on the sea. The next thing we heard of him was that his beautiful wife was dead, and then that he had got that good fellow Bolton to supply her loss, as far as teaching the poor unfortunate children went. And this he really did, and certainly gave a most excellent account of them both, as far as learning went. But now comes the extraordinary part of my long story. There will always be gossiping, you know, in every place, and, of course, there was gossiping here, and the gossipers said that Rixley treated this natural son like a brute, and that the young man was driven half mad with it. But, be this as it may, the finale was horrible on the other side. When the young man was about seventeen or eighteen years old, I believe, or thereabout, Rixley, the father, who had been away for several months, came home, if it was his home; at any rate, he came to the Warren House, and, as the servants said, had a most violent quarrel with his son. The next day the miserable children were left in peace, for he spent the whole day on the sea, and when he came home he ate his supper and went to bed. But from his bed he never rose again; when his old housekeeper went to wake him in the morning, she found him a corpse. The doctor was sent for, but dead he was; and then the parson was sent for, to tell them what they were to do next. 'But where was the son?' you will say. Gone, Captain Hackwood—vanished— and nobody knew where. The only trace he left behind him was the open window of his bed-room, with his sheets knotted together, hanging from one of the hinges of the casement. As it was well know that there had been a most furious quarrel between them, this scampish running away of the young man created a very strong suspicion that this very sudden death of the father, who had been in the most perfect health the day before, might have been the act and deed of the run-away son. In one word, to shorten a very long story, a post-mortem examination of the body was loudly called for, the result of which was that the unfortunate man had died from swallowing poison. I was applied to for a warrant to arrest the son, within an hour, I believe, after this verdict was recorded, and the warrant was given accordingly. But from that hour to this the scamp has never been heard of. As to the young heiress, she was immediately taken possession of by an uncle, of the name of Rixley; but she, as Bolton told me, had to take the name of Beauchamp, as a condition, I believe, of inheriting the property. And here ends my story; and now, if you like it better than more claret, we will join the ladies in the drawing-room."

It would have been difficult for Squire Bingley to have found any man unconnected with the parties more likely to listen with interest to such a narrative than Captain Hackwood. Of the relationship between his heartily-detested rival and the fair possessor of Beauchamp Park, he as yet knew nothing, but the having picked up so strange and eventful a history concerning the lineage and the history of a lady so important in her neighbourhood as Miss Beauchamp, was felt as a positive blessing by him, and the value he attached to it was manifested by his declaring at the breakfast-table on the following morning that he had received letters which obliged him, much against his inclination, to return immediately to London.

And to London he accordingly went without loss of time, and was greeted, infinitely to his satisfaction, by finding at his lodgings an invitation to dinner at a house where he felt sure of meeting society sufficiently distinguished to be worthy of being the first recipients of the bit of racy gossip which he had been fortunate enough to bring to town with him.

He felt that it was too good to be muttered to his next neighbour while the act of dining was still in process, but when this was over, he began, with the tact of one versed in the business, of making himself valued for his little anecdotes, to relate all the circumstances he had learned from Mr. Bingley, in a voice sufficiently distinct to be heard by the whole table.

As one of the guests seated at it was Colonel Maurice, it will be easily believed that his narrative was not listened to with indifference. Colonel Maurice, however, was a man who had great command over himself, and he steadily listened to the close of it. The last sentence was in these words, "It's a strange history, is it not? However, the fact of the run-away brother having committed the murder seems to be established on all hands. In fact it seems to me very difficult to understand how there ever could have been any feeling of doubt about it."

"Then permit me to enlighten your understanding now," said Colonel Maurice, in a voice not loud, but of that clear and distinct quality which makes itself heard, when louder tones fail of being so; "I am the run-away brother, but I deny the fact of having committed the murder; and if you feel any difficulty in believing my assertion, I will beg you to say so immediately."

The first effect of this rejoinder was to make Captain Hackwood, for a moment, look extremely pale, but in the next his complexion more than recovered itself, and he said, in a voice which, if not quite steady, was perfectly audible, "Upon my word, Sir, I am at a loss how to answer you with propriety;" then turning towards the master of the house, who was himself a highly distinguished military man, he added, "This is no place, is it, Sir, for such an altercation?"

"Certainly not!" returned Colonel Maurice, rising. "You are not, I presume, Captain Hackwood, about to leave town immediately?"

"Oh dear no, Sir," replied Captain Hackwood; "I have no thoughts of it."

"Then I will do myself the honour of calling upon you to-morrow, when I trust you will be so obliging as to inform me from what source you derived the statement upon the strength of which you have thought yourself justified in branding me as a murderer."

To this speech Captain Hackwood answered not a word, nor did he look as if he had power to do so, for he was again as pales as ashes.

Colonel Maurice then turned to his host, saying, "I am sure, General, that you will, under the circumstances, forgive my taking an abrupt leave of you; but it is already getting late, and I have business to get through before to-morrow morning which makes it necessary that I should return to my lodgings as soon as possible. You are lodging in Jermyn Street, I think, Captain Hackwood?"

The only answer he received to this was an affirmative nod of the head; and at the same moment General Pace, at whose table this very disagreeable discussion had arisen, stepped up to

Colonel Maurice and, cordially extending his hand to him, said,
in a voice which he evidently intended should be heard by all
his guests, "Good night, my dear Maurice. If I can be useful to
you in any way, let me know it. I shall always be at your
service."

CHAPTER LIX.

Captain Hackwood had been made fully aware that Colonel
Maurice had achieved immediate success in the quarter where
he had met immediate failure, and the hatred he conceived
towards him was as sincere as the mortification he had received
was bitter.

That he was startled, and—as much as a young gentleman
could be—that he was frightened, by the manner in which
Colonel Maurice addressed him, after having listened to his
Crumpton narrative, is certain; but it is not less so that hate
very speedily conquered fear; and that the hour which succeeded
the breaking up of General Pace's dinner-party, during which
important hour he was at liberty to indulge his own cogitations
without the least danger of being broken in upon by the stately
apparition of his ireful rival's figure, was the happiest which
Captain Hackwood had ever known.

It was, perhaps, impossible for one man to hate another more
heartily than Captain Hackwood hated Colonel Maurice, for the
rivalry between them in love made the least part of it. Captain
Hackwood was as fully aware of the striking contrast in all
respects between himself and his rival as George Harrington
had been when he attempted to describe them both to Helen:
and, for his torment, he was aware, also, that whenever they
appeared together he was himself forgotten, while Maurice
seemed the centre upon which every eye—masculine as well as
feminine—was fixed; and his hatred was in due proportion to
the acuteness and the justice of the remark.

To a man of such a temperament, and in such a state of
mind, the discovering that the rival he so envied and so hated
was a base-born felon, was likely enough to be agreeable, and to

Captain Hackwood it appeared like the consummation of all the dearest wishes of his heart.

Both gentlemen left the table of General Pace with the consciousness that they had a great deal of important business upon their hands, and they both set about performing it with energy.

The first occupation of both was to write letters. As Captain Hackwood completed his dispatches first, they shall be first noticed. The first he indited was to Colonel Maurice, and was as follows:—

"Sir,

"There may, perhaps, be some doubt whether I am not transgressing the laws and regulations of good society by addressing myself in any way to a man standing in so infamous a position as yourself; but as such a man as General Pace has shared in the delusion which has enabled you to thrust yourself into the presence of gentlemen, I prefer the chance of sinning against etiquette to the danger of having my conduct misunderstood. You had the insolence, notwithstanding the frightful disclosure which had taken place, to threaten me with a call at my lodgings. I now write to give you notice that you will not find me there. I hope within an hour to be in the train that will convey me to the mansion of my friend Mr. Bingley, near Crumpton. But as I scorn to take an unfair advantage of any man, I deem it proper to inform you that he is a Justice of the Peace; and a very active one; so that if you should have the rashness to follow me thither, you would probably be in the hands of justice within a few minutes after your arrival.

"I remain, Sir, &c.,
"Richard Fitzgeorge Hackwood."

His next epistle was addressed to Sir Richard Knighton, at Knighton Hall; and this need not be given at length, because it only contained a repetition of the statement respecting Colonel Maurice which he had given at the table of General Pace, together with the intelligence that " the said Colonel had found it impossible to deny his identity with the fearful parricide of the Crumpton Warren House, and that probably before the present letter could reach its destination he would be in the hands of justice."

Having completed these epistles, and placed them in the hands of a trustworthy agent, to be duly forwarded on the

25

morrow, Captain Hackwood and his carpet-bag got into the cab, that had been summoned for him while he wrote, and drove to the railway station in excellent time to be conveyed by the night train to Crumpton.

Colonel Maurice, meanwhile, was also occupied in writing. His first act was to write to his sister, telling her of the scene which had passed at the dinner-table, and begging her not to be unreasonably vexed about it, as, though decidedly disagreeable, it would only be considered as one of those bare-faced slanders to which disappointed men sometimes had recourse when they could hit upon no better expedient, to soothe their vexed feelings.

He wrote also to Agnes; but to her he was less explicit. A repugnance, which he could not conquer, to the idea of her knowing that such accusations had been brought against him, seemed to chain his pen, and to render it absolutely impossible for him to enter upon any detail of what had passed. It was not, however, that he had the least intention of concealing from her what had taken place; but it was his purpose to see George Harrington early on the morrow, to whom, of course, it was his intention to communicate everything that had passed; and he greatly preferred the idea of her learning it from her brother than from himself.

Having written this letter, he resumed his pen, and set about making his will. In his case, at least, he felt, or fancied, that a duel was inevitable, and, despite the immensity of sound philosophy which he knew might be brought against such a mode of proving innocence, it appeared to him morally impossible that he could have recourse to any other. But in deciding upon this, he was so far ready to confess himself less magnanimous than he might have been, that in his short preface to his short will he confessed the act to be a proof of human weakness which he should probably blame in another, though he was not strong-minded enough to avoid it himself.

His will gave all he died possessed ot to his sister, save five thousand pounds (the half of what he had inherited from the grateful Captain Maclogan), which he bequeathed to Agnes Harrington. The witnessing this document was of necessity postponed to the following morning, as by the time he had finished it everybody in the house had retired to rest except himself.

And then he retired to rest also.

Neither a tranquil conscience nor an undaun.... spirit were

wanting to ensure to him some hours of tranquil repose, but even this sufficed not to obtain it, for the thoughts of the frightful charge against him, which he had heard that day, and the effect which it might produce on his affianced wife, his friend, and his sister, haunted him in a thousand different shapes, and his night was very nearly a sleepless one.

The first event which occurred to him on the following morning was the receiving the letter of Captain Hackwood, which was given to him as soon as he left his room. The contents of it caused him immediately to change all his plans. The letters he had written he did not send to the post, but he got his own servant and the mistress of the house to witness his will, and then he set forth, not to ask the friendly assistance of General Pace in a duel, but to tell the whole story to his friend George Harrington.

That this interview was a painful one will be readily believed, for the prevalent feeling in the minds of both the young men was sympathy with the agony which it would cause to the dear ones whom they had hoped so soon to meet, and to greet with all the happiness that love and hope could give.

The contrast was indeed terrible, and George Harrington declared, with great sincerity, that he thought himself the most to be pitied of the two. And, perhaps, he was right, for even the feverish agitation of those dreadful moments could not prevent Colonel Maurice from seeing and appreciating the perfect sympathy of his friend with every feeling of his own heart, nor could that noble heart itself more indignantly reject the calumny which caused them so much misery than did that of the man to whom he had revealed it. But no verbal explanations were resorted to on either side, either to express or to welcome this sympathy; one glance exchanged between them, one momentary pressure of the hand, was quite enough, and they parted after an interview wonderfully short, considering the importance of it, with the mutual consolation in the heart of both that each had a friend whose attachment might atone for much sorrow.

And so they parted, George Harrington setting off upon his melancholy journey homeward, and Colonel Maurice upon his strangely eventful return to the place of his birth.

CHAPTER LX

It was no fault of George Harrington's that Colonel Maurice set off upon this tremendous expedition alone, for he had earnestly, and even vehemently, urged his friend to permit his going with him; but he yielded, at length, to the unanswerable argument that Helen and Agnes would need his presence more than he should do.

"That I shall not want you as my second in a duel with Captain Hackwood is made sufficiently evident, as you must, I think, allow, by his leaving town after what passed between us last night. I not only very distinctly told him that he would hear from me this morning, but General Pace very kindly declared, with equal distinctness, that he was perfectly at my service if he could assist me in any way. This was intelligible enough, you will allow, to keep him in London, if he had had any intention of fighting. It is evident that he prefers police-men to pistols, and if he really believes the statement he made at the table of General Pace, it would be difficult to say that he was wrong. But, at any rate, George, it is clear that I shall not want you in the capacity of my second, and in no other case can my claims upon you be equal to those of these dear girls. I shall, I am quite sure, find my old friend Bolton ready and willing to help me, if help be needed; and, fortunately, I have just recovered a letter which I promised to deliver to him in person, but which has been delayed by the box, which contained it, having been put on board the wrong vessel when I left the Cape. So you perceive that I really have business at Crumpton, besides that which Captain Hackwood has provided for me.

These arguments, very calmly stated by his friend, were too unanswerable to leave room for any further discussion.

Never, perhaps, was any arrival more completely unexpected than that of Colonel Maurice at the house of Mr. Bingley, for it was there that he ordered himself to be driven in the Crumpton post-chaise, immediately upon leaving the train which brought him to the entrance of the little town.

He had left London before mid-day, and, having travelled by an express train, arrived at the end of his long journey, while the family party, of which Captain Hackwood made one, was still at table.

The servant, who opened the door of the house to him, had stated, on his inquiring for Mr. Bingley, that the family were at dinner.

"It is necessary that I should immediately see Mr. Bingley," was Colonel Maurice's reply to this information, "but if you will permit me to go into the drawing-room, I will wait for him till his dinner is over."

The servant, though a very prudent and discreet servant, did not, as it seemed, suspect that the individual who stood before him came there for the express purpose of being sent to the county gaol and tried for his life. On the contrary, he bowed very respectfully, took a lamp, which stood upon one of the hall tables, and lighted him to the drawing-room door. "What name shall I say, Sir?" said the man, after stirring the fire, and setting a chair beside it.

"My name would give him no information, for he does not know it," replied Colonel Maurice. "Only tell him, if you please, that a stranger is here, who wishes to speak to him upon business, but that I beg him not to hasten his removal from table."

The servant again bowed very respectfully, for still it did not occur to him that the stranger was come there for the purpose of giving himself up into the hands of justice; and having quietly replied, "Very well, Sir," left the room, and closed the door after him.

Colonel Maurice sat down, and very rationally employed the interval which followed in warming his feet, which, in consequence of English railroad carriages not having yet adopted the delicious warm-water system of French ones, were suffering from cold.

But the civility of the worthy magistrate did not permit him to wait long before the drawing-room door was again opened, and three ladies and three gentlemen entered; thus evidently breaking through the customary ceremony of dividing males and females in order to prevent the awkwardness of letting the ladies introduce themselves to the "strange gentleman," whom the footman deponed he had never seen before.

No sooner did Colonel Maurice see the ladies than he became conscious of his indiscretion in not having asked to see Mr. Bingley alone; and his not having done so was a proof of his having been more occupied by the hope of immediately seeing

Captain Hackwood, and witnessing his dismay at his arrival, than by any other idea.

Nor was he mistaken in thinking that the astonishment of this gentleman, at seeing him there, would considerably exceed his satisfaction. " D—n—n!" was the first articulate sound which greeted his ears after the entrance of the party, but this welcome Colonel Maurice did not think it necessary to acknowledge, beyond casting upon him one look of recognition, not, perhaps, quite unblended with a smile; and passing on to the elderly gentleman, who entered the room the last, and whom he readily divined to be the master of the house, he said, " I beg your pardon, Sir, for not remembering, in my eagerness to bring myself before you, that it was possible that you might have company with you. But, as I learnt, not many hours ago, from that person," pointing to Captain Hackwood, " that you had stated me to stand charged with the crime of murder, and that you formerly issued a warrant for my apprehension, which was not executed because I was not to be found, I have hastened hither, with as little delay as possible, in order to surrender myself for trial. I am Colonel Maurice, Mr. Bingley, the natural son of the late Mr. Beauchamp, of Beauchamp Park, better know in this neighbourhood, I believe, as Mr. Rixley, of the Warren House, in the parish of Crumpton. As this gentleman," he added, turning himself round, and facing Captain Hackwood, " thought proper to declare, when he narrated the history of my father's death, yesterday, at the table of General Pace, that he felt it impossible not to believe the foul charge made against me, my first purpose, as I immediately gave him to understand, was to call upon *him* for an explanation of the words he had thought proper to use; but by his immediately leaving town, it is evident that the more business-like and prudent way of treating the matter would, in his opinion, be to place me safely, and with as little delay as possile, in the hands of justice. And, perhaps, he was right."

The three ladies had already left the room in obedience to a signal from the master of the house; and the door being closed after them, Mr. Bingley approached his self-constituted prisoner, and said, " Your conduct, Colonel Maurice, is such as would fully justify me, in my own opinion, if I were to decline such a course: believing you entirely innocent of the crime laid to your charge, I do not consider myself as in any way called upon to interfere with your freedom. But it may be that you will not yourself consider this as a sufficient exoneration from the charge."

"Certainly not, Mr. Bingley," returned Colonel Maurice, with a smile. "But, while I reject your offer, let me thank you for it. It is consolatory to feel that all my fellow-creatures do not, like Captain Hackwood, consider it absolutely impossible that I should be innocent."

"I rather think, Sir," replied the old gentleman, returning the smile, "that if all your fellow-creatures were brought to the poll, I should be found in the majority. But what is the course you wish me to pursue?"

"Nay, my dear Sir, it is not for me to dictate to you on that point; all I can do in order to assist the course of justice, is to place myself in your hands, and I am here expressly for that purpose."

"I really think that the best course we can pursue," said Mr. Bingley, after the silent meditation of a minute or two, "will be for you to accept an apartment in my house for to-night. To-morrow, I shall meet my fellow-justices at Crumpton, when all the circumstances of this strange case can be laid before them, and the proper steps to be taken may be decided on by more competent authority than my own. Will you do me the favour of accepting hospitality so strangely offered?"

It was now Colonel Maurice's turn to pause before he returned an answer. There was something very decidedly the reverse of agreeable in becoming the fellow-guest of Captain Hackwood; nevertheless, he felt that it would be more disagreeable still to decline being *garde-à-vue*, a position, which the offer, however courteously made, necessarily involved. He, therefore, replied, after a moment's consideration, "Assuredly, Mr. Bingley, I will; it will evidently save trouble to us both, not to mention the pleasure I shall feel in cultivating the acquaintance of a gentleman who has treated me with so much consideration, under circumstances so every-way disadvantageous to me."

This acceptance was as graciously received as it was given, and as Captain Hackwood had very judiciously joined the ladies, who had taken refuge in the dressing-room allotted to his sister, an hour or two was passed by Bingley father and Bingley son, with their strangely-situated guest, in a manner much less disagreeable than might have been anticipated.

When it was drawing to a close, however, Colonel Maurice, of necessity, alluded to his position, by saying, "I owe you much gratitude, Mr. Bingley, for your kindness under circumstances in which I fear few persons would have ventured to show it; but I am constrained to ask still more at your hands.

I have one personal friend in your neighbourhood, to whom I wish to communicate both my arrival here and all the circumstances attending it. This friend is no other than your worthy minister, Mr. Bolton, and I not only wish to see him on my own account, but also because I am the bearer of a letter to him which I promised the writer on her death-bed to deliver into his own hands. May I, therefore, request you to let him know that you wish to see him here as early as possible to-morrow?"

Mr. Bingley readily promised that the message should be transmitted to the parsonage at an early hour in the morning; and the next important occurrence was the separation of the party for the night; Mr. Bingley escorting his guest to the door of the handsome apartment prepared for him with as much ceremony, or, more properly speaking, with as much respect, as if he had not been a " prisoner at large."

CHAPTER LXI.

The following day was an eventful one. Mr. Bolton, whose early habits made an early visit no matter of inconvenience to him, obeyed the somewhat urgent summons of Mr. Bingley, by appearing before the family party had separated after breakfast. Colonel Maurice, though as little disposed as any gentleman under the circumstances could be, to make any fuss about the singularity of his position, nevertheless, felt more repugnance than he thought it worth while to conquer, against being formally introduced to the assembled family of the Bingleys at the breakfast-table; he had, therefore, requested, without making any great ceremony about it, that his breakfast might be sent to him in his own room. This was immediately done with the most observant attention; but in about ten minutes after his coffee reached him, the servant returned to inform him that Mr. Bolton had arrived. His wish to receive his former master alone had, no doubt, assisted his decision respecting his manner of breakfasting; and his reply to this message was a request to Mr. Bolton to come to him in his room.

On hearing of his arrival Mr. Bingley immediately rose from the breakfast-table, and met him at the door. Colonel Maurice had expressed a wish, on the preceding evening, that Mr. Bolton should not be told who it was that wished to see him, and Mr. Bingley himself conducted the good clergyman to his former pupil's door, in order to prevent inquiries being asked, or, at any rate, answered.

The words "Come in!" by which Colonel Maurice replied to his host's gentle tap at his door, were immediately obeyed; Mr. Bingley as immediately retired; and Mr. Bolton and his old pupil stood face to face.

They stood thus for a moment, silently and earnestly gazing at each other; but there was nothing approaching sympathy in their feelings: for whereas Colonel Maurice felt at his heart that he should have recognised his old master anywhere, Mr. Bolton felt equally sure that he had never seen the stately stranger before.

"I beg your pardon, Sir," said Mr. Bolton, very respectfully, "but I think my friend, Mr. Bingley, must have made some mistake. I understood, from what he said, that it was an old acquaintance who wished to see me."

"And have you no lingering recollection of me, my dear Mr. Bolton?" said Colonel Maurice, holding out his hands towards him, with a friendly smile.

The smile did more than any words could have done towards awakening the recollection of his old friend. Mr. Bolton looked at him from head to foot, as if measuring his noble stature; and feeling that this could not help him, fixed his eyes on that smiling face, and then exclaimed, "If it were possible, I should believe that I saw William Rixley before me!"

"It is more than possible; it is most soberly certain, my dear old friend, that I am the William Rixley who owes you such a measureless debt of gratitude. I am at this moment, in some respects, under very disagreeable circumstances; but, nevertheless, the seeing you again, looking so well, and so little changed, too, gives me a greater degree of pleasure that I can easily express."

"And your sister, my dear William," said Mr. Bolton, drawing a chair and placing it opposite to that which Colonel Maurice had occupied near the fire. "Has she had the great happiness of seeing you?"

"Yes! Thank heaven, we have, at last, met again! But it has only been very recently. You shall hear all my adventures at full length, if you will, my dear friend; but it must be when I have more leisure to recount them than at the present

moment. My situation, just now, is rather a strange one.
Your friend, Mr. Bingley, has been exceedingly civil, and,
under the circumstances, I must say, exceedingly considerate
and kind; but, nevertheless, my dear friend, I am here rather
as his prisoner than his guest. It seems that he issued a
warrant against me nearly nine years ago, but as I was not to
be found, the warrant could not be served, and it has, therefore,
become his duty, I believe, to issue another. I am accused of
having murdered my father, Mr. Bolton."

"I know it, William! I know it!" replied Mr. Bolton, in
great agitation.

"But you do not believe it, Mr. Bolton, do you?" said
Colonel Maurice, looking earnestly at him.

"No more than I believe that I murdered him myself!"
replied Mr. Bolton, earnestly.

"Then do not look uneasy about it, my dear friend!"
returned the young man, cheerfully. "If I am brought to
trial, be very sure that this strange annoyance will end there.
An English jury will not bring me in guilty, my good friend."

"No, no! I do not fear it—I cannot fear it. But my confidence in the result will not reconcile me to the idea of such a
trial."

Nor can it reconcile me to the idea of it either, my dear Mr.
Bolton," replied Colonel Maurice, passing his hand across his
lofty brow with a greater appearance of painful feeling than he
had yet manifested. "But I know of no method which it would
be possible for me to adopt by which it can be avoided. I need
scarcely tell you that my suffering under such circumstances
would be more than doubled by the suffering of my sister. But
this is not all, dear friend. Listen to me for a few minutes and
I will make you understand what my position actually is, or
rather was, before I knew of any such frightful charge having
been brought against me."

Colonel Maurice then gave, with great clearness, but with
great rapidity, a sketch of his history from the hour in which
he let himself down by his sheets, from his bed-room window, to
that in which he had listened to Captain Hackwood's statement
at the dinner-table of General Pace; and, then, without giving
his attentive auditor time to make any observation on the eventful narrative, he added, "And now, dearest Mr. Bolton, tell me,
I entreat you, in what manner, and with whom did the idea of
my having committed this dreadful crime arise?"

"In the first place, the examination of your father's body

proved, beyond the reach of doubt, that he had died from the effects of poison. You must, I am sure, remember that his habits of life had made him very popular among the sailors, and no sooner was his death made known among them, than a whole host of them, headed by a man known by the title of Commodore Jack, rushed to the Warren House, and into the room in which the corpse lay, calling for vengeance on his murderer. Your clandestine flight during the night, of course, became immediately known to them, and you were immediately accused of being the culprit. A warrant for your apprehension was issued, and a most persevering search made, with what success I need not tell you. Nothing has ever transpired to throw light upon the mystery. My own opinion very decidedly is, that your father destroyed himself."

"I doubt it," replied Colonel Maurice, "I do more than doubt it, Mr. Bolton; I disbelieve it utterly: notwithstanding the unfatherly and unfilial terms we were upon, I knew him better than most lads of seventeen know their fathers; but he, and his wild ways, were a study to me, and nothing, I am confident, will ever persuade me that he destroyed himself."

"Then how is it to be accounted for, William?" said Mr. Bolton, with a look of painful anxiety.

"Nay, I know not, my good friend," returned Colonel Maurice, shaking his head; "but if I am to be brought to trial, I certainly will not owe my safety to the suggestion of such a fallacy as that. I feel confident, that a man who is not guilty will not be declared to be so by an English jury! and I must trust both my honour and my life to that."

"You may be right, William, nay, I believe you are so," returned Mr. Bolton, in a voice which spoke, however, neither of hope, confidence, nor contentment. "But the trial—the trial itself—to a man situated as you now are, is a misfortune too great to contemplate with philosophical composure."

"I feel it to be so," returned the unhappy young man; and for a very painful interval they both remained silent.

At length, Colonel Maurice roused himself from a state of mind that was very unusual to him, and said, firmly, if not cheerfully, "If this heavy misfortune of being tried in a court of justice for the murder of my father be inevitable, dear Bolton, it must be borne, and, with God's help, I will bear it manfully. Would that the task of bearing it fell upon me alone! I was taught to bear a good deal when I was young, and am, doubtless, the better able to endure suffering now. But there are others . . ." and there he stopped, and, for a few seconds, perhaps, was completely overcome; but he did rally manfully, and, with more perfect self-possession and composure than most men could have commanded under similar circumstances, he commissioned his friend to learn from their host what it was his intention to do respecting him.

Mr. Bolton immediately left him, promising a speedy return; but it soon became evident that the decision of Mr. Bingley was not likely to be a prompt one, for more than an hour had elapsed before Mr. Bolton returned to him.

"Mr. Bingley seems greatly embarrassed, my dear William," were his first words on entering; "so much so, indeed, that he altogether declines doing anything on his own responsibility, anything, at least, beyond requesting you to remain where you are till he has taken legal advice upon the subject."

"Poor gentleman!" replied Colonel Maurice, with a smile. "He certainly has, on the whole, behaved extremely well; but there is something rather ludicrous, is there not, in so very civilly requesting a gentleman, as a personal favour, to be so obliging as to stay where he is, in order to be brought into court and tried for murder? However, his confidence in me, if he really feels it, shall not be abused. There is no danger of my repeating the frolic of escaping through the window. Pray tell him, dear friend, that I am willing to stay here for three hours longer, which will give him time, I think, to consult a lawyer, and summon a quorum; but that the keeping me here beyond that time would look a little like false imprisonment. Don't you think so?"

"I will tell him what you say," replied Mr. Bolton, returning the smile; "but I do assure you he is very much in earnest in wishing to do exactly what the law exacts from him, though he is certainly in some doubt as to what that may be."

"Let him take his time, by all means—let him take his time!" returned Colonel Maurice; "and by-the-by, my dear old friend, you must not leave me again till I have fulfilled a promise made to an old acquaintance of yours on her death-bed. You remember poor Sarah Lambert, our good old nurse, do you not, Mr. Bolton?"

"Yes, certainly. I remember her perfectly," replied the good man, with the stiff sort of gravity with which people are named whom we do not wish to talk about.

"Are you aware that she left her country in the hope of finding me?" demanded his companion.

"I was told so at Falmouth," returned Mr. Bolton; "but the statement appeared to me too improbable to be true."

"But it was true, nevertheless," resumed Maurice: "and she not only sought, but found me; and nothing short of death, I believe, would have parted us again. Her health was already failing when she found me, and she died before she had been with me many years. In all my various campaignings, I always contrived to keep a fixed home for her, good soul; and when she died, she left me, as a legacy, *all her property!* Poor dear woman! She was most devotedly attached both to Helen and to me! I have never yet had leisure to inquire what all her property amounted to, poor dear soul!"

"And did she never tell you, during all the years you passed together, of the imputation which had been thrown upon you at the death of your father?" said Mr. Bolton.

"Never!" replied Colonel Maurice.

Then, suddenly starting from his chair, he exclaimed: "Your question, however, suggests a solution to a mystery which has long puzzled me. During the whole of her residence with me, and especially upon every occasion when my rapid promotion in the service suggested the probability of my return to England, she unceasingly repeated to me, 'Do not go yet, my dearest William! Wait! wait only for a year or two, and then your going may be a blessing to yourself and your sister, both. But not yet, William! It would not be a blessing to either of you as yet.' I perfectly comprehend it now, my dear friend. She fancied that a year or two longer, together with my change of name and station, would suffice to prevent any danger of this frightful charge being brought against me."

"I have no doubt but that you understand her rightly, now," said Mr. Bolton, sadly. "She would have done better had she told you the whole truth."

"The whole truth would not have prevented my returning to England, Mr. Bolton," replied Colonel Maurice, quietly; "but I have not told you yet that she seemed to change her mind about all this when she was dying, for she gave me a letter for you, which would have been delivered long ago had not an accident occurred to my baggage; and when she put it into my hands, which was but a short time before she breathed her last, she said, with great earnestness, 'Now, dear William, now the sooner you go back to England, and to your dear sister, the better it will be for you both.'"

Colonel Maurice had taken out his pocket-book as he spoke,

and he now drew a letter from it, which he placed in the hands of Mr. Bolton.

There was no great eagerness in that gentleman's manner of receiving it. The writer had forfeited his esteem, and a farewell letter from her was more likely to be painful than interesting. He put it quietly in his pocket, saying, " I shall be more at leisure to read it when I get home."

He then took his leave, promising to deliver the message he had received from Mr. Bingley, and to repeat his visit at an early hour on the morrow.

CHAPTER LXII.

Mr. Bolton kept his word, and did deliver the message of Colonel Maurice very distinctly, and then took his leave, saying that he should take the liberty of returning on the morrow, to learn what further steps had been taken.

Captain Hackwood was present when this message was delivered to his host.

" Insolent ruffian ! " he exclaimed; " does he hope to escape the gallows by bullying? If I were you, Mr. Bingley, I would have him safe in prison before sunset."

" I don't think so badly of him as you seem to do," replied the old gentleman, quietly; " but, nevertheless, I am quite aware that it is my duty to prevent his again escaping from an investigation which the circumstances certainly call for. I have already dispatched a messenger to Falmouth to desire Mr. Lucas, the lawyer, to come to me; and my son is himself gone in the carriage to bring over Sir Thomas White from Crumpton Park. He is one of our best-informed and most active magistrates; and I daresay that between us we shall make out what we ought to do. After which there will be no delay in doing it, you may depend upon it."

The measures thus promptly taken were immediately effectual; and the result of the consultation which followed the arrival of these gentlemen was, that a warrant for the detention of the person now calling himself Colonel Maurice, but formerly known as William Rixley, should immediately be made out.

The next step was, of course, to commit the unfortunate object of this decision to the county gaol; and the worthy Mr. Bingley, with very sincere regret that he could do nothing better for his service, ordered his carriage out to convey him thither. This order was already obeyed, and the carriage was already at the door, when Mr. Bolton was seen approaching the house with every appearance of violent haste and agitation.

Colonel Maurice, who was already at the hall-door in readiness to depart, was rather pained than comforted by seeing him, for he doubted not that his old friend had already heard of his committal, and was hastening to take leave of him before the doors of a prison were closed between them.

The moment was one in which everything tending to awaken feeling had better be avoided; and the unfortunate Colonel Maurice was so fully aware of this, that when Mr. Bolton stretched out his hand, apparently to impede his stepping into the carriage, he said, "You mean this visit most kindly, my dear friend; but if you would spare me all unnecessary suffering, do not attempt to delay my departure at this moment."

The triumphant eye of Captain Hackwood, who was standing on the door-steps, was on him as he spoke—a circumstance which, no doubt, added to the earnestness with which this remonstrance was uttered.

But this earnestness did not produce its intented effect on Mr. Bolton. On the contrary, he persevered with a degree of vehemence, very unusual in him, to retain the arm of Colonel Maurice, which he had seized, endeavouring to draw him back by main force into the house. "What the devil are you about, Sir?" exclaimed Captain Hackwood. "Do you mean to resist the warrant?"

"Yes, sir, I do," replied the clergyman, immediately recovering his self-possession.

"You both know me, gentlemen," he continued, turning to the two magistrates; "you both know me too well to doubt that I have some reason for what I do. I hold a document in my hand," he added, drawing a letter from his pocket, "which will show you that the sending this gentleman to prison, after it has been offered for your perusal in evidence, may be attended with inconvenience to others as well as to him."

"And you must know us too well, my dear Sir, to doubt our feeling well pleased at anything that may lawfully impede our performing so unpleasant a duty," said Sir Thomas White. Whereupon he himself re-entered the house, followed by the whole party.

Mr. Bolton was too eager to achieve the business he had to perform to wait till they had passed through the hall before he placed the important letter in the hands of Sir Thomas; but that gentleman had the discretion not to open it till he had entered the drawing-room, waited till all the party had entered it also, closed the door, and put on his spectacles.

This done, he opened the letter, and, at the request of Mr Bolton, read it aloud. Its contents were as follows :—

"HONOURED SIR,

"I know my own position, and I know yours, much too well to obtrude myself upon your recollection, unless I had such a reason for doing so as might justify the act in your eyes.

"You already know the terrible secret of my sinful life; you already know that, while living as the servant of the late Mrs. Rixley, and as the attendant of her children I was the mistress of her husband, and their father.

"Thus much I have already confessed to you, and I confessed it with shame and sorrow, a shame and a sorrow as genuine as was ever felt by a repentant sinner.

"And I have now, Sir, another confession to make to you; but though the deed which I am now obliged to disclose is considered, I believe, as worse than any other, the remembrance of it causes me neither shame nor sorrow. I loved my master passionately, and devotedly, and I loved his children devotedly too, perhaps because they were his children. My love to the father was of that unprincipled kind which utterly obscures the judgment, making that appear pardonable in him which, in another, would have appeared hateful beyond the reach of forgiveness.

"His cruel neglect of his faultless wife, and his utter indifference towards his children, I more than forgave, for I believed both to be the result of his overpowering attachment to myself.

"But my judgment became clearer when, upon his return to the Warren House, after an unusually long absence of several months, he coolly informed me that he was immediately going to be married.

"It is no part of my task to describe the feeling which this announcement created in me. If it was hatred, it was not strong enough to have led to the catastrophe which followed, for it is certain that I should not have acted as I did act, had not his children been very dear to me.

"In talking to me of his approaching nuptials, which he did without even affecting the slightest consideration for my feelings, he informed me for the first time that his real name was Beauchamp, which he had taken upon succeeding to a large estate—this estate, he gaily told me, would be inherited by the son, which he flattered himself would be born to him within a twelvemonth, adding, however, that he had, nevertheless, made a will, leaving the property to his daughter Helen, in case this male heir was never born. The whole of the following day my master spent, as he often did, upon the water, leaving home early in the morning, and giving me orders to pack up clothes for him to take with him to London on the following day.

" He also ordered me to prepare a supper for him at night.

" How I got through that dreadful day matters to no one. Perhaps I was mad. I sometimes think it was so; but mad or not, I was not idle. I made my will. I went to Falmouth. I purchased some poison at a druggist's shop, and I came back to the Warren House. Having reposed myself for a while, I prepared my master's supper, and that so skilfully, that if he ate but a little, and drank but a little, I knew that when he lay down to sleep, he would rise no more, and that Helen, and not a son and heir, would inherit his property.·

"It was I who poisoned George Rixley, of the Warren House, alias George Beauchamp, of Beauchamp Park.

"The departure of poor William was an accidental coincidence. He went, poor boy, because his brutal father had treated him in a manner too bad to bear. The dear boy had often told me, that he thought he should be driven to run away at last.

"I repeat, Sir, that I do not feel any remorse for having prevented the father of Helen from leaving her destitute. I may have been mad, and I may be so still; but I firmly believe that I did more good than evil."

" Signed Almeria, commonly called

" Sarah Lambert."

It will readily be imagined that this strange document was

not listened to with indifference by any of the persons present at
the reading it.

The feelings of Colonel Maurice, though certainly not unmixed with pain, were those of deep thankfulness for this
sudden change in his destiny, from he hardly knew what of
misery, to the recovery of a degree of happiness which he most
sincerely believed to be greatly beyond the ordinary lot of
mortals; and as he thought of the change which this wonderful transition brought to the distant dear ones, whose fate hung
on his, the happiness he felt seemed to become as unselfish, and
as holy, as it was intense.

The deep joy, and the delightful feeling of relief experienced
by the truly sensitive heart of Mr. Bolton, may be easily enough
conceived by all possessed of human affections and warm sym-
pathies; and the other gentlemen present, with the exception
of one, unquestionably experienced a very sincere feeling of satisfaction, at the happy turn which the disagreable affair that
had brought them together had taken.

The exception, as may easily be guessed, was found in the
person of the deeply-disappointed Captain Hackwood. But even
at that very discouraging moment, the spirit within him did
not leave him altogether without resourc e, for in the midst of
the congratulations which were pouring in upon Colonel
Maurice, he gently touched the constable on the arm, and said,
"Take care what you are about, my good fellow. It is likely
enough to come out, I think, that this very improbable epistle
has been concocted at the Parsonage, within the last twenty-
four hours."

Captain Hackwood could not have addressed himself to a
more promising subject, for the constable was both timid and
punctilious.

"Thank you kindly for the hint, Sir," replied the man; "it
would not be the first time that such a trick may have been
played, I'll answer for it."

And then, turning to Sir Thomas White, he said, "I ask your
pardon, Sir, but when a prisoner has been given over to my
keeping, I must take care not to let him go without having
to show good and sufficient cause for the same. Now it
seems to me, your Honour, that we have not got any
good and sufficient proof as to when that there letter was
written. Even if there was anybody here to prove the woman's
handwriting, we don't know but what she might have been
persuaded by the young man to do it when she was dying,

because in that case it might do him a deal of good without doing a bit of harm to her."

This speech was listened to by all with, perhaps, more attention than it deserved; but the effect was not lasting, for our old acquaintance, Mr. Lucas, the Falmouth attorney, immediately drew another letter from his pocket, together with the will of Almeria Lambert.

The letter, which was addressed to " William Rixley," expressly stated that it was her purpose to avenge herself, and him, by destroying his father by means of poison, which she had already procured, and which it was her fixed purpose to administer before she again closed her eyes in sleep. " By this just act of retribution," she added, " I shall ensure to your dear sister the noble fortune to which she was born, and which, if he lives, will in all probability be given to another." This letter was not only dated the day before the late Mr. Beauchamp's death, but Mr. Lucas was ready to depose on oath that it had been confided to him on that day. He offered, also, to swear that it was in the handwriting of Mrs. Lambert.

.This seemed to satisfy everybody, except Captain Hackwood; but he evidently continued to entertain doubts as to its authenticity, for after casting a look of the utmost contempt upon Mr. Lucas, he turned on his heel and walked out of the room.

The rest of the party, however, seemed, one and all, to be exceedingly pleased with this happy termination of the disagreeable business which had brought them there, and it was not Mr. Bingley's fault if they did not all stay and dine with him. But Colonel Maurice pleaded the absolute necessity of his returning to London by the next train, together with his earnest wish of passing the short interval before he started, with his old friends at the Parsonage.

The carriage which still stood at the door, ready to convey the gallant Colonel to the county gaol, was now offered to take him and his old master to the Parsonage, and his meeting with Mrs. Bolton was as happy as that with her husband had been the reverse.

Yet, nevertheless, Colonel Maurice took care to be ready for the train, and in a time so short as would have seemed fabulous to our fathers, he found himself once more at Beauchamp Park, and surrounded by all that he loved best on earth.

*　　　*　　　*　　　*　　　*

And now my story is done.

Need it be added at full length that the double wedding came off exactly on the day originally fixed—exactly as it would have done if Colonel Maurice's flying excursion to Crumpton had never taken place ?   The only difference was, that Mr. Bolton came to perform the double ceremony; and then he learnt, happy man, that Helen had, several years ago, purchased the next presentation to a capital good living in her neighbourhood, the incumbent of which, at the time of the purchase, had already numbered nearly four-score years.   The only consolation for this long delay was to be found in the evident salubrity of the spot that was to be his future home.

The Warren House may be seen still standing in its desolate loneliness; but neither William nor Helen have ever taxed their courage so far as to enter it.   And they acted wisely, for their present happiness is too perfect to require any contrast with former sufferings to increase their enjoyment of it.

THE END.

W. H. SMITH & SON, PRINTERS, 186, STRAND, LONDON.

www.ingramcontent.com/pod-product-compliance
Lightning Source LLC
Chambersburg PA
CBHW032149110726
47902CB00003B/756